DIRE COVENANTS
A Dombrowski

&

Callahan Case
M. D. IRONZ

Published in the United States of America.

Professorial Holdings

professorialholdings@gmail.com

Second Edition

Michael J. Moriarty

Stephen Landry

Also by M.D. Ironz

Table of Contents

CH 1

———

THE YELLOW CRIME SCENE tape stretching across the driveway was a glaring affront to the dignity of such an exclusive neighborhood. Two marked police cars flanking the large house sat silent, no longer flashing their blue and red overhead strobes, no longer disrupting the placid ambiance of the meticulously maintained community.

Nonetheless, a small gathering of neighbors had responded to the unexpected wail of police sirens that had shattered their Sunday morning. They now huddled together in small groups, whispering in hushed and shocked tones, lingering self-consciously nearby in tastefully landscaped yards. Some thrust cell phones forward, digitally capturing the scene.

The buzz would travel quickly and the media would descend any time now—provided, of course, they could circumvent the contracted twenty-four-hour guard service manning the elaborately wrought gate at the community's sole entrance.

Detective First Class Katie Callahan guided the unmarked cruiser past the two uniforms lifting the tape, and rolled to a stop in the driveway, as her partner peered through the windshield.

"You know," Detective Sergeant Donald Dombrowski offered as he twisted in his seat and fumbled with the seatbelt release, "these gated communities abhor any hint of crime and the inevitable negative publicity. This is really gonna piss somebody off."

"Why'd we catch this one anyway, D? We weren't up. Why couldn't the day shift handle it? I'm dog tired—I hate working midnights."

"Don't whine, Katie, it's unbecoming. Maybe we got it because the call came in before eight, and we were still on the north side, *comprende*? So, quit complaining and let's see what's what."

1

They approached a patrol officer holding a clipboard.

He looked up, smiled, and offered the sign-in sheet. "Hey, Big D! Hi'ya Katie! So, y'all caught this one?"

"Yeah, Steve," Dombrowski grumbled, signing them in. "You know, no rest for the weary. What've we got?"

"Apparent suicide; middle-aged white male, in the garage, late model Cadillac, outta gas, ignition on, and a hose from the tailpipe into the interior."

"I don't see any garage." Katie shrugged. "Is it a separate building or rear entry to the main house?"

"Only one building," the officer explained. "The garage entrance is at the rear of the house. My partner, Baker, is at the garage door, keeping the scene secure."

"Tyrone Baker?" Katie asked. "We went through the academy together; he's your partner?"

"Yeah, for about a month now—"

"That's great, Steve," Dombrowski interrupted and got back on point. "We got ID on the *vic*?"

"Yeah, but it's tentative. Hold on." He paused, looked at his notes, and held up his cell phone to display a photo. "One Gregory Adamson. We ran the plate. Dispatch pulled an old DL pic from the DMV. It kinda looks like him. The DL address is about a mile from here. That's all we've got for an ID right now."

"Well, that's a start," Dombrowski acknowledged. "If the DL is still good, the photo can't be any older than eight years."

"Wait! This isn't his place?" Katie probed. "Hell, is it his car?"

"Nope and yep," Steve answered grinning. "He doesn't live here. The house is vacant, and has been for almost ten months; it's a foreclosure. A bank, Consolidated Federal, owns it. As for the vehicle, the plates are current, and the car is definitely registered to him."

"Wait a sec—*foreclosure?*" echoed Dombrowski, "In this neighborhood?"

"Hey, times are tough all over, D," Katie offered. "It's not like this economy is roaring back."

"Right. Well, who found the body?"

Steve again consulted his notes. "Real estate agent, uh, Abigail Fonseca, nice lady, but she's a little excitable. Ramirez and Harmon have her calmed down in the kitchen. She said she came to inspect the house at the request of the bank to list it or something. She babbled something about short sales; I'm not real sure. Anyway, she found the car in the garage, and the body. She made the 911 call on her cell phone."

"Did she know him, the decedent?" Katie asked.

"I really don't know. She didn't say so, but then we didn't ask her."

"All right, we'll take a look at the scene, and then take her preliminary statement. Katie, we'll need gloves and booties; and get the big flashlight from the trunk."

"Got it. Be right back."

"Steve, if the house has been vacant, is the power on, the water?"

"Yeah, Sarge, both are—strange, too. I'd thought they'd be off. Maybe the bank's been carrying the utilities?"

The big detective raised his eyebrows in response.

His cell phone rang just as his partner returned.

"Dombrowski . . . Yeah, Lieutenant, we're gonna need CSI here . . . Yeah, if you would, sir, that'll save me a call to the M.E.'s office . . . Oh, coupla hours, I think . . . No, sir, we got this . . . Right . . . Yes, sir, you got it. Bye."

"Sarge, did the boss just offer to send out the day shift to take this case," Katie asked as she handed him the gloves and booties, "and you turned him down?" A hint of petulance in her voice hovered just below the surface.

"Uh, well yeah," he admitted, mildly chagrined. "Not to worry, we'll wrap this up pretty quick, just like the brass wants. This looks like a real ground ball."

Her lips thinned in mute resentment and she stormed off in the direction of the garage.

"Whoa, Sarge," cautioned Steve. "I don't think your partner is too happy with you right now. Is everything cool?"

Dombrowski paused. *Something's bugging her, but I'd best keep that to myself.* "Oh yeah, we've just worked ten days straight of midnight to eight. She's not really a night person, a little tired is all; she'll be fine. This was supposed to be the start of her four days off. No big deal—I'll pep her up with my famous wit."

"R-i-ght." Steve chuckled. "Good luck with that!"

———————

DOMBROWSKI FOUND KATIE talking to Officer Tyrone Baker in front of the open garage door. The patrolman towered over the diminutive detective and yet appeared to be uncomfortable under her scrutiny. Neither was smiling; the sergeant immediately knew something was wrong.

"Problem, Detective?"

"My fault, Sarge," Officer Baker admitted. "I opened the garage door after we found the body. Sorry—wasn't thinking."

"Touch anything?"

"Just the opener button by the inside door." He pointed to a closed door on the rear wall of the garage. "But I used the tip of my pen in case of prints."

"No harm, no foul," Dombrowski assured him. "Don't sweat it, Officer Baker. Were the fumes bad?"

"Well, not really. I mean, you could smell exhaust and all, but the car wasn't running, outta gas. No idea how long. I didn't touch the hood, but I could feel the heat coming off it when I went to the driver's side to look in."

"Ty, did you or Steve call for an ambulance?" Katie asked.

"No. We were gonna; but when I called the Patrol Desk and told the desk sergeant what we had, he said to sit tight and wait for Homicide."

"It was that obvious, huh?" Katie winced.

The hulking patrolman grimaced and said, "Yeah, you'll see. Let me know when you're gonna open that car door. I'll switch posts with Steve. I don't want that stink getting on my uniform; I got a whole shift to work."

"Really, dumb-ass?" Katie teased. "So you let him catch the stink? You still gotta ride a whole shift with him. And you know, I think it's gonna get pretty hot today."

"Aw, crap," Ty groaned.

"Enough, you two," Dombrowski declared, shaking his head and grinning. "Under the circumstances, I think we'll let CSI and the M.E. crew open the car and process what they can. We'll just take a look and then interview the real estate agent."

The dark blue Cadillac sedan looked new, but was actually four years old. Somebody took excellent care of its appearance at least. A garden hose was duct-taped into one of the tailpipes. The other end of the hose was wedged between the uppermost part of the passenger side window frame and the glass. Another strip of duct tape sealed the length of the remaining inch-wide gap.

Katie pointed. "Sarge, you ever see that before?"

"Not exactly, not duct tape; cloth or pieces of clothing, yeah—anything to make a seal. I guess you can't beat duct tape, though."

The body was slumped toward the console, head lolled forward and canted to the right. The hands rested on the thighs, palms upward. The cloying odor of corruption was barely discernible, hovering at the edge of perception.

Dombrowski knew it would not be wise at this juncture to venture a guess how long the victim had been dead since decomposition would accelerate appreciably in the summer heat, especially in the confinement of a sealed car. Thankfully, determining the approximate time and actual cause of death were going to be the medical examiner's problems; but it sure looked like a classic suicide.

Hoping this one would be as simple as it appeared, Dombrowski nudged Katie. "All right Detective, what do we see?"

"Pretty much what we'd expect for a suicide, I think. Do the dash lights look dim to you?"

"Yeah, they do. Ignition's still on, so the battery's probably going down. Anything else?"

Moving around to the left rear passenger door, she played her flashlight beam throughout the interior. After a moment she looked up with pursed lips and knitted brow. "D, lemme ask you, if you were gonna commit suicide—"

"I'd eat my gun," he interrupted with a wry grin.

"Yeah, no shit. Listen, I mean do it this way, car exhaust, would you sit on your seat belt—you know, the clip part?"

"Huh? Show me."

"Look, follow the line of the shoulder belt, forward over the seat back, down and behind the body. It's not clipped into the latch, there by the console, so it has to be digging into his back—or his butt. I don't know about you, but I'd find that pretty uncomfortable."

"Yeah, me too. It might be nothing, but let's make sure we note it."

His phone rang.

"Dombrowski . . . Yes sir, Captain . . . Ah, no, we haven't started a canvass yet; we've still got to interview the woman who found the body . . . Yeah, well sure . . . Okay, thank you, sir . . . Right, as soon as we finish that interview . . . Yes, sir. 'Bye."

Katie's eyebrows rose in an unspoken question.

"Yep, that was the captain. It seems we are going to get some help on this case. Two teams from the day shift are on their way. No, don't look too happy; we're still the primaries. They're supposed to help with the legwork, the canvass, and any other interviews that might be needed."

She scowled, but kept silent.

He relented. "Look, I can see that something's bugging you. Want to tell me about it?"

She sulked and glanced askance toward Officer Baker, now standing just beyond the open overhead door. "No, not now, maybe later. Did the captain say anything else?"

"Yeah, we're supposed to report to his office as soon as we conclude the interview of our real estate agent, Ms. Fonseca."

"Okay, you got any clue why?"

"Nope, not yet, but something about this case has already rattled somebody's tree."

"Somebody in this neighborhood, you think?"

"It wouldn't surprise me. This is pretty exclusive real estate; some pretty influential people live here."

"So what? A case is a case," Katie spat and scowled. "The rich can go to jail, too."

"Oh, I can see your mood is improving. Can we dial down the *proletariat indignation* maybe just long enough to interview our anxious and excitable witness?"

Katie smirked, rolled her eyes, and offered her best mock-Russian accent, "*Da*, of course, comrade Sergeant."

CH 2

LT. WATERS SAVORED the last drag on his cigarette and crushed the butt into the gravel beneath his heel. The Criminal Investigations Division parking lot was the only place he could feed his habit these days—the whole damn building was now a smoke-free zone. He wouldn't quit if he could; it got him out of the office at least half a dozen times a shift. People expected to see him out here smoking; so, no one should think it unusual in the least. That was good, because he needed to catch Dombrowski and Callahan before they saw the captain.

He didn't have long to wait; their car pulled in and parked.

"HEY, LT," DOMBROWSKI hailed. "What're you doing still here? Weren't you off duty like two hours ago?"

"Yeah," added Katie, *sotto voce*, "like when we should've gotten off, too."

Dombrowski gave her *the look*. She shut up.

"I'm waiting on y'all. This Adamson case, did you get anything worthwhile from your interview with the woman who found the body?"

"Not really. She doesn't know the victim. She found the car in the garage and saw the body in it, didn't touch anything except the front door of the house and the interior door to the garage. She made the 911 call on her cell. We'll pull her records to confirm."

Waters nodded and asked, "Still look like a suicide?"

"Well yeah, it looks like it, but we'll wait for the M.E.'s final word. The ID is from a DMV pic, so it's still tentative, but probably good. The CSI crew started recovering evidence when we went on the interview, so they'll have anything the victim might've had on him, you know, like a wallet or cell phone."

"The day shift teams were starting the canvass," Katie added. "We haven't heard from them, so there's probably nothing to tell, not yet anyway."

The lieutenant pursed his lips and sighed. "That's it?"

"Yeah, LT, that's it so far," Dombrowski acknowledged. "Why the sudden interest in this case? Something we need to know?"

"The captain has guests in his office, *Feds*. I'm here to catch you before you report to him, in case there are any surprises. You know how he hates surprises."

The big sergeant only grinned. One never surprised Captain Walker, especially in the presence of guests.

"They're here on this case?" Katie queried.

"That's right," Waters confirmed, and pulled out his phone. "Kill a coupla minutes at your desks before going to his office. That'll give me time to make some calls and get him brought up to speed."

"You got it, boss," Dombrowski said. "Are you gonna be in that meeting?"

"Yeah, right after I talk to the CSI sergeant. And Detectives?"

"Sir?"

"Speak to no one else about this case."

"Yessir," they replied in unison.

Nudging her partner as they entered the building, Katie asked, "What the hell was that all about?"

"Damned if I know; but I suspect we're gonna find out soon enough."

DOMBROWSKI'S POLITE knock was answered by Captain Walker's familiar bellow.

"Come!"

Two men in suits rose as the detectives entered.

The captain started to make the introductions. "Detectives Dombrowski and Callahan, this is FBI Special Agent Carlson, and—"

A thin man wearing horn-rimmed glasses interrupted the captain and thrust out his hand. "Hi, call me Fred."

Shaking the offered hand, Dombrowski caught the flash of irritation that marred the captain's expression. It was not wise to interrupt the boss.

"*And,*" Capt. Walker grumbled, "this is Deputy U.S. Marshal Gonzalez."

The Deputy U.S. Marshal smiled and shook hands with the detectives, but remained silent.

"These detectives have just returned from the scene, having concluded an interview of the sole witness, Ms. Fonseca," the Captain intoned. "I understand she had little information to add. Correct, Sergeant?"

"Yes sir, Captain. Aside from her original statement, that's what our report will reflect."

"These gentlemen from the Department of Justice are here to provide us with some additional information regarding the decedent. It seems our identification inquiry tripped some flags in several databases. Agent Carlson, would you care to elucidate?"

"Ah, yes, of course. Your decedent, Gregory Adamson, is a retired U.S. Air Force officer, a former O.S.I. investigator. He's been retired for almost ten years. He had a high security clearance. We keep track of people who held that sort of clearance. Thus, your query got our attention."

Dombrowski glanced toward his boss. "Captain, if I may?"

"Of course, Sergeant," Walker replied, obviously pleased at the overt display of protocol courtesy.

"Agent Carlson—"

"Fred—call me Fred."

"Ah, right, Fred. Can you officially confirm the identification? The decedent is Adamson? You know him, personally?"

"Ah, no, I don't know him personally, but I've read his file. There are photographs, fingerprints, his Air Force I.D. and such."

"I believe I can also help you with that, Sergeant," offered the Deputy U.S. Marshal. "I have photos and prints as well. I've met him—even interviewed him about eighteen months ago. I'd be happy to make an ID for you, at your convenience."

"What can you tell us about next of kin?" Katie asked. "So far, we have his last known address from the DMV records, but no information on any family. We still have to make the notification."

The FBI agent flipped through the file and announced, "The subject is married, but separated; a divorce is pending. The wife is living in an apartment on the west side, with her sister. There are two adult children; a daughter living in Florida, married with no kids, and a son, single, attending college in Virginia."

The Deputy U.S. Marshal handed Katie a slip of paper. "The wife's name is Marian. Her sister is Louise Hesterly, a widow. This is her address and phone number."

"We appreciate that," Dombrowski said sincerely, "but I gotta ask, Deputy. I can see why the FBI might keep track of people with high clearances, but why is the Marshals Service interested?"

"Fair question, Sergeant—and you can call me Emilio. Did you notice the neighborhood where your scene is located—pretty nice, no? Well, we have a U.S. Circuit Court Judge who lives about two blocks away, and our Mr. Adamson had some strained interactions with members of the judge's family a while back."

"Okay," the sergeant acknowledged. "So, our dead guy had 'interactions' with a federal judge, or members of his family?"

"Right. Consequently, Mr. Adamson came up on our radar. We did a cursory protective investigation. It was subsequently determined that he was not a viable threat."

"So, you interviewed him in the course of your investigation? What about his wife?" Katie pressed.

"Certainly," the Deputy U.S. Marshal replied. "We interviewed their children, and her sister, who's about fifteen years younger. Although at the time, Marian was still living with her husband."

Dombrowski lifted a finger. "Okay. Uh, Fred, you told us that Adamson was retired; but was he working anywhere, post-retirement? Did he currently have a job?"

"No, there's no record of any employment, no social security or tax withholding. He wasn't working," Fred assured them.

"Well, not exactly," Emilio cautioned. "He didn't have a paid position, but he did volunteer. He served on the board of the neighborhood home owners association, or HOA, if you will. He also chaired their architectural review committee, or ARC. In fact, it was certain related activities that brought him to our attention."

"How so?" asked the captain.

"Let's just say that Mr. Adamson took what he believed to be his duties and responsibilities with the HOA and the ARC very seriously. This HOA covers a number of adjacent neighborhood communities in a specific geographic region. These communities have covenants, rules and regulations about almost everything, way beyond basic housing codes. If you've ever lived in a condo you know what I mean. It can vary just how involved they get. In some cases there's tremendous emphasis on the appearance of properties in the neighborhood; and, it's very restrictive. I mean the landscaping, the color of the house and its attachments, window treatments—almost anything that can be seen from the street is regulated. If a homeowner fails to comply with a covenant standard they can be fined. Ignore an assessed fine and in some cases it doubles every thirty days. The HOA can elect to correct the noncompliance issue and bill the homeowner—they can even put a lien on the property."

"Is that even legal?" Katie gasped.

The Deputy U.S. Marshal nodded and shrugged. "Afraid so. Covenants are contracts, and contract law prevails. People sign these agreements at settlement, along with a pile of property transfer documents. Most of them just want to get the settlement session over with and never bother to read the fine print.

"Dealing with strict HOAs can get pretty ugly, pretty quick. See, any time you want to change or repair something—like put in a flower bed, plant a tree, repaint shutters, or put on a new roof—you have to submit a written request for consideration and permission to the relevant architectural review committee. Without that permission, you can't do anything."

"And Adamson?" prompted Dombrowski.

"He would drive around the neighborhoods on his own looking for covenant violations. He'd take pictures and start files on homes in question. He'd knock on the door to notify the homeowner of the violation. If no one was home, he'd leave a warning citation on the door. Thereafter, he'd have the ARC or the HOA send the homeowner a letter threatening fines if the violation wasn't corrected by a certain time."

"What if he found someone at home?" Katie pressed.

"That was sometimes a problem," Emilio acknowledged. "He tended to be rather assertive, even outright confrontational if someone disagreed or argued with him. But that was usually with the men—although sometimes with women, too. He was known to be a bit flirtatious with younger, attractive women."

"Was that the sort of thing that happened with the judge's family?" asked Dombrowski.

The Deputy U.S. Marshal nodded and his eyebrows rose. "Essentially, yes. The judge wasn't home. His daughter, seventeen, was helping her mother in the front yard, planting some bulbs and trimming some bushes. Her mother was in the house on the phone when Adamson approached the girl and initiated a conversation. Suffice to say, her mother took umbrage at this and ordered him off the property. They had words, some of which may have been construed as threats, HOA fines, liens, and such. He left her pretty upset. She called her husband. He called my boss; and, we commenced our inquiry."

"Did she, the mother, know who he was?" Katie asked.

"No, not at that time, but she was later informed in the course of the investigation."

"So, what finally happened? Did you lock him up?" the captain asked.

"No, it never had to come to that. When we interviewed Adamson's putative boss, an attorney who ran the HOA, he had the good sense not to run afoul of a federal judge. That was pretty much the end of it. Adamson was instructed never to return to the judge's home. And as far as we know, he never did. We closed our case; but of course, it remains accessible in our database."

"An attorney ran the HOA? Is that unusual?" Katie wondered aloud.

"Not really," he said with a shrug, "especially in these high end communities. The lawyer's name was Walter Farrell. As far as I know he's still the HOA honcho."

Three brisk knocks sounded on the door, and Lt. Waters poked his head in. "Oh, sorry, sir—didn't know you were in a meeting."

Dombrowski and Katie shared a knowing glance, as the captain feigned surprise. "Oh, it's quite all right, please join us. Gentlemen, this is Lt. Waters. Lieutenant, have you any news on this Adamson matter?"

"Yes, sir. The M.E. cleared the scene; the body is on its way to the morgue. He can do the postmortem first thing tomorrow. The media showed up, but never got past the entrance gate. CSI is still on the scene, but they're almost done."

"Good. What else?"

"The day shift teams have completed the initial canvass and are on their way back in. The guard service, who mans the gate, keeps some records of who comes and goes, contractors and vendors mostly, but not residents. The decedent isn't a resident of that particular neighborhood, so his comings and goings may have been noted. However, the guard service wasn't very cooperative, citing their privacy policies. We'll need a subpoena for their records. The rest of the teams' reports will reflect that quite a number of residents had interactions with the decedent, none of which were characterized as pleasant."

The captain steepled his fingers and rocked back in his chair. "That comports with what Deputy Marshal Gonzalez has been telling us. Did these interactions have to do with the decedent's activities on behalf of the home owners association?"

Lt. Waters nodded. "Precisely so, sir. It appears he was universally disliked. I understand that the terms 'abrasive' and 'rude' were frequently heard during the canvass."

"That still doesn't sound like a good reason to commit suicide," Dombrowski mumbled.

"No, it doesn't," echoed the captain. "You and Callahan cover the autopsy tomorrow. Then backtrack his movements and let's find out if he had another reason."

Dombrowski nodded affirmatively and noticed that Katie stifled a scowl.

"Captain," offered the Deputy U.S. Marshal, "if it's convenient for your detectives, I can meet them at the Medical Examiner's Office tomorrow, prior to the autopsy, and make the necessary identification."

Captain Walker looked to his detectives, who both shrugged and nodded in unison. "That'll work. Thank you, Marshal."

The FBI agent weakly cleared his throat. "Ahem, uh, since I don't think I'd be of any further assistance with the, uh, identification at the Medical Examiner's Office, I'll leave that to Deputy Marshal Gonzalez."

"Oh, that's okay, Fred," Dombrowski said, surreptitiously winking at his partner. "I'm sure you'll be with us in spirit."

CH 3

DR. PARKER, THE CHIEF Medical Examiner, strode into the staff lounge to find Detectives Dombrowski and Callahan holding foam cups of coffee and staring vacantly at a television screen set against one wall. The Weather Channel played on in silence, the sound muted. They glanced up as he reached for the coffee pot and poured himself a cup.

"So, tell me, Doc," the sergeant probed, "are we done yet? Can we wrap this one up? Katie wants to go home."

His partner elbowed him in the ribs, forcing him to juggle his coffee.

"Ignore him, Doc. It's just that this was supposed to be the start of four days off—time I really needed. Never mind. Where do we stand, Doc?"

The M.E. pursed his lips, cocked his head, and blew gently on his steaming coffee. "Well, I've got good news and bad news. I've finished the postmortem; that's the good news. The bad news is that this is still a suspicious death, definitely not a suicide."

"Oh, crap," Katie mumbled and sighed.

Dombrowski shrugged in resignation. He had no plans of his own, but he did feel sympathy for Katie. She hadn't told him what she had planned, but he knew she felt it was important. "Sorry, kiddo. So, what's the word, Doc?"

"I did not find what I should have, no carbon monoxide in his blood or lungs. The lividity was inconsistent as well. Katie, you were correct in regard to the seat belt clip; it put a severe dent in the dermis just above the lumbar. He was dead, maybe an hour or more, before he was placed in that vehicle."

"So, she was right," Dombrowski acknowledged. "It's staged to look like a suicide. What was the true cause of death?"

"I'm not completely sure, yet. There are no obvious wounds or signs of trauma. To be honest it looks a lot like a stroke, but I'm not certain. I did find traces of gases in his lung tissue that I suspect will prove to be phosphine and chlorine. That analysis is underway. I'll know more shortly. My best estimate for time of death is between forty-eight and seventy-two hours ago."

"A stroke? Could it be a natural?" Katie mused aloud. "And then staged? No, that wouldn't make sense, not if there's insurance. Most don't always pay on a suicide. Damn!"

"Good point about insurance," Dombrowski noted. "We'll have to look deeper into that. I think the staging points more to a murder that might hopefully be overlooked. How rare are those gases, Doc?"

"Chlorine isn't rare at all; it's in lots of common household products, bleach for example. Phosphine can be a bit rarer. It's found in some pesticides and fumigants; and it's used in the semiconductor industry. It can exist in nature as a result of decaying organic matter that contains natural phosphorus. Both chemicals are used in the textile industry. Pure phosphine gas can be quite volatile—very explosive in the presence of oxygen. Breathing enough of either chlorine or phosphine can be fatal."

"So, can that cause a stroke?" Katie pressed.

"Maybe," the M.E. cautioned. "It is arguably a possibility. As I said, I'll know for certain when the analysis is complete. By the way, where's your friend, the Deputy U.S. Marshal? Was he here only to make the identification?"

"Yeah, he had to go back to his office. I'll call him and our bosses with this update. I already know what they'll say; we'll still need a confirmation on the COD."

"I'll advise as soon as I know."

"Okay, thanks, Doc. Come on, Katie, we've got some calls to make."

———————

DEATH NOTIFICATIONS to next of kin can be unpredictable. Some people take the news with stoic calm, while others may react in a dramatic display of unbridled emotion. Of course, most fall somewhere in between. Marian Adamson fell definitely closer to the stoic side of the bell curve.

Sitting on the sofa, holding hands with Louise, her sister, Marian blinked as tears welled in her eyes. She took a deep breath and thrust her chin forward, the barely perceptible quiver betraying the anguish in her heart. "I—I'm sorry, Detective, but I haven't spoken to my husband in months. I can't believe he's . . . he's . . . "

"We're sorry for your loss, ma'am," Dombrowski soothed. "Please understand that we have to ask these questions."

Louise plucked some tissues from a box on an end table and pressed them into her sister's hands.

"When," Dombrowski asked, "did you last see him?"

"Oh, months ago, in my attorney's office. We are—*were* divorcing . . . It was a meeting to work out the division of property, our things . . . I guess that doesn't matter any more, does it?"

"So you haven't spoken with him, even over the phone, since then?"

"No. We only communicated through the lawyers. Mine is Preston Harris. My husband is represented by Walter Farrell."

Dombrowski and Katie shared a quick and knowing look.

"Louise, could I trouble you for a glass of water?" Katie asked.

She followed Louise into the small kitchen.

———

"FORGIVE ME, LOUISE," Katie whispered, "I'm not really thirsty. I got the sense there was something you wanted to say, but perhaps not in front of Marian. Am I right?"

"Well, it's just that she won't speak ill of the dead—we weren't brought up that way. But that man treated her terribly. She put up with it for years—for the sake of the children, I'm sure."

"Can you be more specific? What did she put up with?"

"He was unfaithful! And he made little effort to hide it! It was just shameful—she didn't deserve that. I urged her many times to leave him, but she stayed—as I said, for the children."

"When did the divorce idea finally take hold?"

"About eighteen months ago, when their son left for college. You know they have a lovely daughter—she's the oldest—married and trying to start a family of her own down in Florida."

"Yes, good for her. How did the son and daughter get along with their father?"

"Hmmph, they didn't! They couldn't wait to get out of that house. Their father was an overbearing disciplinarian who was just impossible to please. I wouldn't have anything to do with him if I could avoid it. I'd try to visit with Marian only when I knew he was away—and that was often enough. Lord knows what he was up to . . . "

"I see. Do you know if he was ever violent?"

"Do you mean did he hit them? No, not that I know of." Louise leaned toward Katie and whispered, "I'm sure Marian would have told me—she tells me everything."

"Of course. She's been with you for the past few days?"

"Oh, we haven't been anywhere but here for the past two weeks." Louise shrugged, her hand going to her throat. "Oh, we went to the grocery store; we probably should do that again soon. The best coupons come out in tomorrow's paper—we always shop with coupons. You can save so much if you're careful."

"Oh yes, I know just what you mean. Thank you, Louise. I know you're going to be a big help to your sister in this difficult time. Shall we rejoin them?"

LT. WATERS PINCHED the bridge of his nose and considered slipping out of the office for a quick cigarette, but he spied Dombrowski and Callahan heading for his door and knew his craving would have to wait.

"You ready for us, LT?"

"Yeah, sit down. What've you got?"

The big sergeant flipped through his notebook and cleared his throat. "The M.E. says it's still suspicious and not a suicide. He thinks it looks like a stroke. The decedent was already dead when placed in the vehicle. He found traces of gases in the lungs but not carbon monoxide. So, COD is still pending."

"Ha!" The lieutenant scoffed. "You know a stroke might make it a natural—unless it was induced. But the car exhaust, I don't get. If our victim is already dead, he's not gonna inhale any carbon monoxide. I guess most people don't expect us to check that close if it looks so much like a suicide."

"True," agreed Dombrowski. "Most people, when contemplating suicide, don't really think it through—"

"Or when trying to stage one," interrupted Katie. "Remember, the M.E. didn't say asphyxiation, much less carbon monoxide poisoning."

"Yeah," her partner agreed and shrugged. "Anyway, we found the wife and made the notification, absent any specifics, of course. Her reaction was kinda what we expected; surprised, hurt, but composed. They were going through a divorce, and had been split for over a year, only communicating through the attorneys. We haven't talked to the lawyers yet. Her sister was present; but Katie managed a separate interview. The two can alibi each other out, for at least the last two weeks."

Katie picked up the narrative. "The younger sister, Louise, didn't like the decedent and strongly resented the way he treated her sister. He was unfaithful, and blatant about it."

"Hmm, that sounds like motive for the wife and the sister," Lt. Waters mused aloud. "Will their alibis hold?"

"Good question," Dombrowski conceded, "since they can essentially alibi each other, I don't know. I don't see how we can corroborate or refute with what we now have. We confirmed the adult children's alibis; the son is still away at college, and the daughter is in Florida."

"There is insurance," Katie added, "an old policy, a holdover from his military service, but it's a modest payout, about a hundred grand, payable to the wife and kids in equal portions. The policy has a suicide exclusion clause, so any payment will be contingent on the results of our investigation. If it's a natural death, why would a family member—a beneficiary—stage it as a suicide? It makes no sense."

The lieutenant shrugged and slid a large envelope across his desk. "Here are copies of the canvass reports from the day shift teams. Funny thing—there were quite a few vacant homes in that neighborhood. The teams discovered that by knocking on doors and looking in windows. Outside, the lawns and all looked normal and well maintained."

"Well, our scene is in a vacant house, too," Katie remarked. "In fact, it's a foreclosure."

"Yeah, and the power and water were on," Dombrowski added. "So, somebody is footing the bill. It's not the bank involved in the foreclosure proceedings, Consolidated Federal, at least not directly. We checked with the water and power utility companies. Payments are coming through a corporate credit card issued by another bank based in Delaware. They're not very cooperative absent a subpoena. We think it might be the HOA, you know, keeping up appearances. We'll look into it."

Lt. Waters nodded and pointed to the envelope. "You'll see that your decedent was definitely not a popular guy. You'll also find copies of what CSI found; everything in his wallet, some cash, a few credit cards, and a list of phone numbers from his cell phone memory. There are some camera images. We're getting a subpoena for the full phone records to include toll calls."

"That reminds me, did we get anything from the on-site security company yet?" Dombrowski inquired.

"I'm glad you asked." Lt. Waters grinned and slid another envelope across the desk. "Here's that subpoena. The attorney of record is Walter Farrell, the same attorney in charge of the HOA. Weren't you going to interview him anyway?"

"Oh yeah, and by the way," Katie quipped, "he's also the attorney representing our decedent, Mr. Adamson, in his divorce proceedings. The Clerk of Court's office confirmed it."

Dombrowski grinned and nodded as the lieutenant's eyebrows rose. "Trust me, LT, he's on our list."

"Well, first," Waters countered, tossing a set of keys on the desk, "I'd go have a look around Adamson's home; these are his keys. They were in his pocket, so they're evidence. You have to sign a chain of custody form, from me to you. Bring them back to me after you secure his place."

"We're on it," Dombrowski assured him. "We'll check in with you from that location."

CH 4

THE HOUSE LOOKED NO different from its neighbors on the quiet street. Lawns were well maintained and neatly trimmed to near military precision.

However, the interior of this house was a study in chaos.

"What the hell?" Dombrowski mumbled from the doorway. Reaching along the wall, he flipped a light switch. Nothing happened. "Crap! Lights are dead—probably no power."

Katie stepped inside and pulled open the curtains covering the front windows. "Holy shit! Sarge, look at this place! Somebody tossed it, but good! Hey, there's an alarm panel—it's dead, too. I can't tell if it's monitored. Shouldn't there be a battery backup?"

"Yeah, I dunno where, though. We've still gotta look around, but let's try not to disturb too much."

"Think it's a crime scene?"

"Dunno, maybe. Use gloves."

Sunlight bounced off overturned furniture, shredded cushions, and scattered papers. If someone had been searching for something, they'd been in a hurry. Every room in the house was in a sorry state. Even the refrigerator door stood open, its discarded contents strewn across the kitchen floor. What should have been cold had long been at room temperature. It was clear from the sour stench that whatever happened here had occurred some days ago.

"Sarge, in here—back bedroom."

He found Katie squatting behind a small desk near the far wall, holding a series of wires in her fist.

"What?"

"Phone line's dead. These wires are AC power cords and Cat-6 cabling. The power cords are plugged into a wall socket, but not connected to anything." She stood and traced the Cat-6 cabling to the top shelf of a closet. "Here's the router. Here's the main alarm box, bolted to the back wall of this closet. Uh-oh, the ground wire to the battery's been cut."

"That figures," Dombrowski groaned as he got down on one knee and peered under the bed. "There's a busted up wireless printer under here—looks like it was kicked—better leave it for CSI."

"Makes sense," she agreed. "There's no computer. My guess is they took all the hardware; monitor, keyboard, and drive tower. Or maybe he just had a laptop or tablet; but whatever, it's not here."

Stroking his chin he asked, "So, you think that's what they were looking for, his computer?"

She gestured at the dishevelled room. "Yeah, I'd say so. I don't see any storage media either, no discs or backup drives. Think about it; as nice as he kept that Caddy, and the way this home looks on the outside, Adamson just seems too meticulous not to have backed up his data. I'd bet they took that, too."

"Well, I gotta agree he wouldn't trash his own place," Dombrowski reasoned. "And we can surmise that he had a computer that's now missing. So, this probably is a crime scene, even though there's no sign of forced entry."

Katie shrugged and reminded him, "Well, we got in easily enough."

"Yeah, using his keys. Wait! Are you thinking someone else used his keys—assuming of course, he didn't do this?"

"Well, why not? Neither one of us thinks *he* did this. His keys have only effectively been in our custody since the body was discovered. Wait—think his estranged wife, Marian, has a key?"

"Probably, but do you see her doing this? Isn't she supposed to have been at her sister's?"

"Yeah, I get it. Besides, I don't see her doing this either. But remember what the M.E. said, there may well be a two day window from the time of his death until discovery of the body. Or, he may not have even been dead when this place was ransacked."

Dombrowski slowly nodded and speculated. "Hell, for all we know he may have even been here when it went down. It could have been someone he knew, someone he let in, or someone he trusted with a key. Maybe he was even coerced, forced to surrender his laptop, or whatever, and any backup files."

"Good points," Katie acknowledged. "We may need to get with the M.E. and have another look at that body."

"Yeah, for sure. I gotta call the lieutenant," he announced, retrieving his phone. "We're gonna definitely need CSI out here. And we're gonna have to find out if this alarm system is monitored."

"Where would the electrical service come in?" Katie wondered aloud. "I'm gonna take another look around the yard just to be sure we didn't miss anything."

"Be careful. Don't touch any wires. We can let CSI trace the power interruption."

"I'm just gonna look, not touch. Don't worry."

———

AFTER WALKING AROUND the carefully landscaped yard, she found the electric meter on the side of the dwelling. Conduits rose from underground sources; there were no overhead lines. Everything appeared to be intact, even the telephone line.

Logically, the incoming service panel would be the next thing to check; but she was no electrician. She'd let the experts deal with this.

Returning to the front of the house, she was surprised to see Dombrowski standing on the front walk, scowling at the home's perfect façade.

"What's wrong?" she asked.

"We've got another body. Let's go."

"Damn, where?"

"The HOA office."

THE HOME OWNERS ASSOCIATION office was a modest suite on the second floor of the glass-fronted office building. The small reception area was crowded with uniformed patrol officers and CSI techs with their crime scene gear.

"Hey Sarge, hello Katie. Here's the sign-in sheet." The young officer thrust a clipboard at Dombrowski for his *John Hancock*, and stole a shy glance at Katie.

Reaching for her pen, Katie followed her partner's lead, knowing that all personnel on the scene were required to record their presence. She handed the clipboard back and tried to ignore the rookie's eager smile. She didn't want to encourage him.

"Thanks, Tim," Dombrowski rumbled. "What've we got?"

"Looks like a suicide; white female, about forty, in the bathtub, no ID. Janitor found the body and called. The office was locked. He came in response to the first floor tenant's complaint about a water leak in her ceiling. He turned the tub water off."

"A bathtub in an office building?" Dombrowski asked.

"Yeah, before this block was rezoned commercial it was residential, apartments and condos. This building, like most along this street, went through renovations a few years ago. Quite a few of these office suites still have full baths. Some are very elaborate; this one's pretty nice—you'll see."

"Where's the janitor, now?" asked Katie.

"In the building manager's first floor office—my partner's keeping him company until you talk to him."

"Good, let's keep him there for now," Dombrowski suggested. "Was anybody else here when he opened up? Damn, Tim, how big is this suite anyway?"

"Not that big, Sarge. Besides the bathroom, there are three more rooms; a conference room with a big table and half a dozen chairs, a file room, and a small office. All were unoccupied."

"Has CSI been in the bathroom yet?"

"Nah, they only looked in from the doorway. They knew to wait for you guys. I understand your office already called for the M.E."

"Okay, thanks Tim. We'll have a look."

Katie handed her partner a set of stretch booties and latex gloves. Thus attired, they stepped into the bathroom.

A fully clothed woman lay wedged in the tub, only her knees and head above the still water. Her head lolled to her right, mouth open, and eyelids half closed.

Dombrowski and Katie stood still and took in the entire room. Pink-tinged water filled the tub to its brim and pooled around its base, covering about a third of the tiled floor. There were no obvious signs of a struggle; nothing seemed out of place, save for a black leather pump lying near the tub.

"Something's way off here," Katie remarked, looking down into the tub.

"Yeah? More than taking a bath at the office?"

Her deadpan expression spoke volumes.

His humor faltered and he capitulated. "Okay, 'sorry. I guess she could have been a lunchtime jogger. Never mind. Go on."

Sighing, Katie swept her hand to encompass the recumbent body. "For one thing, she's fully clothed—and she's still wearing her other shoe. And check this out."

Katie gently dipped her gloved hands into the water. A trace of water sloshed over the tub's lip. Without further disturbing the corpse, she carefully lifted one arm and then the other out of the water. The skin of each inner forearm bore a deep solitary slice from wrist to elbow. "No rigor yet, and only a little wrinkling of the fingers. This is probably a fresh scene."

"Could be," he agreed, carefully stepping around a pinkish puddle so as not to contaminate the scene, or get his booties wet.

Katie eased the corpse's arms back below the waterline and into their original positions. "Another thing, Sarge, if she bled out in this tub, wouldn't the water be darker? This water is still warm."

"So, you think someone put her in this tub?"

"I dunno, maybe. Something's not right. Who would cut both arms that deeply and cleanly? What did she use to cut herself? Do you see anything?"

"No, but we can't see what might be under the body." He pointed to the lone pump on the floor. "What's with this shoe?"

"That's what I mean; why get into a tub wearing one shoe? Hell, why get into one fully clothed? That's just not the way women act; they're more careful about these things. That outfit she's wearing—the skirt, sleeveless blouse, and dark hose—that's business-like attire and expensive. Hell, those shoes alone are worth a few hundred bucks. She'd be more careful with this outfit—even if she planned to die in it."

Seeing the puzzled look on her partner's face, she simply added, "Look, just trust me on this—something's not kosher."

Dombrowski smiled broadly, but kept silent.

"What?" she demanded.

"Nothing," he answered. "I happen to agree with you. Please continue."

"Okay. Here's another thing—there's no note. And where's her purse? She's gotta have a purse."

He shrugged and called out to the other room. "Hey, anybody find a purse? Or any ID?"

A CSI tech answered, "Not in plain view. The M.E. crew is here. Can we start processing the scene? If we find something, we'll holler."

Katie shrugged, and Dombrowski responded. "Yeah, go ahead. We'll be downstairs interviewing the janitor."

———————

LT. WATERS GROUND THE butt beneath his heel and popped a breath mint into his mouth. He was about to return to his office when his cell phone rang.

"Waters . . . Yeah, Captain, at the back door . . . You bet, as a matter of fact, they're pulling in now . . . Yes, sir, I'll send them. 'Bye."

He started toward the detectives before they'd even shut their car off.

———————

KATIE SAW HIM FIRST. "Oh-oh, something's up. Hey, LT, are you looking for us?"

"I am, indeed. Get over to the M.E.'s office. They've already started on the post of your latest body."

"Damn, that was fast," remarked Dombrowski. "We just finished verifying the ID, one Jennifer Halsted, part-time administrative clerk for the HOA. It turns out the janitor, Hector Almanza, knew her and could make a formal ID for us. He had her contact information on his tenant list. He pointed out her car, too—a late model Toyota sedan, still in the parking lot."

Waters scratched his chin and asked, "Did you find any next of kin info, or go by her home?"

"No to both," Katie offered. "We've got the DMV registration data and her license photo, but we wanted to wait until CSI finished with the scene. They hadn't found her purse or any personal info by the time we cleared the scene."

Waters nodded. "The CSI team is done, and on their way in. However, I don't know what was found. Y'all go ahead. I'll call you when they get here and I know more."

"You got it, LT," Dombrowski acknowledged. "We're on it."

CH 5

THE AUTOPSY SUITE WAS kept chilled to an even seventy degrees. Spartan in its appointments, the glaring lights, white tiled walls, and stainless cabinets lent substance to the ambiance of antiseptic proficiency. In fact, it bore a strong resemblance to a hospital operating room, but without the typically narrow operating table. Instead, the recessed stainless table with drains at one end gave a strong hint as to its true purpose. Of course, the woman's corpse lying thereon was rather conclusive.

Dr. Parker glanced up and saw Detectives Dombrowski and Callahan standing patiently beyond the glass doors of the suite. He knew they would not enter until he beckoned.

"THINK WE'VE GOT TIME for a coffee?" Katie asked her partner. "We could wait in the staff lounge."

"Nah, let's wait a minute. He can see us. I think he's gonna invite us in."

No one, save the Medical Examiner's staff entered the autopsy suite absent an invitation, or unaccompanied. The detectives respected that rule, knowing that an autopsy is a search for evidence; and, the integrity of evidence is always a priority.

Dr. Parker stepped away from the table, and waved them in.

"Hi'ya, Doc," greeted Dombrowski. "You called for us?"

"I did. Our Ms. Halsted here—"

"Whoa, that's her?" Dombrowski spouted. "I didn't even recognize her. She sure looks different without her make-up, I guess."

"Yeah," Katie agreed, "it looks like she glammed herself up to go to work at the office."

"Ahem . . . As I was saying, Detectives, Ms. Halsted is not a suicide, as I understand you two suspected. Rather, she appears to have succumbed to a stroke."

"What the hell!" Katie blurted. "Another stroke? Fully clothed in a bathtub? Or was she dead before going in the tub?"

The M.E. shook his head and shrugged. "I can't tell you that for certain. I can tell you the lacerations on her forearms were postmortem."

"Oh yeah? Thus, no blood pressure," Dombrowski deduced. "I guess that would explain why the water wasn't darker with more blood. What do you think made the cuts?"

"Yeah," Katie added. "We didn't see anything at the scene."

The doctor held up a plastic evidence bag; a thin bladed letter opener lay inside. "Your colleagues from the CSI unit dropped this off a little while ago. It was found in the bathtub under the body. It is reasonably sharp—however, not sharp enough. This blade did not make those lacerations."

"Damn, then what did?"

"I don't know, Sergeant, but it was very sharp—more like a scalpel or razor—certainly not this letter opener."

"I wonder," mused Katie, "if CSI got any latents off it. Do you know, Doc?"

"I asked; they did not. I presume you will assume custody and return it to your evidence locker?"

"Of course," she answered as her partner raised a finger.

"What about time of death, Doc?"

"As I said," Dr. Parker cautioned, "I'm not certain as to the exact time of death, but I strongly suspect it was just before she went into that tub. If her heart was beating once she was in the water, it stopped shortly thereafter. The warm water delayed the body's cooling to some degree, so the liver temp wasn't all that helpful. Nonetheless, I would estimate TOD to be within two hours of the body being found."

"So, she dies of a stroke," Katie reasoned. "Someone puts her in that tub, and then slices her arms. We found no blood spatter in the room, just what had diluted in the tub water. So, someone tried to make this look like a suicide, too."

"Okay, two strokes and two staged suicides—all within a couple of days—that's just too damn much to be mere coincidence!" Dombrowski declared.

"Can strokes be induced?" Katie asked, absently chewing on her lip.

The M.E. grinned and crooked a finger. "I thought you'd never ask. Step this way."

Standing at the autopsy table, Dr. Parker pulled the overhead examination light closer to the head of the corpse. Opening the jaw and pulling it forward, he pulled the tongue out and to one side to expose the back of the throat. "I found two small puncture marks in the tissues on either side at the rear of the throat; more specifically, what appear to be hypodermic needle marks. This is the region of the interior carotid arteries. I believe this woman was injected with air in these two arteries causing massive air embolisms, and thus the subsequent fatal stroke."

"Air? That's all it takes?" Katie asked.

"Oh yes," the doctor assured her. "Air, 10 to 20cc or more, creates a blockage that would effectively interrupt a significant amount of blood flow to the brain, in this case, enough to cause death in a very short time. We can be certain that this is the cause of her death."

"We still have a problem," Dombrowski cautioned. "However unlikely it might be for her to do this to herself—as a suicide method, I mean—it is possible, right?"

"That would be quite a stretch, Sergeant. She would have to have had considerable medical skill or training. And it would be extremely difficult to perform two injections. The first one would cause a stroke to one side of the brain almost immediately, but not necessarily death. I have no doubt that a second injection in the other artery would cause death. But in all candor, I think a second self-inflicted injection would be nigh impossible. Besides, she would reflexively fight the entire procedure. I would speculate that she was already unconscious when injected."

"That makes sense," Dombrowski agreed. "Forgive me, but I'm just thinking that a lawyer might argue the point. So, how does she get unconscious in the first place?"

"Yeah, wouldn't she put up a fight?" Katie asked. "I don't see any defensive marks or wounds."

Dr. Parker nodded and grinned. "Neither did I, at first. Then I found this." Lifting one shoulder, he rolled Jennifer Halsted's body up on its side. "See these two red marks, just below the base of the neck, here? These are not insect bites or subcutaneous infections. These are burn marks from an electrical source; I would guess a stun gun. These marks are only reddened because the metal probes did not penetrate her clothing, like the barbs from a taser would."

"Now I get it," declared Katie. "Our perp stuns her, thus rendering her unconscious or at least helpless, and then injects her with air. Oh man, that is just . . . pretty—"

"Sophisticated? Diabolical?" offered her leering partner before she could finish her sentence.

"I was gonna say pretty *creepy*. So, it's definitely a homicide, right Doc?"

"Indeed. And as the good sergeant has duly noted, two stroke victims and two staged suicides, in too narrow a time frame, is simply too much coincidence. So, I re-examined the first victim, Mr. Adamson, and found the same puncture marks in his throat as well. However, I did not find any burns, no stun gun or taser marks. Nonetheless, we can conclude that we definitely have two homicides with a similar method of execution—no pun intended."

"Crap", mumbled Katie, "a serial killer?"

"Oh, man, let's hope not," Dombrowski groaned. "Doc, we were thinking that Adamson might have been restrained at some point. Did you find any marks or contusions on him that might support that notion?"

"No, not marks or contusions, but there was a trace of an adhesive at the base of a thumbnail—uh, left hand. As I recall, it appeared to be a very common soft and gummy kind of glue. It'll all be in my report."

"Common and gummy?" Katie asked. "You mean like on duct tape?"

"Yes, possibly."

The detectives shared a look.

"We had duct tape on the scene—a fair amount," Dombrowski explained. "We'll have to check with CSI to see if it's a match."

"And how it'd get on the back of his thumb?" Katie added. "Maybe we'll get lucky and they found some prints."

"Yeah, other than the victim's. So, Doc, any luck with the lab on those gas traces you found?"

The M.E. brightened and nodded affirmatively. "Yes, Sergeant, we have confirmation of chlorine and phosphine, as we suspected. And in anticipation of your next question, yes, either of which, in sufficient quantities, could render someone unconscious."

"At least long enough to perform the injections?" Katie probed.

"Oh yes, quite easily. But keep in mind that too much of either gas would be fatal. The appropriate dosage to attain unconsciousness would be tricky."

The detectives shared another knowing glance; this was going to be one bitch of a case. Katie gritted her teeth and Dombrowski sighed in resignation. "Damn! So, who are we looking for, Doc, somebody with medical training?"

"Possibly. This technique would require considerable skill. But I wouldn't discount anyone who is used to giving injections. This is a trick that could be learned."

"So, a diabetic could be a suspect?"

"Or any junkie," Katie spat with disgust.

"Oh, I don't know," Dombrowski mused with a grin. "How many junkies carry stun guns?"

———————————

LT. WATERS KNOCKED on the captain's door.

"Come. What is it Lieutenant?"

"The desk sergeant called. He's dealing with a man downstairs who's insisting on speaking with the 'chief of detectives.'"

"Well, that would be Assistant Chief Dunbar, I suppose, since he oversees CID. Why are you telling me?"

"He identifies himself as Walter Farrell, and he's pretty upset about something."

"Really? What?"

"He won't say, not until he speaks with someone in authority. I thought that might best be you, sir."

"I gather this is the same man Dombrowski and Callahan were planning to serve with a subpoena? Where are they now?"

"That's correct, sir. They're on their way back from the M.E.'s office. They should be here in a few minutes."

"Good. Escort Mr. Farrell to the conference room and keep him company. I'll join you after I spend a few minutes with our detectives."

"Yes sir, anything else?"

"Yeah, get him a cup of coffee or tea. I want his prints on something."

Lt. Waters just smiled; the captain never missed a trick.

As he pulled the door open to leave the captain's office, he almost bumped into a pair of men in gray jumpsuits crowding the door, janitors from the cleaning crew. One held a wastebasket while the other pawed through its contents. The two men appeared equally surprised; and Waters quickly apologized.

"Oh, sorry, I didn't know you were out here. Are you guys new? I usually recognize members of the crew. Have you guys been on another shift?"

"Yeah, uh, sir. We've been here a coupla weeks—been rotating to learn the shifts and all."

"And stuff like separating the recyclables," his companion hastily added, hoisting the wastebasket.

"Okay, I see," Waters said as he strode down the hall. "Y'all have a good day."

———————

"SO, YOU WANNA TELL me what was so important about the time off we seem to have been screwed out of?" Dombrowski asked as he drove.

"Meh, it's not that big a deal, I guess," dismissed Katie. "I'd promised my dad I'd spend some time with him and get him out of that place for a while; maybe even take him up to the cabin for a coupla days. I hate to have to disappoint him—again."

"Come on, Katie, he was a career cop with the State Police—he'll understand. Besides, I thought he liked the VA home, doesn't he?"

"Well, he did, when a few of his older friends were there; but people die. And to be honest, his early onset Alzheimer's is getting a little worse each time I see him. It scares the hell outta me to know that someday he won't even know who I am—not even remember me. What time I can spend with him now is precious to me."

"Damn, that's understandable but tough to deal with in this job—there'll never be enough time," he sympathized as he pulled into the CID parking lot.

"Look, D, I'd appreciate you not mentioning this to anyone else. He's very sensitive about his failing memory."

"No problem. Tell him I said 'Hi' when you see him."

Katie gave her partner a sad smile and a nod, just as her cell phone buzzed.

"It's a text from the captain—his office ASAP."

"Hmmph, good timing. Let's go."

CH 6

DOMBROWSKI AND KATIE spent almost twenty minutes closeted with Captain Walker discussing the Jennifer Halsted case. They reviewed the CSI reports, telephone records, and the recently received financial records and credit reports.

"So where did CSI find Jennifer Halsted's purse?" Dombrowski asked, scratching his head.

"Locked in her desk drawer," Katie answered. "I should've thought of that."

"Don't sweat it; at least now we've got her cell phone, too. Man, I can't believe how fast these phone records came in!"

"You can thank Lt. Waters for that," said the captain. "He's got an excellent connection—of course we always follow with the appropriate subpoena."

"Yes, sir, we will, for sure!" Dombrowski agreed.

"Well, now that you've seen everything, shall we go deal with Walter Farrell? I think we've kept him waiting long enough. Callahan, go find the lieutenant and join us. Dombrowski, you're with me; we'll wait for them there."

"Yes, sir." Dombrowski stood. "Lead on."

"MR. FARRELL, I AM CAPTAIN Walker. This is Lieutenant Waters, Detective Sergeant Dombrowski, and Detective Callahan—"

"A captain? Well, it's about time!" declared the intense and clearly agitated man squeezing the half-empty coffee mug. He rose, pushing the chair back from the conference table and balled his fists.

"Sir? Just what—" Captain Walker began.

"My daughter's missing! You have to find her!"

"Excuse me? Please sit down and calm yourself, Mr. Farrell. That's better. Now, please explain."

"She's missing! I just returned home this morning and she's gone! It's her birthday—she knows I was going to be here for her birthday. I'm surprising her with a car; it's being delivered this afternoon."

"Captain, if I may?" Dombrowski asked, and continued after a nod from his boss. "Sir, where were you coming from?"

"The airport; I've been in Chicago for the last ten days. My firm—I'm an attorney—my firm and an associated firm in Illinois had a case in Chicago. I just got home this morning and she was gone."

"I see. And her mother?"

"We're divorced. She's remarried and resides in London or Paris. They—she and her husband—have homes in both cities. We share custody of Amanda, my daughter. She was here to spend the summer with me. She just graduated from high school; she starts college in the fall. I want—"

"Please forgive the interruption, Mr. Farrell," Katie said, "but you said today is Amanda's birthday; how old is she?"

"Eighteen. Why?"

Silence descended upon the room.

Captain Walker leaned forward and spoke softly. "Mr. Farrell, I'm sure you realize that your daughter is now an adult. As such, she must be considered a missing person—not a missing child. Normally, we can act immediately in the case of a missing juvenile. However, we are legally constrained from initiating an investigation into a missing adult, absent extenuating circumstances, until that person has been missing for forty-eight hours."

The blood drained from Farrell's face. "Wh-what? Y-you won't even look for her?"

"Sir, I did not say that. We can begin some preliminary background work in preparation for an investigation should circumstances warrant that we proceed to officially open a case. Do you understand?"

"I—I think so. What can I do?"

"You can cooperate with these detectives; answer their questions."

"Of course, anything."

"Good. Detectives, you may proceed. I shall leave you to it. Lieutenant, we have another meeting, but first see if Mr. Farrell needs another coffee."

"Oh, no thank you," the anxious man declined. "I've had more than enough."

"As you wish," Lt. Waters responded as he retrieved the mug and followed the captain from the room.

The captain proceeded to his office; the lieutenant went directly to the crime lab.

AN HOUR LATER, DOMBROWSKI and Katie rapped on the Captain's door.

"Come."

Lt. Waters was already there. The detectives nodded to him and took their seats.

"He's gone?" the captain asked.

"Yes sir," Dombrowski acknowledged. "Regarding the daughter, it went pretty much as we expected. She's been here a little over three weeks. She spends every summer at her father's home, like she has ever since the divorce, six years ago. The rest of the time she's with her mother and her mother's husband, Pierre Demotte. She attended school in London but was going to go to college here in the States. She has plenty of friends here, so it wouldn't be unusual for her to be out with some of them. He says he's called the ones he knows about, with no luck. As far as he knows, she doesn't have a boyfriend. But you know teenagers; she may not really be missing at all."

"I'm not so sure," Katie remarked. "There's no question that her father is truly frightened for her. He spoke to her by phone the day before yesterday and he says everything was fine. He knows she was seeing her friends while he claims he was in Chicago—"

The captain raised a hand and interrupted. "By the way, Lt. Waters made some calls. We verified that Farrell was in Chicago for the last ten days as he claimed. Please go on, Detective."

"Yes sir. It is possible that Amanda Farrell is still with friends. We have a short list of her friends, at least those her father knows about. We did not ask to be admitted to his home to examine her room, as would be normal procedure; that would be premature at this point."

"He didn't make the offer either," Dombrowski added, "if it even occurred to him. But Katie's right; until we meet the forty-eight hour time requirement, there's little more we can do at this stage."

"All right, we'll have to wait and see. In the meantime, send the preliminary file to the Missing Persons Office," the captain ordered. "What did Farrell have to say about the Adamson and Halsted cases when you questioned him?"

Dombrowski grinned. "Ah, then it got interesting; you should see the video."

He handed the Lieutenant a USB flash drive. "LT, if you could open the file labelled 'Farrell' and display it on the big screen. Thanks."

A moment later, their eyes locked on the large monitor; the display resolved to show the detectives seated across the table from Farrell. Lt. Waters pecked briefly at the computer's keyboard and Farrell's voice was suddenly in the room.

"*. . . of course my staff kept me informed. Most unfortunate, to say the least. I had no idea he was so severely troubled. I was representing him in his divorce,* *of course, so I had some insight—but I can't comment about that. I must admit the news about Ms. Halsted was at first quite a surprise, but upon reflection I suppose I might have suspected they were involved. I mean there were little hints—stolen glances, knowing smiles, that sort of thing. He was frequently there when I stopped by the HOA office. I guess I should have known something was going on. But I had no idea she felt so strongly—I mean to follow him in death. . ."*

The captain signaled for Lt. Waters to pause the recording. "Hold on. He's suggesting that this scenario was a lovers' mutual suicide pact? Is there anything to support that?"

Waters raised a finger. "Not specifically. And if I may, sir, there are two things worth noting. Firstly, neither we, nor the M.E., have released any statement confirming suicide or homicide in either case. The media ran with suicide in both cases without confirmation, most likely because that was the rumor at each scene. Secondly, we know the two decedents worked together at the HOA. The media does not seem to be aware of that fact, at least not yet, otherwise, they would have already run with it. Now, should Mr. Farrell repeat this allegation publicly . . . well, you see?"

"Oh, I do, indeed. The lovers' suicide pact is simply too sensational for the media to resist. At least we'll know who the leak is. But what about my other question; is there any evidence to support the theory that they were lovers? You said *not specifically.*"

"The only thing we have," Dombrowski offered, "is that their cell phones had each other's number in the internal phone books. But that's not unusual since they both worked for the HOA."

"Home numbers or cell phone numbers?" The captain pressed. "And what's the pattern of usage?"

"No home numbers, just cell phones and the HOA office number. The usage pattern is pretty random according to the carrier records." Dombrowski shrugged and shook his head. "I just don't see them as lovers; it just doesn't feel right. He may have been a randy rogue, but her? She had more class . . . I dunno."

It took a moment for Katie to realize she was staring at her partner in surprise—and that she happened to agree with him. She nodded to him approvingly and spoke up. "If I may, Captain, I think he's right. A suicide pact between lovers usually means they intend to take their lives together—or at least simultaneously, or as close to the same time as possible. We know that these are actually homicides, in separate locations and days apart, but no one else should—except the killer."

"Or killers," her partner added.

"Yeah, there is that possibility," Katie admitted. "At any rate, Adamson's cell records show another number that he was calling—a lot. CSI already submitted a request for subscriber information; we're waiting on a call-back. But it's my guess that if he was involved with another woman, this may well be her. We'll certainly look into it. But I agree with the sergeant; I don't believe Jennifer Halsted was involved romantically with Gregory Adamson. There's no evidence to support that notion."

"Okay. Follow up on that number. What else is on the recording worth seeing?"

Dombrowski nodded to the lieutenant to fast-forward the recording. "Take it to the twenty-two minute mark, LT. That's good—right there.

"We wanted to save the subpoena for the neighborhood security guard service records for last, since he might shut down his voluntary cooperation at that point. But he got a little antsy and bowed up when we asked about the utilities being paid on the foreclosed homes in the HOA neighborhoods. It kinda went downhill from there."

At a nod from the sergeant, the recording resumed.

". . . don't see what relevance that has to anything! This is just another distraction that keeps you from finding my daughter!"

"Sir, we're just following up—"

"What you are doing, Sergeant, is wasting my time! Now are we done here?"

"Not quite, Mr. Farrell. As the attorney of record for the guard service, Security Associates, Inc., we now serve you with a subpoena duces tecum for the gate register records for the time frame articulated therein. Do you have any questions, sir?"

Farrell jumped to his feet, snatched the document from the table, and sneered at the detectives. Without another word, he spun on his heel and made for the door.

Just as he left the room, Dombrowski called out. *"You have a nice day now—we'll be in touch."*

Katie and her partner looked at one another, then right into the hidden camera and smiled. They collected their notes and prepared to depart the room.

Lt. Waters stopped the recording.

"Well, you certainly know how to win friends and influence people," the captain observed dryly.

Dombrowski and Katie shrugged and grinned.

"He's hiding something," she declared, "and we all know it."

"That may be, Detectives. However, he is still the father of a young woman who may truly be missing. Do not lose sight of that. Furthermore, he is not without considerable influence. I have been made aware that he has been a generous contributor to certain political figures. It would behoove you to be careful with him, or any lawyer who might appear in the future on his behalf."

"That man is no fool," Lt. Waters warned. "He knows you suspect him of something. Discretion is well advised. Captain, do you have anything else, sir?"

"Just this, I can usually deal with any heat from above so you detectives can investigate thoroughly, but I'd appreciate it if you'd not add unnecessary fuel to the fire and make my job more difficult than it already is."

"Yes, sir. You don't have to worry about us. We got this, right Katie?"

"Uh, yes, sir, of course, sir."

———

AS THE DETECTIVES LEFT the captain's office, they had to skirt a warning placard that urged *caution—wet floor*. They took no notice of the mop-wielding janitor working his way down the hall. However, he noticed them, and watched them carefully until they rounded a corner and disappeared from view.

CH 7

====

UPON THEIR RETURN TO the squad room, the detectives were surprised to find over a dozen cardboard file boxes stacked around their desks. Each box was sealed with a strip of evidence tape, and marked with a case number that corresponded to the Jennifer Halsted case.

Lt. Waters walked up and extended a clipboard to Dombrowski. "Here, you gotta sign for them—chain of custody, you know. While you were conducting your interview, CSI delivered these boxed files from the HOA Office. I signed for them, but it's your case and your evidence. You've got some reading to do. CSI is still processing Jennifer Halsted's car, so that report is pending."

"Oh man, LT," the big sergeant groaned, "that's an awful lot of material to plow through."

Lt. Waters chuckled and commiserated. "Yep, sure is. Who knows what you might find?"

Katie shoved some boxes aside so she could get to her chair. She plopped down in disgust. "It could take a week or more to sift through all this stuff."

Lt. Waters relented and said, "We may have more pressing matters. As for these HOA files, I'll get you some help, but for now, let's put these files on a back burner."

Katie looked up hopefully, as the lieutenant handed Dombrowski a sheet of paper.

"Tomorrow you'll need to follow up on Jennifer Halsted's information. We've confirmed last known address. You might have to make a notification to next of kin."

"Have we identified her next of kin?"

"No, I'm afraid not, Sergeant. Perhaps you'll find something useful at her home."

Turning to Katie, the lieutenant handed her a sheet of paper as well. "Detective, in the meeting with the captain, you mentioned the cell number that Adamson was repeatedly calling; here's the subscriber information from the cell carrier. Since this relates to the earlier case, the Adamson homicide, y'all might want to deal with that first thing tomorrow."

"Yes sir, we'll take care of it!" she assured him.

———————

"WE'RE GETTING TO BE regular visitors to this neighborhood, D," Katie remarked the next morning as she coasted the cruiser down the suburban street. "I think that guy watering his lawn recognized our car. I should've waved."

"Yeah, right." Dombrowski grunted. "The next crossing street should be Buchanan. Yeah, this is it—make a left. Okay, the even numbers are on this side of the street; so, the house should be on our right—3812."

She peered through the windshield and noted the passing mailboxes. "This is the 3900 block. The numbers are going down, so it should be in the next block."

"I think I see it—third one from the corner—the two-storied, what? Dutch Colonial?"

"Whoa," she teased, "listen to you, Mr. Real Estate! The house with the three newspapers lying scattered in the driveway?"

"Yeah, that's not a good sign. Maybe no one's home. What's her name again?"

"Carolyn Silverberg, according to the cell carrier. Park right in front, you think?"

"Might as well; this is just an interview."

Neither the doorbell nor their brisk knocking produced any response. The door appeared secure. Dombrowski studied the lock while Katie stepped into the yard and scanned the windows for any movement. She shook her head.

"Nothing," she said and pointed. "Looks like the side gate is ajar; I'm gonna check out the back."

"Okay, I'll check the other side and see if I can get to the rear from there."

He passed through another gate and rounded the corner to find Katie at the edge of a flagstone patio, pistol drawn. She locked eyes with him, put a finger to her lips, and then pointed to the shattered glass of the open patio door.

Dombrowski drew his own gun, held up a single finger and hissed, "Wait!" He made a quick call on his phone and nodded.

She knew backup would be en route. She was ready.

At his signal, they made a quick entry. She went low right; he went high left. They found the large kitchen empty. Ample daylight streamed through a host of windows, making it easy for them to see deeper into the house. A quick check of the first floor rooms yielded little more information. But for the broken patio door, nothing appeared unusual or out of place. The house was neat and tidy.

Dombrowski pointed to a telephone. She picked up the receiver—dead—and shook her head. He nodded and pointed to the second floor.

They ascended the stairs with practiced stealth, covering potential threats from above and below with the muzzles of their pistols. Only the occasional creak of a stair tread betrayed their progress.

Closed doors along the upstairs hall beckoned. Two of the bedrooms were vacant, as was an adjoining bathroom. To the rear of the second floor, the large master bedroom and en suite bath held the only signs of recent occupancy; an unmade bed, and a couple of towels heaped upon the floor by the shower stall.

"Nothing?" whispered Dombrowski.

"Zip," Katie hissed. "Wait! Has this place got a basement?"

"Maybe, let's check."

Without another sound, they retraced their steps to the kitchen and found the door to the basement.

"Light switch, here on the wall," Katie breathed. "What do you think?"

"We've got flashlights. What the hell—try it."

She flicked the switch. Nothing happened.

The basement stairwell disappeared into a maw of darkness.

"Hold on—lemme check something." He tugged the refrigerator door open and wrinkled his nose. "Ugh! Power's off—coupla days, maybe."

"Shh! I hear something!" she said softly, cocking an ear down the stairwell.

"Yeah, I think I just did, too—but from behind us! Stay here and watch those stairs!"

"What? Where the hell are you—? Shit!" She was alone at the top of the dark stairwell.

She heard it again. *A baby? There's a baby down there?*

Thumbing the switch on the base of her flashlight she sent a wash of light down the steps as far as a mid-flight landing. The stairwell turned to the right where the lower steps were lost in darkness.

She barely hesitated, glancing back just long enough to see that she was still on her own. Against her better judgement, her lips drawn in grim determination, she crept down the wooden treads to the landing. Her light shone down the remaining stairs to a concrete floor.

Had she heard something again? She wasn't sure. She strained to hear the slightest sound; the tension in her shoulders leached upward as the hairs on the back of her neck rose. Her knuckles whitened as she clung tighter to her flashlight and pistol grip.

She descended the final steps and found a short hall. Rough wooden doors stood closed at either end. She tried the one to the right—unlocked. She pushed it open and panned her flashlight around.

The room was smaller than she expected, a utility and laundry room; furnace, water heater, washer, dryer, and utility sink.

She re-entered the hallway and approached the other door. Its rough surface was girdled with wrought iron straps and a heavy set of elaborate hinges. It was not locked. She braced herself and pushed on the wood. The door swung open easily into pitch black.

As she washed the beam of her flashlight across the opening, something howled from within the darkness and streaked forth through her legs! She spun about, bobbling the flashlight, and brought her pistol to bear.

A Siamese cat stared into the light beam, its lowered ears and crouching form betraying its unease.

A cat? What I heard was a damned cat? What the hell?

Ignoring the feline for the moment, she turned her attention to the dark room and let her flashlight explore. She was speechless. It looked like a movie set from some medieval dungeon fantasy.

"Katie! What the hell!" hissed Dombrowski from just over her shoulder, sending a flush of adrenaline throughout her tensely alert body.

Oh just great! How the hell did he get behind me? I never heard a thing!

"Why didn't you wait for me?" He spat and pulled her to one side as two uniformed patrolmen poured into the room, their flashlights augmenting her own.

"Clear!" a patrolman declared, and then mumbled, "Holy shit! What is this?"

"Whoa!" Dombrowski exclaimed. "It looks like a role-playing room for kinky sex—you know, bondage, S&M, that sort of thing."

Shining his light on a narrow wire cage festooned with internal spikes and suspended from a ceiling joist, the other patrolman asked, "Is this stuff for real?"

Dombrowski touched the cage and set it rocking. "Hmmph, plastic. Nah, most of this stuff is just mock medieval décor, just props to give it that dungeon look. The whips, chrome chains, and furry restraints are probably used as sex toys. Be careful not to touch anything."

"It appears," Katie stated dryly, "that someone is into a little domination."

"Does that make this a crime scene?" the patrolman asked.

"No, not in and of itself," Dombrowski answered and swept his hand to encompass the entire space. "And as for the décor, poor taste isn't a crime. None of this is actually illegal."

"Yeah, between consenting adults," Katie groused and aimed her flashlight into a dark corner. "What's that?"

"Looks like a big leaf bag," the patrolman remarked and took a step forward. "See, it's gathered at the top, and tied with, what—a red cord?"

"Hold on! Remember, don't touch anything," Dombrowski warned as he snapped on a pair of latex gloves and retrieved a pocket knife.

He carefully cut the cord and dropped it with the knot intact into an evidence envelope. The gathered plastic remained bunched together as if stuck. The sergeant played his flashlight over the closure. "This isn't a bag; it's a big tarp. Its edges have been gathered and tied to form a bag. Katie, glove up and help me peel the edges back."

"Okay, give me a second."

With the two patrolmen holding the four flashlights, Katie and her partner began to peel the plastic tarp open. The edges were very sticky, and difficult to separate at first, but finally parted. The coppery tang of coagulated blood and the cloying stench of decomposition rose as the tarp opened and revealed its gruesome contents.

The bloodied corpse of a naked woman was tied with coat hanger wire and duct tape to a metal armchair. The body had begun to bloat, but the hallmarks of deliberate and prolonged torture were still clearly evident. And worst of all, her eyelids had been sliced off, so she could not seek darkness. Someone had forced her to watch.

Dombrowski ground his teeth. "This wasn't some sex game. This was torture, probably for information. It looks like someone knew what they were doing, slowly extracting more and more information as her torment escalated until she was begging for death."

"Jeez," whispered a patrolman.

"Even her death could serve their purpose—a message," Dombrowski added. "I've seen this sort of thing before, a long time ago."

"Well, I haven't." Katie fought back a gag and pointed. "Is that . . . you know?"

"Yeah, a *Colombian necktie*. That would have been the perp's final ploy, after he'd gotten all he could from her. He cuts her throat, then cuts out her tongue and stages it poking out through through the incision. Leaving it that way sends a message, or a warning—maybe both."

"Yeah? To whom?" She wanted to look away, but found it hard to do so.

"Good question," Dombrowski admitted. Turning to the patrolmen, he said, "Let's get the entire house taped off—better do the yard, too. Don't touch anything on the way out and make sure you secure the perimeter."

The patrolmen left to carry out his instructions.

"D, do you think," Katie asked, "this is Carolyn Silverberg?"

"Dunno for sure, but my gut tells me *yes*. Look, I'll call the lieutenant and get CSI en route. Can you call the M.E.'s office?"

"Sure, but can we do it upstairs? The smell is getting to me."

"Works for me. By the way, where's that cat? We damn near tripped over it coming down the steps."

She shrugged and looked around. "I don't see it anywhere."

"Screw it. Let's go upstairs."

THE CSI CREW ARRIVED within minutes and began their work in the basement.

Dombrowski and Katie elected to search the master bedroom for anything that might help with establishing the identity of the victim.

The sergeant opened a nightstand drawer and found a diverse collection of sex toys. "Aw, jeez. Glad I've got gloves on."

Katie found a number of purses in the closet, one of which appeared to be in current use. "Got a wallet in this one, D. Hold on. Yeah, credit cards, some cash, and a driver's license—Carolyn Silverberg. But I'm not sure this picture is going to be much help."

"Lemme see. Yeah, I see what you mean, but that's her all right."

Katie shuddered, walked to a window, and stared into the backyard; but that wasn't the image she was seeing.

"Listen to me, kiddo," he said as he joined her and placed a comforting hand on her shoulder. "I know this is a bad one. That picture in your head isn't going to go away. You've got to get over the emotional hump, the brutal horror of it all. You have to think of it as evidence, clinical details that tell you the truth about what happened in the course of the crime. And just as important, think how it can provide some insight into the mind and motive of the perp."

"D, what happened to that woman was beyond horrible, you know. But I get it; it was purposeful, too. Someone wanted information and she was tortured for it! So, what the hell did she know?"

Dombrowski sighed and shrugged. "Good question. The only lead we have is the phone record that links her with Adamson."

"Yeah, and that's too many calls," she noted. "I'm thinking it was personal; they were definitely involved."

"Could be; it would fit." He folded his arms and followed her gaze into the backyards of the houses on the adjacent block. "We know he chased other women. Maybe CSI can find some trace of him here."

"You mean like his DNA on some of her kinky toys?"

Dombrowski grimaced, and reluctantly nodded.

"Hey, it's all good, Sarge," she wryly assured him. "I'm just being clinical."

CH 8

JENNIFER HALSTED'S apartment was on fire. In fact, the entire uppermost floor of the four-storied building was involved. Clouds of dark smoke belched forth from shattered windows and tongues of raw flame licked at the crenellated façade of the roof line.

Dombrowski and Katie stood across the street with the growing crowd of onlookers and watched as the fire department fought the raging inferno. Uniformed patrolmen kept warning people back, away from the fire apparatus. A sudden change of wind sent a blast of hot smoke in the direction of the crowd; they dispersed without further urging.

The detectives moved as well. Dombrowski pulled Katie to the leeward side of a pumper truck, and reached for his ringing phone.

"Dombrowski . . . You gotta speak up, LT, it's loud here. No, we were too late . . . We don't know yet, but we'll ask when we get the chance . . . Tomorrow morning? Okay, that shouldn't be a problem. Yessir, we'll advise when we clear this scene. 'Bye."

He leaned into Katie's ear while keeping an eye on the firefighters lugging hoses around the pumper. "The LT is not happy that we didn't get into Halsted's home to look around. He said they still couldn't find any next of kin info. He wants us to try to find out if this was arson before we clear the scene. And we're supposed to attend the Silverberg autopsy tomorrow morning."

"Crap, like we don't have enough to do. Do you see any of the arson investigators anywhere?"

"I can't tell; all these guys are in full gear. But they're probably here. Let's get out of their way, and get some phone shots of the crowd—you never know. The media's here; so, we can get some of their unedited stuff later."

"I already took some crowd pics. But you're right; the media cameras are a lot better than my phone. Come on, we can go up the block, grab some coffee, and come back when the FD has this mess under control."

———————————

THE WAITRESS POURED a refill and smiled coyly at the big detective. He mumbled his thanks and tried to ignore her. Her lips in a pout, she dismissed him with a soft sigh, and strode away with an exaggerated sway to her hips.

Katie smirked and stirred creamer into her coffee. "Aw, D, I think she likes you—maybe you oughta ask her out. Wha'cha think?"

"Forget about it! I get enough of that crap from my sister. She's always trying to set me up with some of her friends, most of whom are divorced, with kids, or some dysfunctional emotional baggage. Like I need that kind of grief—*sheesh*. I can get my own dates, thank you."

"So, your sister; how is Donna? And the kids? Is Toby still overseas?"

"Oh, she's fine; the kids are fine, too, as far as I know. Yeah, Toby still has a coupla months on this deployment. He can retire the year after next. I dunno if he will though. I haven't talked to him in a while."

"Doesn't their oldest girl graduate high school soon?"

"Yeah, Brittany, next year, I think."

A uniformed patrolman appeared at their booth. "Sorry to interrupt, Detectives. Sarge, you said you wanted to know when the fire department was wrapping up."

"Yeah, thanks. We're coming. Are the arson guys there?"

"They are, Preston and Guerra. They know you want to walk the scene with them."

"Okay, let me pay this check and we'll meet them there."

THE FIRE WAS OUT, BUT the scene was a study in chaos. Smoking piles of debris were still being sprayed down as tired firefighters probed for smoldering embers. Displaced building residents huddled beyond the police line and commiserated with one another. EMT personnel stood vigil nearby, but for the moment, nobody seemed to be in need of their services.

"Hey Dombrowski, over here!" The arson investigator waved from the side of the ladder truck and nudged the tall man standing next to him.

"Hi, Carlos," Dombrowski rumbled as he pumped the stout fireman's hand. "Where's Sammy? Oh, hi Sam—didn't see you there."

The perennial joke wasn't lost on Katie. Sam Preston was almost seven feet tall and rail thin, in contrast to his partner, Carlos Guerra, who barely cleared five and a half feet at two-twenty, most of it muscle. Both had been star athletes on state wide high school championship teams, in basketball and football respectively. They were good friends, and an outstanding arson investigation team.

"Hello, Katie. Are you still putting up with Big D?" Sam asked with a grin.

"Yeah, afraid so—what're you gonna do? Good help is so hard to find." She smirked and haughtily waved her hand.

"Okay, you guys, to business," Carlos said with a chuckle. "No casualties that we're aware of at this point. It appears everyone got out. Someone hit the fire alarm, but we don't know who. We've been completely through once, and we found the point of origin—fourth floor apartment bedroom—definitely arson."

"Petroleum-based accelerant," added Sam, "on the bedding, in the closet, and along the base of the interior walls."

Dombrowski consulted his notebook. "We wanted to see apartment 406. Was that the one?"

The arson investigators nodded in unison.

"Sorry, Sarge," Carlos said. "That's the one. It's not safe to go back up there. The roof is still intact, but clearly compromised. The fourth floor is mostly gutted, and the third floor's not much better. We put a lot of water on that fire so there's gonna be quite a bit of water damage as well. As for that apartment, there wasn't much left; all the movables were tossed." He pointed to a smoldering pile being sprayed down. "We'll be going through it when it's safe. What are you looking for?"

"Damn! Uh, personal records for one thing, and anything else that may have had a bearing on our case."

"Well, you're welcome to join us when we examine the debris, but you know how it is."

"Yeah, I do," Dombrowski admitted. "I know the fire most likely destroyed any personal records. However, if there's the slightest trace of anything left, you're just the guys to find it. Katie and I'll pass on going through the debris with you; we'd just be in your way. Call us if you do find anything."

"We should interview the building manager," Katie remarked. "Is he or she still here?"

"That'd be Mrs. Brodie," Sam announced and pointed. "She's over there, with the rest of the residents."

Offering his hand, Dombrowski thanked the arson team and reached for his ringing phone.

"Dombrowski . . . Oh, hi Donna . . . No, it's okay. Is everything all right? What—this coming Friday? I dunno. Can I get back to you on that? I'm right in the middle of something. Yeah, I promise. 'Bye."

Katie heard him mumble as he shoved the phone in his pocket. She couldn't help but smile. "Your sister? How sweet! We were just talking about her, weren't we?" she teased.

"Don't even go there," he warned. "Come on; let's talk to Mrs. Brodie, the building manager."

———————

THE PETITE WOMAN WAS unharmed, but emotionally hurt and angry; she had learned the fire had been started deliberately. "No, detective, I don't know Ms. Halsted all that well; but, if I find out she has anything to do with this—"

"Uh, Mrs. Brodie," Katie interrupted, "I can assure you that she did not. Ms. Halsted is deceased, as of a coupla days ago."

Hands to her open mouth, Mrs. Brodie gasped. "Oh my, lands sakes—I had no idea!"

"We understand, ma'am," soothed Dombrowski. "We are investigating her death. We had hoped to have a look around her apartment, but that appears to be moot. Could we see what you have regarding her in your tenant files, a rental application, for example?"

The building manager hesitated, clearly uncomfortable with the request.

Katie intuitively recognized the woman's dilemma, and offered the obvious solution. "If it'd make you feel more comfortable, we can get a subpoena. Would that help?"

Mrs. Brodie pursed her lips, and cocked her head. "Look, I'm supposed to call my boss and the company lawyer. But, let me ask you; do you think this would help to find out who did this to my building?"

Dombrowski and Katie looked at one another and shrugged.

"I can't say for certain," he admitted, "but it is possible. Of course, the sooner we see the file, the sooner we can act on what we find."

"That's good enough for me! Some bastard just made a bunch of good people homeless—and I want him caught! I'll probably get in trouble with the company; so, if you find anything, you may have to get that subpoena. Will the firemen let us in the building? My office is on the first floor."

Katie smiled and announced, "I know just who to ask!"

AS EXPECTED, CARLOS and Sam insisted on leading the way with powerful LED lights as the detectives accompanied Mrs. Brodie to her office.

"This is Jennifer Halsted's tenant file," she said, handing the folder to Dombrowski. "It has her rental application, storage contract, and payment record. She was a good tenant, always paid on time."

"Excuse me, storage contract?" Katie echoed.

"Yes, we offer storage space in the basement level; lockable rooms, eight by twelve feet, of private storage for an additional monthly fee. Most tenants don't take advantage of the optional extra storage."

"And Ms. Halsted had a storage room?"

Reaching for the file, Mrs. Brodie asked, "May I?"

The small office was very quiet.

"Why, yes. Here it is, ninety-six square feet, room BL7. I have the master key. Would you like to see that room—if it's safe, of course?"

Dombrowski grinned widely. "Yes, ma'am. Carlos, Sam, is that okay with you?"

"Yeah, should be," Carlos agreed. "But we'll go with you. Don't be surprised if there's some water down there."

There was water, still trickling down through the walls from the fire damaged floors, pooling on the concrete floor. Room BL7 was no exception. They found a growing puddle covering the entire floor, but assorted plastic tubs stacked ceiling high kept everything dry. Most were stuffed with clothing, shoes, and fashion accessories.

"Wow, that's a lot of clothes for one person," Dombrowski remarked. "Crap! Look at all the shoes!"

"D, don't start!" Katie warned. "You're a lifelong bachelor, so you have no clue. Women and their clothes will always be a mystery for you; so just accept that. These are winter clothes; her summer wardrobe was probably in her closet. Remember how she looked and dressed for work? Her appearance was very important to her."

"But why would anybody need this much—this many shoes? I just don't get it."

"Stop trying," Sam warned the big detective. "It'll only make your head hurt. This is like an arsenal for a huntress, tools of the trade. Women have to feel they're attractive."

"What do you mean huntress?" Dombrowski pressed. "What's she hunting—a husband?"

"Maybe, or somebody else's husband," Katie remarked.

Carlos and Sam snorted with laughter; Dombrowski just grinned.

Katie kept a straight face and tried not to smile. She knew she wouldn't derail the slightly sexist train of thought the men seemed to be on, so she simply diverted it with a bit of humor—notwithstanding that her observation might be true.

To her way of thinking, men were no different when it came to the hunt. She knew guys her age who had more clothes and hair products than she did—straight guys! But bringing that fact up now would not change her companions' views, and likely only provide more opportunity for gender-bending stereotypical humor. *Men can be such little boys sometimes.*

Atop a stack, a clear plastic tub filled with something other than clothes caught her eye. "Sam, can you reach that one—yeah, on top. Thanks."

She popped it open.

"What've you got there?" Sam asked.

"Not sure, newspapers, clippings, old checks and bank statements, and files? Hey, these are HOA files. I thought we had all the HOA files in our office."

"Evidently not," Dombrowski said as he reached over her shoulder, selected a few, and thumbed through the files. "Katie, each of these is a foreclosed property."

"Yeah, these too."

"Mrs. Brodie, thank you ever so much," Dombrowski suddenly said. "You've been a big help. We'll be taking these with us. If you don't mind, please keep this room locked; this may all be evidence. We'll send someone back for everything in here. And don't you worry one bit, we'll get you your subpoena."

KATIE STARED INTO HER cooling cup of coffee and sighed. She had slept poorly last night and was dragging this morning. The overhead fluorescent lights in the Medical Examiner's staff lounge seemed way too bright. She fidgeted in the uncomfortable plastic chair, looked up, and caught her partner in the midst of a massive yawn.

She sympathized.

"D, I'm gonna ask the LT for the weekend off. I really need the time."

"I know. I could use a coupla days, too. I don't think I'm gonna get out of this dinner Donna's got planned for Friday night. I begged off twice before. Crap, I may as well get it over with."

She smiled and shook her head. "So, who's she setting you up with this time? That yoga instructor she likes, or her friend, the bank teller?"

"Dunno yet. She hasn't told me; and I didn't ask. You'd think she'd take the hint. I don't like these games; but I don't want to hurt her feelings."

"Aw, she just wants to see you happy. She just happens to think that means you should be in a relationship. You know she's got your best interests at heart."

He rubbed his face with his palms and groaned. "Probably so, but her predilection for match-making gets old. And the truth is that none of her friends really interest me."

"Wait! Didn't you go out with a couple of them?"

"Well, yeah, but that didn't work out. I don't know what she tells them about me, but by the end of the evening they're somehow disappointed. And to be honest, I'm bored. What can I say?"

"What about that family law attorney you were seeing early last year, uh, Melanie something? I thought y'all were doing okay."

"Oh yeah, Melanie Dubois. Yeah, we got along pretty good for a while there."

"Well, what happened?"

"Irreconcilable differences . . . She took a position with the Public Defender's Office, and within three months was head-hunted and recruited for a big law firm. She became one of their criminal trial lawyers. It was pretty clear to me that we didn't have much of a future."

She grimaced at the realization that he'd likely broken it off—and probably gracelessly at that. "Well, didn't you part friends?"

"Uh, yeah, I thought so, although I haven't talked to her since."

Katie's eyebrows rose. *How dense can a man be?*

The sergeant's phone rang.

"Dombrowski . . . Yes sir, LT, we're still at the M.E.'s office . . . Yeah, that's right . . . No, Katie interviewed her . . . When? Oh yeah, I agree that's very interesting . . . Okay, got it. Yes sir, will do, as soon as we clear here. Right, 'bye."

Katie put her cold coffee down and opened her palms. "Okay, what?"

"When we interviewed Marian Adamson and her sister, Louise Hesterly, you got Louise aside in her kitchen, remember?"

"Yeah, I remember."

"Didn't she tell you that she and Marian hadn't been anywhere—except the grocery store—for two weeks?"

"That's right. So?"

"The LT advised that the financials and credit reports for both sisters came in, and Louise has some credit card charges within that time frame at an Indian casino about a hundred miles away."

"She lied to me?"

"So it appears. It seems Louise retired when her husband died in a car wreck. There was a big life insurance check. Guess what her career was—surgical nurse."

"No shit? She lied to my face? And to think I thought she was sweet; I kinda liked her." An ember of anger began to flare in the depths of her gut.

"Yeah? Well, I kinda like her for two homicides."

"What? Explain that."

"Think about it. She had motive. She hated the way Adamson treated her sister; she knew he was running around on her. She probably knew Adamson worked at the HOA and thought Jennifer Halsted was the other woman."

"Okay, that might be a stretch, but it makes sense," Katie allowed.

Dombrowski grinned. "She had opportunity. She lied about staying at home for those two weeks—she could have gone anywhere and done anything. And finally, she had the necessary skill set as a former surgical nurse to identify the inner carotid artery and administer a lethal dose of air with a syringe."

"Okay, I see how it all kinda fits," Katie acknowledged, "but there are still some loose ends. Like, how does she render the victims unconscious, give 'em the shot, and then stage the bodies to fake the suicides? Is she working alone? Those bodies aren't light Wait, do you think that Marian—"

"Helped her?" Dombrowski finished, his eyebrows raised. "Damned good question. I do believe we'll be interviewing these sisters once again."

"Damned straight! That lying bitch!" Katie fumed.

The door to the lounge opened and Dr. Parker entered. "Ah, Detectives, there you are. Sorry, the autopsy on Ms. Silverberg took somewhat longer than I anticipated."

"No problem, Doc," Dombrowski assured him. "We already know it's a homicide. So, what's the COD?"

"Exsanguination—massive blood loss—the laceration across the throat severed both jugular veins and carotid arteries. She bled out in a matter of a few seconds. The excision and subsequent staging of the tongue through the wound was postmortem."

"But she was alive and conscious for what happened before, wasn't she, Doc?" Katie probed grimly.

"Sadly, I suspect so," the M.E. admitted. "I have no way of knowing if she was conscious for the entire ordeal, but someone went to considerable effort to administer very painful and specific trauma, short of lethal levels, to extend this woman's suffering for a protracted period of time. The specific details will be in my written report."

"Well, thanks, Doc," Dombrowski said as he stood up. "We've got to get back to our office. We don't have her next of kin info yet; but we'll let you know."

"One moment, Sergeant. There is something else, something I found in Ms. Silverberg's mouth, partially wedged in the back of her throat."

He handed Dombrowski a small plastic evidence bag containing some sort of laminated card.

"What the hell?" The sergeant mumbled as he held the bag out for Katie to see. He reached for his reading glasses as she plucked the bag from his fingers.

"It's actually a current British provisional driver's license, a learner's permit, if you will," the doctor explained.

"Well, it's not her," Katie declared, as she focused on the small DL photo and rotated the bag to diffuse the glare of the overhead fluorescent lights. "And D, you're not gonna believe the name on this license."

"Lemme see," he insisted, as he fitted his glasses on the bridge of his nose.

She gave him a moment to digest the information printed on the card.

"I assume," posed the doctor, "that this is of some significance?"

Dombrowski looked up and grinned at Katie. Her smile couldn't get any wider.

The M.E. discretely cleared his throat.

"Oh, sorry Doc, but yes," Dombrowski explained, "this could be of great significance. Amanda Farrell was, as of yesterday, simply a missing person. But now, she is also a person of interest in a homicide investigation."

"SO, HOW DO YOU WANT to handle it?" Lt. Waters asked as he rocked back in his chair and interlaced his fingers behind his head. "Remember what the captain said."

"I don't see that we have any alternative," Dombrowski offered with a shrug. "We have Walter Farrell's statement that she was staying with him, so that's her last known address. There's still no sign of her as far as we know. I mean, he hasn't called to tell us otherwise, so she's still a missing person."

"And it's been forty-eight hours," Katie added, "so, officially, we now have a case."

"True enough," Waters conceded. "But now she may be involved in the Silverberg case—as what, a principal or possibly a material witness?"

"Anything's possible at this point, LT. Hell, she might be a victim herself," the sergeant allowed. "We really need to talk to her, but we've got to find her first. We have to go to Walter Farrell's home and talk to him."

"He's right, LT," Katie insisted. "That's the last place she's supposed to have been. She's his daughter; why wouldn't he cooperate? He seemed plenty worried before."

"Look, I don't disagree, but I have to brief the captain. And he's gonna have questions, and not just about the Silverberg case. What about the Adamson case—the wife and sister's alibi not holding up? And the Halsted case—the arson and those extra HOA files you found? Not to mention that you haven't even begun to go through all those HOA files in your office."

"LT, you said you'd get us some help with those files," Katie reminded him.

"And I will. But I'm not assigning more teams for that project until the both of you are there and fully focused on those files—after all, it is your case. Understand?"

"Yes, sir, no problem," Dombrowski assured him. "It's just that Amanda Farrell may still be alive—that's got to be the priority here. The other issues will keep."

Katie nodded in agreement; and the lieutenant smiled.

"That, Detectives, was precisely the right response."

CH 10

KATIE DROVE UP THE long driveway and parked in front of the palatial Georgian style mansion. "Wow! Farrell's got himself a nice place here. What do you think, D? Should we have made an appointment?"

"Don't be a smart-ass, Detective. I'll bet he likes surprises. Come on."

Dombrowski ignored the doorbell button and opted for the lion's head knocker of heavy wrought iron affixed to the broad door.

His sharp raps were answered by a uniformed maid who opened the stout door a few inches. "Yes, can I help you?"

Dombrowski held up his credentials. "Good morning, ma'am, Detectives Callahan and Dombrowski for Mr. Farrell. Is he home?"

Before she could respond, another woman's voice called from within the house, growing stronger as she approached. "Who is it, Consuela? There are no appointments this afternoon."

"It's the police, ma'am, some detectives for Mr. Farrell."

"Oh, really? I'll handle this."

The maid nodded and turned away as the door swung fully open to reveal a tall attractive woman in her forties. She was dressed in a rather stern business suit; a pair of wire-rimmed glasses dangled from one hand. "Good morning. I am Ms. Dubois, and I represent—"

Dombrowski gaped. "Uh, Melanie?"

Mildly surprised, she slipped her glasses on and peered at him. "Donald?"

"Uh, yeah. What are you doing here?"

"As I was saying, I represent Mr. Farrell. Now, what are you doing here?"

"Oh, uh, this is my partner, Detective Katie Callahan. Katie, this is Melanie Dubois. We're here to talk to Mr. Farrell about his daughter, Amanda. We have some questions for him."

"I think not. Anything you have to say to, or ask of, Mr. Farrell, you can direct to me. As I said, I represent him."

Dombrowski scoffed. "Look, Melanie—"

"Stop right there!" the attorney warned. "You are here in an official capacity—as am I. You will please address me as Ms. Dubois."

Katie winced. It was pretty clear that this woman bore Dombrowski some heartfelt animosity. *You big lummox! You've got a scorned woman on your hands here. Maybe you deserve a little chastisement—I don't know. But right now, this can't interfere with our investigation.*

"Ms. Dubois, if I may explain?" Katie offered.

"Yes?"

"A few days ago, Mr. Farrell reported his daughter, Amanda, missing. Since then, we have opened a case; and, there has been a development."

"What kind of development?"

"An item that belongs to Amanda Farrell was found. We'd like to speak to Mr. Farrell about it."

The lawyer folded her arms. "That won't be necessary. I am fully aware of your department's reluctance to act upon my client's initial report. My client rescinds his assertion that she was missing. You may close your case."

"It's not gonna be that easy," Dombrowski growled. "Amanda Farrell's identification was found at the scene of a crime. She is now a person of interest in a criminal investigation. If, as you say, she is no longer a missing person, then we need to speak with her—now. Is she here?"

The attorney crossed her arms and stared at him in silence, her lips drawing into a thin line of defiance.

Katie could see this was going downhill fast. She had to try a more reasonable approach. "Ms. Dubois, if she's here, we would very much like to speak with her. If she's not here, please be kind enough to tell us. We just want to clear some things up."

"Detective, I am not at liberty to discuss Amanda Farrell. And before you ask, no, you may not enter and search this home. This is not her residence of record; she was only a guest under this roof. This is a third party property—you will need a search warrant. And I strongly doubt that you have sufficient probable cause."

Katie bit her tongue; there was no point in arguing.

However, Dombrowski couldn't contain himself. "Damn it, Melanie! You don't have to be like this!"

"That's Ms. Dubois to you! We are done here. Good day." She slammed the door.

BACK IN THE CAR, DOMBROWSKI glanced over to Katie. "Well, I hate to admit it, but I think that could have gone better."

"You think?" She rolled her eyes in mock shock.

He nodded and raised a finger to make a point. "At least we know that Amanda's not there—not now anyway."

"What? How do you figure that? We got no further than the front door. All you managed to do was piss off the lawyer—one with whom you have a personal history. She'd like your head on a pike! What if she calls and complains? The captain already warned us!"

"Meh, forget all that," he dismissed with a wave of his hand. "Melanie just told us Amanda's not there. She said 'she was only a guest under this roof'—'was' is past tense. She's not in that house now. I doubt she's been there since before her father made that first report."

"Maybe," Katie cautioned, and started the car. "But now we don't have a complainant, so no missing person case."

"True, but her potential involvement in the Silverberg homicide is more than enough for us to keep looking for Amanda Farrell. I'm gonna ask the lieutenant to get the phone records, and set up a surveillance on the house. Meanwhile, we can check again with her friends to see if there's been any contact. My gut says something's really off here."

A pensive look passed across Katie's countenance. She gave voice to her thoughts. "You know, rich folks tend to overlook the help, the servants and all. They're always around but not always noticed. They usually know everything that's going on in a family. I'm gonna find out who that maid is and see if she'll talk to me."

"Good idea," Dombrowski acknowledged. "We'd better get back to the office."

———————————

THE LIEUTENANT WAS not in a very generous mood. He craved a cigarette in the worst way but he'd have to wait. The captain had just left his office, and he hadn't been too happy either.

The media had run a story about a crime wave—three recent deaths and no arrests. The journalists were playing fast and loose with what few facts they had, and didn't hesitate to speculate and theorize. Even their initial, and erroneous, assumptions about the presumed suicides were now vaguely characterized as official misdirection—notwithstanding that no official statement had ever been released. Another newspaper article was liberally spiced with hints pointing to police ineptitude among references to old unsolved cases. Fortunately, there weren't many of those.

Walking to his office door, the lieutenant looked out at the squad room. Four of his detectives were at their desks, plowing through the HOA files. They'd been at it all morning; nothing of consequence had yet been found.

"Dombrowski! Callahan! My office!"

Both looked up from the files on their desks and acknowledged their boss. Without another word, they filed into his office and took seats.

Lt. Waters rocked back in his chair and sighed—oh man, he wanted a smoke right now. "Okay, status reports; what's the sitrep with the Farrell kid?"

Dombrowski shrugged and grunted. "Hmmph, nothing, LT, no contact with any of her friends, surveillance has seen her father, his lawyer, and the staff, but no trace of the girl. There's nothing on her cell phone dump, no usage at all. The dump on Walter Farrell's home phone was no real help either. We're almost certain—absent a search—that she's not at his home."

Katie nodded in agreement and added further confirmation. "I found the maid, Consuela Ladonez, and interviewed her—with the understanding that we'd keep her cooperation confidential. She said that Amanda hasn't been in that house since the day before Walter Farrell returned from Chicago. Consuela may have a little immigration issue she wouldn't want scrutinized too closely, so she's willing to work with us. She has our tip-line number—the *cold CI line*, not the public tip line. She promised to call if Amanda shows up at the house."

Waters leaned forward and made a note on a pad. "That's good, because I have to pull the surveillance team off, after this shift."

"What?" Dombrowski groaned. "LT, we can't leave that site uncovered. We're only using a two-man surveillance team."

"I don't have a choice, Sergeant. Those resources are needed elsewhere. Your cooperating CI is still in place; that should be sufficient."

"Crap," Dombrowski mumbled.

The lieutenant ignored him and slid a copy of an official looking e-mail across his desk. "There are other developments. As you know, at our request the *Surete Nationale* located and made contact with Nicole Demotte, Amanda Farrell's mother, in Paris. Their interview pretty much corroborated what Walter Farrell told us about the divorce and Amanda's summer visits. We sent word late yesterday that we no longer had an open missing person case, but this morning, the *Prefecture de Police de Paris* advised that Nicole Demotte and her husband, Pierre, had left Paris and are already on their way here."

"Oh boy, that can't be good for Walter," Katie surmised.

Dombrowski handed the e-mail to Katie. "Yeah, I'll bet his lawyer's job is about to get interesting. So, the mother and stepfather are coming here, and they don't know that Amanda's no longer a missing person, or that she is a person of interest in a homicide investigation. When do they get here?"

The lieutenant shrugged. "We don't know yet. Pierre Demotte has his own jet. He filed a flight plan for Paris to New York. Departure was a little over two hours ago; so, they're still somewhere over the Atlantic. Whenever he files a CONUS flight plan, we'll be notified."

"You know," Katie pointed out, "we could arrange for them to be notified while they're in the air. But I doubt that would change their plans."

"No, it wouldn't," Waters agreed. "She's a mother and her child may be in jeopardy—she's coming."

"I wonder if Walter knows," Dombrowski mused.

"You'd better believe it," Katie answered. "I'll bet she's already burned up a phone line chewing him a new one. Hey, he may have already told her that Amanda's not really missing. Of course, that means he'd have to produce her for her mother, wouldn't he?"

Dombrowski just grinned. "This might get very interesting, indeed."

Lt. Waters cleared his throat. "Ahem, let's put the lead on Amanda Farrell aside for the moment. Am I right in assuming we're really no closer to a break in the Carolyn Silverberg case?"

"Afraid so, LT," Dombrowski admitted.

"All right, moving on; the HOA secretary case, Jennifer Halsted?"

"Well, we started this morning going through the HOA files—thanks for giving us Barkley and Johnson to help, by the way. The only thing we've found so far is that there are a lot of covenant violations, most of which appear to have been corrected. But some of the foreclosure files have an extraordinary number of violations."

"Well, wouldn't that be expected, at least to some degree?" Waters asked. "I mean, someone down on their luck wouldn't sweat their lawn not being mowed too frequently, right?"

"You may be right, sir," Katie acknowledged, "but we're finding a lot of citations issued by Gregory Adamson—really broad and subjective stuff like 'yard fails to meet covenant guidelines'. There are names of other volunteers who issued citations, too—but they issued nowhere near as many."

"We don't know if that really means anything, other than Adamson was enthusiastic about it," her partner added.

"So the federal agents told us," Waters reminded them. "I trust you'll look into it?"

"You bet, LT."

"Okay. How about the Gregory Adamson case?"

"As you know," Dombrowski began, "based on the financial reports, specifically some credit card charges at a casino a hundred miles away, the sisters' alibi—being at Louise Hesterly's apartment at that time—isn't holding up. We contacted the security staff at the Indian Casino and got verbal confirmation that Louise Hesterly and Marian Adamson were there.

We asked for their copies of any credit card charges and copies of any surveillance tapes of either sister in the casino. The security staff will comply, of course, but they have to have a subpoena."

"That should be forthcoming today," the lieutenant confirmed. "When will you re-interview these women?"

"Well, we thought about waiting for hard copies of the subpoenaed records, but we already know what they'll show. So, we decided to act today."

That surprised and pleased Lt. Waters. "Today? So soon?"

"Yes sir," Katie answered firmly, "the sooner, the better. Both sisters are coming into our office this afternoon, at our invitation, ostensibly for an update. We'll interview them separately."

"You'll have to Mirandize each one," Waters warned. "At this point, they're both suspects."

"Don't worry, LT, I'll be certain of that," Katie declared.

"Okay, Detectives, anything else?"

Dombrowski shook his head. "No sir, not at the moment."

"Very well. I have to brief the captain now. Oh, and by the way, he's asked me to remind everyone about not speaking to the press or any media people. No problems there, right?"

"Right, LT," the sergeant assured him, "no problems."

"Yeah, we saw this morning's paper," Katie admitted. "I think it's pretty clear they're grasping at shadows. They're not talking to anyone who knows anything of substance. It's all speculation and innuendo."

"I know," Waters agreed, "but it doesn't help; and the captain has to handle the related heat from the upper brass. Sometimes public relations matters too much to some who might harbor further political ambition . . . Crap! I talk too much. All right, get out of here—go fight crime!"

AS THEY LEFT HIS OFFICE and returned to the squad room, Dombrowski nudged Katie. "Hey, I thought you were going to ask for the weekend off? Didn't you say you needed the time? Did you forget?"

"No, I didn't forget. What about you? Don't you need Friday evening free for Donna's dinner? You know, your blind date?"

"Nice try—don't change the subject. So, you didn't ask—what gives?"

She sat at her desk and pursed her lips. He plopped down at his own desk, and moved a stack of files so he could more easily see her face.

"Look, I really do need the time, and I am going to ask for it," she explained. "But first, I want to deal with Louise Hesterly. She lied to my face—and I bought into it. I should've known better."

"You can't let shit like that get to you," he cautioned. "You're pissed because you wanted to believe a sweet little old lady—and you got conned. You lost sight of the fact that everyone has an agenda—everyone. And now, our job is to figure out why she lied. What's she have to gain or hide."

"I know you're right—I am pissed at myself. But she's not that little or that old. Until I resolve this, I'd be poor company for my dad on a weekend outing."

"Hey, it's okay; I get it. This is only Thursday; we've got time to deal with these interviews and do the reports. We may yet salvage some of the weekend."

"With three open homicides? Who are you kidding? You know damn well we're gonna work straight through—we always do," she groaned in mock despair, a wry smile stealing across her face.

"Ah, you know you love it," he declared as they locked eyes in a moment of complete honesty.

Their shared smiles spoke silent volumes. They both loved the work—lived for it, actually—and they both knew it.

"Hey, who knows?" he offered, "Maybe we can squeeze out a few hours and you can take your dad to dinner one evening? I could probably cover for you."

"That might be nice," she admitted. "I could call him. It'd be good for my head, too."

"No problem—consider it a well deserved favor."

"Oh, I'll repay it in kind," she teased. "Don't forget your blind date!"

"Arrg!" he groaned and grimaced. "Jeez, you try to help some people . . . Alas, no good deed goes unpunished. All right, Detective, back to the HOA files. Look lively now!"

"Oh no, you're such a taskmaster! Be careful, Sergeant, you wouldn't want to get a paper cut!"

CH 11

"WHAT NEWS, DETECTIVES?" Louise Hesterly asked as she took a seat in the interview room. "And why did you ask to speak with me alone? Surely, whatever you have to tell me could be said in my sister's presence, couldn't it?"

"We'll be speaking with your sister in a few minutes," Dombrowski explained, "but we need to clear up something you told us, a bit of an inconsistency."

"Why, whatever do you mean?"

"Please understand," Katie began with a sincerity she didn't truly feel, "that we deeply appreciate your willingness to help in this matter, but you don't really have to talk to us. You can consult with your attorney if you choose, or one can be provided if you'd like. Do you understand? Do you have any questions?"

Louise sat back and folded her arms. A scowl replaced her pleasantly bland expression. "I think you just read me my rights. What the hell is going on here, Sergeant?"

"Mrs. Hesterly, when we last spoke, you told Detective Callahan that you and Marian hadn't been anywhere for the prior two weeks. We know that isn't true."

Indignation flared in her eyes. "Just what are you talking about?"

"Would you care to tell us," Katie asked evenly, "about the casino trip?"

Louise Hesterly paled. One hand went to her throat and the other gripped the handle of her purse until her knuckles whitened. Her lips drew into a line of grim determination and her voice hissed through clenched teeth.

"That is none of your business!"

"On the contrary, ma'am," Dombrowski rationalized. "Your whereabouts and activities at the time are very much our business; and the fact that you've lied about it . . . well, that's cause for concern."

"You're a retired surgical nurse," Katie stated. "We've confirmed that. So, you are familiar with certain surgical procedures and support protocols, like giving injections. You told me how you didn't like your sister's husband, Gregory, very much, remember?"

Louise was getting angrier. "So what? What has any of this to do with that bastard's suicide?"

"Mrs. Hesterly, please," Dombrowski tried in his most reasonable tone, "tell us about the casino trip. It could be of considerable importance—to you as well as us."

She was unbowed. She thrust her chin out in defiance. "That is none of your business!"

Katie's patience was sorely depleted. She'd had enough of Louise's intransigence. "Damn it, Louise! We know Gregory Adamson did not commit suicide! He was murdered—and you are a suspect!"

Conflicting emotions warred across Louise's face as she fought silently to maintain her composure.

Dombrowski looked askance at his partner, closed his eyes, and gently shook his head.

Louise took a deep breath and spoke through pinched lips. "I have nothing more to say without my attorney present. Am I free to go?"

Dombrowski and Katie shared a look of mutual chagrin. What little evidence they had was at best circumstantial and clearly insufficient to charge her. There was no way to hold her.

"Yes, ma'am," he intoned, "at this time you are free to go."

Louise rose and demanded, "Where is my sister, Marian? I'm taking her out of here!"

Dombrowski stood and answered evenly. "You can wait for her in the lobby, if you like."

"No! She leaves with me now!"

Dombrowski sighed; but before he could respond, Katie flared and spoke up.

"Louise, listen to me very carefully. You are not an attorney—you do not represent Marian. You are not entitled to be present during our interview with her. Right now, you are free to go. However, if you persist in interfering, that can be construed as interfering with a criminal investigation and obstruction of justice. I will arrest you. You will spend tonight in jail, and see a judge in the morning to have bail set. So, you can wait in the lobby, or be our overnight guest—your choice. Do you understand?"

Dombrowski held the door open as a subtle suggestion.

With barely contained contempt and bloodless lips, Louise spun on her heel and stormed from the room.

He closed the door and resumed his seat. "Well Katie, now tell me, was telling her that Adamson was murdered and she's now a suspect some sort of surprise tactics—or did your short fuse get the better of you again?"

"Maybe a little of both, I guess," she admitted. "If the Miranda warning hadn't shut her down, I figured a more emphatic highlighting of her potential jeopardy would either push her into a more cooperative frame of mind, or else end the interview right quick. I was losing patience with her. Sorry, D, she got to me—again. I don't know what it is about her."

"Forget it," he dismissed. "Get it together. We still have an interview to do."

"I'm good. I assume her sister is still in the other interview room, right? Shall we?"

"HONESTLY, DETECTIVES, I can't fathom why I would want to speak with an attorney. Why am I here?" asked Marian Adamson, her confusion evident. "Don't you have something to tell me?"

"We do, ma'am," Dombrowski acknowledged. "But first we have to clear up a question about the trip you and your sister took a week ago to the casino."

"Oh, okay. How can I help?"

The sergeant and his partner shared a look of surprise. They hadn't expected Marian Adamson's willing cooperation, especially after her sister's refusal. But then, Louise had gone directly to the lobby, so the women hadn't yet had the opportunity to speak. Marian was, for the moment, unaware of her sister's defiant attitude.

The investigators knew they would have to proceed very carefully with this interview.

"So, do you and your sister go to the casino often?" Katie casually asked. "Kinda like a girls' night out?"

Marian smiled and dropped her eyes. "Oh, no, not exactly—I mean that I don't go that often. Louise likes to go and sometimes I'll go with her. I'm not much of a gambler—I usually lose—but I do like to play the slot machines."

"I never seem to win either," Katie commiserated. "So, Louise goes more often. Do y'all stay the night at the hotel?"

"Oh yes, it's too far a drive not to, and it'd be dark. Neither of us sees that well at night these days."

"Oh, I know just what you mean," Dombrowski offered. "I got new glasses and they don't seem to be a bit of help with night driving. So, y'all share a room at the hotel?"

"Well, yes, when I go, but that's not that often. Now Louise goes just about every month, and she'll stay at the hotel."

"Does Louise like to play the slots with you?" Katie asked.

"Sometimes, but she gets bored easily and usually goes in search of other games. We always meet back in the hotel room, although I'm usually asleep by the time she gets there."

"So, you don't always see each other in the course of the evening?" Dombrowski probed.

"Uh, no, not always. The slot machines are on one floor; but the other games, you know, cards, roulette, and such, are on other floors. I stay with the slots; that's more than enough excitement for me."

"When did you and your sister arrive at the casino?"

Marian rolled her eyes and tilted her head. "Um, let's see . . . It was a little after two o'clock, Thursday afternoon, I think. I'm pretty sure, since we left her home right after lunch. She drove the whole way—I offered to drive some, but she said no. She likes to drive. She got a new car last year, a Buick; it still has that new car smell, too."

"That's nice, I love that smell!" He smiled. "And when did y'all return to her place?"

"Oh, about mid-afternoon the next day, um, Friday. We had lunch on the way back at that new restaurant off the interstate . . . I'm sorry, I can't remember the name."

Katie leaned forward for emphasis. "Marian, this is important. Was your sister with you the whole time or were you two separated, like when you were in the casino?"

"Well . . . I guess we weren't always together. I played the slots the whole time while she went off somewhere to gamble."

"When did you next see Louise?" Dombrowski asked.

"Oh . . . I was asleep when she came back to the room. So, I didn't really see her until the morning. Why do you ask?"

Katie straightened in her chair and locked eyes with the woman. "Marian, why do you think Louise would lie about taking this trip?"

"Why . . . what?"

"Your sister denied making this trip. She insisted that neither of you had been anywhere for the past few weeks. Why would she lie like that?"

Marian sat in stunned silence. Her mouth opened, but no sound issued forth. Her brows drew down and her jaw clamped shut.

"Ma'am, are you all right?" Dombrowski asked solicitously. "Can we get you anything?"

It took a moment, but Marian found her voice. "No, I'm fine. I'm sorry, but I have no answer for you. Are we done here? Where is my sister? You told me that I don't have to talk to you. I'd like to leave now."

The detectives shared a glance and rose.

"Mrs. Adamson," the sergeant began, "of course you are free to go. Your sister should be waiting for you in the lobby. However, before you go, there is something we must tell you. Your husband did not commit suicide—he was murdered. You may rest assured we will thoroughly investigate and determine the truth. We will be in touch."

Marian Adamson remained silent. Only the welling of tears in her eyes and the slight quiver of her lower lip betrayed the turmoil in her heart as she rose and walked from the room.

The detectives followed and watched as Marian made her way to the lobby. She strode right past her scowling sister with only the briefest glance and left the building. Louise hastened to catch up. In the parking lot, they were lost from view.

"Damn, D . . . What do you make of that?"

Dombrowski could only shrug. "Don't ask me, Katie. I never claimed to understand women—much less sisters. What do you think?"

"I dunno . . . . There's a strange dynamic with those two."

CH 12

LT. WATERS SIPPED HIS coffee, leaned against the doorjamb of his office, and surveyed the squad room. The only detectives present this morning were Donald Dombrowski and Katie Callahan. She was frowning at her monitor as she typed a report; he was peering through his reading glasses at yet another HOA file.

Waters knew the Adamson investigation had pretty much stalled with the less than productive interviews of the sisters, Louise Hesterly and Marian Adamson. Consequently, Dombrowski and Callahan had little choice but to catch up on reports and delve once more into the towering stack of HOA files.

Unfortunately, Barkley and Johnson, the other detectives Waters had assigned to help in reviewing these files, had court this morning and might be tied up all day. So for now, Dombrowski and Callahan were on their own and swamped. The lieutenant sympathized, but without more manpower there was little more he could do.

His ringing phone pulled him back into his office.

"Lt. Waters . . . 'Morning, Captain . . . When? Yes, sir . . . They're in the office. I'll tell them . . . Thank you, sir."

He hung up, drained his coffee mug, and strode into the squad room.

Dombrowski and Callahan looked up expectantly.

"Detectives, the captain just informed me that Pierre Demotte filed a CONUS flight plan very early this morning. He and Nicole Demotte may already be here."

"What?" Dombrowski exclaimed. "Damn, LT! I thought we were gonna get notified as soon as he filed a flight plan—not hours later."

89

Waters shrugged and shook his head. "What can I say? The notification was late—it happens. The captain's not happy either. Katie, are you still in contact with your CI, Consuela Ladonez?"

"She hasn't called, but that's probably because there's nothing to tell us. Don't worry, LT, she'll call when there's something we should know."

"Okay. Has anything else developed on Amanda Farrell?"

Dombrowski handed the lieutenant a sheet of paper. "All the patrol units got a copy of this BOLO describing her as a person of interest in the Carolyn Silverberg homicide. We've interviewed her friends—still no contact, not even e-mail. Her favored social network sites have been rechecked, but so far, no luck. Her father, Walter Farrell, has lawyered up, so we're stalled on that front."

"But if her mother, Nicole, is here now," Katie cautioned, "things might get very interesting at the Farrell homestead today."

"All the more reason to keep an ear cocked for your CI's call," Lt. Waters said with a grin.

The double ring of the interoffice phone interrupted; the sergeant reached for the receiver.

"Squad Room, Dombrowski . . . Yes, we'll be here . . . No, that's fine. Thanks."

As he hung up the phone and started to speak, the double ring interrupted once more.

"Yeah? Uh, Squad Room, Dombrowski . . . Okay . . . Nah, we'll pick it up. Thanks."

He hung up and stared at the phone, like he dared it to ring again and interrupt him; but it didn't. "The first call was from the CSI unit; they're bringing us some processed evidence that's gotta be signed for. The other call was from the mail room. There's some certified mail that's also gotta be signed for, probably a response to a document subpoena. Katie, if you'll get the mail, I'll sign for the evidence from CSI."

"No problem," she acknowledged, as she stood and rotated her shoulders. "I was getting kinda stiff sitting here anyway. Be right back. Oh, did you have anything else, LT?"

"No, that's it. I uh, might slip out back for a smoke. Then, I'll be in my office if you need me."

———————

UPON KATIE'S RETURN with the mail, she found her partner in conversation with a bespectacled young man in a CSI lab coat. When he glanced up at her, he smiled self-consciously and looked down.

"Ah, here she comes now," Dombrowski boomed, a wry smile teasing the corners of his mouth. "Detective Katie Callahan, meet Officer Kenny Reynolds, newly assigned to the CSI Unit."

The young man blushed, thrust out a hand and mumbled, "Ken . . . just Ken is fine."

She dropped the armload of mail on the desk and shook his offered hand.

Dombrowski grinned and said, "Well okay, Ken. Tell her what you just told me."

"Oh, yes, of course," he stammered, dropping her hand. "Um, the glue—the glue you asked about, that was on the hand—I mean the fingernail."

She stared into him, her impatience awakening. "Do you mean in the Adamson case, the trace of glue found on the decedent?"

"Yes, yes, the Adamson case. The trace of glue is consistent with the other duct tape recovered, uh, I mean the glue on the other duct tape, from the vehicle at the scene."

"Any prints on any of that tape?"

"Uh, no, ma'am, no latent prints."

She bristled. *What the hell—ma'am?*

Sensing her pique, Dombrowski immediately rose, clasped the tech's hand, and shepherded him to the squad room door. "Hey, Ken, we can't thank you enough for bringing this stuff to us. I know your sergeant has you guys hopping, busy as ever, so we'll let you get back to work. You take care, now."

He turned and found Katie at her desk—scowling. He smiled. "Wasn't that nice of him to wait around for you so he could personally tell you the results?"

Her expression darkened. "Everything he said is in the report, isn't it? There was no reason for him to wait for me."

"Ah, but then he wouldn't get to see you, or speak to you, or bask in the warmth of your smile."

"D, don't even go there! That science geek is close to my age—and he called me ma'am!"

Dombrowski sighed and opened his palms. "Seriously, Katie. You're an attractive young woman, single, and a damn fine detective. That impresses these young cops. They're drawn to you—moths to the flame and all that. Of course, you also intimidate them."

She gave him a darkening look, but he was unfazed.

"I'm just saying, you can be a little intense; but that only adds to the mystique. So, you gotta understand that they mean no disrespect. They just don't quite know how to act around you. I gotta admit, sometimes it's just too funny when they can't help acting like shy teenagers."

His candor and sincerity made her feel self-conscious and mildly uncomfortable.

"Aw, come on, D."

He held his hands in an attitude of prayer and intoned in mock solemnity, "Partner, it's just your cross to bear—it's not your fault you're awesome."

She stared at him, and then snorted with laughter. She never took herself that seriously, and knew her partner didn't either. In truth, they both knew that a well-honed sense of humor was an unwritten requirement for this job. "All right already," she gasped in surrender. "What else did he bring us?"

He handed her a large envelope marked EVIDENCE. "Well, there's the report on the duct tape glue, and about a dozen photographs that were recovered from the damaged wireless printer that was found under the bed in Adamson's bedroom. Apparently, these images were from files that hadn't been printed but were still held in the printer's memory. CSI developed and printed copies. They're all shots of houses from various angles—nothing I recognized."

"So, what do you think—covenant violations? Didn't Adamson take pictures of those?"

"Yeah, he did. We'll look closer later—maybe try to match them with some HOA files." He pointed to the stack of mail and asked, "What'd we get in the mail?"

"Dunno, let me open it. This is Adamson's financials and credit reports. Let's see, these are patrol reports, upcoming court schedules, and witness summons."

"Anything else?"

"Yeah, this package. Oh, these are videos from media crews who were on the scene of the fire at Jennifer Halsted's building," she announced as she held up a set of DVDs.

"Good! We can put those with the cell phone camera shots that you took of the crowd. We can look at that stuff this afternoon. Is there anything else?"

"Nope, that's it. Hey, it's coming up on noon. Are we gonna get some lunch?"

"Sure, Mexican?"

"Hold on," she cautioned. "Isn't tonight your sister's dinner party? Do you know what she's serving? We shouldn't get Mexican if that's what she's having."

"Oh crap! I'd forgotten all about that. I have no idea what she's gonna have. I guess it won't really matter; I'll eat whatever she serves."

Katie patted his arm. "That's sweet. You're a good brother. No doubt that'll impress your blind date. Still no idea who it's gonna be?"

He grimaced and shook his head. "No, and don't remind me. I really wish she wouldn't pull these stunts."

"Look, you know she means well. I know you don't want to offend her—and it is only one evening. It'll be okay—you might even have fun."

"Yeah, maybe. What about you? Have you planned anything with your dad yet?"

She brightened and nodded affirmatively. "Yeah, as a matter of fact. I know the LT said we'd probably have to work the weekend; but, you know—time. So, if we don't have to work too late tomorrow afternoon, I'm taking him to dinner at that little Italian restaurant he always enjoyed."

"That's great! Look, if we do have to work a little later tomorrow, I could cover for you if you need to slip out a bit early. We could even clear it with the LT. You've got your cell phone if we need you."

"That's a sweet offer, D. I may even take you up on it. Of course, I'd do the same for you—you know, so you can make it to Donna's dinner party. After all, you wouldn't want to disappoint your date."

Dombrowski could only chuckle and shake his head; Katie always seemed to get the last word. So of course, he couldn't resist. "No, ma'am."

Her pinched scowl reluctantly disintegrated into a wry grin.

The sudden triple trill of the confidential informant line echoed through the otherwise empty office.

Katie lunged for the phone. "I got it!"

Dombrowski closed the door to the hall as Katie settled herself and picked up the receiver.

"Hello? Yes, this is Detective Callahan . . . Calm down and speak slower . . . Who? What did you hear? They both left—together? Okay. What about his lawyer, Ms. Dubois? No, you did fine, Consuela . . . Yes, if something changes call back on this number. It won't matter—you can talk to whoever answers, okay? Good. No, you just follow your normal routine . . . Yes, I'll be in touch. Goodbye."

Lt. Waters had come into the squad room and now stood with Dombrowski. Both looked to Katie expectantly.

She smiled. "That was our CI, Consuela, on her cell phone. She said that Pierre and Nicole Demotte showed up at Walter Farrell's house a little while ago. She heard a heated argument, raised voices and shouting. She couldn't discern the words, but she's sure it was Farrell and Nicole arguing. A few minutes ago, Nicole and Pierre Demotte left the house together. Walter Farrell has locked himself in his study. He's alone; but she could hear his voice, like he was making phone calls, trying to find someone. His lawyer, Ms. Dubois, hasn't been at the house today. That's all our CI knows for now. She'll call back if there's anything new."

Waters smiled and nodded. "Well done, Detective, good move with the CI."

"What do you bet," Dombrowski mused aloud, "that Farrell's calling around, trying to contact his lawyer right now?"

Katie shrugged and answered, "It wouldn't surprise me. But there's no way of knowing since we don't have a tap on his phone."

"It may not matter at this point," Waters remarked with a sigh. "I don't see what else we can do now but wait and see."

"Yeah, you never know, LT," Dombrowski agreed. "Nicole and Pierre Demotte may be the wild cards in this deal. Now that they've stirred the pot, give it some time to stew and we'll see what surfaces."

"Shouldn't we interview them?" Katie asked.

"Oh yeah, definitely," her partner agreed. "Does our CI know if they're staying or where—a hotel maybe?"

"No, I'm sure she told us everything she knew," Katie reasoned, "but if she calls back, I'll double check."

"I can make some calls, check with a few hotels," the lieutenant offered, "that is if you'll bring me back some takeout. I heard y'all talking about Mexican for lunch; a taco salad with some chips and salsa would be fine."

"You got it, LT," Dombrowski declared as he stood.

———

BY MID-AFTERNOON THE two detectives had reviewed all of the raw footage newscast videos and still shots taken at the fire scene. It hadn't been too difficult to preliminarily identify all the people present. They were displaced residents, concerned neighbors, or fire fighting personnel.

"Well, that wasn't too fruitful," Katie groused.

"Now Katie, you know it's just as important to close out an unproductive lead as it is to follow a good one," Dombrowski reminded her.

"I know, I'm just tired. What's next?"

He reached for the short stack of photographs from the CSI Unit, and started thumbing through them. "We may as well start on these new shots of houses that came from Adamson's home printer, and try to match them with the HOA files. Hmm, that's funny."

"What?"

"Uh, most of these pictures are of the fronts of houses—you know, front lawns and stuff," he murmured as he flipped through the stack once more. "But these three are of a backyard; I think it's the same backyard."

"Lemme see."

He handed her the photos; she studied them.

"Yeah, I think you're right. You can't see all of the back of the house, but a good part of the yard is visible. That's the same deck and the same pool. That pool is pretty dirty, really funky. Maybe that was the violation?"

"Maybe," he allowed, "but without knowing the street address—the numbers aren't on the back of the house—we're gonna have a hard time matching it up to a file."

"Aw crap," she groaned. "Hey, maybe not. What if it's the backyard of a house in one of these other pictures?"

"Could be, but we've still got to match it to a file. Is there anything else in the photos that might help us?"

She studied the prints and gnawed at her lower lip. "Look here, D. In this shot, you can see a part of what looks like a commercial van with a name painted on its side—*something* pool cleaning? Maybe CSI can enhance this shot and we can identify the pool cleaning company. We find them, and they might have a record of this job, don't you think?"

"Yeah, good thinking, Detective. I'll call CSI."

As her partner spoke on the phone, Katie spread the three photographs out before her. Something was nagging at her, something she couldn't put a finger on. The lighting was different in each picture, and shadows were of differing lengths. No doubt each photo was taken at a different time of day and under different weather conditions. She rummaged through her desk for a magnifying glass, and scrutinized the prints. In the lower left corners she found the faint time stamps and rearranged the photographs chronologically.

"Hey, D, have a look at this."

Dombrowski concluded his call and came to stand over her shoulder. "Okay, what?"

"Use this glass and look close. See the time stamps? These photographs were taken over the course of five days. First this one, shot in the middle of the afternoon. Then this one, with the van in it, shot two days later, earlier in the day. And finally, this one, shot three days later, late in the afternoon."

"Yeah, go on," he urged, as he leaned closer.

"Let's check these time stamps against the security company's gate records that we got via the subpoena. Weren't they supposed to document or record the comings and goings of contractors and vendors? Maybe we can ID the pool company that way."

"Yeah, maybe," he cautioned, "but we've got two problems. This house might not be in that specific neighborhood, or not even in a gated community. But even if it is . . . well, you saw those records and you know how sloppy their documentation was. We'll check it out; you never know."

She sagged as she remembered the haphazard nature of the security company's record keeping.

Her partner pointed to the barely perceptible smudge that was the time stamp on the nearest photograph. "But you know what? If we can find the time stamps on the other pictures, the ones that depict the fronts of houses, and the times are close, maybe we can come up with a street address."

She bent to the task and spent several long minutes studying the prints. Sighing, she looked up and shrugged. "I can barely make out some of them, D; I'm not real sure. Do you think the CSI lab can enhance the time stamps?"

"Dunno, we can ask," he acknowledged. "It's worth a shot. What? Is there something else?"

"Well, maybe it's silly. But, if the pool cleaner showed up on this day," she reasoned pointing to the middle picture, "why is the pool still a funky mess three days later? See, it still looks like a neglected fish pond."

His eyes followed her finger as it came to rest on the final photograph. "Now, that is interesting. Maybe he turned down the job?"

She scoffed. "In this economy? Come on, nobody turns down a job these days."

"You're probably right," he admitted with a shrug. "That's something we can ask when we get the company identified. I've asked the CSI lab to try to enhance the photos."

She stared, her brow knit in concentration.

"What?" he asked. "Is there something else?"

"I dunno. Something's still bugging me about this," she admitted. "Maybe I'll just let it gel, put it on a back burner and it'll come to me."

Lt. Waters entered the squad room and approached the detectives. "I'm returning this HOA file. I didn't find anything of note."

"Oh yeah, the house we found Adamson in," Katie acknowledged. "There wasn't much in that file, like a lot of them."

"Hey, LT," hailed Dombrowski. "Any luck finding out if the Demottes are staying, and where?"

"No, but you can ask them yourselves; the Demottes are in the captain's office. I'll join you there in a few minutes. I have some calls to make. Report to the captain."

"Yes, sir, we're on our way," Dombrowski acknowledged.

"Oh, I bet this is going to be interesting," Katie murmured as they walked down the hall.

"Yeah," he agreed, "I gotta admit I didn't think we'd get to talk to them this soon. Maybe they've got a lawyer with them."

"Nah, the LT would've told us," she assured him. "I'm thinking we're about to meet a mama lion who's concerned about her cub, and heaven help anyone in her way."

CH 13

———

"DETECTIVES, THIS IS Mr. and Mrs. Demotte," announced Captain Walker, standing at his desk, and gesturing to his seated visitors, a smartly dressed blonde woman and her lean jawed husband. The man, attired in an expensive yet understated business suit, rose and nodded, but did not offer his hand.

The captain continued, "This is Detective Sergeant Dombrowski and Detective Callahan. They were looking into the whereabouts of your daughter, Amanda, before her father, Mr. Farrell, withdrew his report that she was missing."

"She is still missing—maybe kidnapped—despite whatever my ex-husband might say!" Nicole Demotte anxiously spat, sitting ramrod straight in her chair, her fists balled tightly in her lap. "I want her found! Now just what are you doing about it?"

Pierre Demotte resumed his seat, laid a calming hand on his wife's arm and tilted his head toward her. He said nothing, but she seemed to regain her composure under his touch.

"Sergeant," the Captain asked, "can you enlighten Mrs. Demotte?"

"Of course sir. Mrs. Demotte, there is no evidence that Amanda has been kidnapped, nor has there been any ransom demand. Nonetheless, we have not abandoned the search for your daughter. It is true that her father, through his attorney, rescinded his assertion that she was missing. However, we suspect otherwise, so we are still investigating. Can you tell us why you believe she's missing, and not gone off somewhere of her own volition?"

Nicole Demotte leaned forward, her barely constrained anger fuelling her intensity. "Why? Because she would have called me by now! We're close! We keep in touch, even when she spends time with her father—especially when she spends time with her father. It's been over a week! He's no damn help—he didn't even look for her! Some father—the fool thinks he can buy her affection with some stupid car. He didn't even call me when she . . . she . . . went missing!"

"Yes, ma'am, we understand that's very upsetting," Katie soothed. "Please understand that we have to ask, has Amanda ever, uh, been out of touch with you for this long before?"

"No, never! As I said, we're very close . . . I . . . " Nicole's voice broke, and she fumbled in her purse.

Her stoic husband offered her his monogrammed handkerchief.

She dabbed at her eyes and cleared her throat. "I apologize. It's just that I'm very afraid for her . . . I'm not usually so emotional . . . but she's my little girl . . . I'm sorry."

"There's no need to apologize, ma'am, truly," Dombrowski assured the stricken mother. "As we understand it, Amanda was supposed to spend the summer here, with her father, and then go to college in the fall. Is that correct?"

"Yes, yes, that's right," Nicole confirmed. "She has some friends here, and this was to be their last summer together before they all went off to college."

"Did you know her friends?" Katie asked.

"Well, yes, I should think . . . I know some from when I lived here, of course. And I know those who have visited us. She talks about most of her friends all the time. And I've seen many of their pictures on her cell phone."

"Was there a Carolyn Silverberg among them?"

"No, I don't think so. That name isn't familiar. Why?"

Dombrowski ignored her question and asked one of his own. "Mrs. Demotte, did Amanda recently get a driver's license?"

"Why, yes, she did . . . a provisional license—a learner's permit. She was quite pleased with herself. It is a bit of an accomplishment for a teenager in the UK, you see."

"Yes, of course." He smiled. "Teenagers are the same everywhere, I suppose. A symbolic rite of passage—one attains a level of freedom, and all that, right?"

"Quite so," Nicole agreed, a bit wistfully.

"Mrs. Demotte, if you know," Katie probed, "did Amanda bring her new license with her when she came to stay with her father?"

"I should say so," Nicole confirmed. "She was so proud; she wouldn't go anywhere without it. Why do you ask?"

The captain gave Dombrowski and Callahan a knowing look and nodded.

"Mrs. Demotte," the sergeant began gently, "it appears that we may have found Amanda's driver's license, but there was no sign of Amanda."

"What? Where?" Nicole exclaimed.

Dombrowski stole a glance at his partner, and considered his next words very carefully. "It was found in the home of a woman, Carolyn Silverberg, in her possession."

"That's why you asked if Amanda has a friend by that name? Does she know where Amanda is? Why would she have Amanda's license?"

The big sergeant could only shrug and admit, "I'm sorry, but we don't know."

"And why not? Surely, you questioned this girl; what did she say?"

"Ma'am, we did not have the opportunity to question her. We found Ms. Silverberg deceased."

Nicole gasped and paled. "A-amanda?"

"As I said, we did not find Amanda—only her license. There was no other indication to suggest that she may have been there. We do not know that any harm has befallen her. We are still looking for her."

A host of emotions washed across Nicole Demotte's face as she struggled to maintain her composure. Her husband rose, stood behind her, and placed his hands upon her shoulders. Clearly she took great comfort in his presence. She soon found her voice.

"This Silverberg... person... h-how did she die?"

The captain raised a hand and answered before Dombrowski could respond. "I am sorry, Mrs. Demotte, but that is an ongoing investigation; and as such, I'm afraid we can't discuss that case at this time."

Nicole's face spoke volumes; clearly she suspected the worst, and everyone knew it. Lips drawn in a grim line, she rose. "I see. In that case, I don't feel there is much more we can accomplish here and now. I trust you will keep looking for my daughter—and you will keep us informed."

Pierre Demotte slid a card onto the captain's desk and simply said, "Call this number."

Without another word, the Demottes left the office.

The captain studied the card and then handed it to Dombrowski.

"It's a satellite cell phone number, international carrier," the sergeant observed, "and doesn't tell us where they're staying."

"It doesn't need to," announced Lt. Waters, stepping into the room. "They've taken a suite at the Preston Arms Hotel, for an undetermined duration."

"I'm not surprised," offered Katie. "That woman is not going anywhere until her daughter is found."

"True that," Dombrowski agreed. "I got the impression she thinks her *ex* knows more than he's telling. I know I do."

"Perhaps, but Walter Farrell is represented by counsel," Waters reminded everyone. "You may recall we have been put on notice that any further inquiries of Mr. Farrell are to go through his attorney, Ms. Dubois. Is that clear, Sergeant?"

"Of course it is, LT—no problem."

Katie looked askance at her partner, but kept silent.

"If that's all," concluded the captain, "I'm sure you have other open cases that need your attention."

"Yes, sir," they replied in unison and departed.

———————————

BACK AT THEIR DESKS, the detectives stared at the mound of HOA files yet to be reviewed.

"We've still got a lot of files to plow through, and no more help," Dombrowski grunted. "It's gonna take days."

Katie sighed in resignation, just as Lt. Waters entered the squad room with a package in one hand and a clipboard in the other.

"Problem, Detective?"

"Uh, no sir, LT. Something we can do for you?"

"Yes, you can sign this chain of custody form for this package. An officer from the Tribal Police delivered it while you were in the captain's office. I understand it's the security recordings from the casino security office that you requested via subpoena in the Adamson case. I signed for it in your absence."

As Katie signed the form, Dombrowski thumbed through his notebook and mumbled to himself. "It ought to be more than that. I remember we asked for the hotel registration and credit charges, too."

She heard him and chuckled. "Patience, D, at least let me get it open, then you can whine if it's not here."

"I don't whine," he insisted over a protruding lower lip.

"Ah, here's a letter with attachments, and a DVD from the Tribal Police. Okay, it's the surveillance record from the casino." She read the accompanying letter. "This tells us the digital time marks when either of the sisters is visible on camera. And these attachments are certified copies of the registration and credit card charges."

"Hey great!" he exclaimed. "Thanks for signing for that, LT. We really needed it."

"No problem, Sergeant. I'm going outside for a smoke."

"Say, D, how about we take a break from the HOA files," Katie suggested, "and review the casino security recordings to corroborate or refute the sisters' alibis?"

"Good idea. What's the run time for the DVD?"

She stared at the disc, her puzzlement evident. "I dunno. I think this is a compilation; we don't know if the source was old-school analogue tape or current compressed digital, or a combination of both. Plus, it depends upon what speed it was recorded."

"Huh? What do you mean?"

"Commercial security stuff is typically recorded at as slow a speed as possible. It's cheaper, see? It allows for more time coverage on a single tape or disc but the resolution or clarity could suffer—hell, it usually does. This disc might hold many hours worth of motion activated data. We've got the time stamp information in the letter, but you know we're still gonna have to watch the whole thing."

"Damn, it's already after three," he groused. "I've got that thing this evening."

"Hey, no worries, big guy. I told you I'd cover for you so you wouldn't disappoint your sister. Let's get started on this, and you can leave whenever you need to. I can watch the rest and brief you in the morning. That'll work, won't it?"

"Yeah, I think so. I really appreciate this."

"Oh, it's *quid pro quo*—I may need the same favor tomorrow. Remember my dinner plans with my dad?"

"I didn't forget, Katie. No sweat, I've got you covered."

"Thanks. Come on, let's get started."

CH 14

KATIE LOOKED UP FROM the morning newspaper to see her frowning partner enter the squad room and head for the coffee pot. Hefting her empty cup, she hailed him. "Good morning, Sarge! If you're pouring, I could use a refill."

"Gimme your cup," he mumbled as he detoured past her desk.

She watched him pour and studied his pinched face. She could see that he hadn't slept well, again. She knew he wasn't a morning person to begin with; but when he was short on sleep, he could be downright cranky. Naturally, she couldn't resist. "So, how was Donna's dinner party last night? Did you meet anyone interesting?"

Squinting at her as he placed the hot mug on her desk, he grumbled, "Don't ask." He plopped down at his desk, closed his eyes, and sipped from his own steaming mug.

"Too late," she countered brightly. "What's wrong, D? Rough night?"

He waved his cup and shook his head. When he opened his eyes, he found her smiling impishly. He sighed in resignation. "Ahrgg . . . Have you no mercy? I got home too late and didn't get much sleep."

"I can see that, D. Come on, I want the details. Who was she, any of Donna's friends I might know?"

"You've got it all wrong, Katie. It was nobody I knew, or anyone you know. She was some new acquaintance from Donna's yoga class . . . uh, Eloise . . . *something*. Crap! I don't even remember her last name."

Katie's eyebrows shot up and a smirk played across her face.

Dombrowski blanched and sputtered. "Wha—? No-no! It wasn't like that at all!"

Katie shrugged and retorted innocently, "Hey, whatever you say. It's not really any of my business after all."

"Damn it, Katie! Look, she was one of those new age mystical types, talking about crystals, psychic energies, and all that *woo-woo stuff.* She talked incessantly! Worse, it turned out that, without asking me first, Donna had promised her that I'd drive her home after the dinner party. I was stuck giving her a ride. She never shut up the entire time she was in my truck."

"Ouch! I'm sorry to hear that," Katie commiserated. "I guess that meant no good-night kiss at her door?"

"Not even a handshake," he said in relief. "Enough about my evening—what did you learn from the DVD?"

Katie was still chuckling while she slipped the DVD into her computer. "I gotta warn you, all the surveillance feeds are in black and white, and they're not exactly Hi-Def."

"Well, it's better than nothing. Go on, play it."

She rummaged through her notes as an interior casino scene resolved and displayed on the large monitor screen on the squad room wall. "Okay, I found both sisters, but they're not always together.

"Marian Adamson stayed at the slots from mid-afternoon through the evening and well into the night, a little over ten hours, which essentially corroborates her statement. There are a few gaps, all of which are under ten minutes. But those are just her trips to the ladies' room."

The sergeant sipped his coffee and stared at the screen. "What about the other sister, Louise? We do have her on camera, right?"

"Yeah, we do, three times, and on multiple cameras. Give me a second . . . Here we go; the first time, the two sisters are sitting together at the slots for about half an hour. Then, as you can see, Louise leaves the casino, enters the hotel lobby, and gets on an elevator. After that, she's off camera for a while. Hold on, I'll fast forward."

As the digital image flickered, Dombrowski drank the rest of his coffee, and stared at the time stamp readout as it frantically accelerated. A lot of time was passing. "Damn! How long, in real time, before she shows up on camera again?"

"Actually, it's just over fifteen hours—the next morning," she answered with a wince.

"Are you kidding me? Don't we have her getting off the elevator? Or in the hotel hallways—like going to her room?"

Katie shook her head and explained. "No, we don't. Unfortunately, there's no recording of upstairs hallway foot traffic. On all the hotel floors above the main lobby there are fixed cameras at either end of the hallways. They're monitored, but they're not set up to routinely record, so no joy. But that's not the issue that got my attention."

"What do you mean?"

"It's coming up . . . Yeah, here it is; the next morning, first floor main elevator lobby. Just watch."

The highly decorative doors of an elevator slid open. A tall man in a suit took half a step out, scanned the immediate area, and stepped back into the elevator car where a woman stood waiting. He whispered something to her, and then embraced her. They kissed. He broke the embrace, stepped out of the car, and walked swiftly to the right and out of the camera frame. The woman primped for a moment, exited the elevator car, and stood for a moment looking in the same direction the man had taken. Clearly, it was Louise. She then turned to the left and walked out of view.

"Well that's certainly her," Dombrowski acknowledged. "Can you back it up so we can see him again?"

"Yeah, wait one . . . here you go." She paused the DVD just as he stepped out of the elevator, his face clearly visible.

"Now just who do we have here," he asked, his interest flaring, "a mystery man?"

"Dunno yet," Katie admitted. "I wanted you to see this before we made any inquiries. I didn't make him. Do you recognize him by any chance?"

"Nah, I don't know him. I guess we'll ask the Tribal Police and casino security to follow up. He's gotta show up on other security feeds, you know, like a parking lot. If he had a car maybe we could get a tag number. If he was a guest at the hotel, maybe he was registered."

"Yeah, that's what I was thinking, too."

"You said that Louise is on camera three times, right? What's the third?"

Katie tapped a few keys on her keyboard, and the digital image flickered once more. "The sisters are together again when they check out. Ah, here they are, at the front desk, see? This is only a few minutes after Louise says good-bye to her mystery man. Marian had already come downstairs and was waiting for her in the lounge area of the front desk lobby."

"I see. Well done, Katie. So, for about fifteen hours, Louise is unaccounted for—her alibi just collapsed."

"It did indeed," she agreed. "She had ample time to come back here, kill her brother-in-law, and return to the casino."

"Unless her mystery man provides her another alibi," he felt compelled to point out.

"Hell, he's probably an accomplice!"

Dombrowski winced. "Is your temper—" He stopped when he saw her smirking. "Okay, you almost got me . . . So, no assumptions. I'll admit it is possible, but let's just see where the evidence leads. I've got some ideas how we can play this. I think it's time we brief the LT."

"Brief me on what?" Lt. Waters asked as he poured himself a mug of hot coffee.

"Good morning, LT! That's good timing!" Dombrowski declared, reaching for Katie's empty cup. "Lemme get us some refills and we'll bring you up to speed."

HALF AN HOUR LATER the coffee pot sat empty, the briefing concluded. Waters leaned back in his chair and absently fingered the pack of cigarettes in his breast pocket—soon, he promised himself, soon.

"All right, I can't see any reason not to proceed. And, to be honest, I don't really think we have anything to lose at this point," the lieutenant allowed. "The Tribal Police will cooperate, I trust?"

"I checked; they will," Dombrowski assured him. "But it's gotta be an official request from you, first thing Monday. The lieutenant you need to speak with is off on the weekend. Which reminds me, why are you in here today? It's your weekend off, too."

"Ah, yes, about that," Waters began. "I got a curious call from the captain. It seems one of our federal friends, Deputy U.S. Marshal Gonzalez, wants to meet with you two."

Dombrowski couldn't hide his puzzlement. "Emilio? He wants to meet with us? About the Adamson case?"

"I presume so. He'll be coming by this afternoon, sometime after lunch. That's all the captain told me. I'm to call him after the meeting. I'm afraid that's all I know."

"I was under the impression," Katie mused aloud, "that the feds gave us pretty much everything they had on Adamson."

"As was I, Detective," Waters agreed. "I guess we'll find out soon enough. Since it seems I'm going to be here for the better part of the day, is there anything I can help you two with?"

Dombrowski grinned and Katie smirked.

Too late, the lieutenant realized he'd stepped in it.

"As a matter of fact, LT," Dombrowski said genially, "we still have a bunch of HOA files to review. So, anything you could do . . . "

Waters shook his head and smiled. "Sergeant, your dubiously subtle persuasion skills have not diminished with time. But first, I'm going to step outside and enjoy a cigarette. You may as well put another pot of coffee on."

Katie jumped up and collected the empty cups. "I've got that covered, LT. You go enjoy your smoke."

"Need any help, Katie?" her partner asked.

"Nah, you always make the coffee one scoop too strong. I've got this."

The big sergeant chuckled and reached for yet another HOA file.

———————————

THE AFTERNOON SUN HAD begun its slow slide toward the west when the Deputy U.S. Marshal stood in the doorway and politely knocked on the jamb. He waved when the detectives looked up from their desks.

"Hey Emilio!" Dombrowski called out. "Welcome! So you're working on the weekend, too? We heard you wanted to see us. What's up?"

"Coffee?" Katie offered.

"No thanks," the Deputy U.S. Marshal declined. "I just came from an overly long lunch meeting where I drank too much iced tea. Is Lt. Waters here? I'm supposed to brief him too."

"He's in his office," Katie answered, as she stood. "I'll get him."

Dombrowski tugged a chair from another desk and gestured for their visitor to sit. "Here, take a load off. Is everything all right?"

"Most likely. This is more of a courtesy-call visit. Think of it as an informal heads-up."

Before he could sit or elaborate, Katie returned with the lieutenant, who thrust out his hand in greeting. "Ah, Marshal Gonzalez, it's good to see you again. To what do we owe the pleasure?"

Emilio smirked in response as they shook hands. "Thanks for the promotion, Lieutenant, but I'm just a Deputy—I have to work for a living."

Everyone chuckled politely at the old joke, and then took seats near Dombrowski's desk.

"Now what can we do for the Marshals Service?" Waters asked.

The Deputy U.S. Marshal scanned the room; the four of them were alone. He paused, studied each in turn, and began to speak. "It may be more about what I can do for you—in terms of some information. Now, much of what I am about to tell you is classified as *Law Enforcement Sensitive*. You've been cleared for this information, but its further use is to be restricted and shared only on a need to know basis—that includes your chain of command. Your captain has also been cleared and may be made aware of what I am about to tell you. If a need arises and you feel you must share this information outside your agency, please contact me first. Are there any questions at this point?"

There were none.

"You may already know the U.S. Marshals Service is the U.S. liaison with INTERPOL. We have personnel permanently assigned to the INTERPOL Headquarters in Lyon, France. We handle international investigations per INTERPOL requests in the U.S. and abroad. What is not generally known is that we participate in a rather expansive criminal intelligence network of global proportions. While most folks are aware of our primary responsibilities, we get involved in a lot of other things, so we pay close attention to current intelligence data. Some related information has come to our attention that you should be made aware of, since it may relate to one of your open cases."

"Which one?" Waters asked.

"Amanda Farrell, an alleged missing person, and a person of interest in your Carolyn Silverberg homicide investigation."

"Well, you are certainly well informed," the lieutenant remarked coolly. "Her status in the Silverberg case hasn't been shared outside of this department."

"I know," Emilio admitted. "Your BOLO got our attention. All I can say is that it linked with other data in a probability matrix that posited a proactive lead that proved fruitful."

"I won't even pretend to have understood any of that," Dombrowski grumbled. "What are you trying to tell us—in plain English, please?"

The Deputy U.S. Marshal smiled and continued. "You had a meeting yesterday with Amanda's mother, Nicole, and her husband, Pierre Demotte, here in this building. I don't know what transpired at that meeting, but I suspect you shared what you could with Amanda's mother. I also suspect that Pierre Demotte had very little to say, if anything. Am I right?"

"Pretty much," Waters admitted. "He gave us his card and said we could contact them at the number on the card."

"A satellite phone based with a European carrier, right?"

"Yes, that's right. We haven't called the number, because there is nothing new to tell them. We know they're staying at a local hotel. How is this related?"

The Deputy U.S. Marshal shifted in his seat. "This is where the information gets sensitive. Pierre Demotte is a very careful man. He's a French citizen, and apparently a legitimate businessman with holdings in France, the UK, Hong Kong, and Australia. He doesn't get involved in the day-to-day operations, although he does closely monitor his banking interests. Some of his enterprises, like the import-export and shipping businesses have been routinely scrutinized by various oversight authorities. There has never been a shred of evidence found that would suggest any illicit activity. As I said, he's a very careful man, and as far as we know, he's never been implicated in anything illegal.

"However, he has a younger brother, actually a half-brother, Rene Pasqualle, who has quite an INTERPOL file. He claims Swiss citizenship; the facts are vague, but may be legitimate. He's a ten-year veteran of the French Foreign Legion. Upon his discharge, his brother, Pierre, fronted him the seed money to start a contract security service that essentially capitalized on his military contacts.

"Basically it's a temp agency for mercenaries. They specialize in doing the kinds of jobs legitimate governments or public corporations don't want to be associated with or suspected of—all for a price. The company has been suspected of illicit arms trading, assassinations, corporate espionage, and various violations of international law—to include black ops stuff.

"There have been investigations, of course, but nothing ever seems to have come of it. The company has been reformatted and reorganized several times, changed names, and moved from country to country as it deemed fit. Now it claims no country of origin and exists only in cyberspace, conducting its business online by referral only. They no longer even use a name; we understand they just refer to themselves as *the group*. We know they still do business, but getting any information about their activities is a real challenge."

"No country of origin? Does that mean they're paying no taxes?" Dombrowski asked.

"Yes, among other things," Emilio admitted, "but we're getting beyond the scope of my briefing. I can't elucidate further in that regard."

"Well, what do you have on this Rene?" Katie asked.

Emilio shook his head and shrugged. "Sadly, not much. As far as we and INTERPOL are aware, Rene is the only known public face of the group. I know his name has come up in several open cases in Eastern Europe. The group has recently been implicated in a series of assassinations of tribal leaders in the Mideast. When Rene was questioned last year regarding a failed coup in a third-world nation, he claimed total ignorance and denied the existence of the group. He's still under suspicion.

'We do know that they maintain no permanent staff. Instead, they'll draw upon a pool of available mercenaries for ad hoc assignments. When the job is done, the operators are paid in cash, and everyone just disappears. They keep no records that we're aware of—and trust me, plenty of people are looking."

"Okay, this is fascinating and all," Dombrowski remarked, "but I don't see the correlation to our case."

"You will," Emilio assured him. "Last night, Pierre placed an international call to a third-party routing service in Zürich. Our people in Lyon have determined that Rene is on the move. We believe he is coming here."

"What—here?" Waters exclaimed, sitting bolt upright. "Let me be certain I understand what you're saying. Pierre Demotte isn't satisfied with our ongoing effort to find Amanda, so he's sent for his brother, Rene—a man of dubious, if not notorious character—to commence his own search in our jurisdiction. Is that what you're telling us?"

The Deputy U.S. Marshal had the grace to appear chagrined. "Ah, yes, sir. That is what we suspect."

"Well, isn't he wanted somewhere—can't you arrest him?" the lieutenant demanded. "We can't have him mucking around in our case."

Emilio opened his palms and shrugged. "Actually, no, he's not wanted anywhere at this time. As I said, he's under suspicion, so it's possible that we'll be tasked with some level of covert surveillance. But unless a warrant is issued, in Europe for example, and INTERPOL acts to request a provisional warrant in the U.S., Rene would have to break a federal or state law here to face arrest. He knows the ropes, and he's not stupid. It's entirely possible that he might not get personally involved with your case."

"So, why else do you think he'd come here," Dombrowski grumbled, "maybe just to lend moral support to his family?"

"Maybe, but admittedly, not very likely," the Deputy U.S. Marshal conceded. "You see, we don't think he's likely to come alone. While he might travel by himself, it would be unwise to assume he wouldn't have made arrangements for other assets and resources to be available."

Dombrowski scratched his chin, leaned back in his chair, and posed a question. "Emilio, this organization, this *group*, do they do hostage or kidnap rescue missions?"

"It is our understanding that they do—or would for the right price."

"Do you know if they have?" Katie probed. "And if so, what's their success rate?"

"We simply don't know. We're looking into those very questions. Unfortunately, most of the missions attributed to the group have been characterized by a significant body count. We don't know if they consider that as an intrinsic measure of success. I'm sorry, but that's all I've got."

"Crap," mumbled the lieutenant, his hand unconsciously reaching for his pack of cigarettes. "Can we assume you'll advise us if and when this problem arrives?"

"When I know, you'll know. I'll check with our best sources and put together a file on Rene; recent photos, prints, the works. You'll have it within 24 hours. I wish there was more, but as I said, that's all I've got. Any questions?"

There were none; because, at this point, they all knew there were no answers.

CH 15

DOMBROWSKI STOPPED to pick up a Sunday newspaper and a couple of large coffees on his way into the office. Katie's comment about his habit of brewing the office coffee overly strong had irked him. So, he decided to bring her a rather exotic Colombian blend from the local coffee shop that he'd grown fond of, something he favored for what they called its robust character.

If she thought my office brew was strong, just wait until she tries this Colombian morning boost—this'll wake her up!

He found her at her desk, already perusing another HOA file. "Good morning, Katie! Here, you gotta try this—it's black and hot. If you want creamer or sugar, you'll have to hit the office stash."

"Coffee, huh?" She peeled the plastic top back and inhaled deeply. "Oh man, that smells good. Thanks, but I'm not gonna drink it black." She stood. "I'm going for the creamer. Do you want anything?"

"No, I'm good. Is anyone else here?" He sat at his desk and opened the paper.

"Nah, it's just us in the CID offices this morning. Two of the day shift teams are on the street, working their own cases. The LT said to call him if something comes up. Sunday was scheduled as his day off, so he's at home today," she explained, stirring powdered creamer into the tall cardboard cup.

Her partner blew across the surface of his own cup and sipped tentatively. "Oh, that's good. I guess he had enough of these files yesterday. I think we got quite a bit done, don't you?"

Katie sat down at her desk, sipped from her cup, and gestured to the stacks of files. "Yeah, actually we're almost through. I started separating the files with foreclosure notices, and the ones with outstanding covenant violations, from the rest. The stack on your desk is all we have left to review."

He stared in resignation at the pile of files. "And how is it that these files got stacked on my desk? Are you trying to tell me something?"

"Me? Perish the thought!" she retorted and smiled. "You weren't here yet, and I needed the room. These stacks on my desk are the outstanding covenant violations, about a hundred and forty files."

"Damn, that many? What about the foreclosures?"

She pointed to two stacks on the floor next to her desk. "There's about fifty of them; and, from what I can tell, a lot of those houses are vacant, almost half. That's why there are two stacks, occupied and vacant."

He peered around his desk to better see the stacks and stroked his chin. "What about the ones that have been sold, you know, the short sales and such? Remember, the witness in the Adamson case, Ms. Fonseca, was a realtor who was supposed to list and sell that house for the bank. Are we tracking those?"

"Well, yeah, in a sense, but as far as I can tell, there haven't been any sales, or at least I haven't found any yet. There are some notations in a dozen or so of the vacant house files to the effect that a realtor's been contacted for listing purposes, but there aren't any copies of listing agreements."

"Oh, yeah? The same realtor, by any chance?" He sat up, discarding the newspaper, his interest growing.

"Nope, sorry, different realty companies. But I did find another commonality; invoices from a contractor, Associated Construction, who did repairs and renovations on quite a few of the vacant homes."

"Hold on a sec." He gathered up a handful of vacant files and started thumbing through them.

"What?" She picked up some of the remaining vacant files and mimicked his actions. "What are we looking for?"

Gazing at the three files open in his lap, he pursed his lips and knit his brow. "Now, if a foreclosed house has gone back to the mortgage holder—the bank—why would a contractor send an invoice, the bill for repairs and renovations, to the HOA?"

She glanced through a few files and found the same documentation. "I see what you mean. Maybe the HOA has an arrangement with the bank, or the contractor, or both. Remember, the HOA can repair covenant violations and bill the homeowner. The bank would now be the homeowner, right?" She flipped through a few more pages. "I don't see any indication of a bill going from the HOA to the bank, do you?"

"No, I don't either. Who's the bank in those files? It's Consolidated Federal in these."

"Yep, same bank, Consolidated Federal. Do you think there's something off here?"

"I dunno, maybe—at least let's keep it in mind."

He looked over at the long line of stacked file boxes along the wall and jerked a thumb at them. "So, I guess we're done with all those, the rest of the files that have been reviewed, right? They're just regular HOA member files that I'm not sure we're going to need; and they're taking up a lot of space. What do you think, should we keep them here?"

She glanced at the boxes and shrugged. "I see your point. If we don't need them, why not return them to the HOA office? We can hold onto those we want, at least for now."

"Okay," he agreed. "We'll have to list what we decide to keep. I'll ask the LT to have the rest sent back tomorrow." He leaned back in his chair, rolled his shoulders and stretched his arms out to his sides. "I've spent way too much time behind this desk lately. By the way, how did dinner with your dad go last night?"

She brightened. "Quite well, actually. He seemed like his old self for most of the evening. I know he likes to get out now and then. And he likes that little restaurant—he always did. He just forgets . . . things. I told him you said 'Hi' and he remembered you."

"Hey, that's great! I'm glad he's doing pretty well. Are you still worried about his meds? Did you have a chance to speak with the VA doctor?"

"No, not yet. I'm gonna call him this week. I think the dosage level or the combination of whatever he's taking is still too much. He gets so tired so fast. By the time we had dessert, he was calling me by my mother's name. I don't know—I'm hoping adjusting his meds will help."

Dombrowski nodded sympathetically. "Katie, you know, if there's anything I can do?"

"Yeah, I know, D, and I appreciate it. For now, let's just knock out the rest of these files and see if we've got anything here."

Dombrowski smiled, took a long drink of coffee, and handed his partner a handful of files from the stack on his desk. He reasoned that in all likelihood she was right. Focusing on work right now was probably the best thing for her—and maybe for him as well.

He considered mentioning the two phone calls he'd gotten at home late last night. Only a few minutes apart, there was only silence on the line each time. But he knew someone was there, someone who hung up after a brief moment. Caller ID only registered unknown number for each call and he hadn't tried the old *69 call return trick. It might have been nothing, he told himself, but he wasn't truly convinced.

He glanced at Katie over his coffee cup. He could sense the emotional turmoil and concern she harbored for her father. Hovering just below her façade of professional calm, her disquiet festered unabated, obvious to anyone who knew her well. He understood she was worried and angry at her own helplessness in the face of her dad's incremental yet inevitable decline into Alzheimer's; and there wasn't a damn thing she could do about it.

No, this was not the time to mention anything as insignificant and trivial as those phone calls. He pulled a file from the stack and dismissed the calls from his mind.

BY MID-AFTERNOON THEY had completed reviewing the HOA files. They decided to keep one hundred and ninety-six files, the outstanding covenant violations and foreclosures. The remaining files would be returned to the HOA office.

Katie was carefully arranging the foreclosure files in chronological order when the office phone rang.

Her partner lunged for it. "I got it—you keep doing your thing. Squad Room, Dombrowski . . . How y'doin', LT? Yeah, we've been here all day working on the files; we're pretty much done. Most of them can go back to the HOA . . . No kidding, when? No, not a peep . . . Okay, will do. See you tomorrow. Bye."

Katie set the last file in place and looked to her partner. "LT, huh?"

"Yeah," Dombrowski leaned back and swivelled in his chair. "Remember Rene Pasqualle, Pierre Demotte's brother? He entered the U.S. around noon today. He came into Detroit by bus from Windsor. It appears he was alone when he cleared Customs. The feds didn't expect him to come through Canada, so they didn't get a tail on him in time."

"So they lost him in Detroit, but they still think he's coming here, right?" she probed.

The big man shrugged. "LT didn't say that, but . . . "

"Yeah, I get it. What else?"

"He wanted to know if we'd heard from your CI."

"My CI—oh, Consuela?"

"Yeah, you heard; I told him not a peep. You worried?"

"Nah, she's pretty savvy. She wouldn't call unless there was something worth telling us. I might check on her next week, just to be sure though."

The phone rang once more.

"Squad Room, Dombrowski . . . Hey, Sarge . . . Okay, where? All right, we're on our way . . . Yeah, thanks."

Katie stood and stretched. She could sense what he would say before he even opened his mouth. "We got a body, right?"

"Yeah, patrol unit found a female. We're up."

"Aw shit! How old? You don't think—"

"I dunno—no details. Something's up. The desk sergeant said they radioed the other in-service CID units, but they advised him to pass the call on to us."

"Is it related to one of our cases, or are they just passing the buck?"

He met her scowl with one of his own. "Does it matter? We're up anyway. Come on, let's get to the scene. You know it's a waste of time to speculate until we can see for ourselves."

"Yeah, you're right. I'm driving!"

CH 16

KATIE PARKED THEIR cruiser behind a marked patrol unit near the front of the building that bore the address of their crime scene. The edifice was fairly new; an awesome structure of fifteen floors, a towering glass and chrome monument to some architect's Spartan interpretation of neo-modern design.

As they approached the front doors, Katie craned her neck to peer up at the highest floors. She squinted as the lowering sun glinted off the vast reflective expanse. "Oh man, not my style at all, but I'll bet the views are impressive. There's nothing nearby that's more than half that tall."

Dombrowski looked up, winced, and shook his head. "Oh crap," he muttered.

Alarmed, she quickly looked around. "What is it? What's wrong?"

He stopped just as the glass panels of the double doors hissed open. "I know someone who lives in this building."

"Yeah? Who?"

"Melanie Dubois . . . Walter Farrell's lawyer."

"No kidding? She lives here? This place has only been open for little over a year. I hear there are still a lot of vacancies. Have you been in her place—her condo, or whatever?"

"Yeah, just once, right after she moved in. It must've been soon after the building was finished. She was still in the unpacking stage. There were a lot of boxes. I don't really remember too much."

"Oh, D, are you saying that was when you broke up with her?"

"Well, yeah," he admitted. "Anyway, that was the first and last time I was in this building."

She shrugged and nodded to the uniformed patrolman waiting for them in the lobby. "Well, come on then. I can see Ty Baker waiting for us."

The tall patrolman grinned as he saw the detectives approaching. "Hey Sarge, hi Katie. I was told you guys were coming. The CSI crew's upstairs standing by; and the M.E. is en route." He dangled a set of elevator keys and pointed to the open car. "The scene is on the top floor, one of the four penthouse suites. I'll take you up."

"So, Ty," Katie asked as they boarded the elevator, "I gather you guys were first on the scene? Where's Steve?"

"Yeah, it was our run, a response to an anonymous 911 call. My partner's upstairs, keeping the scene secure. He's got the sign-in roster."

In the hallway of the uppermost floor, the knot of CSI techs parted for the detectives and the patrolman as they approached the open apartment door.

"Yo, Steve!" Ty called out. "Homicide's here! Where's the sheet?"

Another uniform appeared in the doorway and thrust a clipboard at Dombrowski. "Here y'go, Sarge. Hi, Katie. So, once more into the breach, huh?"

Katie noticed that Dombrowski was uncharacteristically quiet as he added their names to the roster. "Hey there, Steve," she teased. "Y'know, we really gotta stop meeting like this."

He accepted the clipboard back from Dombrowski and grinned at Katie. "Don't I know it! Two bodies in two weeks—that's some bad karma, at least for me. This body is in the kitchen, propped up in a chair, with gunshot wounds to the chest and head. It's a white female, about forty. We don't have an ID because we haven't touched anything yet. The building manager said that this suite is leased to a law firm; but as far as he knows, just one woman was the only tenant. He's digging up the paperwork now."

"So, you guys found the body?" she probed.

"Yeah, we did," Ty responded. "There was no response to the doorbell. So, I knocked harder with my fist, and the door just swung open—it wasn't even latched."

Steve nodded his head in agreement and continued the narrative. "So, we announced and came in. We found the body in the kitchen and cleared the rest of the place; two bedrooms and two baths. No one else was here. We didn't touch anything, called it in, and secured the scene. That's it."

"What about neighbors? You talk to any of them?"

"A couple down the hall poked their heads out when we were knocking at the door—you know how nosy folks can get when the police show up. They said they hadn't called us, or heard anything coming from this apartment. That was it."

"Okay," she acknowledged. "We'll have a look."

———

MOMENTS LATER THEY stood in the kitchen doorway. Katie leaned into Dombrowski and sighed heavily. "It's her, isn't it?"

"Yeah, it is . . . Somehow I think I knew as soon I recognized the building." He stepped into the kitchen and studied the scene. "Damn, I hate it when it's somebody I know, but this is even worse."

"Do you think this was staged," Katie asked, "or was she shot while sitting in this chair?"

He frowned and leaned over the small café style table. Near the center sat an ornate sugar bowl, its delicate top laid aside. A small spoon lay nearby. A half-full cup of coffee sat before the dead woman. He held his hand over the cup. "This coffee's cold."

Careful not to touch anything, Katie held her open hand near the coffee maker on the kitchen counter. "This has been off for a while, too. It's still got coffee in the carafe. I know most of them have timers and shut off after two hours or so."

"Yeah," he agreed, "mine does that, too."

Katie leaned over the kitchen counter. "There's another cup here in the sink. It looks like it's been rinsed out."

He looked over her shoulder and grunted in agreement.

Katie stepped to the table, looked into the half-full cup, and asked, "Do you remember how she took her coffee—you know, black, cream and sugar, or whatever?"

"Huh? Uh, just cream or milk, I think. She was into health foods, so she avoided sugar . . . At least she did back then."

Katie scrutinized the tabletop, and pointed to the spoon next to the sugar bowl. "Look close. There are granules of sugar still on the spoon. Somebody put sugar in their coffee. If she lives alone and didn't use it, she had a guest who did."

Dombrowski squatted behind the vacant chair on the other side of the small table, drew his flashlight, and let the beam wash across the tabletop. "There's a tiny trail of sugar granules coming from the bowl in the direction of this vacant chair. I think maybe someone spilled a little when sweetening their coffee."

Katie pointed to the trace of sugar sparkling in the spot of roving light. "Here? Yeah, I see it. That would fit with the other cup being in the sink."

Dombrowski couldn't distract himself any longer. He stifled any emotions, steeled his resolve, and looked into the dead woman's face. Aside from her pallor, and the bullet hole in her forehead, she almost appeared alive. He momentarily balked; her wide-eyed expression disturbed him. Nonetheless, he found his voice. "She kinda looks surprised, like she didn't expect this. I think she was shot right where she's sitting."

Katie peered over his shoulder and shuddered. "Yeah, her eyes wide open like that—that's creepy. I'll bet she was surprised. I think she let somebody in, somebody she knew, and likely trusted."

He cocked his head and considered that very scenario; it made sense. "You think?"

"Sure," she answered. "She's not wearing any makeup. The last time we saw her she was wearing plenty—almost too much—you know, at Farrell's house."

He shrugged. That wasn't the kind of thing he'd typically remember about a woman; but he knew Katie would.

She wasn't finished. "Look at how she's dressed; T-shirt, thin sweatpants, and barefoot. Those are comfortable clothes for schlepping around the house. She wasn't planning on going out or entertaining. I think she got a visit she didn't expect."

"Yeah," he grumbled, "and at least three bullets; two in the chest and one in the forehead. Not much blood though." He slipped around the chair the body was in and examined the woman's back. "I don't see any exit wounds on her back, or her skull. I'm thinking low velocity rounds."

Katie motioned toward the hallway where the patrolmen and CSI techs waited. "Steve and Ty said that the neighbors hadn't heard anything. So, you're thinking low velocity—maybe subsonic? Think maybe a suppressor?"

His lips drew into a grim line as he considered the implications. "It's possible. Do you see any spent brass?"

She scanned the floor of the kitchen and the immediate area where a shooter might have been. "No, nothing—maybe CSI will find something."

"Yeah," he agreed and gestured to the victim. "Maybe we'll get a little lucky and the M.E. can recover the rounds intact. That could tell us something."

"Don't forget the sugar spoon and the coffee cups," she reminded him. "Maybe the CSI guys can find some DNA."

"We can always hope," he groaned. "Come on, let's look the rest of the place over and let the techs do their thing."

Katie found a purse in one of the bedrooms. Probing with the tip of her pen she hailed her partner. "I got a purse here, D; wallet, cash, credit cards, ID for Melanie Dubois. Doesn't look like robbery is gonna be a viable motive. Here's a cell phone—funny, it's turned off. She left it in her purse. I'll leave everything for CSI to recover. You find anything else?"

He stood arms akimbo in the living room and scanned the space one more time. "Nah, nothing of note. It doesn't even look like anyone tried to search this place. Did you find a laptop, tablet, or briefcase?"

"No, I didn't," she answered from the bedroom doorway. "That's funny—no computer and no briefcase. I can't imagine a lawyer without either one."

Ty poked his head in the entryway door and called out. "Hey Sarge, could I see you and Katie out here for a second?"

As soon as they stepped into the hallway, the patrolman put a finger to his lips and motioned for them to follow him. Two CSI techs trailed in their wake.

Back near the elevator alcove, Ty whispered as they gathered around. "Your cell phones—do y'all have your cell phones transmitting right now?"

Puzzled, Dombrowski and Katie fished their phones from their pockets.

"No," he said. "It's on but I'm not making a call, so it's not transmitting."

"Same here, why?" she probed.

One of the techs held up a meter with two short antennae and pointed to a digital readout. "This is a very sensitive RFI detector. While we were waiting for you to examine the scene, I was getting our gear ready. I got a GSM transmission reading from somewhere inside that apartment. If you two weren't making any calls—not transmitting—it shouldn't detect your cell phones in standby or reception mode. I'd have to change the detector's sampling parameters—switch to another scale, or—"

"Wait a minute, Kenny Reynolds, right?" Dombrowski interrupted. "Yeah, I remember you. Are you saying that there's like . . . an open phone line in there? Someone could be listening to us? Do you mean like a bug?"

Reynolds nodded and pointed to his meter. "Effectively, yes. Based on my readings, it's more likely that it is a phone. The GSM protocol is very common and used by a lot of cell phone carriers. Using a pre-paid burner with lots of minutes is a pretty cheap and effective way to bug a room. It works as long as the battery lasts—figure eight to twelve hours on a full charge."

"Well, we did find a cell phone, probably the decedent's, in a purse," Dombrowski reasoned. "But it was turned off . . . Right, Katie?"

"Yeah, it was. But some people have more than one cell phone. We didn't find another one, but then we weren't doing a very thorough search. So, for all we know, there might be another phone belonging to the decedent. She might have left it on by mistake. Let's not jump to conclusions."

"True enough," her partner agreed. "But transmitting? I'm the cynical sort. The only reason I can come up with for someone else to deliberately bug the place is to listen in on her—or worse, us, and learn what we know."

"Us? Oh crap! I get it," Katie acknowledged. "Someone could plant the phone while she's distracted with the coffee—or after they killed her. Or, maybe there were really two visitors. Whatever, we'll have to watch what we say when we're in there."

Dombrowski nodded and turned to the tech. "Ken, so your detector can find the bug—phone, or whatever?"

"Sure thing, Sarge. If it's in there, I can find it."

"Okay, you come in with us; but you let Katie and I do all the talking."

In the condo, Dombrowski pulled Katie to one side and watched as the CSI tech began a systematic sweep of the apartment.

"Well, that's that," Dombrowski began. "I guess there's nothing else for us to do but wait for the M.E. So, tell me all about the dinner you had with your dad. What did y'all get to eat?"

She grinned and launched into a detailed recitation of the menu offered at the little Italian restaurant.

In less than five minutes the tech found the simple cell phone. It lay on a wireless charger behind a tissue box on a bookshelf in the living room. The charger would keep the battery up and the line open indefinitely.

Dombrowski was about to reach for the phone when Reynolds stopped him. Pointing to the hallway, he bade the detectives to follow him back to the elevator alcove.

"Sorry, Sarge, but I think there's something else. My meter's telling me there's another cell phone in there—and I mean other than mine, yours, and Katie's."

"What—another bug?"

"Maybe, but I think this one is in standby mode—it's not transmitting. However it's on, so it can receive."

"You can find it?"

"You bet. But don't touch the one we've found. I don't wanna take the chance they're somehow linked, or alert who might be listening."

"Hold on, the phone we found—the open line," Katie mused aloud, "can it be traced?"

"Hmm, maybe," Kenny hedged. "I'd have to see if we brought the right gear, and I should check with our office. But first we gotta identify this other signal source."

"Okay Ken, you're the expert," Dombrowski declared. "Go find it. Come on, Katie, we'll go back in there and resume our snappy patter."

"Okay," she agreed wryly, "but this time you get to run off at the mouth. Tell me all about your sister's dinner party."

It took Reynolds almost ten minutes to find the second cell phone, hidden in the back of a lower kitchen cabinet next to the gas stove. He then motioned the detectives to join him.

The phone was identical to the one they'd already found. However, this one was taped to a series of blocks of plastic explosive. A mass confusion of wires went from the open back of the phone to blasting caps embedded in the blocks and a black box wedged into the center of the explosives. The tech took several pictures with his cell phone.

Dombrowski had seen enough. He stood and pushed Katie and Reynolds out of the apartment. He gently closed the door behind them and beckoned the patrolmen and the CSI techs to follow him to the elevator alcove area.

Once huddled around him, he addressed everyone in a hushed tone. "We have a bomb, and it looks like it's remotely activated. Evacuate the building—and do it quietly! No audible fire alarm and no panic. Go door to door and keep the people as quiet as possible. There are some vacancies, but try every door. Katie, go to the first floor lobby, call the bomb squad from there, and stop the M.E. from coming up here. I'll be in the hall across from the apartment door to keep the scene secure. The rest of you start with the other three penthouse suites on this floor and work your way down. Tell the tenants it's a suspected gas leak and don't let them make any calls. Stay off your phones and radios, too. Go!"

The bomb squad arrived in less than ten minutes, but it took longer to clear the entire building.

Dombrowski looked up to see Katie coming down the hallway. She was alone. "What the hell are you doing back up here? I told you to stay in the first floor lobby!"

"How else can I tell you what's going on—no phones or radios remember? The building's clear and the manager's ready to shut the elevators down. The bomb squad's suiting up and they'll be on their way up with their gear in a few minutes. They've decided from looking at Kenny's cell phone pics that the device is probably booby-trapped, and that it'll be safer to blow it in place. But before they get here, I've got this idea—just bear with me—I don't have time to explain."

She opened the door and entered the apartment.

"Katie! What the hell?"

She spun around, her finger to her lips. He balked, but remained silent.

She went directly to the open line cell phone hidden behind the tissue box and picked it up. She carried it carefully as she returned to the hallway, and bade him to follow. At the elevator alcove she covered the phone's microphone with her hand, tugged him close, and whispered in his ear. "Follow my lead, okay?"

Reluctantly he nodded his compliance, but his confusion was evident as she placed the phone on the floor and pulled him several feet away.

She smiled, winked at him, and spoke in a clear conversational tone. "Hey Sarge, I just thought of something. Let's have another look around the kitchen. I keep thinking we might've missed something important."

She bobbed her head up and down, mouthing *say yes!*

Still confused, he trusted her. "Yeah sure, can't hurt."

Seconds later, a sharp explosion rocked the building.

CH 17

===

DOMBROWSKI GENTLY NUDGED open the door to Katie's hospital room with his right elbow, careful not to spill the coffee sloshing in its flimsy cardboard cup. His left arm hung constrained across his chest in a sling. A large bandage covered the bridge of his nose. Dark smudges beneath his eyes were just beginning to yellow at the edges, the first fading remnants of his facial bruising.

He was surprised to find her sitting up and staring out the window. "Hmmph, it figures you'd wake up when I'm out getting something to eat."

"Hey, D. Did you bring me something? I'm starving."

"Afraid not. How are you doing?"

"Oh, I'm okay, a little stiff and sore. You just missed the doctor. He says I'll be fine but I gotta stay until tomorrow. He wants to keep me under observation one more night."

"Well, that sucks. I know you don't like hospitals."

She shrugged gingerly. "Yeah, well, wadda y'gonna do? But, what about you? I see you're wearing street clothes. You've been discharged?"

"Yeah, early yesterday afternoon. They only kept me overnight for observation. I told them I could just sleep in the chair in your room and save them the bed space, but the doctor just laughed and said no. So, I got stuck in another room. You were still out of it, so I had to deal with visits from the guys from the squad and the lieutenant. Donna came, too."

"Your sister?"

"Yeah, that was kinda nice of her. But then she came back with this nurse in tow, this friend of hers who just happens to work in this hospital and is recently divorced. Sheesh, like I need her matchmaking right now."

Katie smirked. "Aw, I think that's sweet. Maybe she thinks you need a nurse? Ha, I'd bet you couldn't wait to get out of there."

He shook his head and snorted. "You'd better believe it! So, yesterday, the doctor says I'm good to go, but I've gotta follow hospital protocol. As you can see, I can walk just fine, but they still made me use a wheelchair and get rolled all the way to the front door. That shit makes no sense. Anyway, once out the door I turned around and came right back here, to your room, but you were still asleep. Actually, you've been pretty much out of it and sleeping a lot."

"Wait—how long have I been here? What's today?"

"This is Tuesday afternoon. They brought us both in late Sunday afternoon. So, it's been about forty-eight hours."

"Two days? What the hell?"

Dombrowski slid the sole visitor's chair over to her bedside and sat slowly with a painful grunt. "Oof, damn . . . Listen, the doctor told me you might lose a little sense of time. It happens a lot with concussions; it's temporary. It's gonna be okay; you're already doing better."

"No! That's not it! I gotta call my father—I talk to him every day. He'll be worried!"

"Relax, I've already called him. I told him you were okay, just needed some rest, and would call him in the next day or so. There's no need to worry. You can call him today if you want."

"Oh man, D . . . Thank you, I will."

He could see the wave of relief wash over her. He'd anticipated her concern for her father and made the effort to contact him. *No problem, that's what partners do.*

"So, D, what happened? I can't seem to remember."

He shrugged and stared past her, his focus on the memory—disturbing as it was. His eyes found her again, but his voice grew flat, his response terse. "Short answer; the bomb detonated—but you knew that the moment you woke up here."

Her gaze dropped to her lap and her voice grew contrite. "Yeah . . . So, what's the long answer? I know you're pissed—and I'm sorry. Did anyone else get hurt?"

"Nah, just us. I've talked with Kenny Reynolds—but I wanna hear it from you. By the way, we owe him. He and the bomb squad guys pulled us out of that mess. The brass is gonna want to hear from both of us, too. But right here, right now, it's just you and me—so, explain."

She eased back into her pillow and sighed. "It was all about trying to trace the open phone line. When I was in the lobby I asked Kenny if it could be done with the gear they had on the scene. He got all technical on me, but basically he said there was a way he might be able to do it."

"Yeah," Dombrowski grunted, "he pretty much told me the same thing—if he could send some sort of hidden tracer signal out on the open line. It would be tricky because then he'd have to track it piecemeal from cell tower to cell tower."

"Right," she acknowledged. "But he didn't want to initiate the trace too close to the other phone, the one taped to the bomb. We were running out of time. The bomb squad had decided to use some sort of special containment blanket and blow the device in place, so we only had a narrow window of opportunity. I told Kenny to get whatever equipment he needed and meet me in the elevator alcove of the top floor; the phone would be there."

Dombrowski pursed his lips; disapproval tainted his voice. "So, that's why you snatched the phone out of the apartment? What about the possibility the two phones were linked in some way?"

She puffed her cheeks and blew out a thin stream of breath. "Remember the pictures of the bomb that Kenny took? The bomb squad studied them and didn't think the phones were linked. So, I figured that was a chance worth taking. And I was pretty sure you'd never go along with it if I asked first.

"But what's done is done; if there's rip in store for me, I guess I'll take it. But I was sure it would work—besides, if we didn't get that one phone out of there, it might be damaged or even destroyed in the blast. We'd lose our only tangible link to the perp."

His dark scowl spoke volumes. "That was a dangerous and foolhardy thing to do."

She shrugged and waved her hand at the room they currently occupied. "Considering our present circumstances, you'll get no argument from me . . . I really am sorry. So tell me, did we save the phone?"

He sighed and looked askance at the closed door. "In a manner of speaking . . . It came apart when the shock wave hit, but CSI recovered the pieces. They think it'll prove useful."

He pointed to the door. "Someone's coming."

An orderly entered bearing a tray of hospital food, and pulled a rolling tray table over to Katie's bed. "Hello, here's your lunch. You're to eat what you can and drink plenty of water. Do you need anything else?"

"No, thank you," Katie responded, her stomach growling. "I'll be fine."

The door softly closed on the departing orderly.

Dombrowski posed another question, "Why did you want us to keep talking once you had the phone out of the apartment and we were in the hallway?"

She wolfed down what appeared to be lime gelatin and wiped her mouth with a paper napkin. "Actually, that was Kenny's idea. He said we would need some cover noise—our voices would work—when he deployed the tracer signal. I figured it would also keep whoever was listening from getting suspicious. So, I thought talking about examining the crime scene again would be a logical thing for us. You know, we'd be expected to do something like that. It was just something to say, to start a conversation going and keep our listeners on the open line."

His brows knit, Dombrowski sat in silence.

She looked up from her food, gestured to his sling, and asked, "So, what happened to you? How were you hurt, exactly? You haven't told me about that, either."

He straightened his back and sighed. "To be honest, I don't really know. I must've gotten slammed into a wall or something. My left shoulder was dislocated and my nose is broken. I had a concussion, too; but, I never lost consciousness. I guess it wasn't as severe as yours for some reason. As I said, they only kept me here overnight. When I talked with the lieutenant, he said we should take a couple of days, but he wants a full report. I'm thinking maybe by the end of the week, especially if you're getting outta here tomorrow."

She stopped eating and stared at him. "A full report? D, uh, look . . . I don't want to get Kenny jammed up in any way."

"Uh, yeah, about that . . . You know he went along with your stunt without talking to his sergeant—and he's only recently been assigned to the unit. Not too smart, was it?"

"Oh, man," she groaned. "What have I done?"

Dombrowski let her stew for a few moments. "Katie, you gotta be aware that some of these young guys would do damn near anything for you. You gotta be careful what you ask of them. Do you get that?"

She said nothing, but he could see that she got it—and it sucked. She'd let her impetuous and impatient nature get the better of her good judgement, again. And worse, someone else—a rookie tech—might have to pay the price.

"Oh, D," she moaned, "Shit! Poor Kenny! What's gonna happen? This is all my fault. How could I—not thinking . . . "

Her partner sensed her emotional spiral and took a modicum of pity on her. "Well, it's not like I'd want to see him in trouble with his chain of command either—and we do owe him. So, all I've initially said to Lt. Waters was that Reynolds and the bomb squad guys saved our asses when somebody remotely detonated the device. I told him that you were there because we couldn't risk using radios or phones, so you'd come upstairs to tell me that the building was clear, the bomb squad was on their way up, and we could leave."

She nodded, flushed with gratitude. "I see; that'll be the gist of our written report?"

"I don't see why not. It's factual, albeit carefully parsed, but essentially what happened." He leaned forward for emphasis. "However, we will brief the lieutenant on the plan to trace the open line. You know—that plan that we did not have the opportunity to execute? We will also recommend that, as a strategic tactic in the ongoing investigation, such sensitive information should be withheld from the official report pending the results of the CSI tests and lab results. After all, we wouldn't want the media to learn prematurely that we've recovered one of the suspect's phones. Of course, Kenny's chain of command will have to get on board with this, but it'll be better if the lieutenant carries that ball, *capisce?*"

She smiled. "Okay, that works for me . . . and thanks."

He squirmed in his seat. "Katie, there's something else you need to know. I probably should have told you earlier, but I didn't think it amounted to anything—at least, not at that time."

She scooped up the last of her fruit cocktail, pushed her tray away, and gave him her full attention. "Okay, what?"

"I got two phone calls at home Saturday night. Unknown number displayed on my caller ID—maybe blocked, I dunno. Caller didn't speak and hung up after I said hello a coupla times. It wasn't dead air—I knew someone was there."

She tilted her head and shrugged. "So? Didn't you try *69—you know, to reverse dial and see who answered?"

He dropped his eyes and shook his head. "No, I didn't think it was worth the trouble—probably a wrong number or some kids playing with a phone. I let it go, and forgot about it."

Hearing regret in his voice, she gently prodded. "Go on. It wasn't kids or a wrong number, was it?"

He looked up, his battered face drawn and haggard. "No. When I got home about mid-afternoon on Monday, I had a message on my machine from Melanie Dubois. She said she needed to speak to me face to face, that it was important. I was to call her at home as soon as possible. She said it took her a while to muster the courage to do what she felt she had to do, but she couldn't back out now—whatever that meant. The time on the message was a few minutes after nine on Sunday morning; so she was alive as of then."

"I see," Katie acknowledged. "So, do you think she's the one who made those calls to your home Saturday night?"

"I know it was her," he declared. "We subpoenaed her phone records, hard line and cell. The LT went to his phone company sources and had the information within hours. She used her hard line phone in her condo for all three calls. For some reason she stopped using her cell phone a week ago."

"What do you think she was going to tell you? Did she give any hints?"

"None, I have no idea what she was going to say; but I suspect that somebody did." He stared at a blank spot on the wall above her head.

"Who?" she breathed, her focus intense.

"I don't know. I've had little to do but think about this stuff for the past coupla days. While some things are becoming clear, others aren't. There's a sense of too many coincidences. I think we may have missed the obvious."

"What do you mean *we?* I've kinda been out of it for the past two days, remember? And you didn't even know about Melanie's message until Monday afternoon, right?"

"Yeah, that's right. I know I might be a little fuzzy on the details at the moment, but just hear me out, okay?"

"Okay, sure," she acquiesced. "I'm listening."

"Remember the anonymous 911 call late Sunday afternoon? A patrol unit responds to the scene, and subsequently calls in for a homicide unit. Only two teams are on the street, but they're busy with their own cases and can't respond. However, we're in the office, so we get the case, despite being up to our necks in HOA files. Once we're on the crime scene, we find a hidden cell phone being used as a bug listening in on us discussing our case. Then just a bit after we announce that we're gonna have a closer look in the kitchen, someone remotely detonates an IED that was hidden close to the body and any evidence."

"Oh crap!" she exclaimed, sitting straight up, and flinching at the flare of pain in her ribs. "Someone thought we were still in the apartment, mere steps from the kitchen . . . Someone tried to kill us!"

He nodded slowly. "Yeah, that's my thinking; and I suspect there's more than one person involved."

"More than one?" she interrupted. "What do you mean? Oh yeah, didn't we speculate that there might have been more than one visitor in Melanie's apartment?"

He held up his good hand to beg patience. "Yeah, that may be, but hold on—I'll get to that—just bear with me. It's pretty clear to me that someone killed Melanie before she could pass on some sort of information. That suggests that someone knew she called me. Somehow, they knew we'd get the case. They bugged the scene to hear what we said; they wanted to know what we know or suspect."

"Yeah, but how do you know," she countered, "that it wasn't really coincidence that we got the call out? We were the only team in the office at the time; the other teams were in the street working their own cases, remember? How would anyone, other than the dispatcher, know that?"

He leaned back in the chair and tried to find a more comfortable position. It didn't help. "I've been wondering about that, too. Admittedly, it's always possible that it was just a coincidence. But let's assume it's not, and someone specifically wanted us on that scene. Now, if somebody didn't know for sure we were in the office or available, it wouldn't be too hard to find out. And then they could still try to orchestrate it so we'd get the call. Let's face it, if we hadn't gotten it, another team would've eventually had to respond. Maybe the perp would've blown the IED sooner to destroy the evidence. Or, maybe he'd have held off on the detonation altogether."

Katie raised a single eyebrow and scoffed. "Oh, bullshit, D! What *whack job* builds a bomb and doesn't blow it? Come on, that's a lot of speculation based on a shaky assumption—and you know how to spell assume, right?"

He smirked. She was right; they both knew it.

"Yeah, exactly. So, I did a little checking. That afternoon we got a call from the LT, remember? While I was on the phone with him, the Patrol Desk took a call asking who was available in the homicide office. The desk sergeant knew we were in the office, said so, and forwarded the call. It never rang in our office because it either got disconnected or the caller hung up."

Her eyebrows rose. "The caller, was it a man or a woman's voice?"

"The desk sergeant said it was a man's voice, but very soft spoken and kinda hard to hear. If the caller got disconnected, he never called back."

She chewed her lower lip and asked, "What about the anonymous 911 caller—man or woman?"

"Good question," he acknowledged. "The 911 Office thinks it's a woman; but, they advised that the recording's not very clear—a lot of static or something, like a poor cell connection. The message was pretty simple, only that someone needed the police and the address. I understand the timing was about the same time, or just after, I was on the phone with the LT. The 911 office will send us a copy; it'll be time stamped. Maybe CSI can get something useful from it."

"So, two calls—a man and a woman—two perps?" Katie cocked her head and grinned. "Okay, now I see why you think there's definitely more than one person involved. Do you think our 911 caller knew about the bomb?"

He scratched his chin with his free hand and nodded. "Dunno for sure, but my gut says *yes*. I don't think Melanie's murder and the bomb are mutually exclusive. It's possible the IED might have been intended just to eliminate any evidence once they'd heard enough over their impromptu bug—but I don't think so. Remember, they waited a few seconds, after they heard us say we were going into the kitchen, to detonate. They wanted to be sure we were in there."

She shuddered and involuntarily glanced at the door. It was still closed. "So, that means we're a threat. We're getting close—but to what, exactly?"

"Damned if I know. The blast and the fire pretty much destroyed Melanie's apartment. The bomb squad had the gas to the building cut off, but the residual fuel left in the building's pipelines fed the flames until the gas was depleted. The arson investigators and CSI are still going through the debris, but I wouldn't be too hopeful."

She raised her head. "Listen D, about what you said—you know, about your conclusion that someone tried, or is trying, to kill us? Who else knows about this theory? Have you discussed this with anyone else?"

"Nope, just you. If the brass found this out, you know they'd probably take us off this case. We'd be stuck in the office—or worse, saddled with a protective detail. I know neither of us wants that."

"Damn straight! I want a piece of these bastards!"

He smiled; his partner was getting her fire back—a good thing for them, and a very bad thing for their adversaries.

"When you get out of here, hopefully tomorrow," he cautioned, "you'll have to take it easy—it'll be expected."

"Sure, I get it." She grinned wryly and leaned toward him. "So what's the matter—you never heard of working from home?"

CH 18

THE BRIGHT SATURDAY afternoon was unseasonably warm and humid. Dombrowski wondered if thunder showers might cook up before sunset. He wouldn't mind that one bit, especially since the air conditioner in his pickup was once again acting up.

Damn, the refrigerant is probably low again—gotta be a leak. Someday, I'm gonna have to spring for the repairs; but not today.

He parked at the low curb in front of the modest bungalow and peered up at the beautifully landscaped yard. He smiled in appreciation of his partner's eye for floral aesthetics. Katie certainly had a green thumb—a genetic gift, she'd often declared, from her late mother. He had come to expect that something would always be in bloom at the home in which she'd grown up.

He allowed himself a moment to muse. He knew that when Katie was only thirteen, she'd lost her mother to cancer. A dozen years later, her father's worsening Alzheimer's virtually mandated his placement in an assisted care facility.

She now lived here alone, determined to maintain the family home. She was meticulous in the upkeep of the house and small yard, as if such dedication were a subconscious effort to preserve her sense of family, a lonely quest indeed for an only child whose life seemed beset by tragedy.

His gaze lingered on her late mother's delicate climbing roses that clung like a verdant stole over a traditional trellis arbor; their first fading blooms slowly succumbing to the encroaching heat of an early summer. Katie paid constant attention to her roses. Unlike the tea roses, which she called her problematic prima donnas, the climbers were carefree and among her favorites. Vicarious wish fullfillment?

He scoffed at his idle analysis—he could easily be wrong. It could be no more convoluted than that she just loved to garden, and was good at it.

146

He shook himself free of his ruminations. This visit was more than a mere social call. He needed to determine for himself if she was ready to get back to work, and not just physically. Her mind had to be clear, sharp and focused; notwithstanding the ordeal she'd just been through.

The truth, he begrudgingly admitted to himself, was that recent events had taken a toll on both of them.

He tucked some file folders under his arm, scooped up a warm pizza box and a six-pack of beer from the passenger seat, and made his way to her door.

It swung open before he could knock.

She stood before him, grinning and wiping her hands on the tail of her oversized T-shirt. She was barefoot and wearing cut-off jeans shorts. She looked no worse for wear, having been out of the hospital for only a few days. "Hey D, good to see you. I saw you pull up. Excellent, you brought pizza! Thanks!"

"You're welcome. I figured you could use a hot meal—my version, anyway."

"Oh yeah, it'll do. Are those our files and reports?"

"Yeah, I figured we could review our open cases and get the status reports signed before we meet with the LT on Monday. Did the doctor clear you for full duty?"

She spoke over her shoulder as she led him into the kitchen. "He called about an hour ago—I'm good to go. He was harping about me getting more rest, but he kinda mellowed out when I explained we were gonna be working four to twelve and I'd be sleeping in most mornings. How about you—are you cleared?"

Dombrowski sat in a kitchen chair and leaned back. "Yeah, I'm good. The LT ran me outta the office when he found me at my desk drafting these status reports on Thursday. He said the doctor had told him that I wasn't supposed to be back to work before Monday. So, I just took the files home and worked on them there."

She opened the freezer and pulled out a pair of frosted beer mugs. He nodded approvingly as she opened a pair of long neck bottles and poured with practiced skill. They clinked mugs in an unspoken toast and sipped the robust lager appreciatively.

"I vote we eat first," she announced. "The pizza's still warm, and the files can wait."

He grinned and raised his mug. "I concur."

And so, they did.

THE FILES LAY SPREAD out before them. Dombrowski signed each status report as Katie handed it to him, her own signature affixed. He slipped each page into the corresponding case file, and arranged the files in a row.

"Okay, that's done," she observed. "So, where do we really stand on these cases?"

He drained the last of his beer and waggled his empty mug hopefully.

She smirked, retrieved two more cold ones from the fridge, and teased, "Oh, signing reports is such thirsty work."

He shrugged and retorted, "Alas, a sergeant's work is never done."

"The cases?" she prompted.

"Okay, okay . . . In Adamson, we've reviewed most of the HOA files, but there's a few left. We'll get to those next week, I'm sure. We're waiting for the Tribal Police to alert us if the sisters, Marian Adamson and Louise Hesterly, make another foray to the casino. If they make advanced reservations or just check into the hotel, we'll be notified. One of their detectives may have a tentative ID on the mystery man with whom Louise met, but he wants to confirm before we act on it—he's gotta protect his source. Anyway, if they show up at the hotel, I think we can proceed."

She sipped her beer and tapped a finger on the Adamson file. "You know they're hiding something—we both do. They think they can play us. I'm not gonna let that slide."

"I don't disagree," he cautioned, "but we have to move carefully. The Tribal Police are a little hinky about something, but I don't know what. I'm thinking it kinda has a political feel to it; so, we've gotta watch ourselves."

"All right, I can be patient. What about Jennifer Halsted, the HOA secretary, anything on that case?"

"Unfortunately, nothing new," he admitted. "We got the final autopsy report, nothing we didn't already know. We got the arson investigators' report; the fire at her apartment was definitely arson. We've got no new leads."

"Crap," she mumbled. "Oh well. What about the woman who was tortured, Carolyn Silverberg, anything new?"

He slid a file toward her and sighed. "The M.E.'s preliminary report is in there; we'll get the final Monday. He's waiting on some digital charts from the tox screening results; they were upgrading their computer system last week. We already know what to expect—zilch, nothing new, I'm afraid."

"Damn, you didn't bring any good news, did you? What about Amanda Farrell, is she still missing?"

He leaned back in his chair and steepled his fingers. "Yep, still missing. We haven't heard anything from her family; neither her mother nor stepfather—who are still here, by the way—and nothing from her biological father. I think it's time to reach out to your CI and check on things."

"I'll do that," she assured him, reaching for her phone.

"Wait!" he warned. "Neither one of us is supposed to be working until Monday—the LT was pretty firm about that. I think we've already rocked the boat too much lately. We should probably wait until we're back in the office, on full duty, before we shake that tree."

"Oh, yeah, okay," she conceded. "By the way, how's Kenny doing—with all that's happened, I mean?"

"Who? Oh, you mean Kenny Reynolds, the CSI tech who called you ma'am—that Kenny? Is it his welfare you're worried about now? Is that sweet, or what?"

Her scowl and pursed lips could not dim his impish smile. Soon she was shaking her head and smiling as well. "Okay, so he's not as big a dork as I thought he was—and he did save our butts. I just wanna know if he's okay, that's all."

"Sure, you do," he teased. "Not to worry; he's fine. His sergeant went along with the info withholding strategy as proposed by Lt. Waters. So, it's all good. But, I gotta wonder, don't you suppose he's been worried about you?"

"All right, enough already," she capitulated. "Let's move on to the elephant in the room—Melanie Dubois. What's up with that case?"

He straightened in his chair and his mouth drew into a grim line. "It's been re-assigned to Johnson and Barkley. The LT really had no choice once we were injured. He saw her phone records, knows she tried to call me. He knew she and I had—"

"Had dated?" Katie softly finished for him.

"Well, yeah."

She flattened her hands on the tabletop and leaned forward. "Does this case re-assignment have anything to do with your theory?"

"You mean about someone targeting us specifically?"

"That's exactly what I mean. Did you tell anybody—like the LT? Is that why he did it?"

"No, I haven't told a soul. Come on, Katie. You know he had to re-assign the case because interviews of the building tenants and Melanie's co-workers have to be conducted in a timely fashion. Besides, BATF had to be notified.

The investigation can't stall just because we're temporarily out of the game. You know that."

"So, are you telling me we're out completely, or can we get back on this case?"

He shook his head and shrugged. "To be honest, I don't really know. I don't even know what, if anything, the interviews Johnson and Barkley conducted have produced. I guess we'll find out on Monday."

She stood and paced the length of her kitchen. She stared out the window over the sink and turned to face him. "There's no question, D—we have to be back on this case! The lieutenant has gotta see that there's really no choice."

"What do you mean? Am I missing something here?"

She came back to the table and swept her hand across the display of files. "All of these cases, including Melanie Dubois, have something in common—and you know it."

He couldn't help but smile. Yes, she was ready. "And what might that be, Detective?"

She gave him a wry smile and strode back to the sink. She turned, faced him, and sneered, "Walter Farrell."

———————————

LT. WATERS CLOSED THE last file and leaned back in his chair. A quick glance at the wall clock told him he'd have to wait another fifteen minutes for the evening shift roll call. After that, he promised himself a cigarette. He sighed and considered the two attentive detectives seated before him.

"Okay, Sergeant, Detective. I'm satisfied with these status reports. You're both medically cleared and officially returned to full duty as of this evening's shift. I know you're eager to get back into the Dubois case, but Johnson and Barkley are gonna stay the primaries for now. You can assist, as your other open cases allow."

Katie started to object, "But—"

"Yes, sir, LT," Dombrowski interrupted. "Understood—we'll help in any way we can."

She shot him a murderous look, but kept her mouth shut.

Waters produced a large manila envelope and let it thud on his desk. "This, Detectives, you'll have to sign for, a subpoena response from that bank in Delaware."

Dombrowski hefted the envelope and nodded. "Oh yeah, the Adamson case. Thanks, LT, we've been waiting on this."

"Refresh my recollection, Sergeant," Waters suggested. "Why did we need this subpoena?"

Dombrowski handed the envelope to Katie and fished out his notebook. "The vacant houses, about a dozen of them, are linked to this bank in Delaware through a credit card account. We needed to track who was footing the utility bills on the foreclosed properties, and why."

"Okay," Waters acknowledged. "I remember now. Well, they've certainly sent a lot of material in their response."

Katie removed the envelope's contents and thumbed through a few pages. She passed a handful to her partner and held up the remaining stack of papers, almost two inches thick. Her voice held a trace of petulance. "Damn, this is all fine print text, spreadsheets, and crap. This is gonna take some time to decipher."

"Oh man!" her partner groaned, staring in utter confusion at the papers in his hand. "Katie, we may have to ask for some legal or accounting help with this."

"Hey, that's fine with me," she agreed. "I'm almost cross-eyed from staring at those HOA files as it is."

A knock sounded on the office door, and Captain Walker poked his head in. "Ah, here they are. Forgive me, Lieutenant, but Deputy U.S. Marshal Gonzalez is here to see Detectives Dombrowski and Callahan. May we?"

"Of course, Captain, please, come in."

After handshakes all around, they settled in chairs, and the Deputy U.S. Marshal began. "I was sorry to hear about your recent misfortune, but I'm glad to see you're both all right."

"And back in the saddle," Dombrowski quipped.

"So I see. Ah, you should know that I did not come alone. BATF Special Agent Brittany Brathwaite is with Detectives Johnson and Barkley, as we speak, briefing them on BATF's findings. Essentially, the IED was composed of an old batch of Semtex made prior to 1990, a set of anti-tampering mercury switches, common electronic detonator caps, and a cheap cell phone."

"We saw it on the scene," Katie offered. "I was guessing it was C-4. I know we have some photos, too."

"Yes, I understand that was very helpful in the identification," Gonzalez acknowledged. "C-4 is fairly common, but it's an off-white color. Semtex is orange, almost a red, and that's what was in those photos. Lately we've seen a lot more Semtex than C-4. It's been more prevalent in Europe, the Middle East, and Africa. But these days, what can I say? It can show up almost anywhere."

"I gather it's not as closely controlled as C-4?" Dombrowski wondered.

"Ah, yeah, something like that," Gonzalez conceded. "The point is that the explosive is not that hard to come by—if you know where to look for it."

The captain interrupted. "Let me be clear; this is to be kept confidential. BATF has elected to follow our lead on this and make no public comment. The public and the media are under the impression the explosion was the result of a gas leak—probably because that was the ruse used on the scene to facilitate the evacuation. The building's security cameras were somehow off-line at the time, so absent any other explanation, the media is sticking with the gas leak story. We are not inclined to correct that mistaken impression at this time. Am I clear?"

Once everyone acknowledged affirmatively, he continued. "Good. The media is also ignorant of the fact that we recovered one of the cell phones used—although I'm sorry to say that it may not be of much use. CSI determined when and where it was bought, two of them, actually, for cash. Unfortunately, there was no video surveillance. That's all we have right now. I have another meeting in a few minutes, so I'll leave you all to it. Lieutenant, please continue."

As the door closed behind Capt. Walker, Lt. Waters addressed the Deputy U.S. Marshal. "That's not all you're here to tell us, is it?"

"No, it's not. Rene Pasqualle slipped into the US from Windsor. He's not currently on any terrorist watch list. Neither we, nor the FBI, anticipated or had the right assets in place in Detroit. We did pick up his trail in St. Louis; and we know he was here within the last few days. As I cautioned you before, he's not currently wanted anywhere, so our surveillance efforts have been, uh, how shall I put this—subject to budgetary constraints? Absent any evidence of criminal activity, we've had to pull back."

"Wait a damn minute!" Katie blurted. "What do you mean pull back? Based on what we do know about this guy—his background, his paramilitary group of mercenaries—isn't he a potential suspect in this bombing?"

"Easy, Detective," the lieutenant cautioned. "That may seem somewhat obvious to you, however, the bombing falls primarily under BATF's investigative jurisdiction and ours, not that of the Marshals Service."

"Right," Gonzalez acknowledged. "We only had an INTERPOL request to periodically 'locate', which means to keep a loose eye on his public activities. It does not mean to initiate a full blown surveillance. Now, BATF Special Agent Brathwaite happens to feel as you do, but suffers from similar budgetary constraints. Consequently, her bosses have decided that BATF will take a support role and let your agency take the lead on this investigation."

"So, that's why," Dombrowski deduced, "she's in with Johnson and Barkley—"

"Because," Katie spat in interruption, "they're now the primaries on the case!"

"That's enough, Detective!" Waters scowled at her. "If Johnson and Barkley require your assistance, they'll ask for it. You have open cases that need your attention. I suggest you begin with the subpoena response from that Delaware bank."

"LT, if I may?" Dombrowski interjected deftly as he hefted the stack of papers. "Katie and I are really gonna need some help deciphering all this financial stuff. I don't pretend to understand any of it."

"Uh, Lieutenant?" the Deputy U.S. Marshal offered. "Perhaps I can redeem myself. We work closely on occasion with FinCEN, the Financial Crimes Enforcement Network of the U.S. Treasury, investigators and forensic accountants who focus on and investigate financial crimes, like money laundering, bank fraud, and such. I could ask a friend with FinCEN to take a look, and maybe help your detectives out."

Dombrowski smiled broadly and elbowed Katie. "Hey Emilio, that'd be great! Wouldn't it, Katie?"

Before she could respond, Waters raised a cautionary finger. "As helpful as that might be, Emilio, this material is in our hands pursuant to a subpoena. So, the District Attorney's Office will have to authorize access; and that will be on a restricted need-to-know basis. I'm sure you understand."

"Of course. It's pretty much the same in the federal system. If you like, I can try to call my friend and get her on board. She'll need permission from her people as well."

Lt. Waters stood, unconsciously patting the pack of cigarettes in his pocket. "Yes, please do that. In the meantime, I have to attend the roll call for the evening shift. Give me fifteen minutes and we'll see if the D.A. is still in his office."

As they filed out of the lieutenant's office, Dombrowski nudged his partner, whose mood apparently hadn't improved. "Come on, Katie, cheer up! I think we just dodged one hell of a paper bullet."

She looked askance at him, but there was the barest hint of a smile in her wry expression.

CH 19

—————

THE EVENING SHIFT BEGAN slowly, as was typical for a Monday night. By seven o'clock, Lt. Waters came to stand in his office doorway and survey the squad room. Only Dombrowski and Callahan were in the office, going through the last of the HOA files. The phones were quiet.

The big sergeant noticed his boss standing there. "Hey, LT, you need something?"

"I was just thinking about getting something to eat. Have y'all got any plans?"

Katie glanced at her partner and shrugged. "I could eat. D, any ideas?"

Dombrowski tilted his head; his stomach rumbled on cue. He grinned. "Mmm, I've got a hankering for lasagna. How about that little Italian place you took your dad to?"

"Lasagna sounds good," Waters echoed. "Do they do carry-out? I'll stay and cover the phones if y'all will bring me something back. Okay?"

Katie closed the file on her desk, stood, and stretched. "Yeah, they do carry-out. My dad loves the place; I think the food's good, too. So, you want an order of lasagna to go, LT? How about their garlic bread as well? It's really good."

"Yeah, get some garlic bread," he replied, fishing a wad of bills out of his pocket and peeling off a twenty. "Here, put this toward our supper—I'll hold down the fort."

Dombrowski held up his hands and deferred. "Oh no, LT, you don't have to do that—we got this."

"Don't argue, Sergeant. Take it. Bring back some sweet tea, if you don't mind. I've had enough coffee."

Dombrowski acquiesced and winked at Katie. "Very well, if you insist, sir. We'll be back in a bit. Is there anything else you need?"

"Nope, I'm good."

AS THEY TROMPED DOWN the back staircase, they ran into Detectives Bobby Johnson and Sid Barkley on their way up to the office.

"Hey, Sarge, got a minute?" Barkley asked as they reached the landing. "We gotta ask you guys about something on this Dubois case."

Katie stood stock still and her lips drew into a thin line.

Knowing how she felt about being taken off this case, Dombrowski sensed her scowl without having to see it.

"Sure Sid, what do you need?"

Barkley had the grace to appear chagrined. "First of all, we're sorry we had to take over this case—with you guys being hurt and all."

"It's not a problem, Sid. Get to the point—we're on our way to supper."

"Right. Well, look, since Melanie Dubois was your girlfriend—"

"Wrong, Sid! We hadn't dated in some time, about a year. I haven't been in touch with her since—"

"Not true," declared Johnson. "We know you saw her at Walter Farrell's home, the week before she was murdered, didn't you?"

"As I was about to say," Dombrowski rumbled ominously, "I hadn't seen or spoken to her since we stopped dating until we unexpectedly ran into her as Walter Farrell's attorney. That encounter is described in our report. Now, is there anything else on your mind?"

Johnson looked like he wanted to argue, but Barkley forestalled any further comment from his partner with a seemingly innocuous question of his own.

"Well, yeah, there is. It's the missing laptop and briefcase that you reported—we still haven't found them. CSI hasn't found any traces in the debris. The decedent's car was still in her assigned parking space, all locked up; but, there was no laptop or briefcase there either—"

"The real problem," Johnson interrupted, "is that we have no real evidence that they even exist—just your report that they were missing."

Dombrowski's voice cooled as he turned toward Johnson. "All right, Bobby, just what are you trying to say?"

Barkley deftly elbowed his partner aside and held up his open palms. "Easy there, Sarge. Here's the thing—how do you know she had a laptop or briefcase? Did you ever see them?"

"Sure, in court. Haven't you?"

"I mean at her place—you know, when you had occasion to be there."

Katie's ire exceeded her patience. "Really, Barkley? Don't be an idiot! What lawyer do you know who doesn't have a laptop or tablet and briefcase? What about her office? Did you find anything there? You did interview her co-workers, didn't you?"

Stiffening at the vehemence in her retort, Barkley hesitated. But Johnson felt no such restraint. "That's not your concern! This isn't your case! You will not—"

Barkley grabbed Johnson's arm and cautioned, "That's enough!"

Johnson huffed, but said no more.

Barkley turned back to Dombrowski. "All we need to know is if either of you ever saw this laptop or briefcase recently. It'd help if we knew what we're looking for, see?"

Katie glanced at her partner and shook her head. Dombrowski shrugged and offered a candid response. "No, we didn't see either one."

"Like I said, try her office," Katie repeated. "It's clear to me you guys haven't even been there yet."

Barkley sighed and spread his palms. "Okay, fine. Sorry to keep you from your supper."

Without another word Barkley and Johnson ascended the stairs.

Katie stared after them and hissed, "What the hell is their problem? What was that all about?"

Finger to his lips, Dombrowski motioned for her to follow him downstairs. Once in the parking lot, she tried again to ask, but he forestalled her.

"Not here, not now. Come on, let's go eat."

———————————

THE FOOD AT THE LITTLE Italian restaurant was good; but that wasn't the reason they ate in silence.

As the waiter cleared their plates, Katie spoke up. "Lorenzo, we're gonna need an order of lasagna and garlic bread to go, okay?"

"Oh, and a large sweet tea to go, too," Dombrowski added.

"You bet, one dinner special to go," the waiter repeated. "Anything else?"

"Nah, that'll do it," she answered. "Thanks."

As the waiter departed, Dombrowski plopped his napkin on the tabletop. "Boy, now that was good. Hey, lemme ask," his voice dropping, "have you heard from your CI?"

She quickly scanned the room, leaned forward, and matched his volume. "Consuela? No, not yet. I left two messages on her cell phone today. She's already got the cold snitch line. I left her my cell number—but nothing yet."

"She lives at Farrell's house, right?"

"Yeah, maid's quarters. Think we need to go out there and check on her?"

"I dunno, maybe—let's give it a couple of days, first. We'll need some pretense to be there anyway since Farrell rescinded his assertion that his daughter, Amanda, was missing."

"Yeah, but Amanda's still a person of interest in the Carolyn Silverberg case. Isn't that enough?"

"Yeah, should be. But I'd be more comfortable getting the LT on board first. Besides, it'd be the smart thing to do—*CYA*, you know?"

She pushed back from the table and studied her partner as he slurped the last of his sweet tea up through a straw. "Okay, D, I get that. So, Barkley and Johnson—what are we thinking?"

He leaned forward, elbows on the table, and lowered his voice to a near whisper. "I'm not sure, but something's up."

She leaned in, mere inches from his face. "Look, they definitely inferred there was more to your involvement with Melanie. Do they know about the calls she made to your home, her message on your answering machine?"

"Probably. That's in the report; and it's supported by the subpoenaed phone records. I'm sure they've seen it by now."

"Oh, yeah. They've probably got the whole case file. However, that doesn't mean they've read everything yet. It's obvious they've yet to do interviews at her law office—and yet here they are, focused on you because you used to date her."

He sat back and waved a hand dismissively. "Look, it might be nothing. Come on, you know the drill; any current spouse, significant other, or *ex* is always gonna be looked at."

"Yeah, but you've got nothing to hide," she asserted. "So, why the adversarial tone with their questions? Hell, it wasn't even subtle!"

"Barkley was subtle; only Johnson was adversarial."

"Johnson is an anal retentive asshole!"

He winced and shook his head. "Ouch! I'm sure you meant to say that Detective Johnson is an extremely detail oriented investigator, who may be prone to bouts of intense focus, sometimes to the exclusion of other pertinent, and perhaps relevant, matters."

She couldn't help but smile. "Yeah, what you said. So, Bobby's being the usual asshole. What do you mean that Barkley was subtle?"

"Well, let's say he was subtle compared to his partner. The questions about the laptop and briefcase, it's like someone suggested that he ask. It shouldn't be that big of a deal. We never saw them at the scene; for the most part we're speculating that they even exist because it's only logical. Yet Sid and Bobby seemed to be unduly focused on them. Why?"

"Hah!" Katie scoffed and put a thumb to her chest. "Well, I think they exist, and are conspicuous by their absence. Like I told Sid, who ever heard of a lawyer without either one?"

He grinned in agreement, and nodded over her shoulder. "I don't disagree; but let's keep this to ourselves. Now, here comes Lorenzo with our to-go order. We've gotta get back to the office."

———

LT. WATERS WAS ON THE phone when they returned to the squad room. Pushing his reading glasses up the bridge of his nose, he scribbled a quick note. He waived the detectives into his office as he concluded the call.

Katie placed the white plastic bag and large covered cup of sweet tea on his desk. "Here y'go, LT. The lasagna should still be warm, but Lorenzo said it was okay to nuke it in a microwave for about three minutes on half power."

"Thanks, I appreciate this. Listen up—that call was from Detective Sergeant Greenway with the Tribal Police." He glanced at his hasty note. "Louise Hesterly made a reservation at the Casino Hotel for tomorrow night. Y'all asked to be notified, right? This is the Adamson case, right?"

Dombrowski pulled up a chair and nodded. "Right, LT, the two sisters, Marian Adamson and Louise Hesterly, their alibi is looking shaky; and they've stopped cooperating. We're taking a closer look at their alibi; the Tribal Police are helping out. We know from the surveillance recordings there's an unidentified man involved; we're gonna follow up on that."

Waters opened the bag and inhaled deeply; his reading glasses fogged slightly from the food's warmth. "Oh, that smells wonderful! So, you like both sisters, or just the vic's sister-in-law, for the Adamson killing?"

Katie sat in the other chair and answered in a tight voice. "Possibly both, but Louise Hesterly, yeah. She's got motive, the right skill set, an alibi that isn't holding up—and worse, she lied to *m*— uh, us."

Dombrowski stole a glance at his partner. Her jaw was set, and there was no question as to her focus. Now if she could just keep her temper in check. "So, if it's okay with you, LT," he interjected smoothly, "Katie and I will make the trip tomorrow and see if we can wrap this up. Will per diem and lodging be authorized if it takes more than a day or so?"

Waters glanced up over the rim of his glasses and scowled. "See that it doesn't. One day is authorized. Don't blow your per diem at craps and slots. If you run into further issues, call me. Understood?"

"Yes, sir, no problem," both detectives assured him in unison.

Waters chuckled and shook his head. "All right, now get out of my office and let me eat in peace."

CH 20

THE DETECTIVES FOUND that the Security Office at the Indian Casino & Hotel was smaller than expected. Beyond the glass doors, they could see a tastefully furnished reception area that fronted a series of private offices and a modest conference room.

A stout yet attractive woman, wearing lieutenant's bars on her tribal police uniform, sat behind the reception desk. She looked up from a computer printout and pushed a lock of grey hair aside as the outer door swung open. She glanced at a wall clock and then greeted the visitors. "Good evening, can I help you?"

Dombrowski displayed his credentials. "Hi, we're Detectives Dombrowski and Callahan. Sgt. Greenway is expecting us. Is he available?"

"Oh, he will be. He said you were coming." She rose and extended her hand. "I'm Lieutenant Bernice Knighton. I run the *fishbowl*—the video surveillance operations center."

"Good to meet you, I'm Donald Dombrowski; and this is my partner, Katie Callahan."

"Hello, Lieutenant," Katie said, as she shook the woman's hand and returned her smile.

"Y'all can call me Bernice. At this moment, Sgt. Greenway is in a meeting with Captain Tafoya and our Deputy Chief. I don't expect him to be much longer. Would you like some coffee? Since we're open 24/7, there's always a fresh pot on in the conference room. There are restrooms in there, too."

"Yeah, coffee would be nice," Dombrowski acknowledged. "Thanks, Bernice."

Seated at the conference table, Katie sipped her coffee and asked, "So Bernice, where is your ops center anyway? I only see the one big monitor on that far wall."

The lieutenant grinned and pointed to the ceiling. "One floor above us and it's almost three times the size of the space on this floor. We monitor over three hundred CCTV cameras and have the ability to digitally record data from most of them. It's a fairly sophisticated system."

"Aren't most of them," Dombrowski asked, "the cameras, I mean, in and around the casino?"

"True, but just a little over half are deployed in the casino itself. We also monitor the public access areas, like hallways and parking lots."

"What about the hotel?" Katie probed.

Bernice shrugged. "Like I said, public areas; hallways, the lobby and such."

"But not the rooms, right?"

"Oh no, there's no surveillance, no cameras inside the rooms; that would take a court order. Wait a second—that's not why you're here, is it? You don't have such an order, do you?"

"Oh no, Bernice, relax," Dombrowski interjected. "We're just following up on a suspect's alibi—that's all. Didn't Sgt. Greenway discuss this with you?"

"Not really. He told us who to surveil, and said this was a sensitive matter that was not to be disclosed to anyone without a need to know. I don't really know any more than that."

Dombrowski and Katie shared a confused look, but remained silent.

A door at the rear of the conference room opened. A slight middle-aged man wearing horn rimmed glasses and a rumpled suit entered. He nodded to Bernice and thrust his hand toward Dombrowski. "Sorry I'm running a bit late; I was in a meeting. I'm Sam Greenway."

Bernice introduced the visiting detectives.

Sgt. Greenway pulled out a chair and took a seat. Bernice pointed to the coffee pot, but he just shook his head. "I'm good, thanks, Bernice. Now, as I said, I was in a meeting. I've been advised that we are to handle this matter with the utmost discretion."

"I'm a bit confused, Sergeant," Dombrowski began.

"Call me Sam."

"Uh, okay, Sam. We didn't ask or suggest that this investigation be kept secret. So is there something else going on—something that we should know about?"

The Tribal Police detective appeared uncomfortable and parsed his words with deliberate care. "Possibly, let me explain. When my boss got the call from your lieutenant to ask for our assistance in your investigation, it was thought to be just a routine request. Since then, we've learned that it's not going to be that simple. There may be some potentially damaging information—in a political sense—that may or may not be relevant to your case, but that could create some problems, if not irreparable damage for certain interests."

Katie scowled, her patience wearing thin. "So, what are you saying, Sam? That you're not going to help us, or there's going to be some sort of cover-up?"

Greenway blanched and held up his open hands. "Oh no—nothing of the sort! All I'm saying is that we've got to be careful. There are some sensitive considerations involved—that's all."

Dombrowski leaned forward and spoke evenly, never taking his eyes off Sgt. Greenway's face. "What I think he means, Katie, is that they may have already identified our mystery man. And that he may be somebody important, somebody with *clout*."

Katie sat back in her chair and stared into Sgt. Greenway; her gaze smoldered.

One glance was enough for Dombrowski to practically read her mind—and effectively share the same thought.

Somebody important, huh? Ask us if we give a shit!

Bernice sat in wide-eyed silence and cupped her cooling mug.

Sgt. Greenway appeared on the verge of collapsing within himself as he uttered a heavy sigh. "Ah, crap. You have the gist of it. We think we know who it might be, but we're not sure. We may be wrong, as my bosses hope. Unfortunately, until we're sure we can confirm this person's identity, I can't give you a name. I'm sorry, but I have my orders."

"I think I understand, but let me be absolutely certain," Dombrowski cautioned. "We're here because one of our suspects, Louise Hesterly, made a hotel reservation; and you notified us, as requested. Is she here—did she check in?"

"Yes, she's here," Greenway admitted. "She checked in, room 417, just past six this evening; she was alone."

"Hmmph, that was expected," Katie sniped. "We already knew that her sister, Marian Adamson—another suspect in the same case—didn't come with her this time. We checked before we left."

Dombrowski shot Katie a warning glance—*lighten up!*

"Sam, do you know," he prodded, "if our suspect is still in her room, and if she's still alone?"

"She's not in her room. She was at the blackjack tables as of a few minutes ago," Greenway answered, and looked to Bernice.

The lieutenant tapped out a text on her cell phone and then announced, "There's been no change. She's still there, and she still appears to be alone.

We've been watching her since her arrival. Other than a few of the hotel and casino staff, she hasn't made contact with anyone else."

"Okay. So, it's possible," Dombrowski reasoned, "that Louise Hesterly may have plans to meet with this mystery man—whose identity may or may not present a problem for you, or certain interests. Is that roughly it, Sam?"

Sgt. Greenway nodded. "Yes, that's a fair assessment. Look, we have no intention of inhibiting your investigation; on the contrary, we're here to help. However, if it is at all possible, we—our departmental management—would ask that any sensitive matters be handled with reasonable discretion."

Bernice reached out in sympathy and laid her hand on her friend's arm. "Sam, I know you're not happy about this. Let's just wait and see what happens; it might amount to nothing."

He spared her a small smile and patted her hand. "True enough. Forgive me, Detectives; I'm no happier than you are about this sort of thing. I'm more of a 'let the chips fall where they may' kind of guy—and to hell with the politics. But I'm subject to orders as well. I hope you can understand."

Bernice stood, drawing their attention. "Well, then, shall we all go upstairs to the fishbowl and keep an eye on your suspect?"

THE VIDEO SURVEILLANCE operations center was a vast room bathed in subdued lighting. A maze of waist-high cubicles occupied the center. An array of large monitor screens dominated three of the four walls. The scenes depicted on the massive monitors changed in no discernible pattern as any one of the half dozen technical personnel, seated at some of the computer workstations throughout the room, selected different camera views or zoomed in to watch particular patrons.

Bernice smiled with a modicum of pride and swept her arms out to encompass the entire room. "Welcome to our surveillance ops center. As you can see, our techs can pull up any camera and display its view on any of the big screens. Everything so displayed is automatically recorded."

"Wow, this is impressive. I've never seen the like," Dombrowski admitted. "Is this staffed all the time?"

"You bet, 24/7/365," Bernice declared. "All our personnel are qualified technicians and sworn peace officers. They work shifts just like our patrol division."

"I think I'd get bored," Katie grumbled, "you know, just looking at monitors all the time."

Bernice shrugged. "It's not for everyone, I'll admit. But some people have a knack for it. They also get incentives, like pay bonuses for advanced degrees and lots of in-service training opportunities. There's no shortage of personnel who want to work in this division. Remember, besides some R&D and technical equipment evaluations, we do all the surveillance, electronic or otherwise, and that includes field work, that the department needs."

"Okay, I get it now—it's like a one-stop shop for cyber cops; that's pretty cool," Katie blurted. "Uh, no offense . . . "

"None taken. Actually, they kinda like being referred to as the *cyber squad*," Bernice offered with a chuckle.

"Bernice," Dombrowski interrupted, "can you show us our suspect?"

"No problem. Watch the big screen to your left."

She stepped to one of the workstations and spoke quietly to the tech. Nodding, she pointed to the large display.

The scene resolved to depict Louise Hesterly seated alone at a blackjack table. The view zoomed in. As they watched, her modest pile of chips grew over the next few hands. She lost the next hand as the dealer displayed a queen and an ace.

"This is so awesome!" Katie exclaimed.

Dombrowski noticed that comment earned her a glance from the seated tech, followed by a blatant yet self-conscious smile as the young man briefly focused on the very attractive visiting detective.

"So, what's next?" Her partner asked, hiding a smirk. "What do we do now?"

"We wait; we watch," Sgt. Greenway replied.

"It may be a while," Bernice remarked, "so, feel free to make use of the staff lounge. It's through that door. There's coffee, and a window into this room, so you can still observe. There's also a good view of this big monitor. Whatever happens with your suspect, you'll be able to see."

"Sounds good. We appreciate the hospitality," Dombrowski acknowledged. "Sam, are you going to join us?"

"Yes, after I meet with my boss and explain that we've talked—protocol, you know?"

"Yeah, I do. Come on, Katie, let's chill."

SEVERAL HOURS INTO the surveillance Katie pointed. "Look! Louise is gathering her chips. Now, she's moving toward the cashier's window."

"Yeah. She's cashing in her winnings," Dombrowski observed. "What now?"

Sam motioned for them to get up and said, "Come on, we'll watch from the main floor of the ops room. Wherever she goes, she'll be on camera."

Bernice met them at the door to the staff lounge. "Oh, you saw? She's on the move; we're tracking."

They stood below a large screen in the fishbowl and watched as the display suddenly split into four sections—the views from four different cameras.

The cameras tracked the suspect as she left the casino and entered the hotel lobby. She entered an elevator, and the display shifted once again. Louise Hesterly, riding in the elevator car, was clearly depicted in one of the four scenes; the others showed empty hallways. As the car rose, the hallway scenes changed.

"Wherever the elevator goes," Bernice explained, "the other views will change to the floor it's at and the floors immediately above and below."

"It's stopping on the fourth floor," Sam observed. "She's probably going to her room."

Dombrowski glanced at his watch. "It's just after eleven; she's still alone."

Louise strode down the hall and stopped before room 417. She looked up and down the hallway before slipping her key card in the lock slot and opening the door. With a final glance down the hall, she slipped into the room and closed the door.

"Now, we wait—*again*, right?" Katie groused.

"Afraid so," Sam agreed. "We know the room was empty; housekeeping went in to turn down the bed while she was in the casino. If she stays in and has plans to meet with anyone, they're gonna have to come to her—and this hallway is well covered. If she goes out again, we've got that covered, too."

"Well, we can afford to be patient. This is good surveillance," Dombrowski reasoned. "By the way, how did she do at the blackjack table?"

"Give me a sec," said Bernice, who tapped another text on her phone. "She's up a little over two hundred for the evening."

"Does she usually win?"

"Hold on. She does playing blackjack, but never more than a few hundred. She usually loses at the poker tables and slots, though. Overall, she almost breaks even."

"Wow," Katie exclaimed. "That's a lot of information. You track all your gamblers?"

"Sure," Bernice answered with a shrug. "It's no big secret; they know it. They can earn points toward promotional benefits; free food and drinks, room comps, and the like. The data helps marketing and us; we use it to help identify cheats and con artists. Casinos are always a target."

"Oh yeah—'cause that's where the money is', right?"

"Oh man, really, Katie?" Dombrowski winced. "Now you're quoting Willie Sutton?"

"We've got movement!" blurted Sam, pointing to the monitor.

A man, deliberately keeping his head down, was walking briskly down the hall. He went directly to room 417 and knocked. As the door opened, he looked down the hall and then quickly slipped into the room. The door closed, but not before the camera had zoomed in and captured his face.

Sgt. Greenway groaned and sagged. "Damn."

Dombrowski and Katie shared a knowing glance.

"Well, Sam, do we have a problem?" Dombrowski probed.

"Yeah, we do. Let's go back into the staff lounge. Bernice, can you see to it that we're not disturbed—unless there's more to see, of course."

"Sure thing, Sam. I'll be out here if you need me."

───────────

THEY SAT AROUND A SMALL table in silence as Sam rubbed his temples and sighed heavily.

"Okay, Sam," Dombrowski asked evenly, "who is he?"

"It's not good," Sam began. "His name is Jonathan P. Widermark; he's the son of Jeremiah Widermark—"

"What—the state senator? Are you kidding me?"

"Wait a minute," Katie interjected. "Isn't he the same as Apostle Jeremiah Widermark, the television evangelist?"

Sam's pained expression spoke volumes as he found his voice. "One and the same. The son of an ultra-conservative celebrity preacher, who is vehemently opposed to gambling, and also holds a seat in the state senate, is now in a hotel room with your murder suspect."

"This isn't the first time he's been with her," Dombrowski surmised. "We've seen him before, in the other surveillance recording, haven't we?"

"We weren't certain until this moment, but yes, you're right. As I said earlier, we had a hunch it was him; so, we checked and double-checked our records. He has never registered at the hotel, at least not under his own name. And as far as we know, he's never patronized the casino."

"So, how old is this Jonathan? He looks to be in his twenties. Louise must be twice his age!" Katie declared.

"Ah, I believe," Sam mused with a wince, "that Jonathan is twenty-one."

"Louise is a cougar!" Katie blurted.

Sam actually flinched. "Look, we have little control over what goes on behind the closed doors of a guest's hotel room. They're of age—and I assume consenting adults—and they've broken no laws. At best, this is awkward; there could be unfortunate attention, publicity—"

Dombrowski held up his hands. "Sam, we're getting off point here. All we are interested in is whether or not this young man, Jonathan Widermark, can corroborate that he was here with Louise Hesterly at a particular time, almost three weeks ago. All we need to do is interview him."

Sam spread his hands open and spoke with sincerity. "I understand; I just hope you can be discreet in the process. My bosses want to avoid any unnecessary negative publicity. We surely don't want to stir up Jeremiah Widermark—who probably doesn't even know his son has been coming here. That man has been no friend to tribal interests—in the senate or the pulpit."

"If the boy cooperates with us," Dombrowski reasoned, "I see no reason to involve the father. As far as we know, he has nothing to do with this."

"But you don't even know if the boy will cooperate. And if you confront him in the midst of such an indelicate situation as this—hell, you have no idea how he'll react."

Dombrowski leaned forward, mere inches from Sam Greenway's face. "Here's how it is, Sam. He either talks to us here and now, or we subpoena him to appear, with all the attendant pomp and circumstance, before a grand jury. Of course, should the media get wind of such a thing, they'd have a field day. Now, I appreciate how this situation could become embarrassing for all concerned, but this is a homicide investigation—we will see it through to the end."

Sam leaned back in his chair, puffed his cheeks, and blew out a thin stream of air. "I feel like I'm circling the proverbial drain and there's nothing much I can do . . . Shit!"

Katie had been quiet during this exchange. "In my view, this situation calls for a more subtle approach. So, let me make a suggestion on how to deal with this kid. We know he and our suspect are in the room—maybe for the night. We've got good surveillance in place; if either one moves, we'll know it. Right, Sam?"

Confusion clouded his face, but Sgt. Greenway kept silent and nodded his head.

"What are you getting at, Katie?" Her partner grumbled. "You know we've gotta interview this kid."

"True, D, but wouldn't it be wiser to do so when he's away from our suspect, and not under her influence? I've interviewed her, remember? He's young; so, I get the impression that she's the more dominant personality here. Let's wait until he leaves her room—or she leaves, whichever happens first. We can then play the whole thing low key, rather than confrontational."

Dombrowski stroked his chin in contemplation. "You may be on to something here. Younger men—boys, really—like this, tend to want to impress the more sophisticated woman. If she's around, he's liable to get defensive, or deny everything in some misbegotten effort to try and maintain their secret."

"You're right, D. The best way to approach this is when they're apart, even if it means waiting until morning."

Dombrowski reflected for a moment, and smiled. "That idea has merit; we do want him alone for the interview. And if we keep everything on the down low, that should keep your bosses happy, right Sam?"

Sam looked like a condemned prisoner suddenly reprieved. His head bobbed up and down as he looked at them with obvious gratitude. "Yes, of course! Anything I can do? Do you need accommodations for the night?"

"Thanks, but this is right where we need to be," Dombrowski deferred. "If either one of them leaves that room tonight, we'll need to be ready to move."

Katie smiled and raised a finger. "I'll bet you breakfast that they stay in the room for the night. In the morning, they won't leave together—he'll leave first. We can monitor from here and intercept him in the lobby, or wait until he goes to his car. Sam, do we know what he's driving and where it is?"

"Let me check with Bernice."

In his absence, Dombrowski asked his partner, "So, I gather you don't want Louise to know we're even here?"

Katie cocked her head and shrugged. "Yeah, I admit I'm going with my gut here. Much as I'd like to confront her—especially if her alibi collapses—I think we'd be tipping our hand. Who knows how she might react? We're not on our home turf here and I don't want to cause a bad situation for Sam."

"Yeah, he's in an uncomfortable position with his brass already. We'd be wise not to cause him more grief."

Sgt. Greenway returned and announced, "We have his vehicle on camera in the parking garage. It's a rental. We have him recorded as he drove into the structure and parked. Do you want to confront him there?"

"No, I don't think so, Sam," Dombrowski responded. "It'd be best if your people approached him in the lobby—if he's alone, of course—and bring him to us."

"If he's not alone, and she's with him," Katie cautioned, "everybody just backs off until they split up. Hopefully, your people can then get him quickly out of sight for the interview. Maybe we can use the security office conference room—is that feasible, Sam?"

"Yes, absolutely feasible! We can have it all set up and ready."

"You'll also have to maintain the surveillance on our suspect, Louise Hesterly," she insisted. "We don't want her to know we're here, and that we've found her *boy toy*. She'll probably check out and leave the hotel on her own—none the wiser."

"My people can handle the approach in the lobby. Bernice and her team can handle the surveillance—no problem," Sam assured her. "Do you think we'll need to tail her when she departs?"

"Nah," Dombrowski declined. "That's okay. If this goes as planned, we're pretty certain she'll go home when she leaves here. But we'll need to be watchful tonight and tomorrow morning. Now, we just have to be patient."

"Yeah," Katie added, "but this does give us some time to look into Jonathan Widermark and his illustrious father for any connection to Adamson. I'm gonna make some calls in that regard. D, should we brief our LT tonight or tomorrow?"

"I'll call to let him know the plan for tonight, and advise him to expect a more comprehensive briefing tomorrow. We should have more to tell him by then."

"All right," Katie said as she stood. "I'm gonna make those calls."

As she walked to a corner and began using her phone, Sgt. Greenway tilted his head in her direction. "She's really quite good—very intuitive—isn't she? How long has she been a detective?"

"A little over three years." Dombrowski smirked and shook his head. "As for *good?* Sam, you don't know the half of it."

CH 21

KATIE SMIRKED AND POINTED at the monitor. "Looks like you'll be buying breakfast, D. Look there."

A man stepped out of room 417 and hastened down the hall. He stabbed at the elevator call button and looked around furtively. As soon as the doors opened, he boarded. The on-board CCTV camera caught him full-faced as he backed into the corner—Jonathan P. Widermark.

Dombrowski stood, stretched, and groaned. "Oh man, okay, you were right; they spent the night. It's what, almost eight? But breakfast comes after the interview. Sam, you'd better alert your people; he's probably headed for the lobby."

Sgt. Greenway rose and shrugged. "No problem; they're already in place. I'm sure Bernice has already alerted them. Y'all can go on down to the conference room. We'll bring him to you."

Once seated in the conference room, Katie laid a hand on her partner's arm. "D, listen, I think I've got some of this figured out."

"Okay, go on."

"We know Louise is a cougar; they're definitely sleeping together. I'd bet it's been going on for a while—and I mean longer than that earlier surveillance recording. So, when we do interview him, I think it'll be important not to diminish their relationship. I mean that we'll need to treat him like her equal, as if the obvious age difference never crossed our minds. If we don't, he'll pick up on it immediately—in fact, he'll probably be overly sensitive to it. The key to getting his cooperation will be to treat him as more mature than he may actually be. If I'm right, I don't think his father is even aware of their relationship, much less that they're having their trysts in a casino hotel. If that's true, I strongly suspect that our young man has a vested interest in keeping it that way."

Dombrowski chuckled. "Oh yeah! His son with an older woman, carrying on in the very den of iniquity! No doubt that would chap the old man's hide big time—talk about politically embarrassing! Of course, there's little chance the son would bump into any of his father's congregation or political cronies in a casino, so I guess it makes a certain kind of sense."

She scoffed. "Hah! I wouldn't bet on that. You know as well as I that a preacher's sermon tends to wear off after a couple of hours—and now it's been a couple of days! There are plenty of church-going voters who like to gamble on the sly—and don't get me started on politicians!"

Dombrowski couldn't help but grin.

"What's so amusing?" she demanded.

"Oh, I just realized why you're so perpetually cynical; you're a cop's daughter. You sound just like your old man. I get it now; it's genetic. You can't help it."

"Don't be a wise ass," she countered, but she was smiling all the same. "I meant what I said; there's no assurance the kid wouldn't be seen and recognized."

Dombrowski patted her hand and returned her smile. "Yeah, I get it. It'll depend on how well he's known; we have no way to gauge that. But at least they're trying to be discreet."

"Yeah, but that doesn't change our tactics. We also need to be discreet, right? Sam is on the spot, too."

"Sure, there's no harm in playing this a little sensitive. So, the word is discretion all around—it's in everybody's best interests—and mutual cooperation, of course."

"Yeah, let's keep any mention of his father out of this."

"Okay, if we can."

———————

THE DOOR SWUNG OPEN. A casino security guard gestured for the young man to enter, and closed the door behind him.

His anxiety obvious, Jonathan Widermark fidgeted and scanned the room. "What's going on? Why am I here? Who are you people?"

The detectives rose, but before Dombrowski could speak, the young man jabbed a finger at him and blurted, "Do you know who I am? Did my father send you?"

The detectives shared a knowing look—so much for keeping any mention of the father out of this.

"Sir, I'm Detective Sergeant Dombrowski, and this is my partner, Detective Callahan. I'm afraid we don't have anything to do with your father. We need to speak to you regarding—"

"Hold it right there! Do you know who my father is? Do I need to call my family's lawyer?" He began fumbling for his phone. "I have Mr. Farrell's number on speed-dial!"

The detectives shared another knowing look.

"Would that be Walter Farrell, the attorney?" Katie asked blandly.

"Uh, yes. Why?"

"Mr. Widermark," Dombrowski began, "we know who you are; and, we know who your father is. Of course you are welcome to contact your lawyer, but there's really no need. You are not suspected of any crime, and you're not in any trouble. As I was saying, we need to speak to you regarding your friend, the woman with whom you spent the night."

"Uh, who? Louise? Why? I don't understand. What are you talking about?"

"Please, Jonathan" Katie soothed, "have a seat. We're sorry for the inconvenience. We just need to verify something she's already told us. This really won't take very long."

Tentatively, he sat. However, the detectives could see that distrust and reluctance to cooperate hovered just below the surface of his tense demeanor. They said nothing as he squirmed in the chair and tried to appear at ease. Suddenly conscious of his twining thumbs, he thrust his hands into his lap and forced himself to remain motionless.

In that uncomfortable moment of strained silence as the detectives scrutinized him, his anxiety apparently got the better of him. "Well, what is it? She wouldn't have told you about us—she wouldn't have told anybody!"

"All we need to know," Dombrowski explained, "is whether or not she was with you—and I mean in your presence—here at the hotel, several weeks ago. That's all. Can you help us out?"

Widermark began to relax somewhat; but, he was obviously still wary. "That's all? You're sure this doesn't have anything to do with my father? He doesn't know about us, you see—and I don't want him to. Is that clear?"

"As far as we know," Dombrowski assured him, "this does not involve your father; so, we have no reason to involve him. Okay?"

Jonathan stared at the tabletop, took a deep breath, and looked up into Dombrowski's face. "All right. I'll help—*if* you keep him out of it. So, when exactly are we talking about?"

"Ah, very good. Let me check my notes," Dombrowski responded as he paged through his notebook.

A knock on the door was followed by Sgt. Greenway poking his head into the room. "Uh, sorry for the interruption, could I see one of y'all out here for a second?"

Katie nodded to her partner and followed Sgt. Greenway into the hall.

———

PULLING THE CONFERENCE room door closed, Sam motioned for her to follow him to the reception area. Safely out of earshot of the interview, the Tribal Police sergeant spoke softly. "Your suspect, Louise Hesterly, is checking out. We'll maintain surveillance until she leaves the grounds. Still no need to tail her after that?"

"No, Sam, there's no change in plans—thanks anyway. If that's all, I'm gonna get back in there. Are you going to be out here, in case we need anything?"

"Yeah, sure—I can hold down this fort."

"Thanks."

FIFTEEN MINUTES LATER, Dombrowski led Jonathan Widermark out of the conference room. Katie trailed in their wake.

"Jonathan, you've been a big help," Dombrowski declared. "We can't thank you enough. If we need to speak with you again, we'll call on your cell. Don't worry about a thing; we'll be the very soul of discretion. Let me walk you to your car."

With a knowing nod to his partner, Dombrowski ushered the young man out of the office.

Katie, eyebrows raised, looked to Sgt. Greenway. "She's gone?"

Sam nodded. "Yep, ten minutes ago."

"Well then, that wraps up this end of things. I'll give my partner a few minutes and then meet him at our car."

Sgt. Greenway looked puzzled. "Y'all gotta go?"

"Yeah, I'm afraid so," she admitted. "We pretty much knew we'd have to get going as soon as we concluded this interview. But hey, thanks a lot for all you and your people have done—we really appreciate it."

Like she'd seen Dombrowski do a thousand times, she stuck out her hand for that ubiquitous Southern closing handshake. He met her grip and added his other hand over the top, like a preacher's soft sell.

"No problem, Katie. It was a pleasure to meet y'all. You're welcome back anytime. Wait a minute—I thought your sergeant owed you breakfast? I can arrange comps at the breakfast buffet."

She chuckled and shook her head. "Thanks, Sam, but we'll pass. We've gotta get back to our office. Don't worry—I'm gonna make him buy me breakfast on the road."

DRIVING ALONG THE INTERSTATE, Katie gnawed her lower lip.

Dombrowski glanced up from his notebook and asked, "Okay, what is it? Didn't you get enough to eat?"

"Oh, no . . . Breakfast was fine, thanks."

"Then what's bugging you?"

"Oh, the case . . . I don't know," she grumbled. "I admit Louise's alibi seems more solid now with Jonathan's corroboration. But remember the M.E. said Adamson's TOD could have been anytime within a two-day window. So, it is still a possibility—although admittedly it's looking more and more remote that she could've done it. And now this Jonathan Widermark . . . I guess I'm not sure how much I trust him."

He shifted in his seat. "That's two issues you're wrestling with; did she do it, and could he have possibly helped her. Consider a couple facts; it's a least a four hour round trip from the casino hotel to the staged suicide scene, and it'd take some amount of time to move Adamson's body from the real crime scene—wherever that actually is—and then stage it to make it look like a suicide. She'd need help with all the logistics, and the timing would be critical. So, you think maybe he'd help her with the heavy lifting?"

"Maybe," she mused aloud.

"Oh, come on—do you really see him that culpable?"

"Or gullible?" she sneered.

"Come on, Katie, think! What's in it for him—the sex? He's a younger, good looking guy, you know."

"I hear you, okay? Maybe it's the relationship? He's clearly got a reason to protect her. And what about Walter Farrell being his family lawyer—what's up with that?"

Dombrowski sighed and stared through the windshield as the concrete ribbon slipped beneath the cruiser's tires. "Oh Katie, you are entirely too young to be this clinically cynical. I sense that you have not forgiven Louise for lying to you—even though she was, at least in her mind, protecting her relationship with Jonathan."

"Why should I?" she spat. "I don't care about her reason or excuse or whatever. She played me—and that I don't forgive or forget! And by the way, Bernice told me Louise has a *tell*—she touches her throat when she's bluffing or lying! I wish I'd known that."

"No shit? Okay, I understand, and I'm not suggesting that you either forgive or forget. However, I am suggesting that you follow where the evidence leads. We'll look further into Jonathan, his father, and the connection between the Widermarks and Walter Farrell. But understand that Jonathan's statement, assuming it stands corroboration, effectively alibis Louise in the Adamson case. So, unless we find something else, some new evidence that points back to Louise, she shouldn't be your main focus, *capisce?*"

Katie shrugged and mumbled, "Yeah, I know. I'm all right—really. I'm just a little frustrated. I've already made a lot of calls about the Widermarks, but none of my sources have called back yet. I've got to be patient, I guess."

"*True dat!* You tired? Want me to drive some?"

"Nah, I'm good. By the way, aren't you going to call the lieutenant? Or do you think we should wait until we get back to brief him?"

"Yeah, good point, I'd better call him and give him the heads up—he'd appreciate that. Then I can start drafting our report on our way back."

Dombrowski spent the next few minutes on his phone with Lt. Waters. Katie heard her partner's half of the conversation but paid little attention, until she heard the sudden interest in his voice.

"Is that right? No, we didn't . . . He mentioned it at the outset of our interview . . . No, we haven't . . . Yes, sir, will do as soon as we get back . . . See you in a coupla hours. Bye."

Katie glanced at him in an unspoken question.

He grinned in return. "Well, there are a couple of things. Remember the clothing and stuff in Jennifer Halsted's storage room, the one in the basement of her building? We had that stuff sent to CSI. Well, they're finished with it; they found nothing of consequence. Now they want to send all that stuff back to us."

"What for? If they didn't find anything we can use, we don't want it. They can send it back to . . . Oh shit."

"Yeah, exactly. There's nowhere to send it to, no next of kin that we know of, and her condo is history."

"She had a car, too," Katie remembered. "It was in the parking lot at the HOA office."

"True, Katie, but we didn't seize it as evidence. CSI processed it on the scene. Besides, the car has a lien on it, so it'll go back to the bank and likely to auction. But her clothes are another matter."

"D, she had a lot of nice stuff as I recall. Maybe we can look into having it donated to some charity. Do you think that'll fly?"

"I don't see why not," he mused aloud. "If I recall, after six months or so, the department can donate unclaimed or abandoned property—maybe it's a year? I'll have to talk to the lieutenant about it."

"Okay," she acknowledged. "What else?"

"Ah yes, it seems a couple of your inquiries into the Widermarks have already borne fruit; although, some of the responses are coming through the captain's office."

"The captain's office? Why?"

"Politics, I suspect."

"Politics? What the hell?"

"Guess who one of our illustrious state Senator Jeremiah Widermark's major campaign contributors is—Walter Farrell."

Katie's eyes grew wide, and a wry smirk teased her lips. "Oh, really? How major?"

His smirk mirrored hers. "Millions, Detective, millions."

CH 22

WHEN THEY PULLED INTO the parking lot, Katie winced as the sun glared off the windshields of the parked cars, but not before she'd seen someone standing in the shade of the building. "Look, D, isn't that Kenny? You suppose he's waiting for us?"

"*Us?*" Dombrowski scoffed. "Hah! More like he's waiting for you—don't you think? See, here he comes."

As they exited their car, Dombrowski smirked when he heard Kenny's greeting.

"Hi Sarge, Katie. Uh, Katie, could we talk for a minute?"

"Yeah, Katie," Dombrowski insisted, "I gotta get upstairs and file our report. So, why don't you talk to Ken while I do that? I'll see you upstairs. See you later, Ken."

Katie sent him a murderous look that he smugly ignored. Smiling broadly, he entered the building.

DOMBROWSKI FOUND LT. Waters in his office. Taking the chair in front of the lieutenant's desk, Dombrowski slid the draft of his report onto the desk.

"The Adamson case," the sergeant began. "The sisters' alibi might hold after all. Jonathan Widermark's statement corroborates their statements. Katie's made the usual inquiries into him; but, I think the sisters may be in the clear."

Waters leaned back in his chair, his left hand absently patting the shirt pocket that held his pack of cigarettes. "So, what else have we got?"

"Not much, LT. The records from the guard service were basically worthless; they didn't record hardly any of Adamson's comings and goings in the neighborhood. We're certain though, that the Adamson and Halsted cases are linked. We know they both worked for the HOA. Both are homicides staged as suicides; the CODs are similar, and even the TODs are close. We also considered the sisters for the Halsted murder, but the timing doesn't work, especially now with their alibis corroborated."

"So, are you saying you're stalled on these cases?"

"No sir, not at all. You see, there's another link, to the Silverberg case. We know from the phone records that Adamson was frequently talking to Carolyn Silverberg. Just precisely what that relationship was, we haven't determined yet. By the way, the only next of kin we've found for her is a cousin in New York; NYPD will make the notification."

Waters leaned forward and dropped his elbows on the desk. "What about the sisters for the Silverberg murder? Could they be viable suspects?"

Dombrowski shook his head. "Nope, same problem—the timing doesn't work given the TOD."

"Damn! So, we have no viable suspects. Is there anything to suggest a single perpetrator or are we looking for multiple killers?"

"Honestly, we don't know yet. There's no solid evidence either way. One victim, Adamson, knew both Jennifer Halsted and Carolyn Silverberg. However, we can't determine if Halsted and Silverberg knew each other."

"Okay. Anything else?" Waters probed.

"Well, yeah . . . There is one anomaly that contrasts with another similarity; the power and phone lines were fully functioning at the Halsted scene, the HOA office. However phone and power lines were cut inside Adamson's home and Silverberg's home. It might just be that interrupting power and phones at an office building may have been noticed too quickly. That would likely cramp the perp's getaway time. Admittedly, that's speculation because we don't know for sure. But we do know that the HOA office was a crime scene; and Silverberg's home was clearly a crime scene. We also know the location where Adamson's body was found, at the vacant house, was not where he was killed. However, his home was trashed; CSI found the phone and power lines cut. His house has a security system, but it wasn't being monitored; the back-up battery cable was cut."

"So," Waters surmised, "if Adamson's body was staged at the vacant house, is his home where he was killed?"

"It's a possibility," Dombrowski admitted, "but CSI didn't find any clear evidence to support that. And to be candid, my gut's not too happy with that theory. I can't shake the feeling that we're missing something."

Katie appeared in the doorway, a slight flush to her cheeks. "Hey, LT, I'm sorry for the interruption. Sergeant, could I see you out here for a minute?"

Dombrowski looked to Lt. Waters, who simply shrugged. "Go on. We're done. I'll read your final report."

———————

BACK AT THEIR DESKS, Dombrowski sensed that something was amiss with Katie. "What is it?" he hissed. "What's wrong?"

"Oh shit, D, we're gonna be—"

"There they are!" boomed from across the room.

Dombrowski and Katie turned toward the voice.

Detective Bobby Johnson stood in the squad room doorway, pointing at them. Captain Walker, Detective Sid Barkley, and a tall, unidentified man in a dark suit stood behind Johnson.

Lt. Waters came out of his office and stood with his hands on his hips. "Hello, Captain. What's going on?"

"Lieutenant, may we use your office?"

"Of course," Waters responded and stepped aside.

Capt. Walker crooked a finger at the detectives and said, "Dombrowski, Callahan, inside please, and Lieutenant, you as well. Detectives Johnson and Barkley, you may return to your duties."

They filed into the office. Lt. Waters closed the door and gestured for everyone to take seats.

The captain commandeered the lieutenant's chair and took a moment to glare across the desk at his detectives. "People, I am not happy about this, but we will nonetheless proceed. This is Lieutenant Madison; he is on loan from the State Police, Internal Affairs. He is here at the request of the Chief."

Madison said nothing, and made no effort to shake hands.

Walker scowled at his people and continued. "You will give him your complete cooperation, in compliance with policy and procedures."

"Captain, if I may," Waters dared. "What is this?"

"Lieutenant, this is an internal affairs investigation into certain allegations made against Detective Sergeant Dombrowski and Detective Callahan. Lt. Madison will conduct the investigation. The Chief brought in the State Police so that there could be no hint of collusion or impropriety in the course of the investigation."

Katie was smoldering, and Dombrowski sensed it. He slid a foot close and tapped the side of her shoe. She got the message and remained quiet.

"Excuse me, Captain," Dombrowski ventured, "but just what are we being accused of?"

Lt. Madison spoke for the first time in a laconic and disinterested tone. "I'll respond to that question, Captain Walker, if you don't mind."

Walker scoffed and nodded.

Madison continued. "Detective Sergeant Donald Dombrowski, Detective Katie Callahan . . . It is my duty to inform you that you are both alleged to have withheld evidence, possessed controlled substances, and obstructed justice. Understand that neither of you is being charged at this time. These allegations will be investigated; and if substantiated, formal charges may be brought. Charges may be criminal, or administrative. If these allegations are found to be unsubstantiated, you will be cleared and the investigation closed. I will need to interview you each, separately. You may consult with legal counsel, as is your right. You may have your union delegate present if you wish. Do you understand what I have told you?"

Dombrowski and Katie shared a look, and responded in unison. "Yes, Lieutenant."

"Good . . . Captain?"

Walker's scowl had not left his face. It was clear he hated this. He cleared his throat and stood. "Detectives, pursuant to this agency's policy, I have no choice but to place you both under suspension for the duration of this investigation. Please surrender your badges, credentials, and service weapons to Lt. Waters. You are to make yourselves available to Lt. Madison as he sees fit. That is all."

———————————

OUTSIDE, IN THE PARKING lot, Dombrowski fumbled in his jacket pockets for his truck keys. He was still stunned.

What the hell had just happened? Withholding evidence? Controlled substances? What bullshit is this?

"Damned if I know," Katie declared.

Dombrowski winced. "Did I say all that out loud?"

"You sort of mumbled to yourself, but I heard you."

"Oh, sorry about that. Hey, what were you gonna tell me—before the shit hit the fan, that is?"

"Not here," she cautioned. "I've got no wheels here. How about giving me a ride home?"

"Sure, come on."

A few miles down the road, she pointed to a rest stop and said, "Hey, pull in there. Uh, I gotta make a pit stop."

As he parked, she put a finger to her lips and exited his truck. Motioning him to follow, she led him a dozen yards away to a low picnic table.

"Okay . . . What?" he asked

She took a long moment to scan the immediate area and spoke in a guarded tone. "Your truck might be bugged, so watch what you say in it."

"What the hell?"

"Keep your voice down! We're probably okay here, unless somebody's got a parabolic mike on us. Listen, Kenny tipped me that we were going to be the subject of an IA investigation. I didn't get the chance to tell you before it all came down."

Dombrowski let his puzzlement show in his voice. "Kenny? How did he—"

"He was in the lab when Johnson and Barkley brought in a briefcase, a laptop, and two small plastic baggies of crystalline white powder. They stayed while the powder was tested—positive for methamphetamine. He overheard them tell the tech that they'd found all the stuff in our lockers—the briefcase and one baggie in yours, and the laptop and the other baggie in mine."

"Our lockers?" he echoed. "Are you kidding me? That locker room is open to anybody—it doesn't even have a lock! Hell, my locker doesn't have a lock. I don't keep anything in it but an old plastic raincoat."

Katie shrugged and opened her palms. "Yeah, I know what you mean. I don't keep anything but some old running shoes and some sweats in mine. It's not locked either—never has been. So, why would anyone even bother to look in there?"

Dombrowski sat on the bench seat and stared back towards the parking area. He chose his words carefully. "Only one of two reasons, either they planted the stuff there, or they were tipped to look there—"

"By whoever did plant it," she finished. "Bastards!"

"Yeah, more than likely. But, Sid and Bobby . . . "

"What?" She sat next to him and followed his gaze.

"Think about it. Sid and Bobby may not be the brightest lights in the chandelier, but they're honest cops—they wouldn't plant evidence. However, they would follow a tip."

"Okay, I can see that," she allowed. "But who or what is their source?"

"Good question, Katie. If the briefcase and laptop are in fact the property of Melanie Dubois—that's clearly the intended inference—then whoever left them for Sid and Bobby to find, got them from her condo, car, office—"

"Or," she interrupted, "from her personally, which would mean—"

"That person," he finished, "may be our killer."

"All right, that makes sense. But what about the drugs, the meth?"

Dombrowski paused in thought. "I'm thinking that just the briefcase and laptop weren't enough . . . That could have been construed as simply mishandling evidence, like we were late or hadn't had the opportunity to turn them in yet. That might merit an administrative hand-slap. But the dope—that guarantees a suspension."

"So," she reasoned, "somebody wants us off . . . what, the Dubois case? Hell, we're already off that."

"Yeah, I know. Maybe it's one of our other cases?"

"Well, we've got three open homicides. So, which one—or maybe all three? You know they're connected. Come to think of it, if you consider Walter Farrell as the common denominator here, even the Dubois case is linked."

Her point was valid, but he didn't see a direct link between Walter Farrell and Carolyn Silverberg, unless Adamson proved to be an adequate bridge. But then again, Amanda Farrell's license had been found in Carolyn Silverberg's mouth.

He stroked his chin and asked, "By the way, how much meth was found—did anyone say?"

"Kenny said it was only about a quarter gram, or a little less, in each little baggie. The techs weren't happy because they usually like to have more to test."

"Okay, I think I get it now." He crossed his legs and stretched. "Look, we know we're being set up. Whoever is behind it is getting desperate to have us out of the picture. The bomb at the Dubois scene was a far more sophisticated attempt; but it too failed. Now they're trying a different tack."

"What do you mean?"

"The meth gets us suspended, but it's only a trace amount. They messed up—again. You see, the amount is too small for distribution, but enough for possession. If they'd have been smarter they'd have left a larger amount of meth. Then we'd have to disprove intent to distribute rather than simple possession."

"Huh?"

He knew she wasn't seeing the big picture, or the administrative nuances. "Look, it isn't like we're innocent until proven guilty; we have to prove we're being set up. However, this should be relatively easy. We know we've never touched the drugs—or the laptop and briefcase for that matter. Neither our prints nor DNA are gonna be on anything. Unless we're dealing with a far more sophisticated operation than what I've seen leads me to believe—but I seriously doubt it."

"I sure hope not! So, how is this supposed to be easy?"

He needed her to understand how short-sighted this attempt to frame them might actually be. He needed her to focus on the real issues—the real threats. "Think! The small amount of meth suggests personal use, right? So, make an appointment with your doctor; have a full blood panel and urinalysis done. Then you've got proof you're not abusing any drugs. We may have to repeat the process with a doctor the IA investigator or the department selects, but that's no big deal since we'll already have our own proof."

"Okay, I get it," she acknowledged. "But there's still a big problem; we're still suspended!"

"Yeah, but at least it's with pay," he reminded her. "I like to believe we get paid for thinking. Besides, what's the matter—you've never heard of working from home?"

She grinned. "Well, we do have our notes and copies of pertinent stuff from the other cases. Wait—do you think our homes might be bugged like your truck?"

That was a sobering thought, and it gave him pause. "If IA had sufficient probable cause to get an order to bug my truck, they'd likely have enough to tap our phones and bug our homes as well. Hell, they could probably even go for search warrants. But somehow, that doesn't feel likely. In the meantime, we have little choice but to let the IA investigation run its course."

"How long," she wondered, "do you think it'll take?"

"Hmm, hard to say. I'd guess a couple of weeks at least—maybe a little less if this whole set up is really as blatantly obvious as it appears. We'll just have to adjust to the scrutiny."

"Well, I hate it!" she fumed. "This sense of being watched gives me the creeps."

"Meh, don't let it get to you. Where did you get the idea about my truck anyway?"

"Kenny said we should be careful. He saw some people he didn't know—a man and a woman—around your truck yesterday evening when he left work."

"Did he think they were techs? I know we have some female techs in the CSI unit."

"He said he didn't recognize them."

"Maybe they were State Police techs," he offered. "You know, Madison's people."

"Maybe," she begrudgingly admitted. "Somebody else might be involved. We've been bugged before—Melanie's condo, remember? Think we could ask Kenny to do a sweep?"

"We'd better not," he cautioned. "He's already stuck his neck out enough for us. If it's a legitimate order that authorizes bugs and taps, he'll just get jammed up."

"And if it's not?" she probed.

"It's still better if we keep him out of it for now. We're just going to have to be careful. Maybe we could set up shop somewhere other than our homes, someplace our eavesdroppers might not know about—"

"I got it!" Katie immediately brightened. "How about my Dad's cabin at the lake? There's good cell coverage up there now, so the office can still reach us."

"And Madison as well," Dombrowski reminded her. "Let's not forget our Grand Inquisitor, shall we?"

Her face fell, but her enthusiasm recovered quickly. "It'll work! We can forward our home phones to our cell phones; no one need know precisely where we are. We can just answer our phones as we normally would. We'll just have to be circumspect in what we say."

He smiled. It was comforting to see that she was thinking strategically, despite the unsettling events of the last few hours.

"Okay, that's the plan," he agreed. "One other thing, let's pick up a pair of pre-paid burner phones for more secure communications. We can make those doctors' appointments using those phones—no need to tip our hand."

She stood and brushed off her jeans. "Let's do this. We can stop by the big box mega-store on the way to my house. They carry those pre-paid phones."

"Yes, ma'am, I'm at your service."

CH 23

DOMBROWSKI SIPPED HIS coffee and meandered down the rustic dock, past a weathered boat shed. Standing at the end of the pier, he stared out at the morning mist rising from the placid surface of the lake. The forested hills to the east seemed to recede as the sun began to clear their verdant canopies.

Turning his face into the promised warmth of the sunrise, he took a deep cleansing breath. In that timeless moment, the searing orb was swaddled in the remnants of a lingering cloud layer that glowed in a palette of pale pinks and shimmering golds. This magnificent celestial display began to dissipate as he watched. He knew this was special, and he was a little sad that it wouldn't last. He would have liked to have shared this with someone, but . . . He shook off that train of thought and glanced back at Katie's *family cabin*.

Some cabin—a stately stone and cypress house of considerable age lorded over the rural freshwater lake. It was big, much bigger than the modest home in town that she and her father had shared. This house boasted a massive great room—what would be called an open concept today—and four bedrooms. But to Dombrowski's mind, the *piece de resistance* was a library that held his interest almost as much as the magnificent view of the lake from the broad balcony above the wide back porch.

The location was very private; the nearest neighbors were at least half a wooded mile away. The property had been in Katie's family for several generations. Her great-grandfather built the original house almost a century ago. Successive generations had added square footage and improvements over the years.

However, with time, the size of the Callahan clan had dwindled until only Katie and her father remained.

As if summoned by his random thoughts, Dombrowski saw her come out onto the broad rear porch. She stood there a moment, with coffee mug in hand, seemingly lost in thought. Then seeing him, she waved. He returned the gesture and made his way back to the house.

―――――――――

"GOOD MORNING," HE HAILED, stepping onto the porch.

"Morning. I didn't know you were already up. I almost knocked on your door, but I figured I'd let you sleep in."

"Well, I'm not normally a morning person," he admitted, "but since we've been here, I've been waking up earlier. Maybe all this peacefulness is getting to me. I think I like it. So anyway, I thought I'd have my coffee down by the water."

She smiled and waved her mug towards the lake. "I know what you mean. The lake can be pretty special in the early morning."

"Yeah," he agreed. "So, what's on today's agenda?"

She took a long sip before responding. "Seems I've gotta go down to the general store this morning. We've been here four days now and we're gonna be running low on food soon. Is there anything in particular you want me to get?"

"Nah, so long as we've got coffee and stuff to make sandwiches, I'm good. Here, let me give you some cash."

She swallowed a gulp of coffee and shook her head. "No thanks, there's no need. I'm just gonna charge it. We probably ought to keep what cash we've got, just in case, you know?"

"Yeah, okay. That makes sense."

He pulled out his phone and scrolled through the message queue. He squinted at the small screen, grunted in disgust, and fished his reading glasses from his pocket.

"Anything?" she asked.

"No, nothing. I guess I really didn't expect too much over the weekend, but this is Monday morning, right? And still nothing. How about you, get any calls or messages?"

"Nope, I already checked—zip. I'm surprised, too. I really thought Lt. Madison would want to do follow-up interviews by close of business Friday. But he hasn't called."

Dombrowski pulled a bentwood rocking chair from a shaded section of the porch and eased himself into the seat. "You know, I wouldn't worry too much about it, Katie. When he interviewed me, I thought he did a pretty good job; he was professional about it. My impression is he's a straight shooter."

She leaned against a porch rail and stared into her mug. "Well, I don't mind telling you, he sure made me nervous. I was uncomfortable in that interview; I'm usually the one asking the questions. I know we've got nothing to hide—but what the hell! I've never been the subject of an IA investigation. I don't like it one bit!"

"Look, I get it—I really do," he assured her and slipped his phone into his pocket. "But you have to understand that despite how it might feel, IA isn't out to get us. Madison's role is to determine the truth. And as it happens, the truth will clear us of all this crap. So, just relax and let him do his job, okay?"

Her scowl spoke volumes, but he knew her well, so he could only sigh. *Oh, kiddo, you'll have to come to your own peace with this situation.*

She sniffed and turned to face the lake. "Look, I know you're right, but it's still extremely unsettling to be accused—especially when there's nothing I can do about it. I'm now compelled to rely upon others to rectify this situation." Her jaw muscles clenched. "I absolutely hate having to rely on anybody—damn it all!"

Her partner recognized her brooding and snapped her out of it. "Hey! Speaking of the store . . . I just thought of something I could use, a magnifying glass! You know, a good sized one, oh, about this big." He held his hands up to form a four inch circle.

She turned and scoffed. "What—a magnifying glass?"

He plucked his reading glasses off his nose and waved them near his face. "Yeah, I tried to look closer at some of the photos in our file copies, but these glasses just weren't doing it for me. So, I think a magnifying glass would help."

"Okay, if the general store has one I'll get it. Can you think of anything else?"

"Not at the moment. But keep your burner phone on; I'll call on that line if I think of something."

"Oh yeah, we still want to stay discreet about our current location."

"Right you are! We still don't know who's so damned interested in us."

She traced a finger around the rim of her mug. "You know, you could go with me?"

"What? Uh, no . . . It's better if I'm not seen. The folks around here are familiar with you, so it's no big deal if you happen to be seen here periodically. But I'm a stranger; if I'm seen with you, somebody's liable to take note and remember. We've got too much to do; so, we're better off trying to stay below the radar, if not off the grid entirely."

"I get it. Maybe it's a good idea if you stay. I'm not real comfortable leaving the place unattended right now."

"Wouldn't want someone to sneak in and bug us, huh?"

"Yeah, right. Well, come on then. Let's fix breakfast so I can get going. The sooner I go, the sooner I can get back."

———————

KATIE WAS GONE LONGER than he expected, almost two hours. When she returned, she was not alone. Two people, their arms laden with grocery bags, followed Katie into the house.

"Hey, D!" she called to him, a slight edge to her voice. "Look who I found in town—waiting at my car."

Dombrowski entered the kitchen and made no effort to hide his surprise. "Emilio? What the hell are you doing here? And how did you find us? No one is supposed to know we're here."

"Hello, Sergeant," the grinning Deputy U.S. Marshal said, as he set bags of groceries on the counter. He extended his hand. "It's good to see you, too."

Dombrowski shook the offered hand, but didn't immediately release it. "Cut the crap, Emilio. What's going on? And who is this?"

"Ah, right to the point, I see. Uh, you can let go now—everything's cool. Let me introduce my colleague, Rachel MacPherson, an investigator from FinCEN."

As Dombrowski shook the petite woman's hand, the Deputy U.S. Marshal continued. "Remember I said I'd look over the subpoena response from that Delaware bank, and that I might consult with my friend in FinCEN? Well, Rachel is that friend, and she found some of that material very interesting; so much so that FinCEN has taken more than a passing interest in your case."

Dombrowski offered his open palms and shrugged. "Look, we appreciate the assistance; but Emilio, I gotta tell you that Katie and I—we've been suspended. We're under an IA investigation. It's not really our case anymore."

"Oh, we know. We met with Lt. Waters in his office Friday afternoon, when we submitted our written findings. He informed us of your current status."

"He was more . . . candid," Rachel explained in a clear melodious voice, "when we met him later over a few cold beers. He smokes a lot, doesn't he?"

Katie chuckled, but there was no mirth in her eyes. "Ha! That's an understatement. He's good people; we trust him."

Rachel smiled and nodded. "Yes, we could see that he thinks highly of both of you."

Emilio glanced around the room and spoke guardedly. "Look, there are some things you probably need to know. And your boss, well, he doesn't disagree. I think you know he's not happy with this situation. While he firmly believes you'll be cleared of the allegations eventually, he is understandably frustrated with the delay. He has voiced a strong opinion up your chain of command that it would be counterproductive not to keep you informed in the meantime. However, he's constrained by departmental regulations."

"Whereas, we are not so hamstrung," Emilio's FinCEN colleague finished with a smile. "So, we thought a little informal visit might be in order."

Dombrowski could read between the lines as well as anybody; nonetheless, he stifled a smile and kept his voice neutral. "I get it. But how did you find us? Even Lt. Waters doesn't know about this place—or does he?"

"No, that's true, he doesn't," Emilio admitted. "He's under the impression you are both at your respective homes. For now, I see no need to correct him."

"You still haven't explained how you found us," Katie countered flatly.

"Oh come now, Detective, it's what I do."

Dombrowski elbowed his partner and matched her even tone. "Talk about an understatement—U.S. Marshals hunt people for a living, remember Katie?"

"Among other things," Emilio added with a smile.

"So, Emilio, suppose you look at it from our point of view," Dombrowski suggested reasonably, but there was no mistaking the steel in his voice. "Why should we trust you—either of you? We're already suspended and under an IA investigation. We suspect we were being bugged—and not necessarily by the good guys. So, we're trying to stay low profile, somewhere that no one's supposed to know about. But now, you've found us—and you won't tell us how. That doesn't exactly engender trust in my book."

Emilio and Rachel shared a knowing look. She shrugged and he nodded.

"I appreciate your concern, Sergeant. I can assure you both that Rachel and I have nothing to do with your IA matter. We're not here to ask any questions or gather any information in that regard. On the contrary, we're here to give you information that may have a bearing on your open case. If it will help build trust between us, I can tell you it was no great challenge to locate you, once we determined you weren't staying at your respective homes."

"How?" Katie demanded through gritted teeth.

Dombrowski shot her a look—*calm down*.

"Detective, this dwelling," Emilio began, sweeping an arm about the kitchen, "is in your family name; as are the tax records and the current utilities. This morning, both of you used your department-issued cell phones to check for messages. Katie, you charged your grocery purchases with a personal credit card. Your car has an OEM GPS unit with an integrated cellular link. Trust me; you were not hard to find. And for what it's worth, we are the good guys—and we're not bugging you."

Dombrowski and Katie looked to one another and begrudgingly shrugged. They had nothing to lose by listening.

"Okay," Dombrowski grumbled. "So, what do you have to tell us?"

"As I said," Emilio responded, "your lieutenant has our written report which will be available to you when you return to full duty. We can brief you now on our analysis and synopsize our findings. Is this okay with you?"

"Absolutely," Dombrowski assured them. "That's fine."

Katie nodded in agreement and gestured toward the table. "Well then, y'all should make yourselves comfortable. I'll get these groceries put away and put some coffee on."

———————

ONCE SETTLED AROUND the kitchen table, they spent a few minutes in polite conversation about Katie's lake house. With fresh mugs of coffee all around, they got down to business.

"First of all," Rachel began, "understand that FinCEN is an acronym for the Financial Crimes Enforcement Network, an enforcement arm of the U.S. Treasury. The mission of FinCEN is to enhance the integrity of financial systems by facilitating the detection and deterrence of financial crimes. We combat transnational organized crime; investigate financial fraud of any type, to include mortgage and real estate fraud. In short, we administer the Bank Secrecy Act, support law enforcement, intelligence, and regulatory agencies through analysis and sharing of fiscal intelligence. We keep an eye on financial institutions, both domestic and international."

Emilio raised his cup in a toast to his colleague and chuckled. "Well memorized, my friend! But I think they kinda know that already!"

"Stuff it, Emilio!" Rachel spat, a wry smile on her lips. "You know damn well I'm required to recite the agency mission statement—so, give me a break!"

Emilio winked at his colleague and smiled broadly. "Ah, yeah I know—my bad," he teased, and turned to the detectives. "Rachel and I have worked together on a number of task force cases over the past few years. So, she was the first person I thought of when I learned there were banks involved in your case that were cooperating only reluctantly."

"Hey, we appreciate any help we can get," Katie responded, slowly warming to their visitors. "I couldn't begin to understand what that Delaware bank sent us."

"It's not surprising that the response you received was deliberately confusing," Rachel sympathized.

"In this case it's in their best interest to obscure as much as possible—and they're very good at it. The language was very carefully parsed. I found nothing blatantly illegal—no outright violations of current laws—but I found plenty that piqued my interest.

"Two of the banks involved, one in Delaware and one in the Cayman Islands, have come to FinCEN's attention before; but there hasn't been any specific evidence of fraud or money laundering. That's not to say they haven't been under past suspicion and subsequent scrutiny; but there have been no other warning flags in the last year or so—that is, until your case came up."

"So, Rachel, what do you suspect is going on?" Dombrowski asked.

Rachel and Emilio shared a look and seemed to agree to proceed.

"Our written report," Emilio explained, "is a simplified synopsis of the facts gleaned from the response. It states that the Delaware bank hosts certain accounts, ultimately linked to the HOA, that are paying for continued utility services for the foreclosed and vacant houses. HOA dues and 'investor funds' are cited. There are links to another bank, Consolidated Federal, which holds a number of first and second mortgages on these foreclosed properties."

"Of course, that prompted me to dig deeper," Rachel added, "and that analysis is not contained in our written report. You must understand that, officially, this is not a FinCEN case; however, we are interested in following your investigation as there are aspects that may link to ongoing FinCEN investigations. Consequently, whatever we discuss from this point forward should be considered confidential. Are we agreed?"

"We are," Dombrowski answered for both of them.

"Good," Rachel confirmed. "Based upon a number of Suspicious Activity Reports, or SARs, and certain other confidential information available to me, I could see that Consolidated Federal and the Delaware bank have a rather cozy *quid pro quo* relationship in regard to the refinancing, maintenance, rehabilitation, and disposition of these properties.

"I am relatively certain that investment funding is forthcoming from the bank in the Cayman Islands to fuel this enterprise. Now please understand that none of this is illegal—at least not on its face—although we're very curious as to the source of the Cayman funds."

"I'm confused," Dombrowski admitted. "How does the HOA figure in this with all these banks?"

Emilio forestalled Rachel's response with a raised hand. "If I may . . . Sarge, remember how we talked about how stringent HOAs could be? How they could fine homeowners for non-compliance of rules and covenants? Well, FinCEN can look into foreclosures, and you'd be surprised how many were directly impacted by significant HOA fines. A pattern began to emerge, wherein mortgage payments that were reported as missed or late were frequently followed by escalating unpaid HOA fines. They became liens against the property. Simply put, it appeared that some of these struggling homeowners were pushed into foreclosure."

"Some filed for bankruptcy," Rachel countered, "which was smart because that meant the federal bankruptcy court became involved, so the creditors had to back off and wait for the bankruptcy process to grind along to fruition."

"However," Emilio cautioned, "in matters without court oversight, the banks could do as they pleased, within applicable laws and regulations. Here's where it started to get convoluted. Rachel?"

"We think we might know what they're up to, but we still don't have any clear evidence of a crime," she said. "We strongly suspect some foreclosures were manipulated—people were taken advantage of in a tight recession. While that might be morally distasteful and borderline unethical, technically it is not really a violation of law."

"Well, that sucks," Katie observed.

"Oh, it can get worse—and it's all still legal," Rachel warned. "Some mortgage holders will let the owners stay in the house during the foreclosure process, assuming the property will be adequately maintained. However, many mortgage holders don't want any tenants, and will push the residents out as soon as possible. And, of course, there are cases of some owners bailing—just abandoning the property when they know they can't catch up on the loan."

"That helps to explain why there are so many vacant foreclosures," Dombrowski observed.

"True enough," Emilio agreed. "Don't overlook the fact that financial institutions often transfer or sell these outstanding loans at discounts. Whoever winds up holding the outstanding mortgage has effective possession of the asset or collateral, which is the vacant property."

"Right! And that's one of the things I found so interesting about Consolidated Federal," Rachel explained. "You see, it's clear that this bank acquired many such properties at drastically reduced costs by acquiring the discounted outstanding loans. Once the bank had possession, it could do anything—or nothing."

"Nothing?" Katie echoed. "Doesn't that mean they're losing money?"

"So it would seem, since no one is making payments on the loan," Rachel agreed. "However, there are certain tax advantages to taking a carefully considered temporary loss in cash flow—the details are very involved and not really pertinent at this point. What got my attention was the fact that these properties remained in fiscal limbo—and vacant—for too long a period, notwithstanding actual market conditions."

Emilio drained his cup and added, "Yeah, they'd sit vacant for way too long—and then bam!" He snapped his fingers. "Suddenly, there'd be a flurry of activity! Contractors would be brought in and wholesale renovations would commence. Within a few weeks, the property would be listed with a local realty firm and offered for sale."

"That sounds like flipping," Dombrowski remarked. "You know, renovating and selling a house for a quick profit."

"Yeah, except for a couple of things," Emilio cautioned. "Flipping is all about someone—an entrepreneur, for example—acquiring title, then renovating and selling in a hurry, usually in a matter of weeks. The time factor is critical. These homes stayed with Consolidated Federal—no one else acquired title—and they sat vacant for way too long before renovations began. That's not good for a profit margin by any measure."

"There were exceptions, of course" Rachel added. "Some were marketed as-is, with little or no renovation, as short sales."

"Excuse me," Katie interjected, "a 'short sale'?"

The Deputy U.S. Marshal explained. "A short sale is when property is offered for less than the outstanding mortgage debt. The mortgagee—the original borrower—can still be on the hook for the difference if the proceeds don't cover the debt. The bank holding the note has to approve the deal. If it's in a bank's best interest, as a tax write-off for example, it might forgive the difference the debtor is left owing, or not."

"So far," Rachel noted, "none of this is all that unusual in this economy. There are so many foreclosures in some places that vacant houses are commonplace."

"So, what's different about here—our case I mean?" Dombrowski probed.

"A couple of things, but only in a broad sense," Rachel admitted. "It's like when you know something's wrong with this picture, but you can't put your finger on something specific. It's all related to Consolidated Federal and its residential mortgage holdings."

"Yeah, go on," he urged.

"I looked at their current properties as well as those sold in the last few years. Some of these sales, and short sales, piqued my interest. Most of them were foreclosures, all had outstanding HOA liens, and almost all were vacant for a protracted period of time, much longer than normal for the market at the time. And this is important; some remained vacant even after being sold."

"Why is that important?" Dombrowski asked.

"Remember that we're talking about residential property here," Rachel cautioned. "People who buy residential property usually do one of two things; they either live in it, or use it to make money."

"How?" Katie asked, and tried no to fidget. "Sorry, it's just that this is getting confusing."

"I know; bear with me. Basically, to make money, legally that is, they can rent it or resell it—you know, flip it. Letting it sit vacant doesn't make any sense as it doesn't appear to be making any money. Well, there may be a modest increase in equity value, if the market supports it, but that's gonna be minuscule in the short term. The real problem is that there's no cash flow. Unless that house was paid for with cash, somebody's got to pay the monthly mortgage."

"Does that mean there's some sort of fraud going on?" Dombrowski probed. "Is that some sort of flag?"

Rachel leaned back in her chair and shook her head. "Not fraud exactly. You see, there are all kinds of loan fraud; usually they're after the sale proceeds. But I think this is a different scenario; it's much more likely a sophisticated money laundering scheme. I think there may be a *straw man* buyer on some of theses deals."

"What's a *straw man* buyer?" Katie asked, her curiosity fully engaged.

"A fictitious person, someone using an alias—or worse, a stolen identity—who buys the property. Or it could be someone desperate enough to sacrifice their good name and credit rating for some cash. The buyer is paid off with some paltry amount, never moves into the house, and simply disappears. The money launderer makes the loan payments, in the straw man buyer's name, with dirty money. If the monthly mortgage note is paid, the financial institution is possibly none the wiser; and the dirty money used is effectively laundered. As soon as the market warrants, the house is re-appraised at a higher value and offered for sale at a frequently inflated price."

"At that point," Emilio remarked, "they can repeat the process, or opt out and sell the property to an innocent buyer."

"That's pretty slick," Dombrowski observed. "They're making money—or laundering it—at every turn."

Emilio raised a finger in emphasis. "And even better, the financial institution has plausible deniability. After all, if the cash flow is timely and consistent, there's no motivation to look any closer. Remember, mortgages get sold or transferred from one institution to another all the time; and, that's perfectly legitimate."

"So," Katie surmised, "if I'm following all this, a lot of money is changing hands. I mean, I get it with the vacant houses—utilities, landscaping, contractors doing renovations, and so on. The HOA is paying for some of it through an account at this Delaware bank. And this account gets replenished with HOA dues and 'investor funds' from other sources. I get that there's large sums changing hands whenever a mortgage is discounted and transferred or sold. So, I think I understand that you suspect that Consolidated Federal is facilitating and receiving large cash transfers of 'investment funds', mortgage payoffs, and timely loan payments from dubious sources. So, I'm gonna make a deductive leap here and guess that you think this Cayman bank is the source of some, if not most, of this dirty money?"

Rachel smiled. "Let's just say we have our suspicions."

"However," Emilio warned, "we have no proof, at least not yet."

"True," Rachel admitted. "However, it may only take one criminal act, a clear felony, in furtherance of the enterprise to taint the entire process."

"That would make it a conspiracy, under state and federal law, right?" Dombrowski reasoned, grinning.

"It would indeed," Emilio agreed with a smile of his own.

CH 24

THUNDERSTORMS ROLLED in overnight and welcomed the morning with a steady rain. Dombrowski found the sound soothing, but he couldn't drift back to sleep. A vague notion hovered in the back of his mind and refused to be ignored. He surmised it was something he had overlooked, perhaps something important; he was all but certain of it. The thought of sleeping in faded like a forgotten sigh.

He dressed and made his way to the kitchen. Trying not to make too much noise, he brewed a pot of coffee, poured a cup, and settled at the table. The notes and files lay open before him, just as he and Katie had left them last night.

After bidding Rachel and Emilio good-bye yesterday afternoon, he and Katie had immersed themselves in the details of the case. Within a couple of hours, Katie declared a state of hunger and heated up a frozen pizza.

Bolstered by beer and pizza, she and Dombrowski renewed their scrutiny of case notes and rehashed their speculative theories until nearly midnight. By then, the fine print in the files seemed to be swimming on the pages. Mentally exhausted, they'd called it a night. But something had eluded them; they both sensed it.

This morning Dombrowski could no longer ignore that niggling uncertainty. He typically relied on his gut, or *intestinal intuition*, as Katie preferred calling it. And right now, the sense that this was far too important to overlook was growing. Good thing he wasn't one to quit. Grimly determined, he began reorganizing their notes and files, soon losing track of the time.

Almost two hours later, Katie shuffled into the kitchen, drawn to the coffee brewer like a weary moth to a promising flame. "Mmph . . . morning," she mumbled.

Dombrowski glanced up and grinned. He was tempted to comment on her appearance—the tattered jeans, the oversized sweatshirt in some scrambled camouflage pattern, and the ludicrous hot pink bunny slippers—but he quickly assessed her pinched expression and wisely demurred. "Good morning, Katie. Sleep well?"

"Uh-huh, just not enough. What's going on?"

He swept a hand over the table laden with their files and notes. "I've been going over our stuff once more. I think I might've found what's been nagging at me."

"Yeah? Like what?"

He smirked and teased, "Are you sure you're awake enough to focus?"

She scowled and sneered, "Don't even . . . "

He chuckled and reached for the magnifying glass. She gulped down coffee.

"Okay, sorry," he said, and spread three large photographs out before him. "Look, remember these?"

"Uh, yeah, I do." She leaned over his shoulder. "These are the blow-ups of the pics that were found in the memory on Adamson's printer."

"That's right," he acknowledged, peering through the magnifying glass at the time stamps on each photo. "They were taken over the course of several days. Something about these pictures bugs me. Damn, I wish the resolution was better . . . I gotta admit the magnifying glass is a big help."

"You know the resolution's not gonna change just because you had CSI blow up these shots. This may be as good as we're gonna get." She put a finger on the middle photo. "At least we can see the van a little better, but I still can't read any more than the partial sign, 'Pool Cleaning'. Isn't there a name before the word 'Pool'?"

He squinted, but to no avail. "Hell, your eyes are better than mine. There's something there all right, but it's either shadowed or blocked by shrubbery that's out of focus."

"Or," she reasoned, "it's deliberately obscured on the van. Huh, I hadn't thought of that until just now. And look at the pool; it's dirty in all three shots. And the last photo is time-stamped three days later."

Dombrowski glanced up at her. "Yeah, I remember you said that before, back in our office, the first time we saw these in the smaller format."

She straightened and stared at the photographs. She put her coffee down and reached for a stack of papers, copies of contents of HOA foreclosure files. "Give me a minute, D."

She pulled several copies of photographs from those files and spread them out, just above the three enlarged photographs.

"Damn," she breathed. "How did we miss this?"

"Huh? What?"

She pointed to the photographs she'd just spread out. "See these? All these shots from the HOA files are of the fronts of houses. But these three are of the backyard of the same house, right?"

"Yeah," he acknowledged. "We already knew this. So?"

"That's not all that's different—the elevation angle is different. The camera was at street level for all the photos of the fronts of houses, see? But these three pics were shot from a higher vantage point. The camera was in a higher position, looking down into the backyard, see?"

"You're right! Good call, Katie!"

"D, there's more. Look, all three are from the same vantage point. We've seen this view before—this exact view."

"Huh?"

"From Carolyn Silverberg's bedroom window!"

"Oh shit—that's it! I knew there was something about these photos! Adamson took them from her bedroom window."

"Yeah, her bedroom, over the course of several days," she observed. "I think maybe we can now make a reasonable assumption about the two of them."

"Maybe . . . we'll see."

"*We'll see?* Jeez, can you make it sound any more condescending?"

"Huh?" confusion clouded his expression.

"You sound like a parent withholding permission from a child. Damn, I hate being treated like that!"

"Hey, I'm not . . . I mean . . . All I meant was that this is only circumstantial—"

"Fine!" she spat. "Ignore the obvious!"

"It is not wise," he intoned sagely, "for one to leap to conclusions. Have some more coffee—I think you need it."

"Whatever, Confucius."

———

"YOU KNOW," DOMBROWSKI remarked, "this might not be the smartest thing to do, given our circumstances."

Katie spared him a quick glance, returned her eyes to the road, and accelerated to just over the speed limit. The windshield wipers kept an easy cadence with the gentle rain.

"Pfft!" She scoffed. "What do you mean? We're just a coupla friends out for a morning drive. If, out of sheer coincidence, we just happen to drive by and locate this mystery house, where's the harm?"

"You know damn well what I mean! We're suspended! That means we're not supposed to be investigating anything."

She smirked and looked askance at him in the passenger seat. He stared straight ahead through the windshield. "What investigation? Come on, D, we're just driving along here—don't spoil it, okay?"

"Katie, you know I had to say it—we got rules."

"Feel better, now that you got that off your chest?"

He chuckled sheepishly. "Yeah, actually I do. Here's your turn. Hey, the guard shack looks empty."

She let her car slowly drift past the vacant guard post and through the open gate.

"It was empty," she agreed. "Maybe the guy's in the can? They've got one in there, don't they?"

"I guess . . . It's big enough, I suppose."

She drove past rows of large manicured lawns and silent houses. Everything looked a shade darker in the mid-morning rain. The heavy overcast showed no sign of relenting. No one was out or about in the dismal weather.

Dombrowski toggled a map light, slipped his reading glasses on, and consulted a paper map, much to Katie's amusement.

"Jeez, D, where did you find that antique? We've got GPS, you know. What do you need a paper map for?"

"Indulge me, Katie. I happen to like paper maps. They're easier for me to see." He held the map mere inches from his nose.

She smiled and surrendered. "Okay, have it your way. What's my turn?"

"Uh, Crittenden, I think." He squinted more closely. "Streets are alphabetical; Crittenden follows Buchanan."

She peered at a passing street sign. "Okay, this is Buchanan. So, next left?"

"Yeah, then go down a coupla blocks. Silverberg's house was in the 3800 block, third from the end. So, I guess we're looking for a house near the middle of the block."

Katie followed his directions and slowed as they approached a large Mediterranean-style stucco home.

"I think that's it! Yeah . . . Look, the house just past it is for sale. See the sign?" Dombrowski pointed at a home that was evidently vacant, its rather unkempt lawn in need of cutting. "Pull in its driveway. We can act like we're looking at the house that's for sale."

She did as he suggested. They sat there for a few moments and studied the house to their left. A black SUV with heavily tinted windows was parked about midway up the driveway. Another was parked two doors further up the block. Both were unoccupied. There were no other vehicles parked on the street.

"Hey D, look. Can you see those ruts that lead from the driveway through the grass to the street? It looks like another vehicle was parked behind that SUV, near the garage door, blocked in, and someone drove around the SUV to leave."

"Yeah, they must've been in a hurry. They cut some muddy ruts in that grass. We need to get a look in the backyard to be sure that's the right house."

She opened her door and pointed to the front door of the house in whose driveway they were parked. "Come on, let's play real estate agents or prospective buyers and knock here. If we can get in, we can see into the neighboring backyard from the upstairs windows. If we can't get in, we'll just walk around and maybe peek over the backyard fence."

"Katie, you can be quite devious at times. As a supervisor, I suppose that should worry me—but as your partner, not so much. Let's go."

As expected, they got no response at the door. However, the gate to the backyard was unlocked. They proceeded into the rear yard of the sale house as planned. Looking into the neighboring yard was no challenge. Several boards were broken and missing from the privacy fence.

"That's definitely the right place; and that pool is still funky," Katie whispered, as she peered through the fence. "The patio door looks open. Who leaves a sliding glass door open in the rain?"

Dombrowski pointed at the rear of the adjacent garage. "Look, is that another open door?"

"Yeah, and I think I see somebody, on the floor, not moving."

"A body? Are you serious?" He gaped. "You can see a body?"

"I can see something," she insisted, "and it looks like a person, face down on the garage floor."

They stepped away from the fence and faced each other.

"Now what?" she asked. "Doesn't that constitute exigent circumstances?"

Dombrowski winced and pinched the bridge of his nose. "It would," he reasoned, "if we were on the job and not suspended. We need to call this in."

He reached for his phone, but Katie grabbed his arm and firmly squeezed. "No! We can't wait! Someone may be hurt! It might be life or death! We need to check first—then we can call it in, with better facts."

He stared at her, and balked.

I know it's a departmental policy violation. But damn it—she makes a pretty sensible argument.

Her grin was pure mischief. "Hey, let's just knock on the front door of that house and play the real estate buyer bit—you know, asking about this house for sale next door. If everything's okay, then no harm, no foul. How's that sound?"

"You're too damned devious for your own good, young lady," he concluded with a resigned sigh. "Are you armed?"

She scoffed and pointed to the bulge at the small of his back. "Hah! Like you're not—of course I am!"

"Very well . . . Shall we?"

CH 25

KNOCKING AT THE FRONT door was a waste of time. The doorjamb was splintered at the lock. With a knowing glance to his partner, Dombrowski nudged the door and it began to swing open. Pistol in hand, Katie slipped inside and took a position in the shadows to the right. Dombrowski followed to the left.

The foyer was empty, illuminated only by the open door. Without a word, Dombrowski eased the door shut. Katie panned her flashlight around the dim entry hall. Blinds were drawn throughout the first floor, leaving the entire level in colorless shadows. The place stank of stale cigarette smoke. Small piles of crumpled trash and discarded newspapers lay shoved into the corners of the vacant living room. They saw no furniture other than a card table and some folding chairs placed beneath an elaborate chandelier in what was clearly a formal dining room. The irony was almost amusing.

The detectives made their way to the kitchen, where a slight chemical smell hovered in the air, but could hide neither the sour reek of trash nor the coppery tang of spilt blood.

Katie panned her light around. Stacks of old pizza boxes and Chinese take-out cartons covered the counters. In one corner a large black trash bag had tipped over, spilling empty beer cans and stained cardboard coffee cups. Her light found a closed door, from which a trail of crimson spatter led across the wide tiles of the floor to an open door that accessed the garage.

Finger to his lips, Dombrowski pointed to the open door and nodded.

Careful not to disturb the congealing blood, they eased into the garage. There, in the middle of the concrete floor, just as Katie had spied from the yard next door, they found a body lying face down in a large pool of blood.

Katie knelt and let her light scan the corpse. It was a woman, hair tucked under a watch cap, dressed all in black, wearing a shoulder holster. The gun was missing. The detective found no pulse.

Rising, Katie whispered to her partner. "Cold, DOA, bled out. Two entry gunshot wounds that I can see; lower back and right shoulder. There's one exit wound in the back of the left thigh—I'd guess her femoral artery was hit."

"The leg shot likely happened first," he speculated. "She tried to get out of the house, but only made it this far."

Dombrowski shone his light across the floor, near the door to the kitchen. Bits of bright brass winked in reflection. "Spent brass," he said, leaning closer, "9mm . . . I see two casings. Shooter was near that doorway."

Katie nodded in acknowledgement and hissed, "Yeah, and shot her in the back."

She trained her pistol at the open kitchen door. At his nod, she soundlessly took the lead and re-entered to the kitchen.

The blood trail clearly started on the other side of the closed door that likely accessed the basement. Katie took a position to one side and reached for the knob, only to have her partner wave her off and motion for her to follow him.

Near an ascending staircase he breathed in her ear. "Let's clear the second floor before we check the basement. We don't want any surprises from above."

Some of the stairs creaked. There was nothing to be done about it but silently curse and cautiously proceed.

The second floor reeked of the familiar smell of blood.

Their flashlights revealed the bodies. Two were in the hallway, men attired similarly in black, and riddled with bullet wounds. The thick muzzle of a suppressed H&K MP5 submachine gun protruded from beneath the first corpse. The other man lay crumpled against the wall, a suppressed semi-auto pistol in his limp grip, its breech open, magazine spent.

The detectives touched nothing, carefully stepped around the bodies, and moved on.

Inside the doorway to the left, a third man, wearing gray coveralls and rubber boots, lay on his back. A suppressed AK assault carbine lay across his chest, his finger still in the trigger guard. His eyes were open in wide surprise, but the skull above his eyebrows was simply gone. The ceiling in that room, stained with congealing spatter and dripping bits of shredded brain tissue, glistened in the flashlight beams.

At the end of the hall, a stout door sported a padlock and hasp; but it stood slightly ajar. The oversized padlock hung open, dangling from a short chain.

At a nod from her partner, who trained his gun at the door, Katie eased the door slowly open and peered into near total darkness. Her pistol held out before her, she let her flashlight wash across the interior of the small room. She tried a switch on the wall; a bare overhead bulb flared to life. The plywood floor was filthy. The walls were water marked near the ceiling from leaks; strips of torn wallpaper hung in tired curls. The sole piece of furniture was a metal framed bed, complete with heavy leather restraints, the likes of which wouldn't seem out of place in a draconian mental asylum. The thin mattress was musty and stained. The sole window was sealed with a sheet of heavy plywood screwed to the frame. A small empty closet lacked a door.

"Clear," she whispered as she let her flashlight probe beneath the bed. "Whew, smells bad. I think someone was being held in here."

"Yeah. Those are some serious restraints." He cocked his head toward the hall. "Come on, let's clear the basement."

"Right. Lead on."

Standing in the kitchen, before the door they'd deduced led to the basement, Katie wrinkled her nose. "Ah crap—what is that smell? It's kinda chemical, I think."

"It's nothing good," he assured her. "It's probably gonna get worse before it gets better. Watch yourself."

As soon as Katie pulled the door open, a gray blur streaked between hanging strips of heavy clear plastic, past her knees and into the kitchen.

"What the—a cat?" she spat through gritted teeth. "Wait—is that the same cat?"

"What—from the Silverberg scene?" he hissed. "How the hell would I know? I dunno; kinda looks like it."

"Well, I think it is. And what's with all this plastic?" she whispered as she pushed the muzzle of her pistol past the hanging strips and into the darkness beyond.

A sudden whiff of the air in the stairwell washed past them and they both winced.

"Whoa," Dombrowski exclaimed. "That's chemicals, for sure."

She snapped her head back and sputtered, "*Gaak*—the fumes! I think I just answered my own question."

"Shallow breaths," he cautioned. "Is there a light switch?"

She felt along the stairwell wall. "I don't feel one. Maybe it's at the base of the stairs."

"Okay. Go ahead—be careful. If you find a switch, leave it alone. These fumes might be flammable—we don't need a spark."

She descended into the darkness; her partner followed. At the bottom, as she scanned for a light switch with her flashlight, something brushed her ear—she froze.

"Uh, D, I found a light switch pull cord," she whispered in relief, "leaving it alone."

"Good! Careful," he responded. "Watch your step."

More sheets of plastic were suspended from the ceiling at the base of the stairs. As the detectives pushed past them, they were nearly overcome with the strong odors of both chemicals and blood.

"Shit! It's a meth lab!" Dombrowski exclaimed, casting his flashlight beam around the chaos that reigned throughout the basement.

"Glad we didn't try the lights! Crap! This place is wrecked!" Katie blurted.

Broken equipment, overturned tables, and scattered notebooks lay about. Pockmarks of bullet impacts speckled the concrete walls. Spent brass and shards of broken glassware were everywhere.

Katie panned her light behind an overturned table. "D, bodies."

Two men, wearing respirators and clad in gray overalls, lay sprawled by a wall. A pair of suppressed AK carbines lay nearby. Each man sported a bloody bullet hole in his forehead like a third eye.

Katie nudged the two carbines with her foot out of the men's reach. She then checked the neck of each for a pulse, slowly looked up, and shook her head.

Dombrowski shrugged. "Both DOA, huh? And both with single head shots . . . Hold on," he cautioned as he pried one man's hand open. "This guy's got something . . . Damn Katie, isn't this yours?"

She blanched as he handed her one of her business cards. She held it up to her light and flipped it over; a set of phone numbers was scrawled across the back.

"Damn, my own handwriting . . . This is the card I gave Consuela!"

"Your CI?"

"Yes! These guys—whoever they are—know about her! Maybe that's why I haven't heard from her! We've got to go check on her!"

Dombrowski was about to tell her to calm down when they heard a low groan from across the dishevelled room.

Behind a toppled metal cabinet, lay a wounded man, attired in all black. He was barely conscious, suffering from several gunshot wounds. He tried to raise the muzzle of his suppressed .45 semi-auto pistol, but apparently he didn't have the strength. His arm faltered and he passed out.

Dombrowski disarmed him and studied his bloodstained face.

Katie knelt, pressing a finger to the side of his throat. "He's alive but his pulse is weak. Who are these guys?"

Dombrowski fumbled for his phone. "Good question. I gotta call this in. He needs an ambulance; and this is clearly a crime scene."

"D, we're suspended, remember? How are we gonna handle this?"

He stared at her as he spoke to the dispatcher. "Yeah, Dombrowski here, I need a *bus* at my location for a shooting victim . . . Yeah, that's it . . . Gonna need homicide and CSI to respond as well. There are six more *unconscious persons* on the scene . . . No, just one ambulance, the rest can go in coroner vans. I'll remain on site to keep it secure . . . Okay, thanks."

Katie stood with her hands on her hips. "What are you doing? You didn't even give the address! And you didn't even mention me."

"No, I didn't," he admitted. "As for the address, the dispatcher had a GPS lock on my departmental phone as soon as I called her." He held it in his flashlight beam for her to see. "She just read the street address to me."

"Oh, yeah, I'd forgot about that."

"Now as for you, think about it. No one needs to know you're here, at least not right now. You just said you've got to go check on your CI. I'll stay, watch our friend here, and maintain the scene."

"But we still don't know what the hell happened here, or who these people are, or anything!"

"Maybe, but I think I might know what's what. Look, we've got two groups in a house with a meth lab. One group is wearing gray coveralls and using respirators; they're the meth cooks, I'd bet. The other group is dressed like ninjas—and there's been a shootout. Clearly, these two groups are not friends. Everybody seems to be carrying suppressed weapons; that makes me think pros all around. And finally, take a good look at our survivor here. Recognize him?"

She peered closer. "Shit! That's Rene Pasqualle!"

"Right you are! And why would he and his ninja team hit a meth lab?"

"Our intel said he'd be looking for his niece, Amanda Farrell . . . Oh crap! The locked bedroom upstairs—she was being held here!"

He smiled, but it was far more feral than amused. "Yeah, that's my take on this situation. And if we're right, I'd love to know how Rene found her; although it doesn't look like he was successful in his rescue attempt."

"So, you think," she surmised, "that he and his team got in a firefight trying to rescue Amanda?"

"Pretty much," he conceded. "All we can deduce is that it didn't work. Maybe they underestimated their opposition, who knows? If she was being held here, she's certainly gone now."

"Oh, crap—the tire ruts out front!"

"Yeah, somebody left in a big hurry," he agreed. "I wouldn't be surprised if those SUVs out there belong to Rene and his ninja team. They're probably rentals, though."

"Yeah, that makes sense. Hold on! Did you hear that—like a *meow*? I'm gonna see if I can find that cat."

"Katie, forget the cat for now. You gotta go!"

"But, not yet," she argued. "See, if that's the same damn cat, like I think, then we've got one more link to Carolyn Silverberg, whose house is right behind this one."

"But, Katie—" he began, his eyes rolling.

"But nothing!" she spat. "Don't forget what was found in the dead woman's mouth—Amanda Farrell's ID!"

"True, but hold on a minute and think," he cautioned. "The cat will keep. We found your card here—the one you gave your CI—that's important. The only real lead we may have right now is your CI. You gotta find out what happened to her. She may have come to some harm, or have some info that helps us pull this all together."

She thrust her lip forward and furrowed her brow. "Yeah, but I just don't feel right about leaving you here with this mess. You're gonna get jammed up because we're still on suspension."

"So will you if you're still here when the cavalry arrives," he reminded her. "And if we're both jammed up, who's gonna check on your CI? Look, don't sweat the small stuff—I can deal with this. You need to go—now."

Clearly frustrated, she acquiesced. "Okay-okay, I'm going; but I don't like this one bit! Keep your burner phone on; I'll call when I know something."

CH 26

THE RAIN, REDUCED TO an ethereal mist, had all but stopped. However, the humidity was cloying. Katie silently cursed as the eyepiece lenses of her binoculars fogged up once again. Wiping them with a passably dry shirttail she hunkered down and peered through the foliage.

The stand of trees and thick brush she'd chosen as a surveillance post offered a fairly good view of the driveway approach and the front of Walter Farrell's house. Her own car was hidden in the trees some fifty yards down the road. She'd been watching the house for almost an hour, hoping to catch a glimpse of her CI, Consuela.

Repeated calls to the maid's cell phone had gone to voicemail. Katie had initially considered simply knocking on the door, but quickly dismissed that idea as unwise. She was on suspension and had no reasonable justification to be here. There was already going to be hell to pay for the scene she and her partner had found. Besides, if all was well here, she ran the risk of blowing her CI's cover.

Movement at the driveway entrance snagged her attention. She focused her binoculars on the car turning in, a late model limousine. It was sleek and black, and somehow sinister in the mist. Gliding to a stop at the front of the mansion, the limo sat idling.

She couldn't make out the tag number; her lenses were fogging again. She got them wiped off and focused just as the front door to the house opened and a woman appeared—Consuela!

The limo driver got out, popped open an umbrella, and went to open the right rear passenger door. A man of medium height and sporting a shock of thick grey hair exited the vehicle and ducked under the offered umbrella. The two men made their way up the front steps and into the house.

Consuela scanned the front yard and closed the door.

Katie felt an enormous sense of relief; her CI was all right. But who was that visitor? She hadn't gotten a very good look at him. Nonetheless, he evoked a somewhat vague sense of familiarity. Was it someone she knew, or should have recognized?

Another car entered the driveway and made its way slowly toward the house. Squinting through the field glasses, Katie was surprised to recognize it as an unmarked police cruiser. She couldn't read this tag either. Could it be from her department? And if so, who was in it? Try as she might, she couldn't get a clear view of the driver. All she could tell was that he appeared to be alone. That didn't seem right; in her experience detectives usually worked in pairs—as partners.

So, who the hell is this?

As the unmarked cruiser parked, the rain began anew.

The door to the house swung open once again; the pale face of a woman peered out at the new arrival.

Consuela?

A man in a dark raincoat, shoulders hunched forward and holding a newspaper over his head, ran up the steps and disappeared into the house.

Katie scowled; she'd missed him exiting the cruiser.

Damn! I should've been looking at him instead of her! So I still don't know who that was. Now what?

Angry with herself for such a simple mistake, she chewed her lip and forced herself to calm down.

On one hand, she had discovered what she set out to learn, that her CI, Consuela, had not been harmed. Of course, that didn't mean the maid was out of danger. Somebody, the wrong people, had somehow gotten hold of that damned business card of hers. So, the bad guys now knew that Consuela had talked with a detective and had the police contact numbers. Not good; it was only a matter of time before the maid would be fingered as a *snitch*.

Now I wanna know who was driving that cruiser—and what's going on in that house. Maybe I can get closer, snoop around; this rain might be good cover.

Armed with a plan, however risky, she felt better, committed. She needed to tell Dombrowski about Consuela. She tried to call her partner on her burner phone but was met with a low battery icon. No problem; she had the 12v charger in her car. She rose and headed back toward her hidden vehicle.

She broke through the thick underbrush further away from her car than she remembered, and had to follow a winding path that led around a dense copse of cedars.

She broached the bend and saw her car, and another vehicle parked behind it, a white van bearing an obscured commercial sign; *something Pool Cleaning!*

Before she could react, she was snatched off her feet from behind and held suspended a foot off the ground. Her arms were effectively pinned to her sides. A hand clamped a damp cloth across her face. She kicked and squirmed, but was held fast in a vise-like grip.

Realization dawned—a chemical smell! She tried to hold her breath. It was no use. She felt her diaphragm convulse; air rushed into her lungs. Her awareness dwindled into a single point of dim light, and all was blackness.

———————

DOMBROWSKI, EVER STOIC, stood before Lt. Waters' desk. He glanced from his boss to the IA investigator, State Police Lt. Madison, seated in a side chair. Neither man would look at him. The silence stretched uncomfortably. Dombrowski knew he was playing a dangerous game here, but he had little choice.

Lt. Waters sighed resignedly and broke the silence. "Sergeant, I don't know what to make of all this, much less how the captain is going to react. You know damn well you're on suspension. Your statement is decidedly ... terse."

"Yes, sir," Dombrowski acknowledged, "my statement reflects the facts."

"And you know nothing about the security guard found bound and drugged in the guard shack at the entry to the gated community?"

"No, sir."

"You report does not mention your partner, Detective Callahan. Am I to understand she wasn't there? No! Don't answer that! I get the sense that I don't want to know—at least not right now."

The big sergeant smiled. He'd had a hunch the LT would get it, read between the lines, but it was still a risk. True, while under suspension they had stumbled onto a multiple homicide scene, but a life had been saved. Rene Pasqualle was hospitalized. His condition had been upgraded from critical to serious. It appeared that he was going to make it. Of course, he'd be going into custody, as soon as it was medically advisable, to face a host of serious charges, state and federal. It would take time to sort it all out; the meth lab, the homicides, who did what, to whom, and when.

However, possession of fully automatic firearms and suppressors without the appropriate tax stamps were clearly federal offenses. The federal authorities were downright ecstatic with this turn of events. Of course, it wouldn't do to have the investigator who broke such a major case in trouble with his own department.

Dombrowski knew that Lt. Waters knew this; and, he knew that the lieutenant would know that he knew it. He had to stifle a smile; he'd played this one well—despite conspicuous omissions like how he got to the scene. Waters was no fool; he'd know better than to ask, and he'd surely sense that this investigative gambit was still playing out.

After all, the LT likes to remind us that sometimes a little plausible deniability is a good thing. On the other hand, how the captain might react is a real gamble. But then again, Capt. Walker is among the most politically aware and sensitive of the brass.

Turning to the state police investigator, Lt. Waters asked, "Lt. Madison, what's your take on this?"

Madison shook his head and opened his palms. "To be honest, I don't see how any of this has a specific bearing on my investigation. I see no direct connection to the matters I was asked to examine in the Melanie Dubois case. Nothing I've become aware of today would cause me to modify my findings. As far as I'm concerned, my investigation is complete and closed. I filed my final IA report and recommendation this morning. I understand it's now on Captain Walker's desk."

Waters nodded. "That's my understanding as well. Unfortunately, Capt. Walker isn't available. I'm advised he had a meeting. He has yet to review your findings and make his own recommendation up the chain of command."

"Ah, I see," Madison conceded, and started to speak, but demurred.

Waters noticed, and glanced at Dombrowski. "Sergeant, would you excuse us? You can wait in the squad room."

"Yes sir." Dombrowski closed the door behind him, but stayed close enough to hear their muted voices.

———

"SO," WATERS PROBED, "what did you want to ask?"

"I don't want to run afoul of your policies and procedures, of course. But I was wondering; can't you informally advise Dombrowski and Callahan of my findings? Sort of take the pressure off? From what I've learned, they're both good cops and stringing this out any longer than absolutely necessary isn't good for anybody. You know how stressful it can be."

"I do, believe me. But I can't divulge what I'm not supposed to know—not until the captain tells me, and I officially learn their fate. I don't have the authority to change their status. They're still suspended."

Lt. Madison stood and thrust out his hand. "I'm sorry to hear that. Well, I've got to return to my office. Please give the captain my regards, and let him know I'll make myself available if he has any questions."

"Thank you, Lieutenant. I sincerely appreciate all you've done. As soon as they return to full duty, I'll let you know."

"Thanks, I'd like that. Have a good one."

"You too. Come on, I'll walk you out. That way I can catch a smoke in the lot."

———————

UPON HIS RETURN, WATERS saw Dombrowski lounging at a nearby desk, and said, "Sergeant, my office."

Poker-faced, Dombrowski rose and followed the lieutenant into his office. Waters shut the door.

Standing once again before Lt. Waters' desk, Dombrowski kept a straight face. "Yes sir?"

Waters fought a smile but only barely succeeded. "Let's both pretend you weren't eavesdropping, shall we?"

Dombrowski feigned shock. "Why, never, sir—perish the very thought!"

"Enough already! You know the suspension is still in effect; so, don't do anything more to screw up now, okay?"

"No worries, LT."

"Now go! Don't you have something to share with your partner? Where is she, by the way?"

"Ah, actually I really don't know. But I'm sure I can find her."

"Okay," Waters acknowledged. "Just see that you both stay out of any further trouble, understand?"

"Yes sir, of course, sir."

CH 27

KATIE'S HEAD THROBBED; her mouth was so dry that her tongue stuck to her palate. Breathing was difficult; and the air tasted stale. She lay on her side, her hands and feet immobilized. Her covered face pressed against a flat surface that vibrated with the thrum of tires on pavement.

Damn! I'm restrained, and in a moving vehicle—that van? I don't feel the weight of my gun, or my burner phone. Hell, they're both gone! Wait—my departmental phone? No, damn it; that's in my car. What the hell happened? Who was it that grabbed me? More than one, I'm sure. And what was that stuff? Shit! I don't remember anything after that strong chemical smell. Oh man, I feel like crap.

Opening her eyes to mere slits, she could see almost nothing but the rough weave of burlap—some sort of bag that covered her head and felt cinched at her throat.

She tried to test her bonds, but to no avail; she'd been secured by someone who knew what they were doing.

I'm tied with what? It's wide, feels like duct tape. Damn! Maybe I'd be better off playing unconscious for a while. I can't seem to do anything else at the moment. Somebody's driving—is he alone? How many am I dealing with?

An unfamiliar ring tone was answered by a gruff voice. "Yeah?"

"*Quien es?* Who is it?" another voice asked.

"*El Jefe*—now shut up!"

Katie stayed still. Now she knew there were at least two of them.

"No, she's still out . . . No, she's not hurt . . . Well, first we were gonna . . . What? Are you serious? Okay, okay—I'm listening . . . No, no problem, I know where that is . . . Yeah, she should come to anytime now, within the

236

hour for sure. No, no—I understand. We'll deliver . . . Yeah, we'll be there in about twenty minutes."

"So? *Que paso?* What was all that about?"

"*Quien sabe?* Who knows? All I know is we're not supposed to hurt her and we gotta take her to the site of the new lab, *pronto! El Jefe* said they gonna 'recover their investment'—*sabes* , you know, since they lost that other lab."

"So we don' get to have our fun first? Give her some more *sleepy-bye-bye*?"

"No, we can't—not now, anyway. They got some use for her, and they want her conscious. We gotta take her there right away."

Katie couldn't hear the mumbled response, but the tone of disappointment was clear, as was the ominous promise in the chuckle that followed.

———————

DOMBROWSKI SAT IN HIS truck, parked in front of the VA Home, growing grumpier by the minute. He couldn't find his partner. He tried calling her home and both cell phones with no luck. He stared at his own two cell phones, the agency issue and the burner, like they had betrayed him.

Stopping by the VA Home in the off chance Katie had gone to visit her father had been his last resort. There were signs in some of the wings that prohibited cell phone use, so he figured it was worth a shot. But that hadn't panned out; she hadn't been here either.

Her dad seemed to be doing well, but hadn't seen her in almost a week. Dombrowski had downplayed it, not wanting to upset her father. But this was one of her dad's more lucid days. The old man was no dummy; he knew something was wrong.

"Don't waste time with me, Donald. Go find her," he commanded. "And when you do, tell her a personal visit will put me at ease—a phone call won't do. Understand?"

Dombrowski could only grin at the retired state police captain; there was still plenty of steel in the old man.

"Yes sir. I'll tell her."

Now, staring at his departmental smart phone in the cab of his truck, Dombrowski was thinking rather unkind things about a phone called *smart*.

Inspiration struck; he quickly made a call.

"Hey, Ken! It's Dombrowski . . . How you doin'? Good, good . . . Listen, I've got something to run by you, kinda on Katie's behalf . . . Yeah, can you meet me in the CID parking lot? No, but I'll be there in about fifteen minutes . . . Okay, great! See you there!"

———————

TAP, TAP, TAP . . . tap, tap, tap . . .

This persistent tapping was getting more insistent and beginning to annoy Katie. She wanted to go back into her dream, but the damn noise wouldn't stop. Now there were muffled voices, too . . . *What the hell?*

"Come on, Katie! Wake up! Open the door!"

She opened her eyes to find herself sprawled across the back seat of her car. Three anxious faces peered through the windows; Dombrowski, Kenny Reynolds, and Emilio Gonzalez.

She tried to sit up, but her stomach lurched and her head began to throb. She took a few deep breaths and eased into a sitting position. She managed to unlock the door and collapsed against the seat-back with a groan.

Dombrowski had the door open in an instant. He grasped her by the shoulders and quickly looked her over. "Are you all right? Are you hurt? I don't see anything. What's going on? What happened to you?"

"I . . . think I was drugged . . . or maybe chloroform . . . Where's the . . . the van?"

"What van?"

Squinting, she scanned the area. It was no longer raining, but the sky was still gray. Her car was still parked where she'd left it, just inside the tree line. There was no sign of the white van. She felt for her gun and burner phone—both were gone.

"What time is it?" she asked, feeling a little better.

"Almost six," her partner answered. "You've been out of touch for hours."

Some of the events of the day came tumbling back like jumbled puzzle pieces. She grabbed his sleeve in urgency. "D, listen . . . I gotta—"

He interrupted with a wave and shook his head. "You gotta try to stand and move around—get your sea legs back. Come on, get out of the car and get some fresh air."

As Dombrowski helped her out of the vehicle, she saw him nod to Ken, who produced an electronic meter and started scanning the interior of her car.

With Emilio and her partner on either side, Katie took a few halting steps. She paused to take several deep breaths, and turned to Dombrowski. "How did . . . how did you find me?"

Emilio pointed off to their left and whispered, "Let's get further away from the car, shall we?"

At what he considered a safe distance, Dombrowski explained. "The short answer is that we found you through your department issued cell phone. I couldn't find you anywhere, so I called Ken to see if he could locate your phone. You know it's got GPS, right?"

"But," she objected, "I had it turned off, didn't I?"

"Yeah, you did. So, Ken suggested I contact Emilio. It seems his people have the ability to locate a phone that's not on. They can turn it on if they want to, as well. Yours was in your glove box—piece of cake."

"Of course," Emilio cautioned, "that sort of information is not for public consumption. It typically takes a court order. This was simply a routine training exercise, you understand?"

She nodded, and remembered her missing burner phone and weapon. "So, is it safe to talk now?"

"It is now," announced Kenny, as he walked up and displayed something small in his open palm. "I've deactivated it—switched it off actually."

Dombrowski pointed and said, "Ken found one in my truck, too, and removed it. Both are bugs with GPS capability, fair quality but of dubious Asian manufacture. Emilio had his people confirm that no law enforcement agencies in this country use them since they don't meet U.S. mil-spec standards and subsequently have admissibility problems in court."

"Then who—" she started to ask.

"Dunno. What we do know is that it wasn't Madison or his people. By the way, our IA investigation concluded two days ago. We're gonna be cleared; all that's left is the administrative red tape."

"Well, that's good to know," she acknowledged with relief. "So Ken, how long has that bug been in my car?"

He shrugged and stared at the device. "There's no telling. It runs on a watch battery, so it could have been under your dash for a few hours or weeks. However, I think this is a relatively fresh battery. This device also has a micro switch to turn it off and on. I turned it off. Range can be an issue, but I don't have that worked out yet. There might be a booster or repeater; I'll have to look into that."

"Oh, okay, I guess," she responded, feeling more vulnerable than ever.

The CSI tech produced a thick brown envelope. "This was crammed under the front seat. Is it yours?"

She broke the envelope's seal and carefully dumped the contents onto her open palm; a digital flash drive, a small white box, and a folded piece of paper. "No, someone put this there."

"So," Dombrowski queried, "What's in the box?"

She opened the box and gasped; a severed human finger lay inside. Her companions were clearly stunned as well.

"The note—what's the note say?" Emilio asked softly.

Katie peered at the precise printing and read aloud. "Five million into the numbered account in twenty-four hours or she will lose one more for each day of delay."

"What?" Ken exclaimed. "Who is *she?*"

Katie stared into the trees without focusing. For just that moment she seemed unable to breathe. The harsh echo of redundant commands, coerced memories, surfaced. "I remember now . . . *She* is Amanda Farrell. I'm supposed to take this envelope to her step-father, Pierre Demotte."

"Whoa, Katie," Dombrowski probed, "what the hell happened to you?"

"Look, this will take a little time . . . I was a little fuzzy before, but more is coming back to me now."

"Katie, I will make the time, don't worry. Come on now; let's go have a seat in my truck."

Emilio tugged at Dombrowski's sleeve. "One moment, Sergeant—if you don't need me any further, I've got somewhere to be. But I would advise caution in regard to this Amanda Farrell kidnapping and ransom demand."

Dombrowski paused, his attention on the Deputy U.S. Marshal. "What do you mean?"

"If you haven't already notified the FBI, I strongly suggest you do so, sooner rather than later. Call our friend, Fred; he is actually quite good at this sort of thing. And now that we know Rene Pasqualle and Pierre Demotte are directly involved, the federal agencies with a vested interest would not take kindly to being out of the loop—especially now that a ransom demand has been made."

"I understand, Emilio, but that's a call my boss is going to have to make. After all, I'm still officially on suspension. But don't worry; I'll have a conversation with my lieutenant before we take any action."

"Good idea. Best of luck, big guy."

As Emilio headed for his car, Ken approached Dombrowski and Katie. "Sarge, what you want me to do with the bug we found in her car? You want me to dissect it like the one we found in your truck?"

Dombrowski paused. "You just turned it off, right? It would still work?"

"Sure, it'll work if turned back on. Why?"

"Would anyone monitoring it know you turned it off?"

Kenny scratched his head and shrugged. "Possibly, but these bugs aren't the best quality, you know? So, it might seem more like it was an intermittent break in the transmission, much like a sporadic signal loss due to vehicle movement or environmental factors like bridges, tunnels, or even pine trees. When the vehicle's being driven, lots of things can interfere with the signal. For example—"

"Uh, that's okay," Dombrowski interrupted, "Katie, wait for me in my truck, okay? Can you make it there on your own?"

"Yeah . . . I'm fine, really."

"Ken, listen, I've got an idea. First, I want you to show me how to work the micro switch. Then I want you to show me where you found it. You're gonna put the bug back exactly where you found it—but leave it turned off."

"No problem. Come on, this'll only take a minute."

A FEW MINUTES LATER, Dombrowski straightened up from a crouch and leaned on the car's fender. "You were right, Ken; that was pretty easy."

The CSI tech grinned. "Told you. Hey, Sarge, let me ask you; is Katie gonna be all right? Should I stick around?"

"Nah, I don't think so; you can go, Ken. See, I'm not sure how all of this is gonna work out, so it'd probably be best for everyone to keep their involvement to a minimum at this point. But listen, man, thanks a heap. As for Katie, I'm sure she'll be okay to drive in a bit. I'll follow her just to be safe."

"Okay, Sarge. Call if you need me. See you later."

KATIE WAS SITTING IN his truck, a grim expression on her face. He climbed in and made himself comfortable.

"I tried to tell you before," she said, "my burner phone and my gun are missing."

"Ah, I see. Why don't you start at the beginning?"

"All right, but then you're gonna explain what's going on with you—I mean from the time I left you with Rene, okay?"

"Sure thing," he agreed and pointed to her, "you first."

"This all started," she began, "when I decided to come out here to check on my CI, Consuela."

AN HOUR LATER, DOMBROWSKI sat in his truck a block up the street from the Preston Arms Hotel, where Pierre and Nicole Demotte were still registered. This was a good vantage point; he could easily see the hotel entrance as well as Katie's car parked across the street.

She'd been inside for less than five minutes when she appeared at the entrance, stuffed her hands deep into her pockets, looked up and down the street, and proceeded to her car.

Those two overt gestures were the agreed upon signal—the Demottes were not currently in the hotel. Now, she would drive to her home, the reactivated bug broadcasting her movements.

———————

AS PLANNED, SHE PARKED in her driveway and entered her home. Five minutes later, she left through the back door, a mere shadow in the dusk, slipped through the backyard hedge, and joined Dombrowski in his idling truck parked on the adjacent block.

"See anyone?" he asked, as he pulled away from the curb and eased down the street.

She shook her head, and turned to scan the block they were leaving. "Other than you, not a soul, not on the way home or in the neighborhood. Hell, I wouldn't recognize those goons anyway; they kept that damned hood over my head the whole time. But I get your point—if they've got active surveillance, they're pretty good."

"Let's hope not—on both counts."

"What now?"

"Scoot down so you're not seen. We've got a stop to make. You got the package?"

She scoffed. "Pfft! What do you think? Of course I do! I got my other pistol, too. I want my other damn gun back!"

"Don't forget your burner phone," he teased.

She scowled and mumbled, "I haven't . . . *bastards!*"

About twenty minutes later, he brought his truck to a stop in a parking lot and scanned the surrounding area. "We're here. It looks okay. You can sit up now."

"What—the VA Home? I told you I'd call him! We don't have time for this now! Amanda—"

"Yes, we do," he retorted. "I promised your dad you'd visit—he wasn't about to settle for a phone call. I told you that! Now go in there, spend a few minutes with him, and put him at ease. I've got some calls to make before we make our next move anyway. So go. I'll wait here for you."

Resigned, she scowled.

Damn him! He's doing it again! He knows I hated being manipulated. But, honestly, is that really what's happening here? Arrgh! The big dummy means well; so, to hell with it! It wouldn't hurt to spend five minutes with my father. We don't know where the Demottes are right now anyway. Damn it—sometimes it galls me when he's right.

In her best mock-Arnold voice she uttered her parting shot. "I'll be back."

The street lights winked on. She slipped through the parking lot, instinctively seeking the shadows, and entered the building unseen.

CH 28

KATIE POURED MORE COFFEE into her cup and glanced over her shoulder at her partner and Lt. Waters.

Seated on the worn plastic couch in the staff lounge of the Medical Examiner's Office, the two men stared blankly at the TV near the coffee bar. The Weather Channel played on, the sound perpetually muted.

"Anyone want a refill? I'm pouring," she asked.

"Nah, I'm good, thanks anyway," Dombrowski uttered as he stretched his legs out.

"No thank you," Waters echoed. "I shouldn't be drinking coffee this late as it is. I'll have a hard time getting to sleep tonight."

"It's almost nine, LT," Dombrowski observed. "Aren't you off tomorrow? Can't you sleep in?"

Waters gave the big sergeant a sour look and scoffed. "Hah! Like I'm not gonna be in this cluster up to my eyebrows! This situation is getting out of hand. I really need the captain to put you both back on the clock—the sooner the better!"

"Still no word from him?" Katie probed.

"Not yet—no answer at his home, and calls to his cell keep going to voicemail." The lieutenant shrugged. "I just don't get it."

Katie and her partner shared a look of resignation, but kept silent. There was nothing they could do about their current suspended status. They weren't even supposed to know that the IA investigation had cleared them of any wrongdoing, at least not yet.

Even asking Lt. Waters to meet them off-the-record here, this late, at the M.E.'s office had been a bit of a calculated risk, perhaps moreso for him than them. However, they had to trust someone—someone within the department.

Waters fidgeted and absently patted the pack of cigarettes in his pocket. Clearly the caffeine was getting to him. "How much longer is the Doc gonna be? Do you think he'd mind if I smoked in here?"

"He would most certainly mind very much!" declared Dr. Parker, the Medical Examiner, as he entered the lounge. "So, don't even think about it."

"As you wish, Doc," Waters surrendered with a sigh. "What can you tell us?"

"One moment, if you don't mind." He paused to pour himself some coffee and sipped carefully from the brimming cup. Taking a seat in the chair to Waters' left, he handed the lieutenant a set of enlarged photographs.

"These depict the severed finger your detectives brought me. It is definitely human, a portion of the small, or pinkie, finger from the left hand of a small-boned person. It's only two bones of the finger; the distal and middle phalanges. The amputation was done at the joint of the middle and proximal phalanges—right here." He held up his hand to indicate the second joint of his little finger. "I can tell you that the original owner of the severed digit was alive at the time of amputation."

"How quickly can we identify the, uh, owner?" Dombrowski asked.

"It depends," the M.E. acknowledged. "The fingerprint is intact; and, we certainly have sufficient tissue to ascertain a DNA profile."

"Assuming, of course," Waters cautioned, "that the print is on file somewhere, or we have a known DNA sample for comparison. Right, Doctor?"

"Quite so, I'm afraid."

"Doc, lemme ask, could that finger," Katie inquired, "be reattached? Like if we found the owner?"

Dr. Parker took a long sip of coffee and pursed his lips. "I suppose it is possible. The amputation was done with some skill; and, it appears to be only a few hours old. There is a time factor involved; typically a maximum of twelve hours, assuming the severed appendage is kept at a reduced temperature—but not frozen. Nonetheless, the patient in this case would have to be located very quickly, I'm sure. Please understand that my explanation is somewhat generic. This isn't my area of expertise; a hand surgeon should be consulted."

"What do you mean that the amputation was done with some skill—how skilled?" Dombrowski pressed.

The M.E. shrugged. "It's somewhat delicate work with a scalpel. So, something beyond basic emergency medical training, I suppose. In my opinion, the level of skill demonstrated suggests that someone was careful and deliberate in an effort to do no further harm. I would speculate that your victim has more value alive than otherwise to the kidnapper, at least at this time."

"We've got to find this girl—right away!" Katie declared. "If there's a chance she can get her finger reattached—"

"Hold on, Detective," Dr. Parker interrupted. "At this point, I cannot definitively determine the gender of the patient. Absent a fingerprint ID, confirmation via DNA analysis will take some time."

"Maybe," Dombrowski acknowledged, "but if we find a teenager whose little finger has been lopped off, it might be a safe bet that's who we're looking for, right, Doc?"

"I wouldn't argue with you, Sergeant. But, since the finger itself is evidence, I'm afraid you'll have to make do with these photographs in your investigation. I'm keeping the severed digit in an appropriate manner in the event you do locate the patient and it can be reattached."

"That's good, Doc," Waters assured them all, "because we're going to do everything we can."

The door to the lounge swung open.

"Sorry I'm a little late," CSI tech Kenny Reynolds announced. "I went by the office to pick up this laptop and a latent print kit. Where do you need me, Sarge?"

"Right here, sit down."

Lt. Waters sent Dombrowski a quizzical glance.

"I called him, LT. I figured we'd want to check everything for prints, and copy what's on that flash drive before Katie gives it to Pierre Demotte. I should've thought of that before she went to the hotel, but lucky for us, neither he, nor his wife, was there."

"I can scan the ransom note, too," Reynolds happily added, holding up a wireless scanning wand.

"I see. So, Sergeant, we're planning to deliver the original note and the flash drive to Demotte?"

"Yeah, LT, I think so. That'll make Katie look more like she's complying with the kidnappers' instructions. She'll be safer if they believe her to be under their control."

"Perhaps," Waters countered, "but have you considered the wisdom of letting such important items of evidence out of our hands?"

"I have, but my partner's safety is more important at this point."

"I don't disagree, Sergeant. However I have another concern; why are the kidnappers demanding ransom from Demotte, and not the victim's father, Walter Farrell?"

"Good question, LT. We think we've got this figured out. Farrell reports his daughter missing, and then changes his mind. In the meantime, we find Amanda Farrell's ID at a homicide scene—"

"Yeah," Katie interrupted, "in the mouth of the corpse, Carolyn Silverberg, no less, whose home *is* that particular homicide scene, and is located right behind the vacant house with the meth lab."

"Right," Dombrowski confirmed. "And we know, through our CI, that Amanda—now a person of interest in the Silverberg case—still hasn't been seen since before her father reported her missing. So, where is she? Nobody is talking. Her mother, Nicole, and her new husband, Pierre Demotte, a man of considerable wealth and means, show up—and it's clear that they believe Amanda is missing—"

"And," Katie finished, "that her father, Walter Farrell, knows more than he's telling."

"So, Pierre Demotte plays his trump card," Dombrowski explained, "and calls in his brother, Rene Pasqualle, a man of interesting skills and connections, and tasks him to find his wife's missing daughter."

"You gotta remember, LT," Katie interjected, "that until recently nobody suggested that Amanda had been kidnapped—only missing."

"Come to think of it," Waters mused aloud, "that's true. She was only considered a missing person."

"But now," she announced, "we think her father knew otherwise, and had his own reasons for withholding the information."

"Think about it, LT," Dombrowski urged. "Without a complainant or any evidence, there was no reason to think of this as a kidnapping. As far as we know, there was no ransom demand at all until after Rene Pasqualle and his crew hit that house looking for Amanda. And by the way, we don't think they even knew there was a meth lab in the basement."

"But, we think they were right," Katie added, "about Amanda being held there, probably in that locked room on the second floor. Somebody moved her out in a hurry, most likely just after the gunfight."

Waters leaned forward and stroked his chin. "That makes sense. CSI hasn't finished fully processing that scene; the meth lab made everything that much more difficult. I suppose they might find some trace evidence of the occupant of that locked room, perhaps some usable DNA."

"Yeah," Katie said, "and don't forget the finger—it might match. We think it will."

Dombrowski opened his palms. "Look, here's the clincher; when Katie was snatched, she was blindfolded, but she came to while the perps were talking and she overheard . . . Well, tell him, Katie."

"It wasn't that much, part of a phone conversation mostly. They were gonna use me to carry the ransom demand to recover the investment since they lost the lab. I played possum while they took me someplace where they were setting up a new lab—maybe a twenty minute drive.

"Once there, they slapped me around until they were sure I was awake, and told me to deliver the ransom demand and a package to Pierre Demotte. Then I was overcome by a strong chemical smell—Doc, here, says it was chloroform. The next thing I know, I wake up in the backseat of my car with my partner tapping on the window."

"I said it was most likely chloroform, Detective," Dr. Parker corrected. "Absent analysis of a timely blood sample, I can't be certain. I still think you should be examined by your primary care physician."

"How are you feeling now?" Waters asked.

"I'm fine, okay," she insisted. "I was kinda foggy for a little while, but I'm clearheaded now."

Dr. Parker scoffed. "Hmmph, you police officers always think you're invincible; you rarely take any medical advice. Well, so be it. I have some paperwork to finish in my office, so I can finally go home. And on that note, I'll leave you all to it."

As the M.E. left the lounge, Dombrowski leaned closer, and spoke in a low voice. "Listen, LT, we've developed a working hypothesis, and it fits what we know so far."

"Yeah, really? Okay, let's hear it."

"We think Rene, who's infamous in certain circles, was recognized by someone who survived the raid. Maybe the guard at the entry gate—he wasn't killed, just drugged and tied up. He's not talking; but we think he was a lookout for the lab operation and Rene's team neutralized him. Or, maybe it was one of the cooks in the lab—somebody probably recognized Rene.

"If so, that, and the fact that there were so many suppressed weapons, suggest a well established and sophisticated drug operation backed with professional muscle.

"That lab could produce a lot of meth—big money. Its loss hurts the operation. So, they change tactics, move on to kidnapping, and demand a ransom, equivalent to their loss to recover their investment, from the player behind the raid—him with the deepest pockets, Rene's brother, Pierre Demotte."

"Compared to Demotte, Farrell is chump change," Katie observed. "This all makes sense only if they were already holding their bargaining chip, Amanda Farrell. Now that begs the question, why would they be holding her in the first place? Remember, no earlier ransom demand. So, why?"

Dombrowski furrowed his brow and lifted a finger. "Only one reason makes sense, to keep Walter Farrell quiet or compliant."

"Okay, that would explain," Waters reasoned, "why he retracted his complaint about her going missing. But what is he hiding? Why would someone want him kept quiet or compliant?"

Dombrowski sighed. "Our theory gets a little thin here, but we think we're close. That meth lab was set up in a vacant house that's in foreclosure, and it's within the HOA that Farrell manages. We don't think this is the first time a lab like this has been established, run for a period of time, and then dismantled and moved to another location. This is more than just a hunch; Katie heard the perps talking about a new lab being set up. It stands to reason they've done this before."

"Yeah," Katie echoed. "They were pretty casual about it, like establishing a new lab at another location was no big thing."

"Exactly!" Dombrowski's head bobbed up and down. "And if you think about it, we know that in just a month or so, a lab of that size can produce enough meth to be worth millions in street value. All you really need are secure, temporary locations, and a means to periodically transfer the essential equipment and chemicals."

"So, who maintains an updated list," Katie asked, "of ideal temporary locations? The HOA does, complete with files of foreclosures and vacant houses in upscale neighborhoods. And let's not overlook that Farrell serves as the attorney for the security company that holds contracts for these gated communities. A good sized lab could be set up anywhere, run for a while, and then moved without the neighbors being any the wiser. Anyone seen coming or going could be explained as contractors renovating and getting the house ready for sale."

"Good sized lab, huh? How much equipment and precursor chemicals," Waters pressed, "would they have to move?"

Dombrowski shrugged and waved his hand dismissively. "Meh, no more than would fit in a pickup truck—"

"Or a van," Katie finished, "especially a van that typically hauls equipment and chemicals, like one that appears to be from a pool or house cleaning service. That wouldn't look out of place in any nice neighborhood."

Waters leaned back against the couch. "You know, this theory is . . . not too wild . No, not at all. In fact, it's certainly a feasible scenario. Do you have any evidence, beyond anything circumstantial?"

"Not yet," Dombrowski admitted.

"So, you think Walter Farrell, through this HOA, is somehow involved?"

"Basically, yes, he's gotta be, LT. Although, for the moment, we don't know to what extent he's involved. It's possible that he could be a major participant. We're pretty sure he has to be of sufficient value to the overall scheme, and ironically, have enough knowledge to be a potential liability to the operation."

"A potential liability? How so?" Waters probed.

Dombrowski and Katie shared an uneasy glance. They knew this part of their theory was more gut-fuelled speculation than proven fact.

"Bear with us," Dombrowski pled. "It's the timing and sequence of events. Look, first we have George Adamson's killing—we know it's a homicide staged as a suicide. He works for the HOA. Then we have Jennifer Halsted's death—another homicide staged as a suicide. She worked for the HOA; and, she was taking and hiding certain documentation, foreclosure files. In our interview with Walter Farrell, he suggested that Adamson and Halsted were romantically involved—an assertion we believe was intended to mislead us. Instead, we find Carolyn Silverberg, another homicide victim, who we know for certain was involved with George Adamson."

"And she," Katie pointed out, "just happens to live behind a vacant home that currently houses a meth lab. We think that while George was visiting with Carolyn, he noticed something about that supposedly vacant house and photographed it over a period of days."

"Remember," Dombrowski interjected, "George Adamson was a retired Air Force cop, an OSI investigator. He was very detail oriented and aggressive in his work for the HOA Architectural Review Committee. We think he grew suspicious and maybe went nosing around that house—"

"And that," interrupted Katie, "may have gotten him killed. Since they were linked to him, Jennifer Halsted and Carolyn Silverberg were loose ends that had to be dealt with to keep the meth operation secure. In a sense, they may have been collateral damage."

Dombrowski nodded and picked up the narrative. "We think that this meth operation had been going on for some time, with nobody the wiser, until George Adamson discovered it. Then the murders begin.

"Maybe at this point, Walter Farrell becomes uncomfortable. He hasn't signed on for this; maybe he wants out. However, his role may be too important in the overall scope of the operation which would very likely include certain aspects of a sophisticated money laundering scheme."

"So," Waters concluded, "they snatch his daughter to insure his continued loyalty and cooperation?"

"You gotta admit it fits, LT." The sergeant opened his palms and nodded.

Katie gave her partner a sympathetic nod and spoke softly. "There's one more thing, LT. We think Farrell's lawyer, Melanie Dubois, either learned of this or figured it out. And at some point, she decided to tell Dombrowski about it, or at least share her suspicions—"

"But they killed her," Dombrowski spat, "before I—"

"It wasn't your fault, D!" Katie scolded, not unkindly. "So don't even go there! Somebody got to her—like they did to everyone else involved. Each of the victims had something in common, a link to one person—Walter Farrell!"

Dombrowski sighed heavily and leaned back against the couch. "Yeah, I know you're right. It all comes back to him."

Waters took a deep breath. "All right, let's consider the implications. If these deaths were indeed all connected, as you have just proposed, the scope of such a criminal conspiracy in support of a large scale and readily mobile drug manufacturing and distribution network could be considerable. If the potential profits are as significant as speculated, there is little doubt that violence—even murder—is possible, if not inevitable; anything to protect the cash flow. Do you agree?"

The detectives bobbed their heads in agreement.

"So, here's the more pressing problem as I see it," Waters reasoned. "If we accept that all these deaths are related to this meth and money laundering enterprise recouping their losses and dealing with loose ends, we can't ignore the looming potential for another tragedy. If things are potentially getting worse by the minute for this illicit operation, this situation can only become more dangerous for the kidnap victim, Amanda Farrell. And now, with Rene Pasqualle's ill-fated rescue raid on this lab, the nature of the game has forever changed. This young lady's life is most likely in serious jeopardy."

"Yeah," Dombrowski admitted, "unless we out-think and out-play these kidnappers, before they decide to cut their losses and disappear."

"You're right. We need to act without delay, and wisely. And I gotta admit," Waters conceded, "the severed finger—it unnerves me. I know we routinely dealt with circumstances of the dead with the dispassionate stoicism of professional homicide investigators, but this remnant token of a still living victim evokes an uneasy knot of visceral horror in my gut."

Waters stifled a small shudder.

"You're keen to give Demotte the original ransom note and flash drive—for Katie's sake, you said. But she won't have the finger. Should she not mention the finger at all? Or do you think giving him a photo will suffice?"

"It'll have to, LT. You heard the M.E. Katie will have to tell them about the finger; and, she'll have to use a photo."

"And only Katie can do this?"

"Yeah, she has to—she's gotta appear compliant. We know her car's being tracked, so it'd be prudent to assume that the kidnappers might try to get eyes on her at some point. They're only using her because they think they can; somehow they know all about her being a suspended cop already in trouble. To them, she's the perfect pawn."

Katie nodded. "Yeah. They told me 'no police'—just me, alone. They gloated, inferring they had somebody on the inside, telling me if I tried to report it rather than follow their instructions, 'new evidence' would surface to implicate me in more serious crimes. I was *pissed*, of course, but I was careful to act good and scared. I think they bought it."

"See, LT?" Dombrowski insisted, "They think they've got her rattled, off balance. We need to keep it looking that way."

"Okay, I get it," Waters admitted. "Listen, the finger—are you sure she won't need it?"

"Come on, LT. You know the doc is right; the actual finger should stay with him—chain of custody at least," Dombrowski reasoned. "We've just gotta find a way around that. Maybe she can use a cell phone picture? Look, it makes a kind of sense that Katie, or anybody for that matter, wouldn't want to carry it around with her. Besides, no one but the kidnappers should even know about it."

"Yeah, I see," Waters allowed. "It would tend to freak someone out."

"Exactly! I think the finger was meant to shake her up as much as the Demottes, and press home the time factor."

"Well, it's working!" Katie spat.

"Easy there, Detective," Waters cautioned, "I agree that the best chance our victim has of having her finger reattached lies with the good doctor keeping it in his custody while we do our best to find her. To that end, we need to know as much as possible, to include what is on that flash drive—before you give it, the ransom note, and a suitable copy of a photograph to Demotte. I doubt he'll ask for the actual finger; but if he does, improvise. Am I clear?"

"Of course, damn it!" Katie blanched. "Er, uh, yes, sir. I meant no disrespect. I'm just anxious to get going!"

"Well, be patient. Until we know where the Demottes are, you have no destination. I'll make some calls while you and your partner work with young Reynolds here to copy and review what's on the flash drive, okay?"

"Yes, sir," she responded, but couldn't resist asking, "But what about our suspensions?"

Waters sighed and stood, his hand absently touching his pocket where his pack of cigarettes resided. "Detective, suppose you let me worry about that. Now help your partner!"

"Yes, sir," she mumbled hastily and huddled with Dombrowski around Kenny's computer.

"How long," Dombrowski asked, "will this take, Ken?"

"First of all, there are no latent prints, other than Katie's, on anything. I ran the print from the finger, no hit on AFIS."

"Can't say that's a surprise," Dombrowski grumbled. "What else do you need to do?"

The tech pointed to the computer's screen. "I've already scanned the ransom note to a protected file on the laptop's hard drive. Now, to copy the flash drive—if it's not transfer protected or encrypted—should take less than a minute. It's a simple USB connection; there we go. Okay, we've got a text file and a video file. I'll bring up the text file first."

Katie peered at the screen and pointed. "Hey! That's the same message that's on the ransom note, and two strings of characters; one of numbers, and one of dots."

Kenny highlighted the first string. "This is a phone number, and a hot link, an executable program. It'll work in range of any accessible WiFi or generic cellular net if you double click it."

"It's an international routing number," Dombrowski observed. "I'll bet the other string is an encrypted account number. You make the call; then using the browser, copy or drag the account number to the appropriate box, right?"

Ken looked up to the big sergeant with newfound respect. "Right, the phone number isn't too difficult to track, but it probably pings off a series of servers

in the cloud, if so it might be a bit more difficult and take a while. The
encrypted account number could be another story; that'll definitely take
some time and effort. I might need a little help, but I think I know who to
call."

Dombrowski grinned. "Emilio?"

Ken nodded. "Yeah, if you don't mind. His people have amazing resources!"

"I know. I think Lt. Waters may have already called him. Listen, there's
something else you and Emilio's people might be able to help with. The perps
who snatched Katie, well, they took her, uh, extra phone. It'd be good if we
could locate it—they might still have it. I don't know if it's on or not. Katie,
you wanna give Ken the number?"

She cast her eyes momentarily downward and then glared at him. "He's
already got it, okay?"

"Oh, really? That's fine—good, good." Dombrowski made no effort to hide
his smirk.

Ken, his cheeks warming, kept his eyes on his keyboard. "Um, I'll pull up the
video file now . . . Oh, shit."

The screen resolved to show a poorly lit scene, a place resembling an
unfinished basement. A blindfolded and gagged woman sat restrained in a
chair. Broad bands of silvery duct tape secured chest and arms to the chair.
Her shoulders heaved; she was panting in fear.

"Is there sound?" Dombrowski breathed.

"Wait one. " Ken made a few keystrokes.

The rapid sound of hyperventilation almost distorted the tiny speakers until
the CSI tech modulated the volume.

"Oh no," Katie groaned. "Is that her?"

The focus blurred and then sharpened. They could now see that thin wires wrapped her wrists and fingers tightly to the arms of the chair—all but for the little finger of her left hand.

The screen went dim, as if someone had stepped in front of the camera. It brightened once more to reveal a pair of hands wearing surgical gloves, and holding a piece of paper. The hands pulled back until the lettering on the paper was in focus.

It was the ransom note.

After a moment, the note disappeared and the camera focused tightly on the woman's face. The tight bands of dark cloth across her eyes and mouth were stained with sweat and tears.

Suddenly, her head snapped back, neck sinews stretched like guy wires. Despite the gag, she shrieked in muffled agony. Her head thrashed convulsively from side to side as she strained against her bonds. She gurgled, paled, and collapsed like a limp rag doll.

The gloved hands reappeared, displaying the ransom note and a freshly amputated finger.

The video ended.

"Was that Amanda Farrell?" Lt. Waters asked softly.

"Dunno for sure," Dombrowski admitted, "but God help us, I think so."

The room was dead quiet.

CH 29

LT. WATERS' CELL PHONE rang; he stepped aside to take the call.

Dombrowski and Katie sat in silence as Ken closed his laptop and placed the small flash drive on the table. The ransom note and photograph lay there in mute testament to the horror and shock of what had just been viewed on the flash drive.

"What now?" the CSI tech asked, clearly shaken.

"We focus," Dombrowski cautioned. "Katie, take a cell phone pic of the finger photograph. If you can get away with only showing that, it might be enough. "

"Maybe, but I'll want that photograph, too—just in case. There's no marking on it that indicates it's any sort of official picture. I'd rather have the option when I deal with Demotte—know what I mean?" She took a picture with her cell phone.

"Yeah, I get it. Okay, we'll put everything back in the original envelope." Dombrowski scooped up the items, to include the photo of the finger. "Now, we need to get a wire on Katie, and take her home. Her car is there and its tracking bug is still active. Once we find the Demottes, she'll use her car to make the delivery. Then, I guess we'll have to play it by ear. Ken, have you got a wire in your bag of tricks?"

The tech rummaged in his kit and produced a small decorative pin, about the size of a dime, which looked a bit like a fancy button. "Here, she could try this. It's a camera and a mike; range is about a quarter mile—maybe a little further with a clear line-of-sight. It takes a watch battery, so it's good for six to eight hours. They're new; we've only had them for a few weeks."

Katie picked it up and gently rolled it around on her palm. "This is pretty cool. How sensitive is it?"

261

"Well, if you put it too close to your heart, the mike will pick up your heartbeat. So, you might want to pin it to your right, like on your collar. Just remember to adjust your stance to keep something or someone on camera. Oh, that reminds me." He bent to his kit once again, and retrieved a standard undercover earwig. "Here, you'll need this, too—encrypted on our UC frequency."

"Thanks. Want to test the new toys?"

"Yeah, give me a sec." Ken opened his laptop and began typing. He looked up to Dombrowski and asked, "Sarge, have you got your radio?"

"Uh, no. But hold on—I'll borrow the lieutenant's. Crap, he's still on the phone. Let's give him a minute."

"No problem. Uh, Katie, you wanna walk around the room some, so I can check the camera?"

"Sure thing," she said pinning it to her shirt.

She roamed around the lounge as Kenny focused on his computer. She sighed and rolled her shoulders, letting the button camera focus where it would. Boredom, frustration, and anxiety were settling in; she needed to *do* something. Every minute that slipped past was another moment of their kidnap victim's life gone forever. Bleak memories arose unbidden; the austere second floor room, the stained leather restraints affixed to the metal bed. Who knew what terrors that poor girl might be experiencing at this very moment?

Lt. Waters concluded his call and rejoined Dombrowski and Reynolds.

"LT, can I borrow your radio for a minute?" the sergeant asked. "We need to check Katie's earwig."

"Oh, yeah, sure." He unclipped his portable from his belt and handed it over. "I'm gonna slip outside for a smoke. Come get me when you're done."

———————

JUST OUTSIDE THE ENTRANCE to the M.E.'s building, Waters was on his phone again. "No, sir. Still no contact . . . Yes, sir, I think we have to. Under the circumstances, that might be the best move . . . Yes, sir, I will . . . I'll advise, thank you, sir. Bye."

"Is everything okay, LT?" Dombrowski probed as he approached.

"Not really. Walk with me."

Lt. Waters strolled away from the building and pulled a pack of cigarettes from his pocket. He almost offered Dombrowski one, but demurred knowing the sergeant had quit years ago. He lit up, glanced around to be certain they were out of earshot, and spoke in low tones. "That was Assistant Chief Dunbar. This is confidential. He thinks the captain has gone missing—but that's on a need-to-know basis."

Dombrowski made no effort to hide his shock. "What the hell? Wait, why are you telling me? Do I have a need-to-know?"

"I believe it's my call; so, I deem you and your partner do. Look, since I had to contact the feds—at your suggestion, I might remind you—I had to pass that up the chain of command. With Capt. Walker unavailable, I had to go to the Assistant Chief. I also took the opportunity to brief him off-the-record about the conclusion of the IA case, and request that he take the appropriate action regarding your suspensions."

The sergeant nodded. "I appreciate that, LT. So?"

"It's complicated . . . A.C. Dunbar confirmed that there's a problem—not just that Capt. Walker is off the grid—but that there's some sort of leak within the department.

"He's been aware of it for some time, and has been directing a discreet internal inquiry. He has determined that our internal comm system, more specifically our IT network, has been compromised."

"LT, are you, or he, inferring that the captain or his absence is somehow linked to this?"

"I'm not, but I don't know exactly what the Assistant Chief thinks. He didn't share any suspicions with me. But that may be irrelevant. What he will do is order an end to your suspensions, and effective immediately, reinstate you and your partner to full duty status. However, this order is verbal only. For now, there will be no documentation or changes to our IT system, that includes personnel records. Everyone else must think you two are still suspended. Consequently, you must both act accordingly."

"I'm confused, LT," Dombrowski admitted. "Am I missing something? Why keep our active duty status confidential? How are we supposed to work this kidnapping? We're gonna need more resources, and we can't even ask for more help if we're still supposed to be suspended. What about Kenny? He's already stuck his neck way out; and, he knows pretty much everything."

Lt. Waters smiled wryly. "First of all, A.C. Dunbar and I have agreed on this strategy since it keeps the two of you out of the official loop—as far as anyone else knows you're still suspended—and you'll be free to operate as needed. You and I both know that you and Katie have been doing pretty well, keeping below the radar so far. I suggest you continue with those tactics. As for young Reynolds, I've been authorized to bring him on board as your tech support; so, I'll advise him of your active duty status and the need for secrecy. All of you will report directly to me, understood?"

"Yes sir, LT. So, we're pretty much on our own?"

"Well, not quite. There's more, good news actually. The federal agencies involved are offering support, but have elected to officially stay out of the limelight, until the time arrives that may be advantageous for their respective cases. DEA is looking into the meth operation. BATF is following up on the Dubois condo bombing and the proliferation of illegal weapons. Homeland Security, the FBI, and the U.S. Marshals are backtracking Rene Pasqualle and the members of his crew. Three of them got into the country illegally, two of whom were Interpol fugitives. They're also concerned that there may be other assets involved, or otherwise available to Rene, that have yet to surface."

"Okay, I get that, LT, but how does that help us with this Amanda Farrell situation? We have more immediate needs, like the location of Pierre Demotte."

"Actually, the feds may have already helped with that," Waters explained. "As you know, Rene is still hospitalized; but he hasn't been arrested—"

"Yeah," Dombrowski interrupted, "because nobody wants to be responsible for his medical bills."

Waters chuckled. The sergeant was right; take someone into custody and you're responsible for their medical care, not to mention the cost of 24 hour guards if the subject is housed in anything other than an incarceration facility. Medical costs these days could become outrageously expensive; every agency has a limited budget. It was often prudent, from a cost analysis perspective, to make an arrest after the suspect was medically discharged—barring extenuating circumstances, of course.

"I have no doubt that was a consideration," Waters admitted, "but that issue became moot when Pierre Demotte informed the hospital staff that he would assume responsibility for all medical costs. Demotte has visited his brother's bedside several times since his admission. Nicole, his wife, has accompanied him, but not always."

"Oh, I see," Dombrowski said. "Rene may not be in custody, but he is under surveillance, right?"

"Precisely, thanks to our FBI friend, Fred Carlson. They're very concerned about the prospect of additional assets at Rene's disposal, so they've maintained a discreet surveillance since he was admitted. Carlson has also arranged for a team to stand by in support of the kidnapping investigation—but it's still considered our case."

Dombrowski smirked. "I gotta admit *'Call me Fred'* Carlson's stock just ticked up a few points. When was the last time Pierre visited Rene?"

"Several hours ago, early this evening. However, there is a strong chance he will return tonight. A.C. Dunbar advised that Rene regained consciousness within the last hour, and that the hospital placed a call to Demotte's hotel."

Dombrowski brightened. "Great! That means Pierre will try to see him right away—but wait, isn't it after visiting hours? Would the staff still let him in?"

Now it was Waters' turn to smirk. "Oh, I think with a word in the right ear, it can be arranged. Agent Carlson is already on site, and can no doubt exert a bit of influence on our behalf."

"That'd be great! Katie can get to Demotte in a somewhat controlled environment—it'd keep her safer."

"I agree her safety is paramount—as well, you understand, as the classified truth of her active duty status," Waters firmly acknowledged. "Remember, she has to appear to be acting on her own. No one, not even the FBI surveillance team, will know otherwise."

Dombrowski frowned. He saw a potential glitch. "The FBI team will take no action? After all, she'll be delivering a ransom demand."

"They will be appropriately instructed," Waters assured him. "To be honest, I'm more concerned with your partner; she's got to be convincing."

"No problem, LT. She can handle it."

"Very well. Now, if and when you need anything else that our federal friends can offer, let me know; I'll serve as your interface." Waters took a last drag on his cigarette, and crushed the butt beneath his heel. "Oh, by the way, you know Reynolds approached me about working with Deputy U.S. Marshal Gonzalez and his tech people. I've made the arrangements; they'll be in touch soon."

"That's good, thanks, LT. If there's nothing else, I should get Katie home. I trust you'll call and advise when we should head to the hospital?"

"Count on it . . . and Sergeant?"

"Sir?"

"Keep her safe."

———————

DOMBROWSKI LOOKED AT his watch, 11:15 p.m., and sighed; no word as yet from Lt. Waters. He glanced over his shoulder. Katie and Kenny sat on her living room couch; she thumbed through the local Yellow Pages phone book, while he tapped the keys on his laptop in rapid spurts. Dombrowski smirked indulgently at their teasing conversation as he peered through the front window curtains at the deserted street in front of Katie's house.

"Katie, this is so much faster," Ken insisted. "My search engine has already found over seven hundred and thirty results."

"Big deal," she retorted. "You still have to go to every website, while I can just glance at a page in the Yellow Pages and see a dozen pool cleaning logos at once. I'll find something before you do!"

"No way!"

Dombrowski rolled his eyes; they'd been at this for almost half an hour. *Who knows? Maybe it'll pay off and they'll find a real link to this unidentified pool cleaning company—at least it's keeping them busy.*

Kenny's cell phone rang.

"Hello, Reynolds . . . Yeah, that'd be great . . . Hold on, repeat the link . . . Got it, typing now. Okay, I'm in."

Katie glanced to Dombrowski in puzzlement.

"I'm guessing," he offered, "that's Emilio's people?"

Ken's grin widened and his head bobbed affirmatively.

Dombrowski motioned for Katie to follow him; he made his way into her kitchen.

"They're trying to get permission to use some special tech to find your missing cell phone," he whispered.

"Oh, my burner phone—good! I hope they can find my gun, too! Losing that really pissed me off."

"Hey, we got a little busy, so I forgot to ask. How was your dad when you visited with him?"

Her face fell. She sighed heavily as she sat in a kitchen chair. "Not great, I almost didn't want to tell you."

"Tell me what?"

"Oh, D, he didn't even remember you'd been there earlier, when you were looking for me."

"Oh, Katie, I am so sorry. I don't know what to say."

"There's nothing to say." She sighed. "It's like there are good days and not-so-good days. But lately, he seems to be losing whole blocks of time almost on a daily basis. I know I was told to expect something like this, but it doesn't make it any easier. One day at a time—you know how it is. I'm gonna try and talk with his doctor sometime next week."

He laid a hand gently on her shoulder. "Katie, you know if there's ever anything I can do . . ."

"I know. I need to focus on something else. Let's turn on the TV and catch the news—if it doesn't distract Kenny."

It didn't. The CSI tech was fully focused on his laptop, his cell phone glued to his ear. Nonetheless, they kept the TV sound level low.

Dombrowski thought Katie was suitably distracted until the familiar face of a young man flashed across the screen, and she grabbed the remote.

The broadcast's volume swelled.

" . . . *his only son, Jonathan Widermark, declined further comment, merely confirming that his father, Jeremiah Widermark, did have an appearance scheduled in Tampa, Florida, at a conclave of evangelical religious leaders. Repeating our top story tonight; a private plane belonging to state Senator Jeremiah Widermark, has been reported missing somewhere over the Gulf of Mexico. It is believed that the Senator, who also holds the title of Apostle within the evangelical community, and unnamed members of his staff were aboard. The Coast Guard has commenced search and rescue operations, but as of this moment . . .* " The newscaster droned on as a picture of Jeremiah Widermark was displayed next to a computerized map of the search region.

"Oh shit," Katie breathed. "That's him."

"That's who?" her partner probed.

She pointed to the TV. "Him! That's who I saw arrive in a limousine at Walter Farrell's house, before I got snatched! I knew he looked familiar, but I couldn't place him!"

Dombrowski leaned forward, peering at the TV. "You're sure it was the father, Jeremiah, not the son, Jonathan, Louise Hesterly's *boy-toy*, remember?"

"I remember Jonathan. I'm not losing it! Jeremiah, the father, is who I saw—I'm sure of it!"

"Wasn't there someone else you saw going into Farrell's house, as well?"

"Yeah, a man arrived a few minutes later," she admitted. "I never got a good look at him; but, the car looked like an unmarked cruiser. Why? What are you thinking?"

He leaned back against the couch and pursed his lips. "Meh, maybe it's nothing, but something the LT said—"

He was interrupted by the ring of his cell phone.

"Yeah, Dombrowski . . . Yes sir, we're both here and ready to go . . . Will do . . . On our way. Bye."

He closed his phone, looked to his partner, and uttered a single word.

"Showtime!"

CH 30

―――

KATIE STARED UP AT the soaring hospital façade, its upper floors lost in the darkness. Only the main entrance was fully illuminated. There were few windows above the first floor that betrayed any glow of lights. That should come as no surprise, she mused, for it was almost midnight.

Squelch crackled in her left ear, followed by a weirdly metallic version of Dombrowski's voice. "Comm check—how copy?"

"Ten-two," she breathed. The micro-mike in her earwig picked up her voice easily. "Are we still a go?"

"Affirmative. Pierre is in Rene's room, 736, but he's not alone; white male, middle-aged, dark suit, no further ID. Wife is a no-show. She's still at the hotel."

"Copy that. I'm going in."

―――

THE LOBBY APPEARED to be deserted. Only a weary woman, her nose buried in a lurid paperback, sat ensconced behind an imposing reception counter. She seemed mildly irritated as the audible hiss of automatic entrance doors closing broke her concentration. She reluctantly tore her eyes from the book only to find the lobby empty. She sniffed and returned to her novel, completely unaware that anyone had slipped past unnoticed. Once more engrossed in her bodice-ripper, the receptionist ignored the elevator's muted ding.

A distracted uniformed guard wandered past, busily texting on his smart phone, oblivious to his surroundings.

―――

STEPPING OFF THE ELEVATOR on the seventh floor, Katie found the lighting subdued, but she could still read the sign on the opposite wall indicating the room she sought was to her right. A few paces to her left she spied the nurses' duty station. A lone night nurse seated behind the tall counter was preoccupied with a hushed telephone conversation, and clearly hadn't seen her.

Katie scanned the long vacant hall. A few soft lights shone from beneath several closed doors. She'd rather remain unobserved if at all possible; but she was not naïve enough to discount the FBI surveillance team. They were probably watching her right now. No matter—she had a mission to accomplish.

The door to room 736 was ajar. She could hear the low tones of men's voices. As she pushed the door open, the voices stopped. She stepped into the light. "Uh, Mr. Demotte, I'm—"

"I recognize you, Detective. If you have come to question Mr. Pasqualle, you will have to deal with Mr. Ferguson, here. He is an attorney, and has been retained to represent—"

"No! That's not why I'm here," she interrupted. "I have to speak to you, and give you this!" She shoved the envelope toward him, but he made no move to take it.

"What is this? Why would the police want to speak to me?" His tone was firm, but his arched eyebrows betrayed his puzzlement.

Katie bit her lip. What could she say? How much could she dare tell him?

Her earwig crackled with her partner's voice. "Parse the truth—just enough to get him to listen."

She sighed and let her shoulders slump. "I'm not here as a cop. In fact, I may not be one any longer—I've been suspended."

The lawyer, Ferguson, whispered something unintelligible in Pierre Demotte's ear. His expression hardened, Demotte straightened to his full height and pointed to the door. "Then you should leave—immediately!"

A weak voice sounded from the bed. "Pierre, no."

Demotte hovered over his brother. Their conversation was hushed and brief, but Katie heard the gist of it. ". . . saved my life . . . hear her out."

Demotte turned and faced her. "Very well, you may speak."

Ferguson started to object, but Demotte cut him off. "I will hear her—do not interrupt again." He studied Katie for a moment and said, "Proceed. I warn you, I do not suffer fools. Do not waste my time."

Her temper flared, but she tamped down the urge to retort. *Arrogant, eh? Then to hell with showing you just the cell phone picture!*

"It's about Amanda," she began, and thrust the envelope toward him once more.

This time he took it. "What about her?"

"She's been kidnapped, as I think you well know. The people who took her took me, too. They let me go to give you this envelope, and a ransom message—five million transferred to a numbered account. The details are in the envelope. I think they may have already hurt her, and promise to do more if you delay paying the ransom."

Demotte opened the envelope. The flash drive and the ransom note slid out easily onto his hand. He peered into the envelope and found the photograph. His face paled; his hand began to perceptibly shake.

She missed none of it. *So, that photograph made an impression—took the wind right out of your sails, didn't it?*

It clearly had; his voice almost failed him. "H-have you spoken to my wife? Has she seen . . . *this?*"

"No," Katie replied, her eyes downcast. "I went to your hotel earlier, but neither of you were there."

"Please, do not . . . tell my wife. I would spare her this."

"I understand . . . and I am so sorry."

"P-Pierre," Rene rasped.

The brothers huddled and conferred once again in hushed tones. Katie could discern nothing, other than that their conversation was in French.

Demotte looked to her and asked, "Do the police know—have you reported this?"

"No," she lied. "I sought you first. Look, I'll admit these people scared me. They threatened to harm Amanda if I didn't comply."

"Do you know them? Did you recognize anyone?"

"No, I don't know who they are. They kept me blindfolded and drugged me. I'm sorry, but that's all I know."

Rene motioned for Pierre to come closer and whispered urgently to his brother. Katie could discern nothing.

Demotte straightened and faced her once again. "Is there anything else you can tell us?"

She shrugged and opened her palms. "No, that's all I know. I am sorry, but I have to go—I can't be seen here."

Demotte made no effort to stop her and said nothing as she left the room.

———————————————

OUTSIDE THE HOSPITAL, and certain she was alone, she spoke into the night air. "Did you copy all that?"

"Affirmative. You've picked up a tail. Sit in your car for a few minutes, then drive straight home. We'll already be there. You'll be followed, but don't try to shake them. We'll let the lieutenant take care of it."

"Copy that. See you there."

———————————

"ARE THEY STILL OUT there?" Katie asked, seeing Ken peer through the blinds of her living room window.

"They're pulling away now. I guess we have Lt. Waters to thank for that, right?"

"Yeah, better believe it," Dombrowski assured the tech as he handed Ken a cold beer and placed one before Katie.

She took a long swig and put her feet up on her coffee table. "I'm bagged, guys. This beer is gonna put me to sleep. Is there anything else we have to do tonight?"

Dombrowski savored a long draught, stifled a belch, and shook his head. "Nah, not that I'm aware of; we gotta wait for the LT's call. In the meantime, I'm glad you've got good taste in beer." He gave her a sly wink.

"Hah! That's some of what you brought over when I got out of the hospital."

"Really? Well that explains it. I knew I had good taste!"

The sergeant's cell phone trilled the opening notes of Wagner's Ride of the Valkyries.

"Whoa, cool ring tone, Sarge!" declared Ken.

"No pun intended?" Katie teased.

Dombrowski dismissed them genially. "Quiet, you Philistines! It's the lieutenant! Hello, Dombrowski here ... Yes, sir, LT, they pulled off, left a few minutes ago ... The lawyer, Ferguson? Okay, got it ... No, I can see that makes sense ... Uh-huh ... Oh, you mean the BATF agent? Yeah, six? Well, that's interesting. Okay, if you think that's best . . . No, it's still on, but Ken said we shouldn't expect the battery to last much longer . . . No, I'm sure we can do that . . . Thanks, LT, we can sure use the rest . . . Yes, sir, talk to you in the morning. Bye."

Ken sat next to Katie on the couch and sipped his beer. Both looked expectantly to Dombrowski for an explanation.

He grinned and plopped down in an overstuffed armchair opposite the couch. "Good news—we are done for the night! He'd like us to stay together. So, Katie, can we crash here tonight?"

"Sure, there's the guest room and the couch; you two work that out."

Dombrowski pointed at the CSI tech and announced, "Ah yes, rank has its privileges, young man. I hope you enjoy the couch."

Katie laid her hand on Kenny's arm in sympathy. "Don't worry; it really is comfortable. I fall asleep on it all the time."

"I'll be, uh, fine," he stammered, and quickly changed the subject. "What else did the lieutenant say, Sarge?"

"He's been interfacing with the feds most of the day. It was no problem to pull the FBI surveillance off Katie. Uh, what else? Oh yeah, the lawyer with Demotte—"

"Ferguson," Katie offered.

"Yeah, Ferguson, he's legit, a member of a big local firm—"

"Not the same firm," she interrupted, "as Farrell, I trust?"

"No, different firm altogether. We don't know if he's worked with Demotte before, but it's doubtful. As far as we know this is the first time Demotte has ever been here. Also, BATF no longer considers Rene Pasqualle a viable suspect in the Dubois bombing, but he'll still face illegal weapons charges. It seems the cell phones used were purchased two weeks before Demotte called

Rene and asked him to come. In fact, neither Pierre nor Rene was even in this country at the time of that purchase."

"Wait! Why weren't we told about exactly when and where the phones were purchased?" she demanded. "Didn't we hear that CSI had determined that?"

Dombrowski sighed. "Have you forgotten? By then, the Dubois homicide was no longer our case; Johnson and Barkley were re-assigned as the primaries. Remember, the LT mentioned the phones earlier, but the purchase details weren't clarified until recently."

"Oh, yeah," she winced, "I forgot, sorry."

"There is more to know now. The LT said half a dozen phones were sold to a single buyer over the course of three days, two phones at a time. BATF Agent Brathwaite found that strange, but indicated it's a pattern they've seen recently. So, she's trying to work it from the staggered purchase angle. But she's pretty sure Rene didn't have a hand in this bombing."

"Well, shit!" Katie exclaimed. "Somebody built that bomb!"

"Indeed," Dombrowski agreed, "And they're still out there. We have to stay on our toes, *capisce?*"

Silence hung heavy for a moment.

Ken tilted his bottle toward Dombrowski. "Sarge, what were you saying about me—you know, about the battery and all?"

"Oh yeah, Lt. Waters wanted to know if that bug in Katie's car was ull active. You heard what I told him, right?"

"Yeah, I'll check it in the morning. I'd be surprised if the batt isn't dead by then. What do you want me to do, maybe remove the bug?

"Dunno, let me think about it."

Katie stood and drained her beer. "Can we worry about this in the morning? I'm beat. D, you know where the guest room is. Kenny, I'll get you a pillow and a blanket; and then I'm going to bed."

"Yeah, I'm bagged too," Dombrowski admitted. "The morning will be here soon enough."

CH 31

THE RAPPING UPON THE door woke Kenny. He experienced a moment of disorientation before he realized that he'd been asleep on Katie's couch. He sat up and rubbed his face. He stood and stretched, tucked the tail of his rumpled T-shirt into his jeans, and made his way to the peephole in the door. Daylight assaulted his retina when he peered through. Another series of sharp knocks startled him, and he tugged the door open.

"Uh, Lieutenant? Um, sorry, I was asleep. It took me a minute to get to the door."

"Where are Dombrowski and Callahan?" Lt. Waters snapped as he brushed past the sleepy tech and scanned the living room.

"I'm here," Dombrowski answered from the hall.

Kenny's eyes widened as he saw the sergeant emerge from the shadows, fully dressed, with pistol in hand.

Dombrowski acknowledged his boss and holstered his weapon. He nodded to the tech. "Shut the door, Ken. What's up, LT?"

"Expecting trouble, are we? Where is Katie?"

Dombrowski shrugged. "Trouble? You never know. Katie's probably in her room. I assume she's still asleep; she was pretty tired. Do you need her? We could wake her up."

Waters fingered a large envelope tucked under his arm. He looked at his watch and mumbled, "It's almost ten. Sergeant, I know she's been with you since she was found, uh, after her ordeal. Are you certain she was here all night?"

"Yeah, she's been with us except for when she went to the hospital last night to find Demotte. After that, we all stayed here, as you suggested. No doubt she's still sacked out in her room." Dombrowski placed his hands on his hips and asked, "LT, what's going on? Do we need to wake her or not?"

"Don't bother," Katie groaned, as she shuffled into the room barefoot, wearing cut-off jeans and an old football jersey. "You guys make enough noise to wake the dead. Is there coffee yet?"

"I'll make some," Kenny offered.

"Bless you," she moaned collapsing into an armchair. "All right, what's going on? What have we missed? What has Demotte done about the ransom demand?"

"Coffee's brewing," Kenny announced.

"The ransom?" echoed Waters. "Demotte has done nothing—yet. Our federal friends now have him under surveillance and have been monitoring the numbered account indicated on the flash drive. As far as we know, he is still at his hotel, and has not yet followed the kidnappers' instructions."

"What could he be waiting for?" Dombrowski pondered.

"It seems that no one knows. However, we have another problem." Waters gestured to the couch. "May I?"

Katie nodded as Dombrowski scooped up Kenny's pillow and blanket and put them to one side.

Once seated, Waters opened the envelope and removed a series of eight by ten inch photographs and spread them out on the coffee table—a car, an unmarked police cruiser with a body behind the steering wheel. "We found Captain Walker, dead, in one of the CID fleet cars, in our own parking lot. The discovery was made early this morning at shift change. He'd been shot in the right chest."

Stunned silence hung in the room like a shroud.

"I know this comes as a shock," Waters said, "but there's more. There was a semi-auto pistol found on the front passenger side floorboard, a Glock 19 that appears to have been fired. The serial number matches that of a Glock 19 registered to you, Katie."

She paled, mouth open; but she couldn't utter a sound.

"Wait! Isn't that the pistol," Dombrowski quickly asked, "that was taken from you when you got snatched?"

Kenny stared at her. "What the hell?"

"Katie, answer me," her partner insisted.

"Yes," she managed.

"LT, do we know," Dombrowski probed, "when he was killed?"

"There is some question about that—he's been out of touch for so long," Waters admitted, "and there wasn't much blood, very little actually. It'll be up to the M.E. to determine the time of death."

"So, that's why you asked if Katie had been with us and here all night," the sergeant surmised. "Somebody thinks she's a viable suspect?"

Waters shrugged, but couldn't hide his concern. "I'm afraid so. It looks like the classic disgruntled employee scenario. A suspended detective, already under IA scrutiny, has an axe to grind with the boss who suspended her. The boss is found shot dead, and her gun is found at the scene. Motive, means, and opportunity—all one needs to become a suspect. Hell, she's at the top of the list!"

"But that's wrong!" Ken exclaimed. "She's not under suspension any more—and she's known that since yesterday! She's been with us—she hasn't had the opportunity! And her gun was stolen from her!"

"All true," Waters admitted. "Now consider that she appears to have been implicated in a kidnapping by delivering the ransom demand."

"That's wrong, too!" Ken blurted. "That was a controlled and monitored tactic in the investigation—she was acting undercover! This is obviously a setup—it's got to be!"

"Every point you've made is valid," the lieutenant conceded. "However, only we, and a handful of people outside this room, know all this. To everyone else, she appears to be a corrupt cop."

"Yeah, I get it. Someone thinks she makes the perfect patsy," Dombrowski observed, "and went to the time and effort to set her up. I just don't know why they'd go to all the trouble. Is that coffee done, do you think, Ken?"

They sat in silence as Ken served them mugs of hot coffee.

"I think I get it now," the tech said as he sat down. "Someone wants Katie out of the way. If she's charged with a crime, that compromises any investigation she was involved in. It would seriously discredit her and anything she might say. No one, other than us, would believe her."

"You're right about that, Ken," Dombrowski acknowledged. "Someone, who doesn't know what we know, wants her out of the picture, her credibility destroyed, and any case she's worked on as a primary investigator consequently sabotaged. Not even the most aggressive prosecutor would take such a case to court."

Ken shook his head in dismay. "Oh man, that's downright devious. That'll kill a law enforcement career."

"Yeah," Dombrowski agreed. "I think we were getting too close to something. So, somebody took advantage of circumstances and carefully crafted this scenario to derail our investigation."

"But why Katie?" Ken asked.

"I don't know," the sergeant admitted. "But it seems pretty clear they've been focused on her. Hell, for all we know it might even be that they have done exactly what they set out to do. Think! Maybe just screwing up our cases was the goal? And now, they may believe she's no longer useful to them, so they want to neutralize her, cast her aside."

"I see, a spent pawn, to be removed from the board," Waters murmured.

"You know," Katie grumbled, "I am sitting right here."

"Oh, sorry, Detective, can't be helped. Sergeant, that strongly suggests," Waters cautioned, "that someone is very familiar with our procedures and those of the court system, does it not?"

"Yeah, I know; and that bothers me," Dombrowski admitted. "Another thing that screams setup to me, the timing is all too convenient. It's no coincidence that the captain's homicide is discovered after she's done what she was compelled to do by the kidnappers. Now with this situation, she's off the job for sure and probably headed for incarceration."

"I think I see where you're going with this. They must feel confident with these tactics that she's no longer a threat," the lieutenant reasoned, "otherwise, they may have just decided to eliminate her."

"But don't criminals say," Kenny quickly interjected, horrified at the thought, "that killing a cop is always bad for business?"

Dombrowski pointed to the graphic photos spread out on the coffee table. "That doesn't appear to faze these people, does it?"

That sobering reality plunged the room into silence once more.

Katie sat upright and declared, "I'm getting pretty damned tired of being manipulated. Enough is enough! We gotta do something! And I think we have to be shrewd, more devious than they are. So, let's keep them in the dark; let them think they've been successful. I'll go low-profile, play the disaffected role—scorned by my peers as untrustworthy, and trying to dodge a potential indictment."

"That could work," Dombrowski admitted. "It would definitely make you seem no threat to them. In their arrogance they'll think their ploy has worked perfectly."

Waters began nodding sagely. "Yes, yes indeed. Well played, this could work out quite well; and, keep our adversary's focus misdirected."

"So, if it appears they've been successful," Kenny reasoned, "and they're not focused on Katie, will we have any other advantages?"

"Assuredly," Waters answered. "Wherever they redirect their focus may give us insights we currently don't enjoy. Don't forget that everyone thinks the good sergeant here is also suspended and out of the picture. Consequently, we will continue to operate under the radar."

Waters' cell phone rang.

"Yes, Waters here . . . Yes, please . . . Uh-huh . . . I see . . . Yes, go on . . . No, I'll be handling that personally . . . No, I'll make that call, when and *if* necessary . . . Excellent, I'll so advise. Thank you, bye."

As soon as that call concluded, his phone rang again. He smiled abashedly and took the call.

"Waters . . . Yes . . . I see . . . Yes, I got it . . . I'll do so immediately. Thank you, bye."

He set his phone down and retrieved a small notebook. He scribbled on a page, tore it out, and handed it to Kenny. "Young man, you asked me to make arrangements with Deputy U.S. Marshal Gonzalez to work with some of his technical people. I understand you've been anticipating the arrival of certain experts and their equipment. Call this number and give the code 'VL49LW'. The person on the other end is awaiting your call."

Ken eagerly accepted the number and reached for his phone; but the lieutenant stopped him.

"Hold on, you all need to hear the rest of the information I was just made aware of. CSI has completed processing the multiple homicide scene where Rene Pasqualle was found. Among things of interest, they found the chemicals phosphine and chlorine—not that unusual, I'm told, in a meth lab or in a pool cleaning operation. I understand Dr. Parker found traces of those respective gases in George Adamson's lungs. CSI also found a roll of duct tape that matches the type found on the car at the Adamson 'suicide' scene. That roll of tape also bears adhesive of the type found on one of Adamson's hands. But the clincher is that they found a partial thumb print of his on a discarded piece of that duct tape in the garage of the house where Pasqualle was found. The decedent, Adamson, had definitely been in that house, and perhaps was killed there."

"Yeah, but," Katie cautioned. "We don't know by whom."

"Hey, LT, that kinda begs the question," Dombrowski mused aloud, "who is gonna handle the captain's homicide?"

Waters sipped his cooling coffee, sat back, and spoke with grim determination. "I am, with Assistant Chief Dunbar's blessing; which effectively means that *we* are. You two will stay below the radar. The autopsy is to begin in about an hour. We'll meet later today with Dr. Parker to discuss his findings."

"What about notification of next of kin?" Dombrowski asked. "I know he's a widower, but I've got no clue as to the rest of his family."

"He has an older brother in Philadelphia. I've already made the call and arranged for the Philly PD to take care of it. I'm not aware of any other kin."

Dombrowski sighed. "Why kill the Captain?" he asked no one in particular. "I mean other than to set Katie up—why him? LT, was he working on anything in particular?"

"No, not that I'm aware of. In fact he was considering retiring next year, maybe even running for Sheriff."

Dombrowski chuckled and shook his head. "Yeah, he's been toying with that idea for years."

"I know—another dream," Waters allowed with a grin. "But lately I got the impression he was thinking about it more seriously." His face fell. "I don't know, maybe it was still just a dream."

Kenny looked around at the glum faces. Each person seemed to be lost in some personal memory about Captain Walker. He'd hardly known the Captain at all, but the sense of loss hung like a tangible cloud in the room. He glanced at the slip of paper in his hand, and remembered. He waited another moment out of politeness.

"Uh, Lieutenant? If there's nothing else, I really need to get on with this search for Katie's missing cell phone."

"What? Oh, yes, of course. Go then. Call me with any results."

"Yes, sir." Ken picked up his cold coffee and made his way into the kitchen to make the call.

———————

KATIE LEANED FORWARD, picked up a few of the photographs, and studied the pictures. "Hmmph, this car . . ."

"Huh?" Dombrowski asked. "What about it?"

"I think I've seen this car . . ."

He guffawed. "Of course you have; it's part of the CID fleet. You've probably seen it in the motor pool lots of times. You may have even driven it at one time or another. Hell, your prints could be in it. Oh, but that might not matter since any of us in CID may have used it."

"No, D, that's not what I mean. I think *this* is the car I saw at Walter Farrell's place, right after the limo arrived."

"You mean just before you got snatched?" His tone was incredulous. "Are you kidding me?"

Waters leaned forward, his brow knit, his eyes intense. "Detective, are you certain? I understood that you did not see the driver, right?"

Katie paused and concentrated. Lingering doubt was dissipating like evaporating steam. *Could it be that simple? Was it that obvious?*

"Look, it was raining, so I can't say I'm a hundred percent sure. But I really think this is the car. In my gut I can feel it. And you're right, LT, I didn't get a look at the driver, at least not his face."

Waters did not relent. "Do you think it could have been the captain?"

"Well, yeah." She was decidedly uncomfortable, being put on the spot like this. She could easily be wrong, but her instincts were otherwise. "It could have been him. I never saw his face. But, somehow, that feels right."

Waters said nothing; he didn't need to. He just nodded in acceptance.

Dombrowski broke the silence. "I got a problem with the car, LT."

"The CID fleet car? How so?"

"The captain is assigned his own cruiser," Dombrowski noted, "So, why would he need to use an unassigned fleet car?"

Waters blew out a thin stream of air and hung his head. "Perhaps because his cruiser is in the motor pool shop awaiting a new set of tires. The captain asked me to have it dropped off last week. It turned out the shop didn't have a full set of the right size tires in stock; so, they had to order a set. They kept the car, waiting for the tires to be delivered. The tires have yet to arrive; and the captain's assigned car is still there."

"So," the sergeant reasoned, "only you, the captain, the motor pool manager and his staff knew about this?"

"Right."

Dombrowski and Waters shared a knowing look, each considering the implications.

Waters broke the silence. "For now, Detectives, I think we need to keep all this to ourselves."

CH 32

DESPITE THE WARM SLANTING rays of the setting sun, the filtered air in Dr. Leonard Parker's private office was overly cool, with just a hint of disinfectant. The M.E. sat stiffly at his keyboard as he typed his final conclusions into the narrative box of the standard autopsy report form. He stared at the monitor and sighed heavily. A glance through his office windows confirmed that it would be dark soon. This had been a long day.

The polite knock on his office door derailed his train of thought.

Lt. Waters poked his head in. "Hi, Doc! Are you ready for us? Dombrowski and Callahan are with me."

"Yes, of course, come in and have a seat. Close the door, please."

They filed in and made themselves comfortable; Dombrowski and Katie on a couch, and Waters in one of the two facing armchairs.

Dr. Parker left his desk and took the other armchair; he leaned toward Waters. "Lieutenant, pursuant to your request, I have not shared the results of Captain Walker's postmortem with anyone, not even my staff. My final report is in an encrypted file, accessible only with my authorization and password. Am I to understand that only the four of us are to be fully informed of my report?"

"That's correct, Doctor," Waters confirmed. "With one codicil, for the time being—I'll be briefing Assistant Chief Dunbar with a synopsis of your findings. That will be a verbal briefing only. There will be no documentation, beyond what is in your secured file, at this time. Nor is anyone to know that Detectives Dombrowski and Callahan were even here. This is required for operational security. I'm sure you can understand. Do you have any questions?"

"Not at this time, but at some point I will have to release my findings," the M.E. conceded. "The law requires it, as you well know."

"Of course. We may only need a few days—perhaps a week at the most," Waters concluded.

"A week at the most—no more. Agreed?"

"Yes, thank you, Doc. Now, what can you tell us?"

"First of all, Edwin Walker did not die from the single gunshot wound to the right side of his chest. That wound was postmortem. I believe he had been dead for twelve to eighteen hours before that event. Furthermore, the cause of death was a stroke, which I believe is attributable to massive air embolisms introduced through the inner carotid arteries. I found puncture wounds on the back of the throat—"

"Like were found on Adamson and Halsted?" Katie blurted in interruption.

Dr. Parker scowled—he didn't care to be interrupted. "Quite so, Detective. Now, if I might continue?"

"Of course. 'Sorry, Doc.'" She cast her eyes downward, but not before she caught her partner's blatant smirk.

"As I was saying, these wounds are consistent with what we've seen in two other cases—as Detective Callahan has duly noted. I also found a pair of burn marks at the back of the neck, consistent with the Halsted case."

As the Medical Examiner paused, Dombrowski winked at his partner and spoke up. "Doc, forgive me. You know how highly we regard your opinion, so we hope to benefit from your insight on that very point. We've speculated before in the Adamson and Halsted cases that those marks might be from a stun gun or taser—electrical burns. Now, with more evidence—another body—well, what do you think?"

"Well, I'd have to say that it is certainly possible; so, my opinion has not greatly changed," the pleased M.E. answered. "However, I would think a stun gun is more likely than a taser; there's no indication of barbs piercing the skin. Also, the distance between the two marks appears to be identical in all these cases; that's rarely the case with taser barbs fired at any distance. These are contact burns that appear to be very much the same in all respects. In fact, there's a fair chance these marks may indicate application of the same device."

"Indeed? We will keep that in mind. What else have you found, Doctor?" Waters prompted.

"I believe, based on lividity, that the body was moved after death and subsequently staged in that vehicle. I think rigor mortis had come and gone before the gunshot. I also strongly suspect that the gunshot was delivered while the body was in a supine position—on its back—and then moved."

"What about the bullet, Doc?" Dombrowski asked.

Dr. Parker steepled his fingers and tilted his head. "Interesting, that. I recovered the 9mm FMJ projectile from just under the skin below the left scapula—shoulder blade—its nose was slightly flattened. It did not strike bone, nor did I find any tissue in its path that would so deform the nose of the bullet. The victim's back was against something firm and hard, possibly a hard floor, when he was shot. Skin is very elastic; the projectile did not create an exit wound. CSI has already taken custody of that bullet. Oh, should I have withheld that as well, as you've requested of my final report?"

"No, I don't think that was necessary at this point," Waters answered. "They already have the pistol that was found. I'm sure they're running the appropriate ballistics tests. There would be no point in delaying that procedure. The results will very likely confirm what we already suspect."

"Ah, I see," Dr. Parker responded, somewhat mollified.

"However, your findings, Doctor," the lieutenant duly noted, "give us a new and more promising direction to pursue in our investigation. It appears that we have a killer who has struck before, and in a most unusual way."

"Of that I have no doubt," the M.E. assured him. "There are two more bodies in my morgue with the same cause of death. In each of those cases, as in this one, the killer has gone to considerable effort to disguise the precise method employed, no doubt to otherwise distract or mislead the investigations, in two staged suicides, and now a staged shooting. Lieutenant, I suspect you are not dealing with a typical serial killer—if there really is such a thing. There is no evidence to suggest he has taken trophies of his kills. This perpetrator is not seeking notoriety, not flaunting his crimes; he does not crave attention. No, I rather think he has an agenda, an endgame known only to himself; and, he is trying very hard to keep it hidden."

The doctor watched his guests carefully for any reaction to his analysis. Their thoughts were plain; there was no disagreement. The sergeant was slowly nodding his head.

"Doc, I think you may have nailed it. We certainly wouldn't disagree," Dombrowski said. "But lemme ask; do you think it's one guy—the same guy—in each case?"

Dr. Parker sat up a little straighter and looked Dombrowski in the eye. "Yes, Sergeant, I most certainly do."

Lt. Waters' cell phone rang. He nodded to the M.E. "Oh, excuse me, Doctor; I've got to take this."

Waters stepped to one side and answered his phone. It was a brief conversation. He closed his phone and approached the Doctor.

"I'm sorry, Doctor. If we're done here for now, we're gonna have to run. Please keep all of this confidential. We can't thank you enough. We'll be in touch."

Parker shook Waters' hand. "Of course, I understand. Good luck."

———————

AS THEY FILED OUT OF the M.E.'s building, Dombrowski asked, "Okay, LT, what's up? Where are we going?"

Waters scanned the parking lot and shook his head.

They got the message—*not here.*

Once on the open road, he provided an answer.

"We're on our way to Assistant Chief Dunbar's home—"

"Oh no!" Katie cried from the backseat—her imagination briefly getting the better of her. "Is he all right?"

Waters glanced in the rear-view mirror. "Relax! He's fine. He just wants to have us meet there rather than at the office. Remember, you are both supposed to still be suspended—you're not even here."

"So, I gather," Dombrowski surmised, "this meeting we're going to is gonna be held under the radar?"

"Assume so. We'll see what this is about soon enough." Waters focused on his driving, keeping his thoughts to himself.

They drove on, with only periodic dispatch transmissions on the police radio disrupting the mood, until Dombrowski fidgeted and broke his silence. "Hey, LT, I've got a question. When the captain was first thought to be missing, did anyone ping his cell phone, or try to get a GPS fix on it?"

"Yes, repeatedly, but they never got a response or a fix. When they found him, his phone was in his pocket but the battery had been removed. It was in the same pocket, but loose."

"You mean like separated and jarred loose? Or deliberately removed?"

"That's unknown," Waters admitted. "There were no prints on the three loose pieces; the phone body, the battery cover, or the battery."

"Not even the captain's prints, eh? Then somebody wiped it down after they removed the battery."

"Would removing the battery," Katie asked, "disable the phone's GPS capability? And what about the CID fleet car—does it have GPS?"

"No, only the marked patrol units have integrated GPS. The unmarked CID cars won't get GPS until next fiscal year, if it's in the budget. As for removing the phone's battery, effectively disabling the phone's GPS, I believe it would," Waters admitted. "But I don't know if any historical GPS data was stored in the phone. CSI was supposed to check."

"Historical GPS data? Now, that information could prove very interesting," Dombrowski mused aloud. "We'll need to trace his movements as best we can." He began drumming his fingers on the armrest as he stared through the windshield. He sat up straight and faced Waters. "When can we get into his home, LT? Or has CSI already been there? We gotta see it, no matter."

"They have, but I think you're right—seeing things with our own eyes is best. If this meeting isn't too long, maybe we'll go afterward."

Dombrowski sat back in his seat, and mumbled, "Oh captain, my captain, what have you been up to?"

"Huh?" Katie asked. "Did you say something?"

"Nah, nothing."

ASSISTANT CHIEF DUNBAR was standing just inside his open garage when Lt. Waters pulled into the driveway. Dunbar waved Waters' car into the illuminated garage, and closed the overhead door as soon as the lieutenant shut off the ignition.

"Chief, what's up?" Waters asked as he exited the car.

Katie and Dombrowski nodded, but kept silent.

Dombrowski always liked Dunbar. He was a big man, even bigger than Dombrowski, and well known for his taciturn demeanor and zero-tolerance for incompetence—or *bullshit*. He'd been a hard-line street cop for most of his career. And now, as second in command, he was very supportive of his troops, and consequently popular with the rank and file. He still enjoyed some heavy street cred, and was fazed by very little. But right now, Dombrowski sensed something in his expression, something unsettling, disturbing, or uncertain—fear?

"Follow me," Dunbar commanded. He turned and led them into his home, down a flight of stairs and into a finished basement, a recreation room. He stopped at a pool table, its balls racked and break ready. With the sweep of a hand he gestured for his guests to gather there. He directed their attention to a large padded envelope on the green felt, to one side of the cue ball.

"This package was delivered to my home—overnight mail. It's addressed to me; I've already opened it."

He tilted the envelope and a small metal box slid out. It looked like brushed aluminum or stainless steel, barely bigger than a pack of playing cards. He carefully separated the box into two pieces. One piece was simply a cover; the other housed a small tape recorder.

Waters pointed. "Chief, is that a—"

"Yes, a NAGRA."

Katie nudged her partner and asked in a stage whisper, "A what?"

Dombrowski smiled and indulged her, much to her chagrin. "That, Katie, is an old school body wire, a tape recorder. We used to use these on undercover assignments, before digital equipment became the norm. It's a very reliable audio recording device—no video, though."

"Chief, have you," Waters probed, "listened to it?"

"I have. You all need to hear it."

He connected a set of small speakers and pressed the PLAY button. There was the sound of clothing rustling, hasty footsteps, and knocking. Dunbar stopped the tape.

"You are about to hear three different voices. One you will no doubt recognize as Capt. Walker. He will identify, in the course of conversation, one of the other speakers. The third speaker, a woman, is unidentified and only appears near the beginning of the tape. Hold your questions until the tape concludes. It runs for just under ten minutes. Are you ready?"

They nodded their assent. For the next ten minutes they listened intently. Katie became increasingly agitated.

Dunbar pressed the OFF button and looked at each of his guests. "Detective Callahan, You have something to add?"

"Yes, sir, I believe this recording was made a day ago at Walter Farrell's home. I recognize the voice of my CI, Consuela Ladonez, when she answered the door. She's the live-in maid at Farrell's home."

"I see. I understand you saw Jeremiah Widermark arrive, followed by Capt. Walker moments later, correct?"

"I was some distance away, but I clearly saw Widermark—although didn't recognize him at the time. I never saw Capt. Walker—his face, I mean—but now I understand that it was him. He was the one wearing the wire, right?"

Dunbar sighed and admitted, "Yes, that seems pretty clear to us, now. You should all know that I knew nothing about this; the captain did this on his own initiative."

"Let's not sell him short," Dombrowski cautioned. "He knew something wasn't right about this meeting. So, he wired himself and had the good sense to get it into the mail, and into the hands of somebody he trusted."

"That's right," echoed Waters. "He always had good street instincts. He spent many years in Narcotics & Vice and used NAGRA recorders all the time. It stands to reason he'd use what he was familiar with and knew well."

Dunbar straightened and balled his fists. "Still, I wished he'd have told me. He wouldn't have had to do this alone."

"Uh, Chief, if you don't mind," Katie broached, "could we hear it again?"

They listened again, several times, until Dombrowski interrupted. "Stop! Back it up a little bit. Yeah, that's good. Now, let it play . . . uh, sir."

Dunbar looked askance at Dombrowski and smirked wryly.

The spools began to spin.

"*. . . this house, Reverend? The owner is known to me. He was recently in our office to report his daughter missing.*"

"*Oh piffle. That was just a rebellious teenager acting out, nothing more. He's my attorney and graciously offered this location for our meeting.*"

"*Won't he be joining us? I know he is a major campaign contributor.*"

"*Ah . . . no . . . He, uh, doesn't get involved with every aspect of the political arena . . . It's just you and I who need to talk.*"

"*About what?*"

"*This run for Sheriff . . . I know I told you the party was amenable to your proposed candidacy, but the situation has evolved. They now have another candidate in mind—*"

"*What are you saying? They won't support me for Sheriff? That software you provided me showed that I was an excellent candidate for that office—you said the party approved!*"

"*No, no—you misunderstand! The Selection Committee, of which I am a member, thinks highly of you. In fact, some members think you may be better suited as a candidate for a higher office—perhaps even Lt Governor.*"

"*Lt. Governor? Are you serious?*"

"*Quite so, I assure you. They already have a candidate for Governor in the wings, an upstanding businessman with a background in real estate development. However, it is felt that the ticket needs a strong law and order element for balance. I think you're just the man. What do you think?*"

"*Well I'm flattered, of course . . . I hadn't really considered anything post retirement beyond seeking the Sheriff's office. I'll have to think this through. When do you need an answer?*"

"*The sooner the better! Of course, there are some minor, uh, administrative issues to be dealt with before I can go forward with the recommendation for your proposed candidacy—things you should tidy up before you retire. Crime statistics can play a significant role in the public relations aspect of a campaign, you know. For example, some recent suicides that your department has handled are still listed as open cases—that bespeaks of sloppy administration, poor attention to detail. That's something we simply can't have in a strong law and order candidate. Get that taken care of, and we can proceed.*"

"*Senator, what are you saying? Are you seriously telling me to close those investigations?*"

"*I'm just suggesting that you bring your statistics in line with what would put you, as a senior law enforcement official, in the best possible light politically.*"

"*I can't— Wait! What are you doing? Let go! Where are we going—*"

"*Quiet! Keep your voice down! Listen, Edwin, it's a simple thing—for the love of God—do as I ask! Do it for both our sakes!*"

"*What the hell? Jeremiah, what are you so afraid of? Calm down. Look, I will look into it and see what I can do. I can make no promises—you know that.*"

"*Please, Edwin—it's vitally important . . . You have no idea!*"

"*Jeremiah, we are done here.*"

The tape ended; Dunbar turned the recorder off.

"Did that sound like a bribe to anybody else?" Dombrowski asked.

"Yeah. Sounds almost like a threat, as well," Waters observed. "I can see why the captain got this recording in the mail right away."

"Which tells us he was alive when he left that house," Katie pointed out. "Do we know what post office he used?"

"We do." Dunbar tapped his finger on the corner of the padded envelope. "See the postmark? It's on his way home from Farrell's house."

The chief nudged the cue ball toward him. He caught the cue ball before it struck the bumper and let his index finger roll it in a small circle on the felt. "You can follow up, but I think that's what happened."

"And now, of those two voices, one man is dead," Dombrowski observed, "and the other is missing, presumed dead. Has there been any further word on Widermark's missing plane? Anything from the Coast Guard?"

"No, nothing," Dunbar responded. He sent the cue ball rolling towards Waters. "Lieutenant, what do you propose to do?"

Waters picked the white ball up and cradled it in his hand. "Our next step, Chief, is to examine Capt. Walker's home. We're aware that CSI has already been there, but these detectives need to see for themselves. Are you going to keep the NAGRA or turn it over to CSI?"

"I'll be calling CSI after you all depart. They may send someone out to pick it up, or more likely, since they're spread a little thin right now, ask me to maintain custody until tomorrow, Nonetheless, I wanted you—all of you—to hear this tape first. "

"Yes, sir, I understand, and we appreciate the opportunity." Waters responded, and carefully placed the cue ball on the head spot. "If that's it, Chief, we'll be going."

"Good hunting and good luck."

———————

BACK IN THE CAR, KATIE succumbed to a head shaking yawn, and rolled her shoulders.

"You all right?" Dombrowski asked.

"Yeah, I'm just tired. I'll be fine. Are we going to the captain's place now?"

Waters looked over his shoulder and shrugged. "Maybe, but, it's getting pretty late and I don't have the keys—CSI does. I've got to call and check. Give me a minute."

As he made the call, Dombrowski turned to face her. "You know, it's after eleven. We've been pushing pretty hard for the past coupla days. We could do the captain's place tomorrow, in the daylight. Hell, I could use a shower, change of clothes, and some rest as well. What do you think?"

She mimicked sniffing in his direction and grimaced. "Whoa! You'll get no argument from me. I wouldn't turn down a nice hot bath. I think I could soak for hours."

Waters turned and shook his head. "Well, you're both gonna get your wish. I can't get the keys before tomorrow morning. So, we're gonna have to call it a night."

Dombrowski shrugged, unfazed. "No big deal. The captain's place isn't going anywhere; and, we'd rather see it in the daylight, anyway. So LT, if you could just take us back to Katie's place, that'd be fine. My truck is there."

"Okay. I'll call you in the morning, once I've got the keys."

"That'll work," Katie assured him. "We'll just meet you at the scene—the captain's place. Okay?"

"That's a plan," Waters agreed.

CH 33

CAPTAIN EDWIN WALKER'S home was a modest bungalow in a bedroom community that predated the Second World War.

Katie thought the Craftsman-style home was quite charming. She nudged her partner as they strolled up the blue slate walkway and approached the wide welcoming porch. "Wow, D, this place is really nice; I like it. Have you ever been here before?"

"Yeah, once, about ten years ago, when the captain's wife died. We all came back here after the funeral, you know, for a sort of wake. That was the only time though."

She didn't quite know how to respond to that. She was spared as the door swung open and Lt. Waters greeted them. "Good morning, Detectives. Please come in. I have news."

"Morning, LT," Dombrowski hailed. "So, what's up?"

"Come on into the kitchen. I found some coffee; I've got a pot brewing. I didn't think the captain would mind."

Seated at the kitchen table, mugs of steaming coffee before them, Dombrowski raised his cup and offered a toast, "To the captain."

"And our commitment to get these bastards," Katie added.

"Hear! Hear!" chimed in the lieutenant.

"Okay, LT, what's the news?" Dombrowski asked.

"It's not good. You remember that our federal friends were watching the numbered account identified in the ransom note; so, we knew that as of yesterday Pierre Demotte hadn't done anything about the ransom."

"I thought that was too strange," Katie interjected. "So, now what's happened?"

"This morning, another box was delivered to his hotel—another finger. And the ransom demand has doubled to ten million dollars."

"Shit!" Dombrowski exclaimed. "How did we find out? Did he report it?"

"Not exactly. This time his wife was present when the concierge delivered the box to their suite. Apparently, she pretty much went ballistic when he finally explained what was going on. The hotel staff, thinking a domestic assault was in progress, called 911. A two-man patrol unit arrived and had to separate the couple—she was pummelling him. The wife would have been on her way to jail had not Assistant Chief Dunbar intervened."

"A kidnapping trumps a domestic," Katie wisecracked.

"How about the deliveryman?" the sergeant asked, ignoring her and sipping his coffee. "Not the concierge, I mean the person who brought the box to the hotel."

The lieutenant blew across his steaming mug. "A bike messenger, just a college student, who picked up the box from a male subject at the bus station. His description of the guy is pretty vague. The kid gets his assignments via text on his phone. His dispatcher just relayed instructions, and charged the delivery fee to a credit card account. It turns out the account is bogus; the number has shown up in a couple of identity theft cases."

Katie wrapped her hands around her cup and murmured, "Big surprise."

Dombrowski took another long sip and pondered. "So, I gather neither the delivery kid nor the concierge knew what was in the box—the finger and the new ransom demand?"

Waters shrugged and opened his palms. "So they both assert, and we have no reason to believe otherwise."

"So," Katie probed, "what is Pierre Demotte going to do now, especially now that his wife, Nicole, knows the truth?"

The lieutenant slid his mug from one hand to the other and sighed. "Our best guess is that he'll comply with the ransom demand, assuming he has the resources. The account is still being monitored so we'll be advised whatever happens. Oh, I should mention that Nicole Demotte made some pretty damning accusations in the presence of the patrol officers—of course, she was extremely upset at the time."

"Oh, she did, huh?" Dombrowski's interest piqued. "Like what exactly?"

Waters took a healthy gulp and smiled wryly. "That her ex, Walter Farrell, was to blame. That he no doubt orchestrated this whole scenario just to get at her new husband's money. That he didn't care one bit about her daughter, that she was just a pawn in some sick game, another wild moneymaking scheme."

Katie raised her cup to her lips and mused aloud. "You know what? Nicole Demotte may not be entirely wrong."

"Yeah," Dombrowski agreed. "Farrell is kind of a strange one. Did she say anything else?"

Waters drained his mug and slid it to the center of the table. "Oh, she ranted and raved for some time. Her current husband wasn't spared any of her wrath, either. He seriously underestimated her response to his decision to not fully inform her of the first ransom demand. As for the fingers, well, they just pushed her over the edge."

"So, I assume," Dombrowski reasoned, "both fingers are now with the M.E.? And this is now an official kidnapping investigation? Do we get to come out of the shadows?"

"Yes, yes, and no," Waters hedged. "It is an official case, but according to Chief Dunbar you two are to stay below the radar. Detectives Walden and Donahue have been assigned, and will be read in to a limited access level. They'll know there are some UC operatives working, but they won't know it's you two. I'll serve as interface and buffer between them and you guys."

"Oh, so we," Katie rationalized with a mischievous gleam in her eye, "won't have to do any of the reports, right?"

Waters shook his head, but couldn't hide his smile. "You would find that a silver lining. Yes, I suppose you're right. Walden and Donahue will be doing the reports."

Dombrowski finished his coffee and slid his empty mug next to the lieutenant's. He sighed and stretched. "Anybody want more java? I gotta lay off or I'll get the jitts."

Katie drained her cup and shook her head. "Nah, I'm good. Shouldn't we start looking around?"

"By all means," Waters encouraged, as he rose and collected the empty coffee mugs. "Look anywhere you like. CSI has already been through here; they didn't find much. I don't think you can compromise anything."

The small house held no surprises. It had obviously been searched by experts, yet was not left in a dishevelled state. After their secondary search, Katie and Dombrowski found themselves returning to the modest den, a cozy room with bookcases lining the walls and a large window overlooking a garden.

Dombrowski settled into a well-worn leather armchair. "This is really comfortable. I think he spent most of his time in here." He swept a hand toward the stuffed bookcases. "He sure liked to read."

"Yeah," Katie agreed. "That's a lot of books. I guess we're gonna have to look through them. Hey, here's his keyboard and monitor on this built-in desk, but where's his PC? Did he have a laptop, too?"

"No laptop; CSI has his desktop computer," said the lieutenant from the doorway, "and any media storage, too."

"Oh, yeah," she acknowledged, "that would make sense. I remember something from the NAGRA recording, something about political software—"

She was interrupted by her ringing cell phone.

"Callahan ... Oh, hi Kenny ... What? Uh, no, it showed low battery so I'm pretty sure I turned it off ... Okay, thanks. Hey wait! We're checking out the captain's house as we speak, and it seems your CSI guys have his computer, right? Yeah, right, the PC housing the drives, and any storage media. Listen, we need to check for some sort of political software he may have used ... Oh, yeah, that'd be great ... Yeah, just call me. Thanks a heap, bye."

She slipped her phone into her pocket and turned to her partner and Lt. Waters. "You both heard, right? That was Kenny. They haven't had much luck locating my missing burner phone. They were under the assumption I'd left it on; but, I'm pretty sure I turned it off. Anyway, they're gonna try to turn it back on in the hope there's enough residual charge to triangulate the signal."

"They can turn an off phone on?" the lieutenant asked.

"Emilio's people can," Dombrowski assured him.

"Yeah, Kenny thinks they're awesome," Katie agreed. "Anyway, it may be nothing, but you heard me ask him to look into that political software thing."

"Indeed, leave no stone unturned," Waters intoned.

———

SOME TIME LATER, THEY concluded there was no more to be learned at the captain's home. Maybe it was just her imagination, but Katie felt the house was somehow sadder now that it was no longer a home.

They stood on the front porch as the lieutenant locked the front door.

"What now, LT?" Dombrowski asked.

Before Waters could respond, his cell phone rang.

"Waters here ... I see ... Yes, of course ... Please let me know right away, would you? Thanks, bye."

Katie and Dombrowski exchanged worried looks.

Waters sighed heavily. "A few minutes ago, Pierre Demotte paid the ransom via a wire transfer."

"The ten million?" Katie interrupted in shock.

"Yes, so it seems. The feds tagged the transfer and are tracking it. They've located the bank—"

"Let me guess," Dombrowski interjected, "a bank we're already familiar with, in the Cayman Islands?"

Waters nodded. "The same. Now, what has not yet happened is any sort of communication regarding the victim's release. The Demottes are waiting to hear from the kidnappers."

"This is not good," Katie breathed.

"Not at all," Dombrowski agreed. "Now there's no reason to keep her alive—especially if there's any chance she could identify anyone involved. This sucks!"

"Damn! What can we do?" Katie demanded, her anger fuelling her anxiety.

"I don't see anything that hasn't been thought of and covered to the best of our ability," Waters reasoned. "Maybe they will release her—"

"Fat chance," Katie spouted. "You know she's only a liability now! They're gonna—"

Her cell phone rang.

"Callahan! What is it? Oh, sorry, Kenny . . . Yeah? Where? That's great! Text me the address *asap*. Thanks, bye."

Dombrowski and Waters stared at her expectantly.

"They found my phone—well, the coordinates. They think it's in a residential neighborhood. He'll text the address!"

"Don't get too optimistic," Waters warned. "The perps may have tossed the phone; some kid may have found it on his way home from school."

His undeniable logic struck home; Katie's shoulders sagged. She desperately wanted to do something—anything.

"However," Waters reasoned, "it's a lead we can't ignore, even if it's just a loose end we need to tie up."

"Hell! It's gotta be more than that, LT," Dombrowski exclaimed. "We all think these are probably the same people who snatched Amanda. We've gotta find her before she comes to any more harm. Maybe this'll lead to her location. We can hope, right?"

"Right!" Katie echoed, with a growing sense of unease.

CH 34

DOMBROWSKI SLOWED AND scanned for oncoming traffic before he turned his truck into the neighborhood. His phone lay on the bench seat between him and Katie. The line was open to Lt. Waters, who followed in his unmarked cruiser a quarter mile to the rear.

"LT, the neighborhood entrance will be coming up on your left. It's not a gated community, but it's real nice. There's nothing parked on the streets. So, you might want to lay low somewhere while we find the address."

"Ten-four. I'll drive past the entrance. There's a gas station at the next intersection; I'll pull in there and get some patrol units headed our way. Advise when you've located the house. Remember to use your phone—not the radio."

"Will do. I'll call you back when we know something."

"Okay, be careful. Talk to you later."

Katie hefted the hand-held mobile radio and declared, "I understand the need to stay off the radio, but I feel better having it with us."

"Yeah, I get it," he agreed, "you never know. Keep it off unless we absolutely have to use it. And for gosh sake, don't lose it; that one's issued to the LT."

"Relax, D, this ain't my first rodeo."

He grinned. "What a smart-ass. What's your GPS say? Are we close?"

She stared at her phone. Looking up, she scanned for street signs. "Yeah, we're one block over. Take your next right and hold at the following intersection. We ought to be able to see it from there; it'll be to our right, third house on the south side."

He followed her instructions and eased to a stop at an intersection with four-way stop signs. A short, bright yellow school bus, now empty of special-needs students, faced them, its flashing turn signal indicating the driver's intention to turn left. Dombrowski waved the driver on. The bus executed the turn and proceeded down the same street, right past the target house. Dombrowski's truck followed in its wake. As he and Katie drove past, they got a good look.

"Whoa, that is one nice house, indeed," the sergeant breathed without turning his head. "Are we sure about the address? Do you see any signs of life?"

"The address is right, but I don't see . . . Oh shit! A white van is parked on the side, back near the privacy fence. Damn! I didn't get a very good look! Do the block!"

"Easy Katie—I'll do the block. You call the LT."

"I'm on it!" She made the connection and had the line open once again in less than a minute.

The school bus continued straight. Dombrowski spared not a moment and took the next right, and the next two successive rights to circumnavigate the block.

"Aw, crap!" Dombrowski hissed. "The damn van's gone! Katie, how many ways are there outta this neighborhood?"

"Hold on!" She checked her GPS app. "Damn, at least half a dozen. What now?"

Waters' voice crackled from the open line. "Sergeant, you and your partner stay on the house. The patrol units and I will do a rolling search and see if we can find the van."

"Okay, LT, we'll stay on the house. Good luck!"

Dombrowski parked in the same block that gave them a good view of the house. Unfortunately, they were the only vehicle parked on the street and a little too obvious.

"Do you think they made us?" Katie asked.

"Dunno, but if we sit here for much longer, somebody will for sure—maybe the neighborhood watch."

"Yeah, your truck is a little ratty for this neighborhood," she teased. "Don't you think?"

"Once a smart-ass," he grumbled, "always a smart-ass."

"Look, seriously, how long are we gonna sit here? We gotta hit that house—Amanda might be in there!"

"We don't know anything about that place. It's a third party residence; we'd need a search warrant!"

"What? Are you kidding me? A kidnapping victim in imminent danger doesn't constitute an exigent circumstance? Besides, we're not cops, remember? We're suspended rogues!"

A slow smile began to work its way across his face. "You know, you may have a point there. And I'm getting an overwhelming sense of *déjà vu*."

"Oh, you do mean, of course," she confirmed, a lone eyebrow wryly arched, "because it reminds you of a certain house we recently found, right?"

"More than likely," he admitted, his smile becoming more blatant. "Well, I guess we could leave the truck here and take a little stroll up the block. Do you suppose it would be polite to knock?"

Her smile was bigger.

THERE WAS NO RESPONSE when they knocked on the front door. Katie peered through the sidelight glass and pressed the doorbell twice—still no response.

"D, the doorbell sounds too loud in there; there's a bit of an echo. This is a foyer or an entrance hall, but I don't see any furniture. I think this place is vacant."

"Might be. Let's check the back."

As they made their way down the side of the house, Dombrowski pointed to the electric meter. "Power's on. The disc is spinning; something is using the juice."

Katie pushed the privacy fence gate open and peered into the yard. "Clear. Patio doors ten yards to our left."

He nodded in understanding. "Go."

The sliding glass patio doors were not locked, only slid closed, not latched. It was as if someone had left in a hurry.

Katie studied the simple latch mechanism and smiled. Silently, they slipped inside.

The house did appear vacant. They could see the first floor was completely devoid of furniture, and harbored a mildly musty odor. Something about the vague smell nagged at Katie, but she couldn't pin it down.

They had a brief surge of hope when they found the garage, but too, was empty.

They found the second floor unoccupied as well. Three of the four bedrooms held pairs of folding cots, similar to old military issue.

Dombrowski pointed to the final bedroom. The door s' ajar.

Katie spied the hasp and dangling padlock bolted to the doorjamb. She pushed the door fully open with the head of her flashlight and let the light beam wash within.

A soiled mattress lay on the hardwood floor; the closet stood open and empty. A sheet of thin plywood was screwed to the lone window frame. The scenario was distinctly familiar.

"Oh, man," Katie whispered, "talk about some déjà vu—check this out."

Dombrowski assessed the entire room in mere seconds and said, "No restraints, and it doesn't smell as bad."

Katie sniffed and agreed. "You're right. Is that blood?"

He leaned closer and played his light across the small string of coagulated spatter. "Looks like it," he agreed. "But it's dry. I can't begin to guess how old it is. See that swipe mark? It looks like there was more, but someone swabbed it up. They must've missed this little bit."

Katie panned her light over the entire floor. "D, over here by the door, looks like another patch of blood, more like a track about half an inch wide and three inches long."

"Yeah, I see. It's like a tire track—something on wheels, maybe?"

She shrugged; there were no answers here, only more questions. And there was still more of the house to search.

"Let's move on," Dombrowski suggested.

"The basement."

"Yeah, quietly."

The basement was quite what they expected; fully finished, carpeted, and furnished with high-end office furniture. A row of incongruous wooden crates were stacked along one wall. That musty smell was slightly more prevalent here, as well

Dombrowski lifted the unsecured lid of a crate and peeked inside. He did the same to each crate, counting as he proceeded. "Hmm, a dozen. They're all empty but for packing material, shredded paper and excelsior. There are marks on the inner walls where something's made contact."

Katie stood in the middle of the room and closed her eyes. She turned her head from side to side, listening and taking short breaths through her nose. When she opened her eyes, she found her partner staring at her in puzzlement. "D, you gotta bear with me, but I think I've been here before, in this room. It feels right."

"You mean when you were snatched?"

"Yeah. It's the feel of this place, and the smell. There's something about the smell."

"They kept you blindfolded—well, hooded—the whole time, right?"

"Yeah, so?"

"Well, it stands to reason that you might remember what you could perceive with your other senses. What did you hear?"

"Uh, there were other people in the room. I could hear them moving around and stuff—it could have been kinda like office sounds. They didn't speak, though."

"Did you sit or stand?"

"Stood, at first, then I was made to sit."

He pulled a rolling office chair over. "Okay, take a seat. What else can you remember?"

She settled into the chair and closed her eyes. She took a few deep calming breaths and relaxed. "Someone kept coming and going through a door, a heavy one, like to the outside rather than inside."

He looked around, but saw no other door at first glance. Moving along the room's perimeter, he methodically searched the recesses of the space. "Found it! There's an alcove back here. It is a heavy door, but it doesn't go outside." He shoved some cardboard boxes aside.

"What?" She was at his elbow. "Where does it go?"

"Only one way to find out." He tried the knob—unlocked.

They readied their pistols and flashlights. After a mutual nod, he twisted the knob and pushed. The door opened; a flight of stairs descended into darkness.

Dombrowski nudged his partner, nodded toward the stairs, and sighed in humorous resignation. "Ah, once more into the breach."

Ignoring the misappropriated quote she started forward.

As their light beams cascaded off each step, the rogue detectives patiently made their way to the lowermost level. They made no sound, nor heard any. At the base of the stairwell, they faced a familiar hanging wall of overlapping vinyl strips—a rudimentary air lock. They knew what to expect; and they were not disappointed.

"Clear!" Dombrowski announced, as his light beam careened around the large unfinished space.

"Clear," Katie confirmed.

"Shit!" He spat. "It's another damn lab!"

"Yeah," she echoed, "in a subbasement. Does it look active to you?"

"You know, it doesn't. In fact, look there; all the glassware is bubble-wrapped. Here's another roll of bubble wrap. Are they packing up?"

"Yeah, I'll bet they are. That would explain those crates upstairs," she reasoned.

"Would all those crates fit in a van?" he pondered, and answered his own question. "Of course they would! They're getting ready to move again. Or, maybe this crew is ready to cut their losses and bug out, could that be it?"

"Let's hope not," Katie cautioned. "Where would that leave Amanda?"

Their eyes locked. They were running out of time. They had to find this girl before she disappeared forever—or worse.

"We don't know for sure she was here," Dombrowski admitted, "but my gut says she was."

"Mine, too," echoed Katie.

"Think she was being held in that bedroom?" he asked.

"Like in that other house? Yeah, I do, but something's different."

"There weren't any restraints, for one thing," he offered.

"And it didn't have that smell, either," she countered. "I don't think they had her here for very long."

"That makes sense," he agreed. "The blood bothers me. All I can think of are her fingers."

"It bothers me, too," she admitted. "I don't even want to go there; but, I'm too afraid we're right."

He shook his head and sighed. "So, the question is; where is she now? Where have they taken her?"

"I don't think it's a coincidence that the van is gone as well," she declared. "She's probably in it, and—"

"We just missed them, damn it!" He kicked at a pile of clothing in frustration, sending it tumbling across the concrete floor.

"What is that?" She asked, letting her light beam settle on the gray material. She bent down and examined what appeared to be a custodial workman's shirt. A pair of matching trousers lay nearby.

"That looks familiar," Dombrowski remarked, joining her. "Is there a company name or logo on that shirt?"

"You're thinking pool cleaning company? Yeah, me too. But there's nothing on any of these. They're just generic work clothes. Hell, I think the janitors in our building wear the same sort of thing—maybe that's why you think it looks familiar?"

"Eh, maybe," Dombrowski mused aloud. "Something about this bugs me. Didn't we find some of our victims in the last lab house wearing gray stuff?"

"Yeah, that's right," she confirmed. "All of Rene's crew were dressed in black; the other guys were in gray. Wait, those were gray jumpsuits—"

"Huh?"

"One piece coveralls—you know, jumpsuits," she explained. "Look, these are separates—pants and shirts. Get it? Individual pieces of a workman's uniform, not a one piece coverall. Jeez, what is it about men and clothes? Sometimes you guys can be so clueless!"

"So, now you're saying this is important?" He truly was growing confused, and didn't see the relevance.

"I don't know, maybe . . . Oh, never mind."

"Oh, that helps immensely," he groused and retrieved his phone. "Crap, I'm not getting a signal down here. Let's go. We've gotta check in with the LT—maybe they found the van."

"Okay, but we haven't found my phone yet," she reminded him and panned her flashlight around.

"We haven't, have we? Hmm . . ."

"D, look, over in that corner. Is that a computer tower?"

Dombrowski added his light to hers. The waist-high black metal box hummed quietly while a series of LEDs blinked randomly.

"Whoa, look here, behind it—there's a rat's nest of wires and connectors" she breathed "Not just a computer; I think this is a server, a pretty sophisticated one at that."

"So, that's why the electric meter was spinning so fast?" he asked.

"Could be; this thing is definitely using some juice. I don't see a keyboard or monitor. Maybe remote access, or WiFi? I bet Kenny would know."

"Yeah, no doubt," he agreed. "Come on, I think we need to get outta here right away. If we haven't blown it, maybe we can still surveil this place now that we know it's a lab and they're packing it up."

"If they have a server here," she reasoned, "it's more than just a lab."

"I know. Come on, let's go!"

CH 35

DOMBROWSKI FOUND LT. Waters parked behind the corner gas station, a thin cloud of cigarette smoke wafting past the upper corner of the driver's open window. The sergeant parked alongside, their drivers' doors only a foot apart.

"Sorry, no luck finding the van," Waters began. "I had to release the patrol units to return to their regular assignments; their calls were starting to back up."

"Ah, that's okay, LT. Is there any word on Amanda Farrell—anything about her being released yet?"

"No, nothing. Walden and Donahue are still with the Demottes; they're sending me periodic updates every couple of hours." Waters tilted his head and lowered his voice. "Listen, I gotta ask; do y'all think that was the same van that was involved in Katie's situation?"

Dombrowski looked to Katie, who shrugged and nodded affirmatively. He answered for both of them. "Yeah, we think so. Hell, if we didn't spook them, the van might even come back to that house. We're pretty sure that's how they move the lab gear around."

Waters took a long drag on his cigarette. "It's clouding up; looks like it's gonna rain. You want to surveil the house?"

"That could be a problem, LT. Aside from the weather getting nasty, we'd probably have to get a willing neighbor to cooperate with us. See, it looks like this might be one of those communities that doesn't allow residents to park on the street—you know, real strict HOA covenants. So, anything parked on the street is real obvious. I'm a little worried that we may have already been made—"

"Yeah," interrupted Katie, "this truck stuck out like a sore thumb."

Dombrowski scowled at his partner and continued. "Anyway, there's no doubt that somebody's packing up that lab, and they're not finished. I think we may as well get a search warrant and take it down."

"A search warrant, really?" Waters asked. "And just what probable cause would you articulate in the affidavit? There's no way you could know there's a meth lab in there—not legally. No, don't say another word—I don't want to know how you arrived at that conclusion."

The sergeant grinned. "Actually, LT, I was referring to a search warrant for Katie's stolen cell phone. Anything found in the course of that search would be admissible. Our probable cause would be the phone's electronic signal coming from within the premises, once it's turned on of course."

"I see." Waters took another long drag on his cigarette and sighed. "Of course, that presumes that Emilio's technical people would be willing, and have the authorization, to make that particular tactic and proprietary technical trick part of the public record, doesn't it?"

Dombrowski's grin faded. He and Katie exchanged worried glances.

"Damn, LT, I hadn't thought about that. Do you think it would be a problem?"

"I have no idea," Waters admitted. "But you should most certainly find out before you compromise what may be classified information. Isn't young Reynolds still with Emilio's people? Shouldn't you try contacting him?"

"I'm on it," Katie declared, and began scrolling through her phone's speed dial menu.

Waters' phone rang; he peered at the caller ID. "It's A.C. Dunbar. I gotta take this."

As the lieutenant took his call, Dombrowski turned to his partner and heard her half of the conversation.

". . . No, I understand . . . Yeah, please, I'll hold."

Dombrowski opened his palms and asked, "What?"

Katie shook her head and explained. "I'm on *hold*. They didn't keep continuous track of the phone's signal. The battery was low, so they briefly turned it on and pinged it. Once they had the location, they turned it off to conserve what little charge was in the battery. Ken doesn't know if the Marshals Service will agree to being named in the search warrant affidavit—he's checking."

"That's not good. Not keeping track of a continuous signal may present a P/C problem for us," he reasoned. "Can they ping it again?"

"Dunno," she answered. "I'll ask."

"Sergeant," hailed Waters, "I have to meet with Chief Dunbar. It seems the Coast Guard has located Senator Widermark's aircraft, or what's left of it. I'm to meet with him so we can participate in a conference call in about thirty minutes. Sorry, but I've got to go. What's your status?"

"Katie's on the phone with Kenny Reynolds and the Marshals Service. We may have an answer shortly on the phone P/C. In the meantime, I think we need to clear this area in case the van returns. We'll probably go to Katie's house. You'll call us there?"

"Affirmative. The patrol units are to notify me if they spot the van. I'll call you immediately. Be safe."

"Thanks, LT, you, too."

As Waters drove off, Dombrowski turned to Katie; she was back on the line with Kenny.

"... Are you sure? Shit! That's not gonna help ... No, you go ahead ... No, just call me back ... Okay, bye."

"Well?" he probed, as sporadic raindrops began to pelt the windshield.

"It's not gonna work out on the affidavit P/C—"

"They won't do it?"

She shook her head and said, "It's not that; the signal's not there any more. They tried to ping it again using the same cell towers as before, but no joy. Anyway, Ken said they're going to try something else. He's gonna call me back."

"Man, that sucks," he groaned. "I thought we had such a great idea going after the phone with a search warrant. Oh, well, we gotta clear this area. Let's go back to your place, okay?"

"All right. I'm hungry; let's grab something on the way."

AN HOUR LATER THEY realized they had made a poor choice in restaurants. Katie finished her diet soft drink with an audible slurp and pushed back from the undersized table. Her partner had commandeered two of the tiny tables for his own use and now sat wedged between them like a contemplative Buddha settling into gastric regret.

"I ate too much, too fast, again." He groaned and added, "Fast food joints can be the bane of street cops; far too convenient for too many calories to be too easily acquired. That burger and fries combo meal was bland and tasteless."

"Didn't seem to bother you while you were wolfing it down," she teased as her phone rang. "Callahan... Hey, Kenny... Really? Are you sure? Great! We're heading to my place now. Okay, bye."

Dombrowski was already on his feet and stuffing his trash into the nearest waste can. Without a word, he followed Katie outside. With barely a glance at the thickening overcast they trotted through the erratic raindrops to his truck.

Once seated, she turned and announced, "They found the signa; it's moving! It's—"

"In the van!" he finished, in a flash of realization.

"Yeah, it's gotta be! He's gonna call if it stops moving and they can get a fix on a location. It should work so long as the battery holds out. I told him we'd be at my house. He couldn't talk more; he said something else was going on and he had to go."

"Yeah," Dombrowski acknowledged, "probably that thing about the Coast Guard and Widermark's plane. Come on; let's get to your place."

THEY WEREN'T IN KATIE'S home for more than ten minutes before her cell phone rang. It was Kenny, again.

"Yeah, give me a second . . . Okay, repeat the coordinates . . . got it . . . No, I'll stand by while you look up the actual street address . . . What? Are you shitting me?"

She scribbled down the address and held it up for Dombrowski to see. His eyes widened and he gestured for the phone. She smiled and held up one finger for patience.

"Kenny? Listen, Dombrowski wants to talk to you—hold on." She handed her phone to her eager partner.

"Hey, Ken, good work! Listen, we need a favor. Can you swing by the office, on the QT, of course, and pick up some things for us?"

Katie looked on in puzzlement, but was soon lost in her own thoughts. She stared at the address she'd written down and wandered into the kitchen. Staring out the window over the sink, she let her thoughts coalesce. Her lips drew into a line of grim determination; now she had some answers—and a goal.

The urgency in her partner's voice confirmed her conviction and drew her back to the living room. "Yeah, we could meet you or you can swing by Katie's. That'd be great, the sooner the better. We'll be here. Thanks, man. Bye."

TWO HOURS LATER, KATIE knocked briskly on the ornate wooden door. The rain was fairly steady now and her hooded jacket was not waterproof. She could feel the clammy chill of a wet trickle run down between her shoulder blades as she waited. She knocked again—this was getting old, fast.

The door finally swung open. Consuela's shocked face peered at her in complete surprise. "Detective Callahan! What are you doing here? Come in—come in out of the rain!"

Katie stepped into the foyer and pulled her soaking hood back. Her limp hair was damp and tangled. A puddle began to form on the polished marble floor around her feet.

"I'm sorry, Consuela." She sighed heavily. "But I'm not a detective any more. I'm sorry for this mess." She gestured to the spreading puddle.

"It is nothing," the maid assured her. "But Miss Katie, why are you here? Are you alone?"

"I'm on my own . . . I came to see Mr. Farrell—I have to talk to him. I-I don't know what else to do."

"But Miss Katie, he—Mr. Farrell—sees no one without an appointment. He is very firm about that; he never makes exceptions. I am so sorry."

Katie wiped her hand across her face and took a deep breath. "Oh, I believe he'll make an exception for me—just tell him I'm here."

"You do not understand—he will not see you. It is simply not done. I am sorry, but I must ask you to leave." Consuela stood firm, hands on her hips.

Katie was not dissuaded; nor would she be dismissed. "I'm afraid you don't understand, Consuela. Please, tell him I'm here—and that I'm on my own. I've figured out what he's doing . . . And I have . . . a proposal. He'll see me—he must, because I won't take no for an answer!"

The maid wrung her hands as her eyes darted about. She was clearly very uncomfortable at the notion of breaking the house rules. She fidgeted for a moment and seemed to come to a decision. "*Ay-yi* . . . Please, you must wait here. I will speak with him."

"Thank you."

Only a few minutes elapsed before Consuela returned to the foyer, but it felt uncomfortably longer to Katie.

"Miss Katie, he will give you five minutes. This way, please."

Consuela led Katie to the doors of Farrell's office study. She knocked twice and pushed the door open. A pair of brass desk lamps provided the only illumination. Walter Farrell sat behind his massive desk and stared at Katie without comment or expression.

With a sweep of her hand, Consuela urged Katie to enter. Katie stepped into the room. Consuela followed and closed the door. Farrell remained silent.

Consuela guided Katie to a spot in front of the desk, between a set of armchairs. The maid leaned in and whispered, "You must tell him why you are here."

Katie glanced at Consuela, who nodded reassuringly and stepped back. Katie then faced Farrell, who had yet to speak. Undaunted, she decided that the direct approach would serve best. She took a deep breath, determined to speak firmly, with conviction.

"I know what you are doing. I figured out what you've been up to . . . I know you're scamming your ex-wife and her husband—and you're using your own daughter as a pawn! You've used me in your damned scheme! You've ruined my life—cost me my job!"

Farrell snorted in derision, but let the unnerving silence stretch on.

Katie was losing patience. "You bastard! Say something, damn it!"

Farrell's eyes flared but his lips did not part.

"Nothing, huh? Well, I've got news for you! Now you're gonna make this up to me! We're gonna reach an accommodation, understand?"

Farrell still said nothing.

She found his silence frustrating in the extreme. She was having difficulty keeping her temper in check. She had to get him to speak. She had no choice—it was time to play her trump card.

"You see, I'm not giving you any choice here," she threatened, as she approached the desk, placed her hands on its surface, and leaned into his face, "because I know all about your meth labs!"

Her eyes raked his face for his reaction. There it was—a shocked gasp! She'd struck home, for certain!

She smiled and her gaze dropped. Too late, she saw that his wrists were duct taped to the arms of his chair.

Sudden pain gripped her in a spasm that flashed down her spine to her fingertips and toes—and back up again. All her muscles collapsed; her head smashed to the surface of the desk, bloodying her nose, and robbing her of conscious thought.

As she crumpled to the carpet, awareness ebbing away, she sensed the dim outline of Consuela leaning over her, the bright spark of a stun gun's discharge, and a whiff of ozone.

The maid's soft voice was like a trickle of water draining away. "Oh, Miss Katie, you poor thing. You really should have taken *no* for an answer."

CH 36

———

SLIPPING THROUGH THE rain and the pervasive shadows of dusk, Dombrowski made his way unseen to the rear of Farrell's house.

He was prepared to force the lock on an access door located on the rear wall of the garage, but luck was with him—it was not locked. The dim garage interior was large, easily accommodating three vehicles; an SUV, a sedan, and the ever elusive white van. He laid a hand upon the hood of each vehicle; only the van held a hint of warmth.

Muffled voices sent him scrambling for a darkened corner. He squeezed beside a tall metal cabinet and hunkered down near a bin of gardening tools just as a set of overhead fluorescent lights flared to life. It was a poor hiding place; but, there was enough random junk stacked along this wall that if no one looked directly at him, he just might remain undetected.

He peered upward. A set of large signs stored in the rafters caught his eye; Associated Construction. *What the hell? Has Farrell got his fingers into the renovations as well? Is this part of the scam?*

Two sets of footsteps approached the van. The side door of the vehicle slid open with a *whorl-clunk*. Someone grunted as something heavy was loaded into the van.

"Oof . . . *Es todo*? This is everything, *no mas*?"

"Yeah, we're ready to roll. We go back and pack up, and then we're outta here. Is there gonna be enough room in here now with this extra box?"

"*Si*, is heavy, but not so big. If we shove in corner, is room."

Another voice called from across the garage. "Hey, if you guys are through screwing around out here, I need one of you to help me. The boss wants the girl brought up to the office. I need help getting that damned chair up the stairs."

"Shit!" the nearest voice softly grumbled. "I get tired of moving that little bitch around."

"Why put her in basement? Just more work for us, no?"

"Eh, the boss said to. I dunno—I just do what I'm told." In a louder voice he yelled, "Keep your shirt on—I'm coming!"

"Is okay, *ese*. You go—I finish here."

As the departing footsteps receded, Dombrowski dared to peek around the cabinet. He saw the van rock on its suspension as the remaining man stepped up into the vehicle to deal with the cargo.

Moments later Dombrowski was waiting for him when he stepped back down to the concrete floor. "Greetings, *amigo*. Show me your hands! Hey, don't I know you?"

The man's shocked expression was quickly replaced by one of panic and desperation. He swung wildly, but Dombrowski was ready and easily blocked the punch. An uppercut palm strike snapped the man's head back; his eyes rolled up into his head. The sergeant delivered a sweeping kick to the inside of the man's right knee that crumpled him like a rag doll.

He was out cold, but Dombrowski still trussed him up with flex cuffs—wrists and ankles—and heaved him into the back of the van. Then he noticed the roll of duct tape. Within a minute, the man's head was completely wrapped in the silvery tape, only his nose was left uncovered. Dombrowski leaned back and considered his work.

"Now, you'll be able to breathe just fine. I think you people did something like this to my partner; let's see how you like it. Besides, I really need you to stay quiet right now."

KATIE WAS DISORIENTED; her head throbbed. She was slouched in an armchair, slumped over its arm, in front of Farrell's desk. There was movement around her; someone was going through her pockets. She felt a rough hand remove her compact Glock 27 from her damp jacket. She thought it wise to remain limp; she had little choice since her muscles weren't yet cooperating and she was dizzy.

"*Pistola,*" announced a man's voice.

"As expected," Consuela confirmed. "Scan her with the radio frequency detector; be sure she doesn't have a transmitter."

Her eyes barely open under blood-stained lids, Katie saw the shape of a man approach and wave some device over and around her.

"*Nada* . . . Is clean," he said.

"*Bueno.* Bring the girl here, to this room. Be sure she is still *compliant. Andele!*"

Katie heard Farrell speak for the first time, the strain in his hoarse voice betraying his desperation. "Wh-what are you planning? Haven't I done everything you asked? What more do you want from me?"

"Your role in this enterprise is not yet complete, *patron,*" Consuela explained coyly, as she took a position behind Katie.

She grabbed the limp detective under her arms and pulled her upright in the chair. She pulled Katie's head back and let it loll against her shoulder. Satisfied, Consuela nodded.

"*Bueno.* We require another service of you, *patron.*"

Feigning unconsciousness, Katie watched through barely closed eyelids as Consuela stepped to Farrell's right side and freed the top two buttons of her maid's blouse. She gently pulled on a golden chain necklace plunging into her cleavage, and retrieved a mother-of-pearl handled straight razor. With a deft flick of her wrist that bespoke of long practiced competence, she displayed the bright blade before Farrell's wide eyes, and smirked at his fear.

"It is time for you to perform that task."

Words appeared to fail Farrell, swallowing emptiness.

Consuela smiled, and with a flash Katie barely saw, the maid severed the duct tape holding Farrell's right wrist to the chair.

He stared at her in surprised relief.

She stepped back, making no effort to free any more of his bonds. She closed the straight razor and let it descend once more into the valley of her décolletage. Suddenly, there was a pistol in her hand, the blunt muzzle of its suppressor aimed at his head.

He gasped in fear. She gave him a wry smile and lowered the weapon.

The door to the room opened, and a man entered. At a nod from Consuela, he motioned for another man to push an emaciated young woman in a wheelchair into the room. He pushed the wheelchair closer to Farrell's desk.

Katie could see the girl was duct taped to the wheelchair. Both her hands were swaddled in dirty bandages. Her head lolled from side to side; she drooled incessantly. Her greasy and stringy hair was plastered to her skull. She was obviously quite heavily drugged.

"A-Amanda," Farrell croaked. He jabbed a finger at Consuela. "What have you done? She was not to be hurt! The ransom was paid! What did you do to her?"

One of her henchmen handed Consuela a zippered black leather kit, the size of a large book.

Her pistol tucked under her arm, she opened the kit and laid it flat upon the desk, directly beneath one of the lamps. In the cone of light, Katie saw a compact medical kit containing various small surgical tools, vials of unknown liquids, and a row of syringes of different sizes.

Farrell gaped and locked eyes with Consuela.

Smirking, she casually gestured to one of the vials. "Amanda was very excitable; it was necessary to calm her down. Phenobarbital made her more tractable and compliant. But you are right; the ransom has been paid. So, be assured, her ordeal is almost over."

Consuela nodded once more, and one of the two henchmen took up a position behind Amanda's wheelchair. The other came to stand at Farrell's left shoulder. Without a word, she placed the pistol on the desk, within Farrell's reach, the muzzle now pointed at Katie.

"Your task is simple," the maid cooed and pointed to Katie. "This person is clearly a threat to your daughter, to yourself, and to us. She knows too much and can hurt us all. You must eliminate this threat—now. Use this gun."

Farrell hesitated, looking from Amanda to Consuela. He stared at the gun.

Consuela leaned forward and hissed, "If you fail to act, your daughter will die—here and now—from an overdose of Phenobarbital . . . And you will watch."

Farrell blanched. He reached out with his free right hand and grasped the pistol grip. Heavier than he expected, the muzzle dipped to the desktop with the weight of the suppressor. He raised it incrementally and centered it on Katie's chest.

Katie had heard enough—she tried to come out of the chair, but only managed to rise a few inches.

PHIFFFT!

A massive weight slammed into her chest. She and the chair were thrown backwards. As she lay sprawled on the floor, her consciousness slipped away; a curtain of darkness descended.

MOUTH AGAPE, FARRELL stared at the crumpled form of the detective sprawled beyond the upended chair. The shock faded as bitterness flushed his senses; stifled anger flared in his gut. Gritting his teeth, he brought the pistol to bear on Consuela's face. Seething, he pulled the trigger.

Click . . .

Her smile was feral. "Oh, come now. You didn't think I'd give you a gun with more than one bullet in it, did you?"

The man at his side slammed Farrell's wrist to the desk. Paralyzing pain shot up his arm; the pistol clattered across the desk.

The henchman reached for the weapon, but Consuela stopped him with a stern command. "No! Don't touch it! I want that pistol found here, with his fingerprints on it. Re-tape his arm to his chair."

As her henchman complied, she turned to Farrell. "You see, that's the gun I used when I visited your nosy lawyer—Melanie Dubois. And now, you will be held to blame."

"But, Amanda," Farrell pleaded. "She's got nothing to do with any of this! Her ransom's paid! You've got to let her go!"

"You fool! I don't have to do anything! You have become unreliable—a liability! You couldn't keep your meddling HOA people from discovering our secrets. True, I have since dealt with them; but, our operations were compromised—our cash flow interrupted! The people I work for do not find that acceptable. I would have had to answer for your mistakes had I not arranged to replace the investment—"

"The r-ransom," Farrell uttered in interruption.

"Of course, you idiot! I actually doubled the expected return from the lab—ten million! So now, I take credit for making a huge success from your failure—me! My employers are pleased, of course; but, they will not be fully satisfied until I tie up certain loose ends."

"W-what are you saying? What loose ends?"

Consuela smiled evilly and gestured to Katie's prone body. "Did you not just shoot the disgraced detective who shot her own captain, kidnapped your daughter, and made the ransom demand of your ex-wife and her husband? Of course you did. Sadly, you were too late to save your beloved Amanda; she will have died of an overdose at the hands of this rogue detective. Not to worry, the damning syringe will be found in her hand."

"No-no . . . not Amanda . . . no, please," Farrell babbled and began to weep.

"Oh, I can see this is really becoming too much for you," observed Consuela sympathetically, as she snapped on a pair of latex gloves. "You shouldn't let yourself get so worked up—you could have a stroke, you know."

Farrell hung his head as his shoulders heaved with his sobs. He squinted through tears and saw Consuela draw a cloudy liquid from a small vial into a syringe. She placed it to one side and reached for a much larger syringe.

"It is so unfortunate," she said with an affected sigh, as she pulled the oversized syringe's plunger back, filling its cartridge with air, "that you didn't take better care of your health. Stress can be such a killer."

At her nod, the henchman standing behind Farrell's chair jammed a stun gun into the base of his neck and pressed the trigger.

Farrell's body convulsed in chaotic spasms! His heartbeat stumbled; his lungs felt locked. It seemed to go on and on. Finally, he sagged, still conscious but helpless.

"*No mas!* I think that's enough," Consuela declared. "*Bueno.* Raul, hold that lamp over here; I need the light. Juan, hold his head back and his mouth open . . . wider . . . There that's better—"

The room was plunged into darkness.

There was a sudden grunt and the lamp clattered to the floor. Another grunt, a low groan, and then sounds of a struggle ensued; repeated slaps of flesh being solidly struck and erratic shuffling echoed throughout the room. *Thuds* of upended furniture were punctuated by crashes of fixtures and décor. Something very large and heavy with glass broke with a resounding crunch and the harsh peal of shattering crystal shards. A low moan was cut off with a vicious *whap!*

The room became ominously quiet.

There was a measured shuffling near the door, and then along the walls.

"Lights!" a deep voice commanded.

A series of bright beams flooded the room—weapons mounted flashlights, held by helmeted men in black fatigues.

In the middle of the room stood Dombrowski, a night vision monocular strapped to his forehead. He raised his open hands and announced, "I'm good! The electric panel is in the back hall—I pulled the main switch. There's another male in custody in the garage, in the white van."

In the next moment the house lights came back on. The SWAT team secured the two unconscious henchmen, and began freeing the oblivious Farrell from his chair.

Lt. Waters entered the room. "Are you all right, Sergeant? Where's Katie?"

Dombrowski scanned the floor, but she wasn't there!

A pile of sofa seat cushions in a corner moved and a muffled voice called out.

"Here! We're here—we're okay!"

Katie pushed the cushions aside to reveal herself and the shaken and pathetic girl in the wheelchair. "This is Amanda Farrell," she announced hoarsely. "We're gonna need an ambulance. She's been drugged—Phenobarbital, they said."

As Lt. Waters made the call, Dombrowski realized that the tactical team had freed Farrell from his chair.

"Hey! Farrell gets locked up! He shot Katie!"

All eyes went to her.

She winced and pulled her jacket and shirt open. "It's okay! I'm okay—the vest saved my butt!"

Dombrowski was instantly at her side. "Are you sure you're all right?"

"Yeah, hurts like hell, but I'm all right. I'm alive."

Dombrowski looked around; the maid was nowhere to be seen. "Oh shit! Where the hell is Consuela?"

One of the SWAT team members poked his head in the room and announced, "Hey, we've got an unconscious female in the back stairwell. There's a syringe in her back."

Dombrowski looked at Katie.

She shrugged and smiled. "Well, I had to improvise—they took my gun."

CH 37

KATIE WAS COMPELLED to spend the night in the hospital, which was standard procedure after her ordeal. Released the next morning, she was sore and badly bruised, but otherwise in good health and better spirits—until she saw the orderly with the wheelchair at the door of her room.

She saw Dombrowski waiting for her just outside the main entrance. He grinned broadly when he saw her being wheeled into the lobby. Her scowl spoke volumes about having to ride in a wheelchair pushed by an orderly who looked like he was barely out of high school.

She tried to bolt from the chair before the orderly was midway across the lobby, but the young man, apparently accustomed to such impulsive patient behavior, gently pulled her back into the seat.

"Now hold on there, ma'am. I am sorry, ma'am." The young man offered an apology in recognition of her obvious pique, as he brought the chair to a stop. "But as I told you upstairs, the wheelchair is hospital policy whenever someone is released."

She grumbled some unintelligible yet apologetic response as she fumbled with the bag in her lap containing her personal items. The orderly smiled and resumed pushing her chair through the outer doors. Once outside, she bolted up from the wheelchair; and he beat a hasty retreat.

Dombrowski's smile was infectious. Her scowl faltered and faded as he gave her a careful hug and held her out at arm's length. "Well, Katie, you look good. How are you feeling?"

"I'm fine . . . okay, maybe a little stiff. Did you hear that orderly? He called me ma'am!"

"He didn't!" he mocked. "Only Kenny is allowed to do that!"

Smirking, she swatted his arm. "Enough already!" She leaned into him, lowered her voice and asked, "Amanda? Did she make it?"

"Yeah, she has so far. I understand her prognosis is guarded but she'll be okay. We did good, kiddo."

Katie felt an oppressive weight lift. She tried to take a deep breath and winced—*bad idea*. She took her partner's offered arm and walked toward his truck.

"So, D, where are we going?"

"I'm taking you home, of course. Have you forgotten that you've been shot? You know you've got some time off coming—a week at least!"

"A week? But we've got this case to wrap up, and—"

"Relax, we got some people meeting us at your place."

She looked at him, clearly puzzled.

"What's the matter," he teased, "you never heard of working from home?"

───────────

WHEN THEY ARRIVED AT Katie's house, they found Lt. Waters and Assistant Chief Dunbar parked at the curb waiting for them.

They all went inside.

About ten minutes later the doorbell rang; CSI tech Kenny Reynolds, FBI Special Agent Fred Carlson, and Deputy U.S. Marshal Emilio Gonzalez had arrived. Katie invited everyone to have a seat at her kitchen table. Dombrowski brewed and served the coffee. With hot mugs all around, they got down to business.

"So, do we have our evidence?" Chief Dunbar asked.

"We do, sir," answered Dombrowski as he produced a NAGRA recorder and placed it before the chief. "Katie gave it to me on the scene. It hasn't been out of my possession; the chain of custody is intact."

Nodding to the federal agents, the sergeant explained. "You see, we took a page from Capt. Walker's book and went 'old school' with a body wire rather than a digital transmitter. We figured the captain knew what he was doing when he opted for the same gear when he met with Senator Widermark in Farrell's house."

"Good thing, too," Katie confirmed, "because they scanned me with a radio frequency detector after they took my gun. They missed the NAGRA completely."

Kenny interrupted to say, "Your Glock 27 was recovered—your phone, too. It was in the van like we thought. They're both in evidence right now."

"Oh, uh, thanks."

He silently mouthed *don't worry—you'll get 'em back.*

"All right, from this point on," Chief Dunbar intoned, "what we share among the agencies represented here is to be considered confidential, and discussed only with those personnel with a verified need to know. Detectives, please provide an oral after-action report. We—that is, all the involved agencies—have agreed that this will be off-the-record for now. Sergeant, you may proceed."

"Yes sir," answered Dombrowski. "As you know, our immediate goal was to locate Amanda Farrell, the kidnap victim, and that locating Katie's stolen cell phone seemed to be the key. You already know that the phone was in the same van the kidnappers were using to move the victim around; and we determined the van was at Farrell's house.

"We concluded that Walter Farrell was integrally involved in several cases, to include the kidnapping. We planned to confront him with a sting tactic, a bribery or blackmail pitch, in an effort to get him to implicate himself on tape." Dombrowski deferred to his partner. "Katie?"

"Right. Since I appeared to be the one most compromised and implicated, I approached him directly. I was admitted right through the front door of his home," she explained. "While I distracted him, my partner approached the rear in the hopes of finding Amanda."

She glanced to her partner, who continued the narrative.

"Of course, it didn't work out the way we anticipated," the sergeant admitted. "It turns out that our CI, Consuela Ladonez, wasn't who we thought she was—"

"That's an understatement," Dunbar interrupted. "Marshal Gonzalez, tell them."

"Yes, sir. Consuela Ladonez is an alias, one of many. In fact, no law enforcement agency knows her real name for certain. However, she is well known among the drug cartels, as a *fixer*, an extractor of information, a torturer, and an assassin. She is called '*Angele de Muerte*', angel of death. She freelances, primarily fixing problems for the cartels—usually permanently—for outrageous fees. Her torture victims are often deliberately staged, intended to be found—"

"To send a message?" Katie asked in interruption.

"Yes, precisely. However, arranging accidents and deaths through apparent natural causes is also her expertise, and, we suspect, her preference. She only works for high end operations."

"Now that she's in our custody," Dunbar added, "We've heard from some very interested agencies."

"Is she all right?" asked Katie.

At a nod from Chief Dunbar, Special Agent Carlson answered.

"Yes, we understand she'll be fine. That syringe held a sizable dose of Phenobarbital, but it wasn't sufficient to be fatal—at least not to her. The doctors advised us it would have easily overdosed Amanda Farrell, who was already heavily strung out on a heavy dose of the same sedative."

"Thanks," Katie acknowledged. "I heard Amanda is going to be all right. Still, this has gotta be tough on her mother and step-father."

"Yes, with time she should fully recover," Carlson agreed. "Unfortunately, the loss of two of her fingers could not be corrected. Her parents are at the hospital and haven't left her side. A team of agents is there for security. Her parents have not been told any details of her rescue, at this time. What we will tell them remains to be seen."

"What about Consuela's three goons? Do we have IDs yet?" Dombrowski asked. "I think one of them looked familiar."

"Before we get into that," the chief cautioned, "I'm curious. Tell me how you managed to deal with them by yourself. I understand Katie was down, having been shot—thank heavens for her vest—so, it was only you until the SWAT team arrived."

Dombrowski squirmed; and Dunbar reminded him, "Remember, this is off-the-record, Sergeant."

"Er, yes, sir. I ran into one of them in the garage—the one I think I recognized—and uh, dealt with him. I secured him and left him in the van. As for Katie, I didn't know right then that she'd been shot—I never heard it. Of course, we know now that Consuela likes to use a suppressed Beretta 9mm."

"That still leaves the other two men and the woman," Dunbar prodded.

"Ah, I found the room they were all in, Farrell's office—that's when I saw Katie on the floor. I didn't know what had happened, just that she was down. I sent the 'GO' message to Lt. Waters via the pre-arranged number, so I knew help was on the way—but I couldn't wait. I could overhear Consuela, and I saw they were gonna kill Farrell; she was gonna shoot him up with air and stroke him out. I'd passed the electric panel in the hall near the garage, so

I ran back and pulled the main switch. Everything went dark, and then I moved in."

"Go on," Dunbar urged.

"Well, we'd asked Kenny—uh, Officer Reynolds—to pick up some gear for us in preparation for this mission, a NAGRA, for one thing. When he dropped it off, he gave us some other things as well, like this night vision monocular." He placed it on the table. "Once I killed the lights, I could still see using this, so I dealt with the other two goons in the dark. What I didn't know was that Katie had been playing possum for a while; when she got the opportunity, she dealt with Consuela using the syringe intended for Amanda."

"I'm still not clear," Chief Dunbar admitted, "how you dealt so effectively with those two men in the dark. You never fired a shot, so I know you didn't use your firearm. However, there was extensive property damage, and both men are hospitalized with serious concussions. Please elucidate, now."

Dombrowski shrugged and gave the boss a wry grin. "To be honest, it was a combination of techniques; a little new school," he slid the night vision monocular forward, "and a little old school." A blackjack appeared in his hand; he placed it next to the monocular.

Asst. Chief Dunbar dropped his gaze and shook his head. He tried, but he couldn't hide his smile. Lt. Waters became very interested in the ceiling, and bit his tongue.

Special Agent Carlson nudged the Deputy U.S. Marshal and whispered, "A blackjack? No one uses those any more, do they?"

Emilio offered a wry smirk. "Well, he did say they were going a little 'old school.'"

"Ah, well, moving right along," Chief Dunbar smoothed. "Can we get back to the man you thought you recognized?"

"Yes, sir, do we have an ID?"

"We do, of a sort. Reynolds, please enlighten us."

"Yes, sir. Enrique Smith is another alias—true name unknown. He is a suspected peripheral associate of several cartels—muscle for hire. You were right, Sergeant—you did recognize him. He and another man of equally dubious background and alias, Pablo Jones—who seems to now be in the wind—have been working part-time as temps for the janitorial service that has the contract for our building. They've both been in and out of our offices periodically for the past few months. When you and Katie came across those janitorial uniforms at the second lab site—"

"You are getting a bit ahead of yourself, young man," the chief interrupted kindly.

"Sergeant, you'll recall that we were looking for a suspected leak in our agency. I'm sorry to say that we found it—in Captain Walker's computer. As you know, personnel of command rank are authorized to access the department's network remotely, even from their home computers. Reynolds, explain."

Kenny sat up straighter and began with a nod to Emilio. "We—the Marshals Service techs and us—found a very well hidden Trojan laden with a host of spyware buried in the code of the political software given by Senator Widermark to the captain. Now, the captain only used it on his home computer; but, the next time he accessed the department's network from home, the malware was lying in wait, undetectable, and it infected our system. It's a nasty piece of work; key loggers, spider bots, code bombs, the works. It's so bad that we're gonna have to scrap our operating system software and start from scratch."

"Did the captain even know?" Lt. Waters asked.

"Very unlikely," Dunbar said sadly, "but we may never know. What we do now know is that his phone's GPS lost contact in the vicinity of the Post Office—the battery was removed. We suspect that was where he was taken. Reynolds?"

Kenny opened his laptop, and pulled up a surveillance video from the interior of the Post Office lobby. In the display Capt. Walker was easily identified entering the lobby and approaching the counter. Kenny froze the frame and pointed.

"We can see the captain enter the Post office. Now I draw your attention to the two people approaching the door from the parking lot. When I restart the recording, you'll see one man come in while the other stays outside and looks around the parking lot. I'll stop it once more when we get a good shot of their faces."

He did as he described; the faces of both men were captured in the frame.

"Those are the two goons from Farrell's house!" declared Dombrowski.

"Yeah," echoed Katie, "but we know now that they're Consuela's goons. So, they snatched the captain?"

"Keep watching," Dunbar advised. "Continue, please, Reynolds."

The recording played on. Captain Walker finished his business at the counter and left the Post Office. The two men followed. All were soon off camera.

"That is the last time the captain was seen alive," Dunbar intoned. "We know, thanks to Dr. Parker, that his cause of death was an induced stroke. There's little doubt that Consuela Ladonez is responsible; it is her preferred M.O. We know the postmortem GSW, with Detective Callahan's gun, and subsequent staging of the captain's body in our own parking lot was the final gambit in the plan to frame Katie, and fatally taint all her cases."

"I should add," offered the lieutenant, "that CSI has a theory about the 9mm bullet. Reynolds?"

"Yes, sir. The 9mm round did not display the tissue penetration we usually see with typical factory loads; and, the nose of the projectile was only slightly deformed—sort of flattened. The M.E. report suggested it hadn't hit any bone. We think it was a subsonic round deliberately used in that weapon—Katie's Glock 19—to be assured of leaving the bullet within the

shoved away. The startled senator barely kept his balance. He hastily looked left and right, and then briskly walked to his left and off camera.

"Is that the same bank—" Dombrowski started to ask.

"One and the same," answered Emilio with a knowing grin.

"So, he faked his death?" Katie wondered. "But why? Is he wanted now?"

"There is no warrant for his arrest, to my knowledge," the Deputy U.S. Marshal admitted. "So he's not running or hiding from us."

"But there must be a reason," the special agent concluded, "for him to turn his back on a multi-million dollar church-based television enterprise. What's that saying? Only the guilty flee when no man pursues?"

Emilio chuckled. "Yeah, something like that."

"So, he's running from the cartels?" Kenny asked.

"Maybe," Carlton allowed. "He was afraid of something; that's evident from Captain Walker's NAGRA tape. Remember that FinCEN has known that certain funding traffic involving this bank links Farrell's HOA and the cartels. We don't think it's mere coincidence that the kidnappers' numbered account is with the same banking enterprise. But now there's another problem—it seems the ransom money is no longer in the kidnappers' account."

"Say what?" Kenny blurted.

Carlson and Gonzalez exchanged a glance and chuckled.

"Actually," the FBI agent explained, "the money was never there—it never left Demotte's bank. Thanks to FinCEN, it was a carefully orchestrated electronic smoke and mirrors illusion that Emilio and I can't really talk about. Suffice to say the bank in the Caymans made the discovery first thing this morning."

"I'm sure that was a rude awakening for someone," the Deputy U.S. Marshal observed dryly.

"Oh, yeah, I see," Dombrowski mused aloud. "So, the senator showing up at that bank this morning—that might not have been his smartest move, eh?"

"He has certainly drawn undue attention to himself," Emilio admitted. "I'd bet whoever is behind the kidnapping—or some cartel—will want to know what happened to *their* ten million. *Someone* is not going to look all that trustworthy, and is very likely going to be suspected of being compromised and subsequently cooperating with the authorities."

"Oh shit," murmured Kenny, "the senator is screwed. How's that for karma?"

"Probably pretty well deserved," Katie groused.

"On the other hand," Emilio continued, "that's not to say there won't be an indictment and subsequent warrants forthcoming. It seems that Walter Farrell is trying to cut a deal; he'll cooperate and testify if he's guaranteed protection."

"We have ample reason to believe," Carlson explained, "that Farrell knows quite a bit about a lot of things, and a lot of people, to include the senator. Consequently, our people are in a meeting with the U. S. Attorney as we speak. If the powers that be agree, Walter Farrell may be entered into the Witness Protection Program."

"What about our open cases?" Dombrowski demanded. "Hell, he shot Katie!"

"Oh, of course he can still be prosecuted. And he would be produced for any required testimony in any of your open cases," Emilio assured him. "That will all be up to your District Attorney and the U.S. Attorney to work out."

"Wait a minute," Katie interjected. "What about Amanda? She was kidnapped! Doesn't she merit protection?"

"An offer may be extended to her as well," Carlson explained. "It'll be up to the U.S. Attorney to work that out."

"But her father—" Katie began.

Carlson cut her off. "Her father, Walter Farrell, won't have any say—she's legally an adult. And to be honest, we don't know at this point if she really has any value as a witness. Also, I understand her mother and step-father want to take her back to Great Britain as soon as possible. But as I said, Amanda Farrell is an adult, so the decision will be hers."

"I understand, but somehow," Katie hedged, "oh, never mind."

Asst. Chief Dunbar cleared his throat and garnered everyone's attention. "Ahem. If we can please now move along, there is more news resulting from our CSI unit's efforts. Reynolds, if you would?"

"Yes, sir. A pearl-handled straight razor was taken from Consuela Ladonez when she was arrested. She had it on a gold chain around her neck. Our techs found bloodstains at the base of the blade, in the hinge area, and inside the handle panels. Results of preliminary testing and typing indicate that we have type matches for Jennifer Halsted and Carolyn Silverberg. We are waiting for DNA confirmation."

"So, Consuela was responsible," Dombrowski concluded, "for the Halsted homicide staged as a suicide, the torture murder of Carolyn Silverberg—"

"And," Katie interjected, "she bragged that the gun Farrell shot me with was the same one she used to kill Farrell's attorney, Melanie Dubois. That's on the NAGRA, and I guess ballistics will prove it."

"Not to mention," Dombrowski added, "that she essentially admitted to 'dealing with' Farrell's 'HOA people', George Adamson and Jennifer Halsted, on the tape, too. And then there's Captain Walker . . . She also took the credit and flaunted how the ransom for Amanda Farrell not only recovered, but doubled the cartel's investment."

"Be that as it may, we still do not know," Chief Dunbar cautioned, "what role the members of her crew may have played, nor do we have definitive IDs on them—yet. There are still arson and bombing investigations to be concluded. However, if Walter Farrell can shed some light on these matters as well, we may well wrap up a number of open cases.

"But more importantly, in capturing this professional serial killer, this *angel of death*, you have solved five homicides, foiled a kidnapping and rescued the victim, exposed a multi-million dollar drug operation and a convoluted money laundering scheme, and finally, uncovered evidence that confirmed the leak in our own department. All in all, good work, people! Now, does anyone have anything else to discuss?"

"Yes, sir," piped up Katie. "When can I come back to work?"

That brought a round of smiles from those at the table and a humorous snort from her partner.

Lt. Waters leaned forward and said, "Well, You've been on the books ever since your suspensions were cleared last week. I believe, with Asst. Chief Dunbar's approval of course, that we can make that part of the official record. But more importantly, what does your doctor say?"

"Um, he'll say that I can come back on Monday?" she offered hopefully.

The lieutenant scoffed. "Really? Okay, you get that in writing and you can start day shift next Monday. But you have to take it easy for the next few days, agreed?"

"You bet, LT. Uh, does this mean that Walden and Donahue will take care of the rest of the reports—you know, with me having to rest and all?"

No one missed her impish smirk and the implied joke.

"Oh, I don't know about that," the lieutenant answered. "Walden and Donahue can only report on their specific activities. You and your partner will be responsible for your own reports, I'm afraid." He winked at her. "Nice try, though."

Asst. Chief Dunbar stood. "If there is nothing else, I believe we can conclude this meeting. Remember, everything discussed is confidential. Special Agent Carlson, Deputy Marshal Gonzalez, I trust we will be in touch?"

"Absolutely," they echoed, and followed him to the door.

Lt. Waters and Chief Dunbar made their way to Waters' cruiser, waved, and drove off. The two federal investigators departed in their separate cruisers.

———————

DOMBROWSKI STOOD ON the porch staring off into the distance, obviously lost in thought. Katie came to stand beside him while Kenny packed up his computer gear.

"What is it?" she asked.

"Just thinking, those janitors . . . They had full access, and nobody ever looked twice. The brass didn't mention it, but, you know—"

"Yeah, I know. Kinda made it real easy to set us up, Didn't it?"

"Too easy," he grunted. "It tends to explain the bullshit tips going to Johnson and Barkley, and some of the strange phone calls to the office, too."

"Makes sense," she agreed. "They were able to keep tabs on us—hell, the whole Criminal Investigations Division—the whole damn time. Shit, D! How did we miss this?"

He shrugged. "We got complacent. We got comfortable in what we felt was a safe place. We got too narrowly focused, to the exclusion of peripheral details. Hell, who knows? We were vulnerable; someone noticed and took advantage."

"So, is it over—at least for now?"

He smiled sadly. "It's never over, Katie, don't ever forget that . . . I'm gonna get going."

She returned his tired smile. "Okay, take care now."

WALKING TO HIS TRUCK, midway down the sidewalk, Dombrowski snapped his fingers, stopped and turned back toward Katie's front door. Kenny had come out onto the porch, and was standing there, talking to Katie.

"Hey Kenny!" Dombrowski called out, "I'm sorry, I should've asked; can I drop you somewhere?"

In that instant, he realized Katie's gaze was smoldering at him. Too late, he knew he'd stepped in it.

"Huh? I, uh," Kenny stammered, her glare now upon him. "Uh, nah, that's okay, Sarge. I've uh, got my own wheels, parked around the corner. Thanks anyway!"

Dombrowski gave them a big smile as he climbed into his truck. "Oh, okay. You kids have fun!"

Katie stared at him, arms akimbo, as he drove off.

In his mirror, he saw her scowl morph into a coy smile, and that little shake of her head.

―――――――――

KATIE TURNED BACK TO Kenny and sighed heavily.

"Hey, are you okay?" he asked. "Can I get you anything?"

"I dunno . . . maybe another cup of coffee? You want one? We could sit out here for a bit?" She tilted her head at the wide porch swing.

"Sure thing!" He beamed. "You get comfortable. I'll get the coffee."

She eased into the porch swing and gazed out at her yard. It had grown a bit unkempt in the last few weeks—what the hell, she'd been busy. Now she had a couple of days off. Maybe she ought to visit her father—or better still, why not bring him here to the house and let him putter around? He used to love that. She could get some yard work done.

"Here's your coffee, I hope it's not too hot." Ken sat next to her on the swing.

He was so polite and solicitous, always a gentleman. She liked that; and yet somehow, if she dwelled too long upon it, it mildly irritated her.

She shook it off—it was better to just be here in the moment.

It was pleasant, just to be outside in the morning. Her encircling hands savored the warmth of the coffee mug, a comforting sensation. Her eyes lingered on her climbing roses. A breeze wafted the fecund fragrance of something in bloom—

"A penny for your thoughts?" he interrupted.

"What? Oh . . . I was just thinking about my front yard."

"Yeah? Well, it does look a little scraggly. You might want to get after that. Wouldn't want to get the HOA all riled up now, would you?"

"HOA? What the hell? Kenny, this neighborhood doesn't have an HOA. We neither need nor want one. So, can't you just shut up and be here—be in the moment, okay?"

"Yes, ma'am."

She rolled her eyes in resigned exasperation and sighed. "Kenny?"

"Uh-huh?"

"Please . . . don't call me ma'am."

THE END

(. . . for now)

She shook it off — it was better to pass the time in the moment.

About the Author

M.D. Ironz is the pseudonym of a former government official, based in an undisclosed location in North America, and now serving as a confidential consultant on matters of intelligence, security, and investigations.

9 781733 759496